Knotty LESSONS

Knotty LESSONS

by

GINNA MORAN

ISBN 978-1-951314-76-7 (soft cover)
ISBN 978-1-951314-77-4 (hardcover)

Cover design by Daqri at Covers by Combs

For Inquiries Contact:

Sunny Palms Press
9663 Santa Monica Blvd Suite 1158
Beverly Hills, CA 90210, USA
www.sunnypalmspress.com
www.GinnaMoran.com

Dedication
To all the dirty girls out there.

Here's a dick pic especially for you.

8============D~~

1

Scarlett

DICKasso

"Nice dick." The beta at the desk beside me leans over, inspecting my drawing. "It's a bit small, though. I think you need a better reference. I'd be happy to help."

I whip my head, and attention, to just stare at the guy, a smile creeping across his face as we both ignore Professor Hart droning on about the significance of Javier García's journey in Madrid and Moonlight had on his life. I'd usually pay better attention, but he'd stopped reading passages, turning from sexy narrator to stuffy professor in a matter of minutes.

"What do you say, Dickasso?" the beta murmurs, leaning closer. Is he serious? Dickasso? Ugh.

I avert my eyes back to my desk, gawking at the life-like sketch I've been working on for the past day. The flaccid appendage hangs sadly between the thin thighs of the scrawny beta guy I saw strolling through the co-ed showers without a towel. I admired his confidence, but the moment imprinted in my brain. The only way I can think of getting it out is to draw it—every tiny blood vessel, curly pubes, and the freckles on the crease between his leg and pelvis.

I shake my head, trying to focus on Professor Hart. I can smell his woodsy floral scent from here, and it does something to me today. It could be the fact that I'm an omega passing as a beta with hormone suppressant lotion or just because he's hot, even for a man my dads' ages. Whatever it is, I need to focus on something else. Like my rendition of a dick pic.

"Don't be embarrassed. You're talented. It's so realistic that I want to gouge my eyes out for having to stare at it." The beta chuckles, his voice echoing over

Professor Hart. He's not even trying to hide his attempt to converse with me anymore.

I hiss under my breath. "I'm trying to focus."

The beta traces his finger on the edge of my desk, scooting his a bit closer. "On dicks? Come on. You know—"

Dropping his book to the desk, Professor Hart startles me with the boom. I frown and try not to draw attention to myself, my body frozen at my desk. I sink lower with the fire flaming my cheeks. This fucking beta. I never thought they were the type not to take hints, but I guess since I'm the one pretending to be something I'm not...

"If you feel the need to talk over me, leave. You will not disrespect me, Mr. Broderik." Professor Hart growls, his deep voice as powerful as his presence, his alpha nature commanding attention.

"My apologies, sir. I couldn't help it. She's distracting me with her cock drawings." The beta hunkers in his desk, clearly acting like the type of fucker that would blame everyone else except for himself if called out. The asshole should've minded his own business. Now I feel the rage of Professor Hart's glare smoldering over me hotter than my blushing cheeks.

"Excuse me?" Professor Hart asks, striding closer. "That doesn't give you the excuse to interrupt my class."

Fear pours through me, Professor Hart's intoxicating scent billowing over me. I take a deep breath, the sudden attention on me making me feel as if I'm as bare and vulnerable as my nude self-portraits filling my folder along with my other explicit artwork. I've been too scared to leave them in my dorm because of my nosy roommate but facing her would be better than this.

This feels like Omega Prep of San Francisco all over again, the strict environment giving me no right to privacy or the ability to express myself creatively. It's why I begged to attend a beta-dominated university while waiting for my parents to find me a pack after I couldn't find any interest myself. It should've happened by now, as I've already hit the age I needed to be married by, but it just hasn't happened. My mom thinks it's because my sisters appear better on paper. I was always average. Not outgoing, not really into afterschool activities that required socializing. I just preferred to draw the world as I saw it and the way I wanted it to be. I didn't get what I wanted, but this private university is good enough. The art program will suffice...unless I'm about to get kicked out. Fuck me.

My phone rings, shocking me out of my state of surprise, and I cringe, wishing I hadn't turned on the volume earlier. I was afraid of missing the call from the coffee shop about hiring me to paint their windows for Halloween. I don't need the money, but it would be the first time someone paid me for my art.

Now, I don't know if I'm going to survive the next sixty seconds.

I scramble to grab my phone from my bag, spotting my mom's name flashing on the screen. "I'm so sorry, Professor Hart. This is an emergency. I'm so sorry." I scoop up my belongings and launch myself from the desk, dodging around my professor and bolting toward the door without waiting to see what unfolds between him and the beta.

I might as well escape before I get kicked out anyway. I'll email him later and hope he can forgive me. The last thing I need is to be expelled. I'm so close to getting my art degree, which I hope will look spectacular to a pack. Maybe. My mom always complained that I should've done something more valuable. Like accounting. Business. Something the pack who chooses me would be proud of since graduating from Omega Prep doesn't seem to be enough. Even if I never use it.

My body goes out of whack, my heart racing, and my palms sweating. I'm absolutely mortified. I wonder if it's even worth trying to apologize to my professor. It might be better to just disappear. Mom would be happy to have me home, so she could berate me and shame me for being on the cusp of being considered unwanted. I'll be another disappointment like my older sisters, who failed to follow the path set before them. This was supposed to be my time to shine, but my internal light dims like my vision as I run into the sun.

I can't see shit as my legs refuse to stop running, and I slam my shins into something solid. I fly forward and tumble, my belongings scattering everywhere. I hit the grass with a thud. The air escapes my lungs with a heave. I blink my eyes, trying not to let the uncontrollable tears fall. This is the worst day of my life. I thought it was every single one before this today because no one has shown any interest in me as an omega, and my mom never lets me forget it, but what the fuck is happening to me now?

"Oh, shit! Miss, are you okay? Is someone chasing you?" The deep rumble of a masculine voice shocks me like a defibrillator, trying to save me when all I want to do is be buried right here on the spot. "Let me help you."

A silhouette of a figure hovers over me, and I rapidly blink, trying to make out who this man is. He squats beside me, his citrusy-lime scent like a salt-rimmed margarita I could desperately chug right about now.

I roll over onto my side, moving out of the way before he can reach for my hands. He doesn't realize that I'm an omega, and his pheromones get to me in a confusing way. I've been rubbing a scent-suppressing lotion on daily for the entire duration of being here. I wanted to blend in. It's not normal for an omega to be at a university after our intensive education at the national prep school.

"I'm fine. I'm so sorry." I scramble to get to my feet, putting space between me and the sweat-glistening alpha, shirtless with tattoos crawling up his arms and around his chest. He only wears a pair of athletic shorts and tennis shoes, one with an untied lace. I can't see much of his face with his sunglasses blocking his eyes and the dark beard with patches of gray obscuring his cheeks and jaw. He must've been running and stopped to tie his shoe.

"No need to apologize. You obviously were trying to get away from something. If someone's bothering you, you can report it to me. I can handle it." The man offers me a small smile, keeping his space as if he thinks I might run again. And I might. Because his gaze trails down my body to land on the grass where the last couple of months of my sketchbook now lies scattered across the grass. In any normal circumstance, I would be unfazed. But this is my dirty little secret sketchbook. The one I would never dare show the world.

And this stranger alpha, someone who probably works at this damn university, now drinks in the sight of my naked self-portraits, erotic fantasies, and a huge collection of dick pics—drawings.

Kill me now.

"Shit! Shit! Shit!" I throw myself on the ground, scooping up all the scattered papers that I can and shove them into my jacket because opening my bag will take too long. "I have to go. I'm so sorry again. I have to go." I sound like a dumbass, stumbling over my words, repeating the same two phrases over and over. My embarrassment turns my brain into mush, and all I can think about is getting the fuck away.

"You dropped one, miss," the guy calls, waving one of the sketches.

I can't get my body to move any closer to him in fear of meeting his eyes. Facing his judgment. My mom would murder me if she found out. Omegas are supposed to be good girls, well-rounded, and ready to give their alphas what they need. I shouldn't have such an obsession with how fascinating I find the human body.

"You can just trash it. It's not important," I yell, peering at him one more time from over my shoulder.

He mumbles something that I can't hear, and I rush forward, clutching onto my drawings for dear life, terrified that my secret will scatter across campus. This is what I get for being idle-handed in class with a professor I find attractive. I can't help that I've already studied world literature at Omega Prep. That's why I wanted to go to an art school, so I didn't have to take a bunch of General Ed.

My side aches from running the near mile it takes to get back to my dorm. My mom refused to pay for an apartment, claiming that if I wanted to be pampered, then I needed to be home. I just wanted space away from my pack, so here I am, sharing a room with a beta who won't say even one word to me that isn't a complaint. It was quite the awakening when I moved in, and she realized I was an omega. After I told her why I decided to attend her university, she called me an entitled brat who should just be appreciative of the life I have been blessed with. Her reaction to learning that I was Scarlett Steele of the Steele sisters, our sort of famous family of all omega girls, made me immediately take on an alias. Scarlett Carlisle is now the one who attends Clearwater University of San Diego, founded by the Clearwater Pack.

I shove the thought away as I rush through the glass door of the dorm building. A man in a black suit with a red tie and shiny dress shoes stands near the Resident

Advisor, and they both look at me. The RA frowns, confusion lining her face. My phone rings again from my bag, and I give up on my art stuff and drop it into one of the chairs in the commons area.

"Sorry, Mom. I was in class," I say, eyeing as the man in the suit and the RA continue to stare at me. It weirds me out, and I turn my back on them.

"You could've left. You know how important my calls are, and this one is what you've been waiting for. I found you a pack! We've been presented an offer for your hand in marriage. There should be a driver at your dorm shortly. They've already paid the dowry, and you're to leave campus immediately. We can't afford you wasting time." My mom spits out the words in one breath. "Don't bother packing any of your things. We will send for them later. You just need to move."

I eye the man in the suit again. Shit. That's probably why the RA looks completely confused. She hasn't been the Resident Advisor for more than two months, and I introduced myself by my alias. I sign everything as Scarlett Carlisle, and the driver must've asked for Scarlett Steele.

"Scarlett? Are you there?" Mom raises her voice. "I can hear you breathing. Say something."

What do I say? I can't believe this is happening. This is what I've been waiting for. This is the moment I didn't think would happen. I thought I just had nothing good to offer on paper, which is why I hadn't received a single proposal. Until now. But why don't I feel as happy as I know I should be?

"I'm sorry, Mama. I'm in shock. I need a second to wrap my mind around it." I haven't called her Mama since I was a kid, and I suddenly feel as if I know nothing. What if I turn out to be a disappointment? What if this pack realizes that they don't want me after all?

I shouldn't care. My sisters would tell me I'm ridiculous.

"Well, knock it off. We don't have time for this. You should be happy. You finally found someone to take care of you. Better late than never. Now you can give up that college nonsense and proudly show your face at home again." Because I was supposed to be married already. And it's only a few weeks until my twenty-second birthday. My mom will lose her entitled life if I'm not.

"You're right. I see the driver now. Thank you for everything you've done to make this happen. I love you." The words feel fake as fuck coming from my mouth, but my mom would yell at me otherwise. It is my duty to be the daughter she dreamed of. I refuse to let my pack down. If only it didn't mean I had to let myself down in the process.

"The driver should have the dress I picked out for you, so be presentable. Don't forget to show them what a fitting woman and omega you are. Be friendly yet reserved. Don't talk unless they do. If they want to immediately welcome you with their affection, do not deny them. They are your alphas. This is your moment to show off how incredible an omega from Pack Steele is. It'll help your younger sisters. Do not mess it up. I've already had enough embarrassment and disappointment with your older sisters." Mom doesn't wait for me to respond before she hangs up, leaving me in a hurricane of mixed emotions.

Squaring my shoulders, I summon my nerve and turn back to the silent RA and the driver waiting for me. "I'm assuming you're my driver?" I ask, wishing with everything in me that he tells me no. "I just need a couple minutes to grab a few things."

"I have strict orders to take you immediately. Your mother said you will not need any of your belongings. I have a privacy shield in my vehicle and the outfit chosen for you." The driver frowns with his words, probably expecting me to lash out and argue. Or maybe he feels bad. Whatever.

"I have already been assigned to gather and ship your belongings. Good luck with your pack, Scarlett *Steele*." The RA bites out my last name, her expression just as heated as her voice. If I made any connections with the other students in the dorm, I'm sure they are now destroyed. People don't like discovering that someone isn't who they thought they were, and I can't blame them.

I blink my eyes and turn my back on the two of them, returning to my chair to organize my artwork to put back in my bag. At least I took it with me today. Because right now, it feels like it's all I have left.

Why can't my brain just accept that I'm about to get more? My life will finally be complete. At least, I hope. There's one thing I know for certain. My happily ever after will never be guaranteed.

2

Scarlett

CLearwater Manor

This can't be right.

This can't be fucking right.

I had expected a far longer car ride. Maybe even a trip to the airport. But the wrought iron gate to the Clearwater Manor looms on the hill just outside of campus and close enough to walk to Clearwater University. There has to be a mistake.

Pack Clearwater founded my university a century ago, and the newest pack leader was recently elected as Mayor of San Diego, the city just south of this university beach town. I knew that I'd end up with a strong, wealthy pack because of my birth into privilege, but to be chosen by Pack Clearwater? What the hell?

Creaking open, the automatic gate sweeps forward, allowing the driver access to the winding road leading uphill. I scoot across the long seat of the limo, unable to resist knocking on the tinted partition.

The driver hits a button, opening the divider. "Yes, miss?"

I grip the wall separating us. "Are you sure we're at the right place? I thought Mayor Clearwater—"

Barking a laugh, the driver glances at me in the rearview mirror. "The reigning pack of Pack Clearwater hasn't lived here in two decades. The university required the estate name remain unchanged."

"Oh." I guess that would make sense. I never really paid attention to the history of the university. All I knew was that it was as far as I could get from my mom without having to leave the state. I love it here, and it's in this moment I realize how grateful I am. This pack must've chosen me because I lived nearby, and maybe they're kind enough to realize just how life-changing this kind of bond is for an omega. It's life-changing for them too. My mom would never let me forget how lucky I am. Because of her fame of being such a fertile omega, we get to reap the benefits by getting selected and married off to the best of the best. We're royalty without the responsibility of running a nation yet obligated to produce heirs for our people. What an honor...fucking and breeding. At least, I might get to enjoy the luxuries of life and get more than I would otherwise.

Be grateful. It's what Mom would say.

It could be worse. I could end up as a rejected omega, teaching how to be perfect to the next generation, all while being reminded how imperfect I am. This way, I'll be well taken care of. A perfect bride for wealthy men and a gift to our people by bearing children to help the diminishing population.

It is my duty to make my parents proud. I need to set an example for my sisters, making sure I don't embarrass our pack. I was never really a rule breaker like some of my other sisters. I was also not as careless as my older sister Violet.

And for the whole breeding expectation? It sounds really fucking fun to me. I've seen how connected my mom is with all of my dads. I know that even though things have been arranged for me, they would never put me with a pack I can't stand. Alphas don't propose to just anyone. They want an omega to love their life. It's in their expectation to take care of us. It's in their deep-seated nature.

I also can't wait to discover what it is truly like to be with an alpha who knows exactly what I need as an omega. The few uneventful times I had sex, when I was enrolled at Omega Prep of San Francisco, was nothing to shout to the world about. One, it was forbidden. My best friend Emma unintentionally got into my head, freaking me out about my first time so much that I just went for it. Meaningless sex to help get over my fear. It was with a beta from a neighboring school that I had a crush on, but he turned out to be…less than appealing, awkward, and quick. A two-pump chump with an ugly attitude after to match his smug, now unattractive face. It's what I get for falling for sweet talk. Emma still teases me about it. So do my sisters. But, whatever. It doesn't matter now. I don't even think it really counts. He couldn't knot with me being a beta, and I couldn't orgasm because he sucked and just stuck his unimpressive cock in.

I shiver at the memory. My vibrator was always the superstar.

What counts now is what happens moving forward. I'll get to learn and bond with alphas who want the same.

Premarital sex is one of those things that is frowned upon, especially by Mom, but many omegas do it. Alphas too. It's completely different when we finally pair up. We are made for each other, and it's an alpha who can fulfill my nature and desire that arises with my heat.

I look forward to it. Because I was not bonded when I hit my first heat just after my twenty-first birthday. It was so awful, and using a knotting toy to help simulate an alpha? Completely unsatisfying. All it helped with was the annoying cramping pain. I wasn't going to risk going through what happened to Violet with her spontaneous, super-early heat, so I was prepared. Then I skipped my second one altogether with drugs.

A toy just couldn't do it, but I didn't have a choice with my first heat. No one wanted me until now. The thought has been wearing on me for months. Mom blamed the fact that I didn't look great on paper, nor was I photogenic. I was an A minus student, but I didn't participate in many extracurricular activities. My interests are more personal with art, and that's not something she had ever listed. I always felt that maybe I wasn't pretty enough or smart enough. I met all expectations at Omega Prep, but it wasn't like alphas were swarming to ask for my hand in marriage.

I shake my head, pushing the thoughts away. That doesn't matter. I have to keep reminding myself. I've been betrothed, and everything I achieved will no longer affect my life. What counts now is being the perfect mate for my alphas.

"Miss? Do you need assistance? You'll have to scoot closer to the door." I jerk my attention to the driver, standing at the opened door, peering into the back of the limo. "We're a bit late, so please hurry. I don't want to upset Mr. Adrian."

I was so lost in my thoughts that I didn't even realize we had pulled up the wraparound drive and stopped under the covered driveway or that he had gotten out.

"Oh, no. I'm sorry. I'm just..." I let my voice trail off as I slide across the seat. I don't need to explain anything to the driver. I don't even know his name.

"Out you go." The driver offers his hand, which I don't take. "Mr. Adrian is surely—"

"Excited to meet my lovely Scarlett." A deep, sultry voice catches my attention. Striding from the double doors of the grand entrance, a man captures my gaze, his sky-blue eyes penetrating my soul. "Thank you for your service and concern about me, Daniel. Next time, please alert me of your arrival. I'd have greeted Scarlett immediately."

"My apologies, Mr. Adrian," the driver says, tightening his jaw.

The driver steps away, giving Adrian the space he needs to fill the door, his over six-foot frame what I'd expect from a voice as demanding as his. He holds out his hand, and I gingerly rest my fingers on his, letting him help me to my feet.

Adrian dips his chin, acknowledging the driver without taking his gaze from mine. "You're excused for the rest of the evening."

"Yes, sir. Thank you, Mr. Adrian." The driver returns to his seat behind the wheel and closes the door softly.

Starting the engine, the driver pulls away, leaving me standing with an unfamiliar handsome man in the soft glow of the porch light. I finally take a moment to really drink Adrian in. Apart from his towering frame, he carries an air of sophistication with his tailored suit. His angular jaw gives him a godly attractiveness, his gaze wise with curiosity. Silver streaks through his blond hair, and small crow's feet pinch the corners of his piercing light blue eyes. A trimmed beard covers his cheeks and chin, and I can't tell exactly how old he is, but there's no way he's even near my age.

I don't know what I was expecting from one of my new alphas, but I thought for certain he'd be at least in his twenties. If I'm not mistaken, he could probably be around my parents' age.

Everything happens so fast that I don't even have a chance to think. Adrian offers me his elbow with a warm smile. "I'm sure you are a bit nervous, so why don't we go inside, and I can show you to your room. It was my understanding that Pack Steele would be shipping your belongings here. Am I correct?"

I nod my head without verbally answering. My mouth dries as my feet automatically follow along beside Adrian as he guides me into the enormous university manor. A medley of fragrances—fresh and light with a hint of velvety warmth—wafts from the vestibule, the grand entrance screaming with luxury. The nervousness I felt before compares to nothing in this moment. This isn't just a mansion. It's a well-loved home of what can only be a pack as sophisticated and mature as Adrian. Dark woods with gold accents fill the entryway. Vases of blooming white flowers line short, decorative tables with leather books. The glass wall of the vestibule separates the entrance from what almost looks like a lobby—something from the commons area of the building housing the university's staff. It's too formal to be a living room, but I have no other way to explain it. There are chairs and coffee tables, bookshelves filled with colorful spines and different statues, and more vases for floral arrangements.

"Please don't mind the in-house museum. It was a requirement of Clearwater University to keep the manor in a certain condition that the public could visit. We sometimes house staff meetings along with hosting our authoritative pack when they come into town from the city." Adrian stops and peers around the museum as if it's the first time he has seen it. "I'm sure you understand that with Pack Steele being a part of the prestigious Pack Carlisle. It was a nice surprise to see your profile come up on Knotty.net. My pack has just decided to finally settle down and bond, and it was incredible to see someone of your age available. Most omegas are so young. We weren't really interested in someone who embodied the purity forced upon them by societal expectations. It's a shame that most packs don't see things the way we do. We wanted to establish great careers and build our home in a way that we would be ready for a mate and be able to supply for all her needs. And you, Scarlett, were quite impressive on paper. Was there a reason you waited so long?"

My body cools at his question. What he just said doesn't exactly make sense. I'm not even that old. Sure,

I've already had my first heat, and I need to be married as soon as possible, but I'm only twenty-one.

"I apologize for being so blunt, but it's important that we're upfront with each other from the beginning. Were you arranged to marry another pack, and it didn't work out? Nothing was mentioned in your paperwork or profile. Your pack shrugged off my questions without reason, and your mother sounded a bit…nonchalant. It's hard to explain. I hope I'm not being too crass. If you don't want to talk about it, that is also fine. I'm just curious. It won't affect anything. Pack Hart knew that someone your age would have…life experience. We can get to know each other better first. I just want you to know that it will not change our offer. You're exactly the omega my pack desires." Adrian touches my chin, guiding my face away from the floor. "Like I said, we don't have the same expectations as some of the younger alphas searching for a beloved. Your age and background suit our pack."

What? I'm so confused.

Fuck.

I'm about to shatter his world because he already has this idea about me, which is not even close to being right.

"I think there's been a mistake." I take a step back, swatting his hand from my face instinctively. My mom would grab me by the hair and scream in my face for such a disrespectful move, but I can't help it. "I don't know what was in my paperwork that made you believe otherwise, but I'm as pure as any other omega up for betrothal. These expectations you have...I'm sorry. I don't understand them."

Adrian cocks his head, giving me a long once-over. "You cannot possibly tell me that you haven't requested assistance during your heat in the last ten years. That sounds utterly torturous."

"Ten years? I've only had one. How old do you think I am?" Embarrassment sneaks into my cheeks, heating my face. This isn't the kind of conversation I expected to have with my alpha within the first ten minutes of meeting him.

I glance at a wall mirror, half-expecting to see my face suddenly aged with wrinkles and other signs of maturity, but I look the same as I always have. Maybe a bit tired. Stressed. But not older...at least, I think.

Adrian purses his lips. "You're thirty-one and absolutely stunning."

"I look thirty-one?" I know he didn't say it, but why would he think that? Now I'm self-conscious, and I can't look at Adrian. Fuck this awkwardness.

"Well, no. Not at all, Scarlett. I'm parroting the information in your paperwork. I can show you." Adrian pulls out his cell phone and taps the screen, his brows scrunching as he scrolls through whatever he's looking at. He turns his phone and holds it out to me. "See. Your profile says thirty-one. You're a Scorpio with your birthday coming in November and almost thirty-two. Your mother didn't correct me during our conversation and arrangement-making. The first thing I asked her was if you would be okay with joining a pack a little bit older. She said you looked over the profiles I submitted and were thrilled to marry us."

A mixture of emotions crashes through me. This sounds as if mom knew about this for a while and she chose not to tell me. I shouldn't have expected anything different. There is no rhyme or reason to how she selects our packs apart from her idea of what a perfect payday is. She cares so little for me. I thought it would be different. I thought that if I were agreeable and more obedient than my older sisters, I'd have a different outcome. But here I am. Blindsided, confused, and now staring down an alpha who might throw me out the second he realizes my mom lied.

My brain screams to suck it up and act as if everything is okay. This isn't the end of the world. Adrian might be older, but he's still attractive. Seemingly kind. He's also honest. It's just all the other stuff. The experience. I'm not who he wanted.

It's unfortunate that my mouth has other plans. "I didn't even know someone proposed until less than an hour ago. I learned your name from the driver. I don't even know how big your pack is or who is on it." I jet my hand out and poke the screen of his phone. "And that's a typo. I'm twenty-one. I guess my mom didn't care enough to actually read through anything and fix it."

I bite my lip and turn around, refusing to face Adrian. I don't want to see his expression. I don't want to see the anger fill his eyes after discovering what a piece of shit situation my mom put us both in. Because I'm clearly not who he and his pack were looking for.

His gentle hand grasps my shoulder. "Scarlett, I'm so sorry. I should have known after my meeting last week when she told me you'd prefer to skip any sort of court-ing. You have quite the respectable pack, but she was a bit off."

"Not off. Desperate. I have an obligation to my pack that my mother has to help me fulfill by being married. Things get complicated if I'm not. She could lose her precious royalty status." I squeeze my eyes shut, trying to wrap my head around everything. "All of this self-doubt because of a fucking typo." I mutter the last comment under my breath, forcing myself to straighten my shoulders.

Adrian reaches out and rubs his thumb across my jaw, drawing it toward my ear to push my dark brownish-auburn hair behind it. "Which is one of the reasons why we picked you, thinking that your pack would have realized how unnecessary such obligations to our orders as alphas and omega are. I mean, Pack Clearwater was quite generous allowing me and my pack mates the opportunity to focus on our careers first to climb their ranks." Because many packs fall under another authority. Pack Clearwater runs San Diego, and I'm sure Pack Hart wants to eventually get to the top of the hierarchy to be able to claim the Clearwater name. This same type of hierarchy helps my sisters and me, pampering and treating us as royalty despite our parents not being a top pack under Pack Carlisle's umbrella. Our family wouldn't be well off otherwise. He continues exploring the skin down my neck, leaving his scent trail behind. It envelops me in something fruity and spicy, like fresh berries mingling with the heat of cinnamon. "I just hope this doesn't turn you off from us. You're a lovely woman, Scarlett."

His closeness overwhelms me in a good way, and I inhale a soft breath, my deep-seated nature as an omega thrilled by the attention this alpha gives me. "I have been preparing for this moment all my life. Everything will be fine." The words come automatically. "If my pack thinks you're a good fit for me, then I trust them."

Adrian remains expressionless, but something dark enters his light blue gaze. "I'm happy to have you here. Let me show you to your room, and I will let you get settled. I'll also prepare the rest of our pack. This comes as a surprise, but what a pleasant accident. I do look forward to our life together. I promise to make you a very satisfied and happy woman if you let me."

His eyes dart down to my mouth and back up, his presence getting to me in a way I never expected. It's as if I can't resist. I stretch up on my tiptoes and brush my lips to his, kissing him without hesitation. The soft, feather-light touch of our lips lasts only a second, and I swallow and smile as I pull away, watching his eyes light up. This is my moment now. It's my duty to be the omega of his dreams. Like my mom would say, I need to be grateful.

Neither of us says anything as he slides his arm around my waist and guides me to the dark, curved double-sided staircase that wraps around to the second floor with another sitting area. Voices murmur from old vents, but nothing is clear enough to hear. I push my spinning thoughts away. This will work out. I know it. I already like how open he is about his feelings toward societal expectations. Maybe the error in my profile was fate.

It's what I have to believe.

"You'll find all the necessities you need in your bathroom, and I'll ensure you get your belongings as soon as possible. If you need anything, don't hesitate to come and find me. All you have to do is follow this hallway around the corner until you hit the library. My wing is just through the double doors. You can also call me. You'll find your new phone with some other electronics at your desk. We didn't want to overwhelm you even more about coming here, so you do have your own space where you can do as you please. We want you to feel at home because you are home now." Adrian opens the door to my room, revealing a beautifully decorated suite, a bright contrast from everything I've seen in the manor so far, with furniture of white woods and a four-poster bed with silver and sapphire-colored bedding.

He leans down and kisses me again as if we've been kissing forever. I never thought such a gesture would feel so normal, considering I just met him, but it does. His kindness and warmth help ease my nerves and give me the courage to step forward and look around at my new life.

"I'll be back in a bit. If you're hungry, you can find the kitchen downstairs. Just follow the way we came in and go through the servant's entrance on the right." Adrian eases away from me and smiles. "Is there anything else I haven't mentioned? I'll print off the profiles you were supposed to have so you can look at them. I'm sure you're anxious about meeting your other alphas."

I only shake my head in response, my words sticking to my throat. Why do I feel as if he's a bit nervous now? Maybe he doesn't want to leave me, but he also doesn't want to overwhelm me or smother me. I'll just go along with things as I was taught until I understand him better. It's all part of Meeting Your Alpha 101 from Omega Prep.

"Like I said, find me if you need me. It's incredible having you here." Adrian nods his head as he exits my suite and closes the door behind him, leaving me alone in the unfamiliar space.

A beep chimes through the room only a moment later, and I spin to watch the printer on my new desk whirl to life, shooting out a couple dozen pieces of paper. It's the profiles Adrian mentioned.

I stride over and pick up the stack, staring at the names and pictures belonging to five men under the Pack Hart name within Pack Clearwater's authority. Many smaller packs band together under one umbrella name, sharing a territory. And these five alphas work at my university.

Shit.

I don't know what this means, but I guess I'll find out. I just hope they can see me as more than a student.

If they can't, this won't work out.

I won't have a pack.

I'll face a life of rejection.

3

Scarlett

PACK HART

Hours pass as I stare at my phone, trying to decide if I want to reach out to my sisters or wait for my mom to share the news. I don't know if I can fake happiness right now, because all I feel is nervous.

"Miss Scarlett? I'm sorry to bother you so late. Misters Hart wanted you to get your belongings immediately. There will be more to come, but a small bag was delivered already. I'll just leave it at the door." The masculine voice cuts off with a double knock on the door.

I hop to my feet and rush to the door, hoping to catch who it is. The figure turns a corner and disappears too quickly for me to get a good glimpse of, and I assume it's one of the off-duty staff members. If it were one of my alphas, he would have stayed. At least, I hope.

Looking down, I spot my backpack with some clothing sticking out from the half-zipped pocket. It looks as if the RA just grabbed whatever she saw in my dirty hamper and stuffed it inside.

Great. This is humiliating.

My phone chimes with the familiar ringtone that belongs to my best friend Emma, and I snap up my backpack and close the door, turning the lock. I don't know why I do it, but it is what it is. I'm not sure if I'm quite ready to face the world anymore tonight, even though Adrian said he would return to me as soon as he could. At this rate, I think it'll be morning.

Psycho: When were you going to tell me you were engaged? What the fuck, Scarlett? I had to hear about it from my pack. My mom said your mom arranged everything weeks ago. I had no idea.

I sigh and click on Emma's contact, opening up a video chat. It's in this moment that I wish she lived closer and not in a different state completely. She's been my best friend all through Omega Prep, and we graduated together. She has always helped talk me down when other omegas were scooped up, and I wasn't. But then she fell in love with some criminals and ran. I wouldn't have stopped her. She was so happy. Her psycho ass found a pack just as adventurous and exciting as she has always been. And to her pack, money is money, regardless of where it came from. A match made in illegal matrimony.

I could use a good shake and a hug from Emma now. Arizona is over six hours away, though, and if I want to see her, I'll have to jump through hoops. She has made it so she's not easily accessible to anyone, and I can't blame her. Not when the law wants her pack.

I straighten my shoulders and wait until Emma's pretty face pops into view, and she narrows her eyes at me.

"Please don't be mad at me. I only found out that my bitch mom accepted a proposal on my behalf today. She threw it on me as if it was some kind of present." I hang my head, cradling my phone. "It's a mess. There was an error on my paperwork, and the pack who asked for me thought I was older. I'm not sure this is going to work out. They are...mature." I don't want to say that Adrian is old, because he's not really; he's just older than me. By over two decades, according to his information.

"Mature? Do you mean you got yourself Pack Grandpa? Shit, Scarlett. Do their cocks even work?" Emma raises an eyebrow and shifts to look over her shoulder at one of her alphas. I can't see them with how dark her room is, but one of them mumbles something that makes her laugh.

I grab the top sheet of paper from my stack and turn the phone toward it, showing her Adrian's formal portrait. "Not exactly."

I turn the phone back to me and remain expressionless, watching as Emma's expression changes and her lips tilt downward.

"Damn, hello Daddy Adrian. I didn't realize I'd think an old guy was attractive, but you got lucky Scarlett. He's hot. Looks a bit prudish, yet I don't think it's a bad thing for you, Scar." Emma smirks at me, once again peeking behind her as if she thrives on teasing her alphas for the reaction. She gets one in the form of a growl.

"It's completely bad. They picked me thinking that I was experienced." I comb my fingers through my dark auburn-brown hair. "I don't know what to do. I want them to like me. You know what will happen if they change their minds. I...I can't handle that."

"It's not like you're a virgin, beta banger. You'll be fine. Just take the damn D. I'm sure it'll be fun." Emma wags her eyebrows and brings the phone closer to her mouth until all I see are her lips. "I'll send you some educational videos. Watch them. You don't have to be a participant to learn a thing or two. Just breathe, Scarlett. I can tell how worried you are, and it's going to be okay. I promise. You've talked about this forever."

I wish I could squeeze the hell out of Emma right now. It's been a while since I've seen her and smelled her apple scent. She might not understand what it's like to be me, but she's here for me and helps me in her own way, which I appreciate.

"Give it a day or two, and if you need rescuing, you know who to call. I know people." Emma blows me a kiss. "And if you need different advice, call Violet. I'm sure she has some suggestions that don't include cum showers. Way better ones than if you called your mom, too. I can't believe she blindsided you like this. I wish there was something I could do to get her back."

I smile and shake my head. "Just being my best friend gets her back. I miss you, Emma. Maybe you can come visit sometime."

She blows me another kiss. "Definitely. Text me if you need anything. I have to go. Love you, Scar."

"Love you, too." I rapidly blink a few times, pushing my emotions away as I click off the line and turn toward my backpack sitting on the floor.

I lift it onto the bed and dump it out, staring at the pile of dirty clothes along with a couple dresses from my closet. No underwear or socks. No jeans. Just random shit that doesn't match or remotely go together, which means I'll be wearing a dress to class—I mean, wearing a dress tomorrow. My university days are over.

What should feel incredible now feels like I'm losing in the end.

My phone chimes again, displaying a link from Emma. I stare at it suspiciously, knowing that whatever educational videos she supposedly sent will most definitely be porn. If I were a cat, I'd be dead, dead, dead from curiosity. I don't exactly want to know what my best friend might watch, but if she thinks it'll help me learn something...

Oh. My. Fucking. Cock. Party.

My phone screams out in pleasure, the omega's voice echoing through the room as the video starts amid a scene unlike anything of my wildest imagination. Hard cocks point in all directions as four naked alphas hold each of the omega's limbs, suspending her midair only to have a fifth man bury his face between her legs, causing her to scream in ecstasy again. A sixth man stands over her head, stroking his hard-on, and the omega tips her head back and opens her mouth, begging for him to deep throat her.

I can't rip my gaze away. Heat blooms between my legs, the sheer raw desire between this pack hotter than I expect.

My nipples pebble, and I run my hand into my bra, touching my sensitive skin, exploring myself as I watch the alphas explore the omega. I imagine what it would feel like to have so much attention and to give in to the needs of someone while they take care of me as well.

I squirm and sit on the bed, scooting back until I rest on the mountain of pillows. The camera shot pans closer, giving me a view of the alphas lowering the omega onto the bed. She reaches out and grabs one of their cocks, gliding her fingers over the length, the shaft glistening with her slick. Again, the shot zooms in, focusing on the omega's thighs and moving to the apex of her legs. I can't stop my wandering hand and work it lower into my panties, sliding my finger over my body like I watch the alpha do to the omega as he teases her, preparing her for his tip.

I moan at the same time as the omega screams out, the alpha sliding his cock between her legs, his girth stretching her.

"What's wrong? Are you okay, Scarlett?" The voice sounds along with several booming thuds to my door, startling me.

I drop my phone off the side of the bed and panic, the video seeming to grow in volume though it's probably in my head.

The omega screams again, sending my heart racing. Now I wish she would just shut up. Someone needs to stick a cock in her mouth or something, or else I'm going to die of embarrassment.

The door handle jiggles, and I thank the universe that I locked it.

"Scarlett?" the voice calls again. "Scarlett!"

I scramble off the bed, scooping up my phone. "Just a—"

My suite door flings open and clatters against the wall. The familiar man rushes into my room and stops short, his eyes widening at the sight of me clutching my phone, my shirt askew, and showing my bra along with my unbuttoned pants showing off my panties.

Fire explodes across my cheeks. I beg the floor to open up and swallow me whole. My phone continues to scream in bliss, drawing the man's attention to the porn Emma sent me. This isn't exactly the impression I wanted to make, especially because I know who this man is.

He's not only a part of Pack Hart and one of my intended, but he is also my World Lit professor and the star of many of my daydreams. It never even clicked in my head when I saw his name as Jonah Hart. His picture is far more formal than I've ever seen him and without his glasses, and now he stands before me, wide eyes and just as red as I surely am with my burning face.

"Ms. Carlisle. I don't understand. What is going on here? This is...fuck." Professor Hart turns around, bolting toward the door, but another figure materializes and unintentionally blocks his way.

I smack my finger to my phone, trying to get the video to shut off. The omega and all the alphas moan in unison as one of them knots with her, and I clasp my phone between my palms to muffle the noise, finally getting the bullshit to turn off.

"What is going on, Jonah? I told you to wait until morning to introduce yourself." Adrian appears behind the other man, and I take a couple steps back, wishing I could disappear into the corner. Why aren't there any secret passageways? I run my fingers along the wall just to make sure, but nothing happens.

"I thought she was in trouble. I heard screaming." Professor Hart rubs his hand on the back of his neck. I expect him to call me out about the porn, but he doesn't. He doesn't look at me either.

"I'm sorry. I was talking to my best friend, and she sent me something, trying to help with my nerves over..." I wave my hand in silence, my voice refusing to say the words out loud. "I'm sorry. I'm so embarrassed."

"This is exactly why I was concerned, Adrian. She's young and shy. We might have nothing in common." Professor Hart flips his switch, my words kicking away his shock and replacing it with annoyance.

"Ten fewer years isn't a dealbreaker. Her profile was everything we agreed on. Age is but a number, anyway. I'm thirty-nine going on nineteen." A deep, husky voice erupts in laughter, and I turn my attention to...oh, no. Kill me now. I wanted to die the first time I crashed into him just as much as I want the floor to open up and devour me. It's the runner. The man I crashed into and unintentionally unveiled my dirty little secret drawings to.

"It matters when she is one of our students! No aliases were mentioned on her profile, not to mention how she's unrecognizable from her picture." Professor Hart roars, his anger booming out.

Whoa. He says it like it's my fault Mom had the make-up artist practically turn me into someone else.

"Like you look like yours either," I whisper, my throat scratchy.

Professor Hart whips his attention to me, catching my retort, but he doesn't get a chance to respond. The runner backhands his shoulder, getting between us.

"Shut the fuck up, Jonah. She's gorgeous either way. We're damn lucky to have found her. Your pompous ass isn't going to ruin it." The runner shoves Professor Hart.

"Leo, this is unethical for him. He's in a position of power with her. He can't be with a student. What if she were in your classes?" I recognize this man, too as he barges into my room, joining one more alpha. Professor Ezra didn't like being called by a formal name in my Art History class during the spring semester. I wouldn't expect him to recognize me, considering I sat in the back row of the stadium-style lecture hall, four times as big as Professor Hart's classroom.

"Damn right, I can't. It was one thing for there to be an error and miscommunication with her age. But this is different. I'm her professor." Professor Hart balls his hands into fists.

My breathing quickens as the five men crowd together, turning their attention away from me. This is it. This is the moment they'll kick me out and leave me floundering, packless, and an utter disappointment to my parents.

"The solution to that is simple, Jonah. You either choose to abstain from bonding with her, or she drops out," the fifth man says, glancing from his pack mates to me. He must be Dominic, the Mathematics instructor who also teaches ceramics. I'd have taken his art class had it not filled up so quickly. Small mercies, I guess.

"That's easy for you to say." Professor Hart groans. "She'll resent me. We need to discuss this more. Things have changed."

I can't listen to their conversation anymore. I'm not far from my old dorm, and I can stay the night there until I figure shit out. I'm sure my roommate will let me in. She has to. I just need time to call Emma and ask her for help. I know I can always rely on my best friend.

I dart my gaze to the door, calculating my escape and how long it will take me to run downstairs and to the driveway. It'll be a hard as fuck trip down the steep hill, but it would be better than listening to these men shout at each other about not getting what they expected from an omega.

Adrian smacks his hands together, trying to draw order with the rest of his pack. "Everyone, calm down. If you can't talk rationally, then you need to go cool off. None of you should be here. This wasn't the introduction we agreed on."

Professor Hart growls again, the noise reverberating through my bones. "Cool off? We spent a fucking fortune—"

I don't wait to hear what else they have to say and spin on my feet, charging toward the door and dodging around them. My heart breaks, and not even because I like these men. I feel utterly and completely rejected all over again. I just don't understand what I'm doing wrong. I didn't think I was that bad. I know I'm not unattractive. If I were ugly, I wouldn't get checked out all the time. I wouldn't have lost my virginity to a beta at a party back in prep school. And just this morning, I wouldn't have been hit on by a classmate.

Maybe I'm boring. Undesirable on paper. My mom told me as much a dozen times.

Obviously, these men are looking for someone older, probably for the experience, and I just have none of it. I've been sheltered and pampered by my pack due to my order. I'm not a great lay or a master with my tongue because of my lack of experience. I'm just an omega with a passion for art and an admiration for things that I have no business really being obsessed with.

My bare feet slap the concrete drive, my mind refusing to comprehend what's going on. I just keep moving. Keep breathing. As soon as I get over the shock of it all, I'll be able to process things. I'll be able to lift myself back up and move on. It's funny. My older sisters weren't into the whole betrothal and finding a pack thing, and I was. Yet our lives couldn't be more opposite now.

A shadow catches my attention in my peripheral vision, and I spot a figure coming into view. A man pops out from between the trees, spreading his arms wide to block my way. I don't have time to stop before I crash into him, but he doesn't let me fall. At least not this time. His salty lime scent envelops me, the runner and apparently one of my alphas now, locking me in his arms.

"Shit, you're fast. I didn't think you were athletic. There weren't any sports listed on your profile." The alpha's beard tickles the side of my cheek as I gasp, my body going completely out of whack with our closeness. Maybe it's the desire lingering from watching the porn Emma sent me or something else. Whatever it is, I can't stop the tingles exploding over my skin. "I'd love to see your skills under better circumstances."

I smack my hands to his back, wiggling. "Put me down."

He doesn't hesitate, setting me on my feet. He bounces on his tennis shoes, following my movements, prepared to grab me if I try to dodge around him to run away again. "I know you're confused and scared because of Jonah's reaction, but he doesn't speak for all of us. I think you should come back inside. I'm sure you're just as surprised by the circumstances. You probably think we're so fucking old and boring. I mean, finding out you're engaged to your Lit professor? Yuck."

Except that's not it. Professor Hart is far from un-attractive. Many people on campus take his class just to hear his passion for books...or how sexy he sounds reading aloud. "No, I don't think that," I automatically say, my mind just wanting to get through this without angering anyone.

He chuckles. "Your mouth says one thing, but your reaction says another. I get it. I'm sure you had your own expectations about who you wanted to marry. I just hope you decide to give us a chance. I'm Leo, if you don't know. From what Adrian said, it sounds like Pack Steele didn't give you any information about us."

"Because it doesn't matter. There are expectations I need to meet. I'm just...grateful to have finally been proposed to...if that's still something. I know about the clause in the contract about transparency. I'm sure my mom lied about a lot of things. Including my advanced education." I cross my arms over my chest, feeling ridiculous as I stand barefooted, in the dark, amid a failed escape plan.

"We are absolutely not going to cancel our proposal. As for the lies? I don't think it was intentional. Your age was a typo. We had just assumed that you had completed some sort of extra education. It's not required to be disclosed." Leo inches closer, respecting my space but also trying to be near me. "And honestly, I didn't read half of the stuff. I like the idea of getting to know you and learning about you as a person compared to setting these expectations that might not even represent you properly."

"Oh." I don't know what else to say, really. This isn't exactly how I imagined things going tonight. I thought I would be a little bit awkward and excited, meeting the men who would be my partners for life. If only I had realized just how significant things would be. I wasn't aware that I had expectations, but I guess I did expect my alphas to desire me because of who I am on paper. It's probably due to my mom's breeding mindset and the government's idea that omegas are completely responsible for our futures, considering we seem to now be the only ones able to procreate and the birth rates have been on a downward trend for a while.

Leo holds out his hand to me. "Come on, Scarlett. It's cold out here. Our pack won't bother you for the rest of the night, and we'll figure out everything together tomorrow. It might not seem like it, but we are happy you're here. I want you to know that. You'll be an amazing addition to our pack."

I don't respond, afraid that if I do, my voice might crack. All of this is so surreal. A small part of me fears letting my guard down. Leo might be welcoming and charming as hell, but he can't speak for the rest of his pack.

I guess I'll take it one day at a time. One moment at a time. Just like I have been my whole life. As always, I'll just have to wait and see.

Scarlett

PACK MEETING

Psycho: Sorry, my phone died. Did you survive the fiasco? How fucking hilarious. They can't think you're so innocent now. You're welcome.

I ignore the message from Emma and tap my finger on the table, my stomach still in knots after last night. I stayed up until almost three in the morning, reading and rereading my new alphas' profiles, trying to figure out how things might be. Leo wasn't lying about everyone leaving me alone. I overslept and missed the alarm for my Biology lecture and then my lab. Not that it matters. I assume my education is now over. Jonah won't risk his career.

Psycho: Hello? It's already past noon. What's going on? Getting the D?
Psycho: You better answer me.
Psycho: SCARLETT!

I stare at the continuous string of text messages from Emma. If voices didn't murmur from the hallway, I'd consider calling her. Right now, I need to awkwardly face the men I'm to marry after last night. It's not how I wanted to start my day, but I need to get it over with. I need to prove that I'm not some immature omega. I'm more than that.

My phone buzzes again, and I lean back, peeking at it resting on my knee. The etiquette teacher at Omega Prep would lose her shit if she saw me now. Phones are considered distractions and rude, especially during a time I should focus my sole attention on my alphas. I should be staring at the doorway waiting for their arrival like a good little girl.

Psycho: Respond to me and let me know you're okay.

Psycho: What the fuck is going on? I'm tracking you now.

Psycho: Don't make me fucking drive there. It's six goddamn hours.

Emma doesn't even give me a chance, her slight paranoia endearing. If something ever happened to me, I could count on her to rescue my ass.

"Looks like you should respond before Psycho comes crashing through a window on an unnecessary rescue mission," Leo says, resting his hands on my shoulders.

I jump in my seat, nearly dropping my phone. "I'm sorry. I know this is poor etiquette, but it's my best friend. I told her about what happened last night and then fell asleep when she didn't respond."

"Etiquette? This is our home, not a prep school. You don't need permission to answer your friend. It's fine." Leo sits beside me, grabbing the pitcher of orange juice to pour us both a glass. "I assume her nickname precedes her?"

"You have no idea." I accept the glass of juice and set it in front of me. "She's...a bit outrageous. Unpredictable. But she's also protective and caring."

Psycho: SCARLETT!
Psycho: YOU.
Psycho: BETTER.
Psycho: BE.
Psycho: DEAD.
Psycho: Or have a cock in your mouth.

I sigh and set my phone on the table. Smirking, I stab my fork into a sausage link on my full plate and then open my camera app. Leo laughs as I snap a picture of me with the piece of sausage between my teeth and quickly send it to Emma.

Me: Not a cock but a sausage. Sorry. I've had a long night. I'll call you later, okay?
Psycho: Fine, but don't forget. You don't want to find out what happens if you do.
Me: Love you, psycho.
Psycho: I know. :P

A tap sounds at the wide entrance of the dining room, drawing my attention away from my message with Emma. My heart races at the scent of sweet jasmine and tangy bergamot tickling my nose. Footsteps thud closer, and the chair on my other side slides from the table before someone fills it.

"Good morning, Scarlett," Professor Ezra says, his smooth voice soft and gentle. "I hope you slept well. Is the food to your liking? I can make you something else if you prefer."

"That's not necessary. Everything tastes delicious. As for me, I'm just a bit tired. I hope you slept well, Professor Ezra." The formality of my voice makes me cringe, and I turn my gaze and look at the man I might've once fantasized about last semester. His dark hair curls around his ears, the mop of strands as carefree as he always seemed to be.

His thick brows lower over his sparkling brown eyes. Running a hand through his black beard, he rubs his lips together. The V of his T-shirt displays his masculine, hairy chest, and I can imagine what he looks like without his shirt because of how tight it hugs his torso, the curves of his abs obvious. These alphas seem to take good care of themselves physically. I would never guess any of them were forty. Unlike Adrian and Professor Hart, Ezra doesn't have any peppering of gray.

"Please, Scarlett. Call me Ezra." Ezra slides his hand a bit closer to mine, but he doesn't try to touch me.

"It'll take me a bit of time to get used to it, considering I was a student in your class last spring." I dart my gaze away, saving myself from his expression.

"Scarlett Carlisle. Yes, I do remember you hiding in the back of the lecture hall. I didn't suspect you were an omega but just from the Pack Carlisle. You scored excellent on the final exam, messing up the grading curve for everyone." He smirks with his words.

I open and close my mouth, shocked that he remembered such details. "They probably hate me."

"I started the curve with the person below you. It just happened to be the first time someone had ever aced my final. And I apologize for not recognizing you immediately. Something's different." Ezra scoots his seat, drinking in my side profile. I know he wants to get a better look at me, but he doesn't want to pressure me either.

This is a moment that I know to give in to his silent question. I've trained for this. Reading an alpha has been ingrained into me.

I turn slightly and push my hair away from my shoulder, showing off the black mini dress that was at the bottom of my backpack. It was one of the few things Emma gave me after her Fall Ball at home. I had never worn it until today, but it was only because I didn't want to put on something dirty.

And now I feel like the sexiest woman in the world with the way Ezra trails his eyes from mine and down my neck and to my cleavage, working his way to my bare thighs, peeking out from the hiked-up hem.

I squirm a bit under his attention, crossing and uncrossing my legs. He flares his nostrils, catching the cherry-vanilla scent emanating from me. Without my suppressant lotion, he'll be able to read my body as if I'm an open book before him. He looks ready to read every single one of my pages with his fingers, his mouth, his...

"Dominic and Jonah better join us for brunch." Adrian's sultry voice shocks my mind back into the present.

I quickly grab my orange juice and sip it slowly, the tangy coolness of the juice helping to smother out the heat burning across every molecule of my body. I never expected to have such a reaction toward an alpha, and it's as if my very nature knows that he will be mine and I'll be his.

Ezra. I repeat his name in my mind, pushing away the thoughts of last semester and my life before this moment. It doesn't matter now. What matters is what happens from this second on.

"I'm here. Joe is pulling into the drive now. You know he had an eight and ten AM lecture. He thought it best not to cancel." Dominic enters the posh dining room, splatters of dried clay peppering his dark complexion like a smattering of stars.

He only wears a T-shirt and jeans, far more casual than I saw him last night. It's a bit strange yet comforting, knowing that he can relax. Adrian remains in a suit, but he is sexy in a sophisticated way. Having the four of them in front of me, no longer shocked or arguing, helps ease my worry.

But then the door slams.

I straighten my back and clutch my fork, bracing myself for Professor Hart to enter the dining room. It can't be easy for him either, considering I've been in his class for weeks now. It's far more intimate, with only thirty students compared to the hundreds of the larger lecture halls. Not many take World Literature, but it's what Mom chose. There is no rhyme or reason to my schedule apart from ticking boxes for a Bachelor of Arts Degree with a focus on general studies despite my desire to work on my skills. It could be worse, though. My mom could've denied me enrolling at all. She could've also chosen an omega program for those who can't procreate and teach at Omega Prep. She did threaten it.

At least I don't have to think about that anymore.

"We're in the dining room, Jonah. Please join us immediately. Scarlett has been waiting long enough for our pack meeting." Adrian slides into the seat at the head of the table, declaring himself as Pack Hart's leader. I kind of assumed as much, but now he looks more authoritative.

"My apologies for being late. I wanted to stop by the garden and pick these up." Professor Hart sets a tissue-wrapped bouquet of fresh flowers in front of me. "I hope you like chrysanthemums. They are quite beautiful this time of year."

I gawk at the bouquet in shock, Professor Hart's gesture surprising me.

"I wish I could take back my reaction yesterday, but I can't, so I will do my best to do better moving forward, Scarlett," he adds, taking a seat next to Dominic across from us.

I scoop up the bouquet and bring it to my nose, inhaling a breath of the herby, earthy fragrance with a hint of musk, unconventional and unlike the sweeter scents of flowers you usually find in a bouquet. "Thank you, Professor Hart. I love them. I also wanted to apologize on behalf of my pack for the way this situation played out."

Leo rests his hand on my shoulder. "First, don't call him Professor Hart. The titles have to go. You're our soon-to-be wife. Second, it's not your duty to apologize to Jonah. You couldn't have known."

I twist my lips. "I still feel as if I need to. I know that I'm not the omega you had desired—"

"Nonsense. You're perfect. I won't allow you to talk any less of yourself." Adrian rests his hands on the table-top, his height commanding attention. "We're happy regardless. We have wanted this for a long time. I have great respect for how you're handling everything. I can only imagine what a shock it is."

"Speak for yourself." Leo scoots closer and drapes his arm over my shoulders. "I look good."

Dominic groans and rests his elbows on the table. "Don't be conceited. It's unbecoming of you, Leo."

A smirk plays on my lips, listening to their banter. "It's okay. He's right...but about all of you." I should just spit it out. The last thing I want is for my alphas to think for even a second that I don't find them attractive. They're hot, smell so good, and have been so welcoming.

"See," Leo says, his smile lighting his face. Leaning in, he kisses my temple, the small gesture of affection warming my insides.

"I guess we'll see if her thoughts remain the same once she's comfortable." Ezra remains expressionless, guarded. "She's been trained to agree to a fault."

I open my mouth to argue but stop myself. He's not wrong. My hesitation comes from my desperation. I need them to accept me. If Mom was unhappy with her pairing with my dads, then she disguised it well. I know that time helps the bond. It gives me hope.

"That's enough. We have more important things to discuss than first impressions and attraction. We need to bring order to this chaos, or I'm going to lose my shit on the next disrespectful beta in my afternoon class." Jonah flicks his attention to me for a second. It reminds me of when the beta started harassing me in class.

"You're absolutely right." Adrian scoops some fruit and yogurt from the buffet-style breakfast the kitchen staff set up upon my arrival. He surprises me by sliding it closer and offering me a bite. "We need to agree on a schedule and decide on how to proceed with Scarlett's education."

"She only has this semester and next before she gets her degree. I think we should allow her to finish." Ezra laces his fingers together, leaning in closer to me. "I mean, if that's what you'd like. You had to have a reason to pursue an education outside of the Omega Prep."

I lift and drop my shoulders. "This wasn't the school I wanted to go to, but my mom wouldn't allow me to attend Shadow Ridge Art School. This had the second-best art program in the area. My single status was an embarrassment to my mom, so I agreed to get as far away as she'd allow."

"You're an artist? That wasn't mentioned in your paperwork. What media?" Dominic perks up, turning his attention away from his full plate.

"Yeah, Dom. She's a damn good one, too." Leo bumps my shoulder. "Mind-blowing."

I purse my lips and side-glance him, praying he doesn't spill my dirty little secret. It's one thing to have him discover my obsession with the human body. It's another to have to show my new pack anything of the such.

Ezra tilts his head, frowning like he might be a bit jealous. "You've seen—"

"I've studied mixed media, drawing and painting, and digital illustration, but my favorite thing is photo-realistic figures with charcoal. I tried to enroll in ceramics to see if I'd enjoy that, but your class is quite popular, Dominic." I don't sound sophisticated as I redirect focus from Leo and Ezra, especially considering one of them is an Art History instructor. "I mostly just like to draw. I haven't had much formal practice since my mom picked an array of courses that all fit under the Bachelor of Arts umbrella."

"That's a shame your pack didn't see the pursuit of your passion as necessary. I'd like to change that. I think I can add another spot in my Friday class if you'd like." Dominic offers me a smile.

"Absolutely not. I know you have good intentions, Dom, but I'd like to suggest pulling Scarlett from Clearwater and taking a more personal approach. There is a great online program." Adrian leans back in his chair, setting his spoon down.

"I have to agree. The risk to our standing with the university and our power within Pack Clearwater is far too great," Ezra says, taking a bite of his food without looking at me.

"I wouldn't mind a little one-on-one education." Leo squeezes my knee under the table. "I think she could excel in athletics under my supervision."

"I suppose you're right. We'd just be testing fate if she were in my class. I can't promise to offer the other students my attention otherwise." Dominic rubs his full lips together, his dark gaze penetrating me as I try not to look at him and his sexy, easy-going smile bright against his velvety dark skin. I think he's flirting, but I can't react.

If I try to speak, my voice might crack. I know they have my best interests in mind, but all I can think about is how I was so close to finishing and how they might accidentally isolate me, keeping me a secret.

I don't want to be a fucking secret.

I just want to enjoy some normalcy with them.

"No. I disagree with all of you, and I'll not allow you to pull Scarlett from the exceptional education she desires. I'm the only one at higher risk, and I will not touch her until she is out of my class. She needs socialization and independence to gain the experience we thought she had. Don't deny her." Jonah stands up and places his hands on his hips, shocking the hell out of me. I thought he would be the first one to demand I unenroll from Clearwater University, and instead, he's on my side even though I haven't said a single word.

Adrian stands up, towering over Jonah as if he wants to use his height to intimidate him as pack leader. "Joe, The rest of us—"

"It has to be unanimous, and I disagree. I think you should ask Scarlett what she wants. If she would prefer to follow through with your suggestion—" Turning to me, Jonah meets my gaze. "And I mean truly want it and not say so just because the rest of them do, Scarlett. If you want to finish up your degree on your current course trajectory, then you should be able to."

Silence fills the room as all five of them stare at me, waiting for me to respond. My instincts say to agree with the majority to please most of them, but then I think about what I truly want. This is the first time I have been asked—basically demanded—to pick for myself.

My mouth dries, and I lift the glass of juice to my lips, gulping until I'm ready to respond. "I'm excellent at keeping to myself, staying under the radar with my suppressant lotions, and I promise to stay out of anyone's business to keep our pack safe."

A cocky smile lights Jonah's face. "I know you will. It's only a couple months."

Dominic shakes his head. "But Jonah, she'll be going into hea—"

"We'll get through all of this. We had our chance to create our perfect life, and I'll do anything to ensure that Scarlett gets hers as our fiancée." Jonah closes the space to me and grazes his knuckles on my cheek. "I hope you find our pack acceptable. The others will handle the schedule and everything else you shall need. I must head back to campus. If I'm not mistaken, you have an afternoon class as well. Would you like a ride?"

I don't know what comes over me, but I nod my head and take his proffered hand. Jonah pulls me from my seat and steals me away, practically making me run as our pack yells his name from behind us.

He doesn't bother to look back, and I just go with it.

I say a silent prayer to the universe. Please don't let this be a big mistake.

Jonah

FORBIDDEN

What am I doing? What am I fucking doing?

It was like something came over me during the pack meeting. I should've been the first one to agree with online studies for Scarlett, but all it took was one glance at her pouty mouth, and I knew it was the wrong decision.

I've only known Scarlett as she permitted the world to see her for a few weeks, but if there is one thing I've learned, it's that she isn't the brainwashed submissive omega I feared. I had my mind set on marrying someone older and not fresh out of one of the many Omega Preps used to keep breeders placid because of it. She's mature, intelligent, and despite her upbringing, on the cusp of breaking the mold she was cast in.

Goddamn it, though.

She's my student.

I've never had an issue with attraction toward any of my previous students, nor have I ever fantasized about being with one...until Scarlett walked in and sat in the back of my classroom, hunkered down and hidden behind her hoodie and cascading mahogany hair. I thought I was crazy with how I couldn't keep my gaze off her. It has been a struggle not constantly staring at her, especially when she'd tilt her head, smiling softly as I read my favorite passages aloud. And now I know why. It was as if my deep-seated nature knew she was an omega, and I desperately wanted to be her alpha.

And of course, fate wanted to torment me. Fate wanted to test me and torture me knowing that I could have her, but at what expense? I don't feel worthy enough to ask her to give up anything when she's already willing to build and create a future. To offer herself as my beautiful mate and the woman willing to be the mother of my children despite not having a chance to truly build a connection. And I want that connection so badly. I think it's why I made the rash decision to use her weakness against her, putting her in the position to obey me as an authoritative figure. It was absolutely wrong of me, but I don't regret it.

Watching her relax in my peripheral vision, sneaking glances at me, gets me right in the cock. Her cherry-vanilla scent wafts around me, intensifying my racing heart. I stomp the throttle and drive faster. I reach the far corner lot of campus, parking under a magnolia tree and away from any cars or students that might see us. I honestly don't know what I was thinking now that I have a moment. I need to come up with an excuse to be around Scarlett. I need a way as to not be suspicious. Maybe she could use extra credit, and I could have her be a teacher's aide. Or maybe I can adjust my lesson plans and create study groups that'll allow me a reason to be where she is.

What am I even thinking? I should just do my best to stay cordial and friendly, using this time to get to know her.

My cock hardens, my balls angry at the thought. I want to fuck her here and now. I just want to take the moment to get it out of my system.

"Thanks for the ride, I guess." Scarlett unclicks her seatbelt, shifting nervously beside me. I've already made her uncomfortable, losing myself to my thoughts.

"Scarlett, wait." I swivel and look at her, studying her peachy lips and pouty mouth like I had the first time she took an exam in my class, and I was able to stare at her without her noticing. "I'm sorry for how this morning has gone. I know I'm giving you whiplash. It's just that...you have unintentionally tested my restraint for weeks now, and it feels as if my fuse is finally burning up. I never guessed your order could be an omega, but let's just say my strong reaction was due to the fact that you're the most beautiful, intelligent woman who has ever graced my class. I shouldn't want you as badly as I do. It could ruin our pack's future. I have worked so hard to get everything we could ever need to raise a family and have a good, fulfilling life. You're my forbidden fruit, and I just want a little taste. But I know better."

Scarlett opens and closes her mouth, her words lost to her. Blush tints her cheeks with a rosy color. I raise my hand and gently test her, seeing if she'll let me touch her. She leans closer, the warmth of her skin so soft and inviting that I cup her cheek and close the space, leaving only inches between our mouths.

"This will be the hardest couple of months of my life, but I know you'll be worth it. I know it's not a good excuse for my previous behavior, but it's the best I can do," I add, trying my hardest to ignore my throbbing cock, the ache enough that the moment I find myself alone, I'm going to have to rub one out.

"I'm sorry." Scarlett pouts, her eyes shining with unshed tears. "Maybe I should drop out and make things easier for all of us. I don't want you to feel so conflicted."

Fuck me. My confession wasn't supposed to make her feel bad. It was supposed to make her feel better about everything.

Now I'm floundering. I don't know what to do or say or how to react.

"No. I will not be the reason you lose something you want. I just...can I kiss you? Just this once. I want to seal my promise with affection, so you know that I'm willing to be the alpha you need and desire." I study her beautiful gray eyes, her scent as sweet and delicious as I'm sure she tastes. My mouth waters at the idea, and I don't know what I'll do if she denies me. I might never recover. I probably deserve it, though.

She responds to my question by bowing close and grazing her lips to mine, kissing me softly, sensually, just teasing me with the cherry-vanilla flavor of her mouth that matches her delectable scent, the gourmand fragrance like the most mouthwatering dessert I've ever experienced.

I kiss her deeper, testing the seam of her mouth with my tongue until she parts her lips and lets me glide my tongue over hers in a way I haven't kissed anyone in years. I've been so focused on work and my pack duties that I've chosen to ignore any sort of relationship since my twenties. This moment is unlike anything I've experienced before. It's more than a kiss with the intention to fulfill my raw need as a rutting alpha or the natural desire and curiosity to explore my sexuality in my youth. This truly is a vow to someone unexpected but highly regarded in my eyes. Scarlett, my untouchable, radiant omega.

She's mine.

I pull away and growl under my breath, my resolve cracking the longer I remain close to her. I need space. I need air. If I get neither of those, I'll undress her right here in the front seat of my car. She wouldn't deny me. She has already accepted her role as my omega, but I want her to truly want me. To crave me. I will not take advantage of her upbringing.

Scarlett whimpers softly, the sound of her building desire striking me in the gut. I've turned her on and now have denied her.

"Please understand why I have to stop, my forbidden beauty. You need to remain unobtainable. If I continue, I won't stop. I'll ask you to take my knot, and I'll never leave your side again. But the world still moves around us and...fuck." I open my car door to bring in some fresh air.

"Jonah..." My name on her lips is like music to my ears and freezes me in place. "Thank you. Thank you for—"

Laughter echoes through the air, cutting Scarlett off, and I turn and spot a couple betas exiting an old, rusted pickup truck. More students will be coming on campus for the afternoon classes.

"We should go. I want you to keep the keys to my car in case something keeps me past my lecture. I'll find my own way home if that's the case." Leaning closer to her once more, I kiss her cheek and smile, hoping to leave things on a good note. "Don't forget to work on your essay. I can't show you special treatment."

Scarlett releases a breathless laugh and nods her head. "I wouldn't expect anything less, Professor Hart."

The way she says it stirs something dark and wild inside me. "Ms. Steele. Tease me with my formal title again, and you might end up staying after class."

What am I doing?

I shouldn't be toeing this line, but I love the way she giggles.

A car horn blares as two sedans nearly hit each other coming onto campus, and I take that as a sign that I need to get out of here before it's too late. Before I won't be able to leave her.

"I'll see you later, my forbidden beauty." I use the term of endearment as a reminder to myself. The woman I want but need to resist.

I stroke my finger along her jaw one last time and exit, staring at her through the window. It takes everything in me to turn my back and walk away.

It kills me that for the next few months, I'll always have to leave Scarlett behind. I know it will be worth it. She won't be forbidden forever.

A knock sounds on my office door two minutes before my office hours end. I growl and drop my pen, wishing students wouldn't wait until the last second to interrupt me.

"Come in," I called out, my voice hopefully capturing my annoyance.

The door swings inward, and in steps my least favorite student, along with two others I don't ever pay much attention to.

"Hey, Professor Hart. You said we could come by and go over our first drafts today." Chaz Broderik meanders into my office, waving a single sheet of paper. It's far shorter than the expected length I stated on the syllabus.

"My office hours end in one minute. That is obviously not enough time, and I'll not stay a moment later to accommodate you and your lack of awareness. You can try again on Friday." I sit up straighter at my desk, remaining expressionless. "You also might want to consider turning that outline into an actual draft. You know it's supposed to be five to seven pages, and I doubt you will be able to clearly state your points within two-hundred and fifty words, Mr. Broderik."

"But the draft is due tomorrow, and you said you had to sign off on them to get the credit before we can even start our final papers," Chaz complains, looking toward the other two betas. "I need the credit."

If he were any other beta, I would just give in and offer an alternative. But Chaz was the one who was harassing Scarlett right before my eyes during a lecture. Just the thought pisses me off, and I grab and clench my pen.

"You should've followed my instructions and not waited to the last second. You've had an ample amount of time to get me to sign off. It's not my fault that you've procrastinated." I narrow my eyes, flicking my attention to the two other betas behind him. "As for you, Mr. Ford and Ms. Harrison, if you show me that you have at least put in some effort with your drafts, I will sign off yours before class tomorrow."

Am I a dick? Absolutely. It's quite obvious that the other two betas have several pages for their essays. It helps that they have never done anything to piss me off. I shouldn't hold a grudge, but the fact that Scarlett is now mine makes everything even worse with my attitude.

"Are you serious?" Mr. Broderik asks, his voice rising with his annoyance.

"Perhaps you will try harder when you repeat my class next semester, Mr. Broderik." A smug smile curves across my lips, and I feel such great relief and satisfaction over his tantrum. He spins and shoves between the two betas, and a feminine cry sounds from the lobby.

"Fuck, Dickasso. I didn't see you. Let me help you up," Chaz says, his voice softening.

I don't even have to see Scarlett to know that she's in the lobby. I can smell her from here, and it takes everything in me not to rush from my place. My legs betray me, and I automatically stand up, trying to peer past the two betas as they face away.

"If you were here to get your essay signed off on, don't waste your time. The fucker won't do it." Chaz groans with his words. "I'm about to fail now."

"Oh, no. That's not why I'm here. I had it signed off already," Scarlett says, reminding me that she did stop by two weeks ago, and I just blocked it out because...damn. She probably thought I was so cold because I barely even read it and just scrawled my name across the top.

Chaz chortles. "Of course, you did. You seem like the kiss-ass type. But I know your secret, Dickasso. Maybe we can get together later and—"

I slam my hands on my desk and stride around it, wanting nothing more than to get this rudimentary student away from Scarlett. Her eyes widen, spotting me, and I catch myself on my doorframe, ignoring how the two betas scramble to move out of my way.

My instincts demand I call Scarlett into my office, but my good senses scream that the best way to get this beta away from her is to give him what he wants. "Mr. Broderik. I've had a change of heart. Please come into my office." Turning my gaze to Scarlett, I add, "I'm sorry, Ms. Carlisle. You'll have to see me before class tomorrow with the others with whatever you need. Email also works well."

Scarlett slowly nods her head, realizing that I need her to just leave the building. I don't know what has gotten into me, but this already proves to be more difficult than I realized it would be.

"Hurry, Mr. Broderik. I don't have all day." I wave my hand at him, demanding that he return.

He whispers something under his breath to Scarlett, and her cheeks flush. I wait until she finally turns around and strides away before I close my door and return to my desk, pointing at the chair across from me.

The second Chaz takes a seat, I lean forward and snatch his half-page essay from his hands. I don't even waste my time reading it and sign the top, marking only half credit.

"You need to rework this entire thing. If you can provide what I have asked for by the morning, I will give you the rest of your credit. Do not procrastinate again. I don't have patience for those who don't want to be here." I slide his paper back to him. "And Mr. Broderik, if I hear you disrespecting another student like you just did, I will fail you. Do you understand?"

Chaz glowers at me but doesn't respond with anything other than nodding his head. He wouldn't. I'm sure if he were to be expelled or fail out of Clearwater University, he would find himself without the power of his pack. Only the most powerful packs and wealthiest send their betas to Clearwater, because it opens positions of power not only throughout San Diego but throughout many different states as we expand our campus with satellite locations across all of the United States.

"Good. Now leave. I have more important things to do than deal with your bullshit." It's not like me to swear in front of students, but it seems that might be the only way I can really get through to him.

Chaz rushes from my office, and I gather my things, not risking getting interrupted once more by either a colleague or other students. I need to get to Scarlett. I need her to know that I will not tolerate people calling her inappropriate nicknames or trying to pressure her into uncomfortable situations she doesn't want a part of.

My cell phone beeps from my pocket as I stare at the full parking lot, spotting my Volvo where I left it. But I don't see a figure inside.

Adrian: FYI Scarlett asked to be picked up from campus. I left your key fob in your tire well.

Me: I told her she could take my car.

Adrian: I was nearby when she asked if she could go to her old dorm. I'm swinging her by since she still hasn't received the rest of her belongings. We'll see you at dinner.

I stare at the text message, wondering if I might have freaked Scarlett out. No, she was probably just anxious and didn't want to wait or leave me stranded.

"Professor Hart, are you okay? You look a bit lost." Chaz stands by the rusted pickup with the two other betas that must've waited for him.

I shake my head and turn away. "Have a good day, Mr. Broderik. It's best if you get to work now."

I stride toward my Volvo and don't look back.

All I want to do now is drive.

Leo

Daddy Issues

There has been so much tension and anticipation in the manor that I feel as if one of us might explode at any second. Even though a couple of days have passed since Scarlett moved in, I still haven't had my chance to get her alone...until today. I've never been so grateful to see my name written on the calendar in our formal study shared by the five of us. I always hated that thing, a reminder of my responsibilities, but Scarlett is far from that. I don't feel as if she's my responsibility. I feel as if she's my treat and my day off from everything. I've always been pretty chill with my schedule as the Director of Athletics, and most of my classes don't need an instructor present all the time. That's what my teacher's aide is for. The sports coaches don't give a shit either, as long as they get the funding they want. Everything is self-run, and I basically just show up to unlock the gym and prepare for the testing every quarter.

It's also nice that my first day with Scarlett falls on a Saturday, so nothing can interfere with us.

I swish mouthwash and spit in the sink, running my fingers through my long beard as I follow my grooming ritual. There is nothing more disgusting than an unkempt, ungroomed beard, and I'd never bestow that shit on the woman of my dreams. I've seen douches not bother to wash their beards in the locker room, and just no. Repulsive.

A soft tap sounds on the door, and I turn away from my bathroom mirror. "Come on in, Scarlett. It's unlocked."

Scarlett cracks the door open and peeks in, not being able to see me in my spot in the bathroom where I can watch her in the mirror. "Leo? I didn't know if you wanted me to meet here or if you were picking me up from my room. You let me sleep in."

"It's Saturday. You can sleep for as long as you want. If you're still tired, hop in my bed. My room is your room." I hang my towel over my shower rod and stroll into my bedroom, spotting Scarlett standing just a few feet into my room.

If I could capture the look on her face forever, I would. Her beautiful gray eyes widen as she stares at me standing naked before her, my body still gleaming with the heat of shower steam.

She doesn't cover her eyes or turn around, proving that she isn't as shy as she acts around my pack mates. And maybe it's because she's comfortable. Or maybe she loves what she sees.

"Oh, you have a Jacob's ladder." Scarlett focuses on my semi, devouring the sight of me as if she plans to draw me later. Maybe she will.

I chuckle and run my fingers along the silver barbells. "I'm surprised you know what that is, my dirty girl."

She ignores my quip and asks, "Did it hurt? I've never seen one in person."

I step closer, puffing out my chest, loving that she is completely unfazed as she stares at me, admitting that she's not naïve, nor is she embarrassed. "Fuck yeah, it did. But it's cool as hell. Extra sensitive."

"You have a lot of tattoos as well. I thought about getting one." Scarlett stares at my cock, tilting her head back and forth, clenching her fingers at her sides as if she's resisting reaching out her hand to stroke me.

I get a hard-on just thinking about it, the idea of her anywhere near me is exhilarating. "I'm not sure my pack mates would agree to allow someone else to touch your body or leave a mark on you even if it's one of your choosing. But I might be able to wear them down."

"You'd do that for me? I mean, it's just a thought. I don't know if I actually want one. I was thinking about doing something I design myself." Scarlett grazes her fingers over my arm, sending my muscles rippling. Fuck, what I would give to feel her explore the rest of me.

It's as if she wants to memorize my body, familiarizing herself with me.

I don't stop her. I know I should, because if she continues, I might seduce her right here, right now.

"Maybe I could design something for you too. You have some space right here." She presses her finger to my hard pec.

I shiver and cover her hand with mine, easing her away. "I'd love it. Whatever you want."

She smiles and giggles, the sweetness of her voice reminding me just what a sugary-sweet dirty girl she is. I've seen the inner workings of her mind displayed through her art. I kept the one she accidentally left behind the very first moment I laid eyes on her as she knocked me off my feet. It's right beside my bed on my nightstand. I can't wait until she discovers it.

"There's a lot of things I want, but especially you, my dirty girl. Keep standing so close, and we're going to get started on our workout right here and now." I playfully growl and take a step away, twirling her toward the bed. She plops down and rests on her hands, crossing her legs.

"If that's what you want." Damn. Her easy submission gets to me in a good way.

I lean forward and get in her face, my lips only a breath away. "If I didn't know any better, I'd think you weren't a virgin."

She stretches her neck, caressing her lips to mine without kissing me. "That's because I'm not. Does it bother you?"

"Fuck no," I automatically say. "I don't want to sound like an ass, but I'm relieved."

"Why?" Scarlett eases away from me, staring into my eyes. "My mom always said that alphas didn't want used goods."

"I don't want to talk about your mom...but fuck that. I don't give a damn about staking a claim on your V-card or whatever. I picked you because of what I liked about you on paper, not for your body or your fertility." I grasp Scarlett's hands. "Though now that you're sitting on my bed..."

Biting her lip, she peeks from me and to my naked body before her, the scent of her desire permeating between us. I've made a huge mistake. I want Scarlett to be comfortable with me, but now all I can think about is climbing on top of her and ripping her clothes off. Our physical attraction is undeniable, and I savor just how flirty she is. My pack thought it was best if we take the first few weeks slow, but I don't think they realize that Scarlett might not be as innocent as we—they—thought. I know her perverse, sexy as hell hobby, and I want to get to know this version of her more, not acting in the way Omega Prep surely taught her how to act.

I shake my head, pushing away the filthy thoughts. "I'm going to regret this, but my pack mates will murder me if I knot with you before feeding you, though maybe—no, we should eat something that isn't each other."

Scarlett tips her head back, her melodious laughter filling the air and giving me a chance to step away from her to get dressed. I can't recall another morning better than this, and I crave a million more. I never expected bringing an omega into our pack would be so easy, but with Scarlett, it's effortless.

Scarlett stands from my bed, sauntering closer, her shadow darkening the wall. "So if we're not going to indulge in each other, what are we going to do? Study? Drive around? Play a game of a thousand questions?"

I zip up my pants and lift an eyebrow. "I should beat up our pack for that shit. They really wasted your time with...adulting."

"I understand they all have things to do. I wasn't expecting all of you to just drop everything with my arrival. And honestly, it's made it easier on me. It's nice still having some freedom. I really thought I would be giving everything up. Not that I wouldn't if you asked me. It's just nice that I don't have to." Scarlett bounces on her feet, suddenly growing nervous as if she's afraid of my reaction.

"As long as you're good, then I'm good. But if you get tired of all the crap, let me know. I have a bit more free time. I could always use another teaching assistant. I can get away with a lot more than Jonah or even Dom at this university. As long as the coaches are happy and my students show up when they are told, then things flow easily." I reach out and caress my fingers to Scarlett's cheek, feeling the warmth of her skin.

"I'm good. Really. I want you guys to be comfortable too. I know that things aren't exactly how you expected them, and I will let you all lead," Scarlett says, drinking me in as if she can't resist. Maybe she still imagines me naked. I'd be lying if I didn't feel even more confident seeing her reaction. I work hard on my body. I'm lucky to have someone appreciate it.

I never really thought about it until now. I'm sure my pack mates are having all sorts of internal struggles about the age gap. I'm more easy-going.

"You might want to take the reins with Jonah and maybe Ezra. If you let them lead, none of you will get anywhere for a while." I grin with my words, wondering how long it will take either of them to break. The masochist, loving the pain of patience.

"Maybe you can help me. I know the whole situation messes with Jonah, and he's afraid of opening up even a little. I think we can still manage to build a relationship despite me being in his class." Scarlett shrugs with her words. "Or maybe not. I don't want to get him in trouble."

"I think Jonah's unnecessarily worried. You deserve to get to know him. If he wants to torture himself, that's fine, but he shouldn't torture you in the process. You could always test him. Get him back for all the essays and exams I'm sure he takes great pleasure in administering." I chuckle with a thought. "I'll take you shopping or something. Pick you out one of those cute plaid skirts. What do you think, dirty girl?"

Scarlett shakes her head, blushing. "I don't know about that. Maybe I'll just start slow."

I hold out my hand to her. "Whatever you want. But let's think about it more outside of this room. Outside of this fucking manor. I want to take you out and stop treating you like a little secret."

Scarlett purses her lips. "Are you sure it's okay?"

"Fuck yeah, it is. No one's going to even notice. Trust me." I guide her toward the door, opening it for her.

She bobs her head, her expression softening with her worry. I know I shouldn't ask her to put so much faith in me, but I will prove myself. I'll earn her trust and be her perfect alpha. She'll see.

"Oh, Scarlett! It's so nice to see you. I was just going to call you about the windows." A woman stands behind the counter of Beach Brew, one of my favorite coffeehouses, tying her apron around her waist. "I didn't mean for it to take a week, but I've been feeling under the weather."

I thought Scarlett was acting nervous when I pulled my Corvette into the lot and parked under the tree in the corner. We're near the beach and not exactly on campus. I thought this would be a great way to start the day. Coffee at Beach Brew and a jog along the waves. It gives me an excuse to see her in the cute sports bra I had Adrian have her pick out.

"Are you feeling better?" Scarlett asks, clearing her throat. "I know that my idea is a bit...dark and wild. I just thought that maybe you wanted to do something more family-friendly for Halloween."

"Family-friendly? Hardly. I'd prefer to keep all the littles away from caffeine. Save their parents' sanities." The woman chuckles and motions to a kid sitting at a small table against the back wall. "Plus, my boy approved. He thought your mockup was the best."

Scarlett lights up, beaming a brilliant smile. "Really?"

The woman grins, nodding her head. "Absolutely. Which means, I'd like to offer you the job. I also was thinking that maybe you could come up with a mural for my back wall. What do you think? That wallpaper really needs to go."

Scarlett squeaks with her excitement and suddenly freezes, tensing beside me. She glances at me and then at the woman. "I'll have to…"

I realize that she probably applied for a job painting the windows for this coffee shop and just got it. And now she's nervous. She doesn't know whether or not she can accept it, considering none of us knew, and it was before we proposed and arranged to marry her.

"We'll have to celebrate. This is amazing, Scarlett." I slide my hand around her waist and give her a shake. "I can't wait to see what you have in store."

Scarlett blinks her watery eyes, her shoulders relaxing. "Really?"

"Yes, really. I'll talk to the others. I'm sure they'll be fine with this, considering that they apparently have a lot of fucking adulting to do." I never knew I could be so proud of someone that I've just met, but I am.

Scarlett steps away from me, smiling like the sun shines from within her. She closes the space to the woman. "I accept. I'm so happy!"

"I'm happy to have you too. I'd like to have it done within a month, if that's okay. In time for the Fall Carnival." The woman eyes me from over Scarlett's shoulder but doesn't say anything. I'm sure she's wondering what an alpha is doing with a...I'm assuming she thinks Scarlett is a beta, considering that she's been passing as one for a while.

"I think I can manage that as long as I can get here every day." Scarlett shifts on her feet and peeks at me.

I nod my head at her.

"Perfect. If you hold on a second, I'll grab the contract and the check for the deposit and supplies you quoted me." The woman spins on her feet, her braid flinging. The door chimes from behind us, and she turns toward a swing door that leads to the back. "Chaz, come watch the register."

Scarlett stiffens and takes a step back, her sudden fear permeating through the air, her cherry-vanilla scent turning warmer like a cherry pie fresh from the oven. I stride a few feet toward her and take her hand again, only to have her yank it away as a twenty-something beta with unkempt hair, a coffee-stained shirt, and jeans with holes in the knees appears from the back room.

The guy, Chaz, ties an apron around his waist and stands at the register. "Dickasso, I didn't think you ever left your dorm. What can I—"

I step forward and block Scarlett, noticing how rigid she is in front of the beta. "I'll take a cold brew with vanilla. Scarlett will have..."

"What he's having," she says softly, finishing our order.

"And two croissants and egg bites. If we want something else, I'll order more." I pull out my wallet.

Chaz narrows his eyes at me. "That'll be—"

"On the house. Scarlett will be painting our windows for Halloween," the woman says, cutting off Chaz and setting a stack of papers on the counter. "That's an extra perk for you, Scarlett."

"Wow, okay. That's awesome. Lucky you, Dickasso. I bet your dad is happy you'll be painting something else that isn't...you know." Chaz eyes me, turning toward Scarlett. "I have some experience painting if you need any help. Or we can just hang out. You look like you could use some fun and inspiration...for all your cock drawings."

"Stop, Chaz." Scarlett flushes, her cheeks turning bright red, realizing I can hear everything he fails to whisper.

It pisses me off more than it should. I don't know what comes over me, but I don't like the way he teases her or calls her names. How he embarrasses her. I don't want him anywhere near her.

I stride forward and grab the front of his shirt, growling in his face. "Don't talk to her like that. Show some respect or you will—"

"Leo, it's okay." Scarlett grabs at my arm, getting me to step away. "Please. It's fine."

But it's not. I'll not let her just take his harassment. She's clearly uncomfortable, and I'm sure there's a reason.

I turn toward the woman. "I don't want him around while she's painting."

Chaz snatches his shirt and rips it from my fingers, stepping back. "What? Are you kidding—"

The woman grasps his shoulder. "Yes, of course. I'm sorry for his behavior. I'll discuss it with him." She turns to Chaz and says, "Go finish unpacking the shipment and take out the trash. After that, you can clock out for lunch."

Chaz throws down his apron. "Yes, Ms. Sandy. See you in class, Dickasso. If Daddy even lets you go. Possessive ass."

I growl under my breath again, not backing down from his scowl.

If looks could kill, we'd go to battle. I silently wage a war as he disappears.

I turn to Scarlett and take her hand. "Let's get it to go."

She only nods.

Silence fills the coffee shop as I collect our coffees and food, guiding Scarlett to the door. I'm pretty sure I just ruined my day with Scarlett, but I'd put Chaz in his place again and again.

"Have a good day, Dickasso," Chaz calls from the dumpster as we pass by.

Scarlett squeezes my hand. "Just ignore him. He's not worth it."

"But you are," I say, glowering at the asshole.

"Please. You don't need to challenge him. He knows he'll never have a chance. I'm yours." Scarlett eases into my side.

Her closeness gives me the strength to let the bullshit go. Because she's right. Nothing has ever been clearer.

Scarlett

UNWANTED ATTENTION

I've been anxious all night, thinking about the art gig at Beach Brew but also about how intensely Leo reacted toward Chaz. He had every right to be upset; I didn't know how to handle the situation either, especially because we need to stay out of anyone's attention, and I know this is another thing we need to discuss.

If only I could've skipped class and slept in.

"I'll see you all next week. Mr. Deeds, Ms. Alabaster, and Ms. Carlisle. Please see me before you go." Jonah strides from his podium and to his desk, plopping down.

I've tried my best not to stare at him the entire time, despite wanting to. I know it'd be more obvious if he returned my gaze, because he'd find it hard to resist, so I didn't want to test him.

A shadow falls over me, and I stiffen, the scent of Chaz's deodorant reminding me of the bathroom spray my dads use to freshen the toilet. It's not exactly something I want intruding on my senses. "Hey, Dickasso. Want a ride to Beach Brew?"

"Please, stop calling me that," I murmur, focusing my attention on gathering my belongings.

"But it fits you. Your dad was super uptight. I'd think he'd appreciate someone like me as your friend. It could save him a trip. Beach Brew is on my way home." Chaz doesn't move from his spot, blocking me in my desk. "You can tell him as much. It was a bit extreme for him to demand I lose some shifts."

I open my mouth to respond, but Jonah calls my name.

"Mr. Broderik, is there something you need? I'd like to get out of here soon, and I need to speak to Miss Carlisle about her essay." Jonah straightens his back, towering a few inches above Chaz.

"Sorry, sir." He turns toward me. "My offer stands. I don't mind waiting."

I shake my head. "Maybe some other time. Thanks, though." I want so badly to be rude to him, but his attention already is terrible enough. I'd hate to know what it would be like if he was even more of a jerk.

"Suit yourself. Maybe Daddy will loosen the reins when he realizes that he can't take care of you forever." Chaz slides past Jonah, tensing as Jonah refuses to move.

Neither of us says anything as Chaz leaves the classroom, swinging the door all the way open, so it takes a moment to close.

"You wanted to see me, Professor Hart?" I ask, tilting my gaze up to him with a smile.

Jonah leans down and presses his lips to mine, kissing me passionately, his body pushing mine into my desk. "I've been thinking about doing this all through class. Why must you torture me by denying me your attention?"

I laugh in exasperation and pat his chest, getting him to inch back. "I was trying to be a good girl and help you stay in professor mode."

"You're so thoughtful yet infuriating." Jonah kisses me again, sitting me up on my desk as he positions himself between my legs, rubbing his hand over my cheek and down my throat. He scents me, desperate to rub away the suppressant lotion I continue to wear.

"And you're a tease, claiming you won't touch me until I'm out of your class, yet you demand I stay after to torture me with kisses." I bite my lip with my words, smiling.

My comment wipes the smile off his face, squeezing my chest in the process. I had intended it to be playful, but he's taking it to heart.

"My forbid—"

My phone buzzes from my pocket, pulling my attention away. Jonah sighs and puts space between us, allowing me to pull it out of my pocket.

Unknown: Last chance, Dickasso.

I grip my phone, reading the text message.

Me: I said, no thank you. I'm not even going today.

Unknown: Then why did Ms. Sandy remove me from the schedule today? She cut my shifts in half

for the next two weeks.

A dozen sarcastic responses flip through my head, but I know better than to respond with any of them.

"Scarlett, who is that? What are they talking about?" Jonah peers at my phone, reading over the text messages.

Leo hasn't had a chance to mention things to the others. He was going to do so today, so I could start the windows tomorrow.

Unknown: Hello? Just come out and talk to me. I know Professor Douche must be done talking if you're replying to me.

My heart skips a beat, and dread crawls up my back. I don't want to deal with Chaz right now. He should've just left. Why didn't he?

"Scarlett? Is that Mr. Broderik?" Jonah asks, his voice deepening. "Did you give him your number, or did he get it on his own? I'm not angry or anything, but those texts seem like harassment."

I swallow and turn the screen off, ignoring another text message from Chaz. "He got it on his own. I just—I'm sorry. Leo said he was going to tell you guys about my job tonight. I didn't mean to throw it on you this second, but I've been hired to paint the windows at Beach Brew for Halloween. I've never been paid for my art, so this—"

"He works there. He's going to continue to pursue you because of the opportunity," he says, ignoring the fact that I just told him that I was hired to paint as if addressing Chaz is more important than the fact that someone thinks my art is worthy enough to display for everyone to see.

"He can pursue me all he wants, but nothing will happen. He's not even going to be working while...wait, how did you know he works there?" I narrow my eyes at Jonah.

He hesitates. "I—I've seen his work shirt."

My shoulders droop with his lie. Beach Brew doesn't have uniforms. All they have to show that they're baristas is their apron with the logo.

Tears burn my eyes. My disappointment isn't even about the fact that he clearly must have looked into Chaz for some reason or another, but he still doesn't grasp how his lack of acknowledgment over my job hurts me.

I sling my satchel over my shoulder and tuck my phone away, ignoring the buzzing. "Why don't you stay here so he doesn't think we're leaving together. I'd hate for him to grow suspicious. I know how important your job is."

"Scarlett, wait. I don't want you to leave." Jonah scratches his fingers through his hair, mussing the neatly combed strands. He removes his glasses and rubs the bridge of his nose. "You're upset."

"Of course, I'm fucking upset. I just told you that I got offered a job because someone thinks my art is good enough, and all you're thinking about is an unimportant beta who will give up when he realizes he's not getting anywhere with me." I slide past him and cross my arms over my chest. I've never used profanity with anyone besides myself, Emma, and my sisters, and it feels as if I'm about to get reprimanded. It's just in my head, though.

Jonah doesn't say anything, remaining in his spot. He won't chase me out. Not with the threat he thinks Chaz poses. His job is important to him, and right now, it kills me a little. I didn't think it would be hard. I didn't realize the challenges we'd face as the secret weighs on us. I can't help it that I feel as if I'm not as important in this moment, and I know it's unfair to think that way. I just... Fuck.

I swing the door open and jog forward.

Chaz tries to block my way. "Dick—"

I dodge around him, elbowing him in the ribs. "Get out of my way. I told you no, and I don't have anything else to say to you. Leave me alone."

Surprisingly, he listens.

I rush from the building and shade my vision, my eyes burning from the change of light and my tears. How the fuck can I feel so sad? It's as if everything catches up to me, and I realize that life isn't as easy as just finding a pack, bonding, and having my happily ever after. I was naïve, after all. I didn't really think about any of the challenges I'd face. I just assumed that if I followed my pack's expectations and my mom's demands that everything would be fine.

I'm an idiot.

Maybe I had too much confidence in the whole proposal. Maybe I should just drop out of Clearwater University. It would make things so much easier, not having to worry about messing up my alphas' careers, careers they need to provide for our family the way they want. Sure, we could get by, but there are expectations. Being betrothed is more than just about breeding. It's about creating ties with other packs. It's about strengthening our society as a whole.

"Scarlett, amore. Slow down." The familiar bass tone of Ezra's voice sounds from my right.

I spot him jogging from the giant lecture hall within the Clearwater art wing. He must've had a class at the same time as Jonah, and I realize that I need to pay more attention to everyone's schedules.

"Jonah told me he thought you'd be heading this way." Ezra manages to catch up to me, jogging beside me in his suit. If I didn't think we'd draw attention, I'd outrun him. I don't need someone defending Jonah right now. "He wanted to follow you—"

"Then why didn't he?" I stop short, surprising Ezra, and he bumps into me.

Grabbing my waist, he stops me from falling and steadies me on my feet. I squeeze my eyes shut, trying to stop my tears. I feel wildly out of control and incapable of processing anything right now. Ezra grasped my hands, holding them gently but securely as if he's afraid I might run away.

I gasp and step into him, pressing my face to his chest, using him as a shield against the world. "I'm such an idiot. I don't know why I'm so hurt by something I already knew couldn't happen."

"Amore, come on. Let me take you inside." Ezra doesn't give me the chance to brace myself before he lifts me off my feet and cradles me in his arms as if I'm a small child. "I'll save Jonah's apology for him to tell you himself, but I don't want you running around so upset."

"It's not a big deal. I'll get over it." I sniffle and wipe my cheek on the back of my hand, hating how I can't stop my tears from spilling.

"Anything that makes you cry is a big deal to me, Scarlett. You don't have to talk about it, but I am here to listen." Ezra pushes through the glass door in the side of the building, leading into a hallway of offices.

He carries me through the first door and shuts it behind us, turning the lock. The faint scent of oil paint and turpentine lingers in the air, drawing my attention toward a lone easel facing the window with a tarp beneath it as if Ezra uses his office as a studio as well. I didn't know he painted, because I know he only taught Art History and nothing else according to his paperwork, but I realize that there's still a lot I don't know about this man.

Ezra sets me down and motions toward a leather couch with colorful pillows popping against the dark fabric. "Let me get you something to drink. Do you prefer water, coffee, or something else? There's a vending machine down the hall."

I rest my elbows on my knees. "Water's fine."

Ezra quickly grabs a glass from a small shelf and pulls a clear decanter from a fridge tucked away in his cabinet. He pours me a cool glass and returns to my side, sitting beside me. He doesn't let me take the water and instead holds it to my lips.

"Take a small sip, amore. You'll feel better in a second. Maybe take some deep breaths. In and out." He inhales deeply through his nose and puffs out of breath through his mouth, the floral bergamot cologne of his body comforting. It reminds me of the jasmine bushes that grow throughout campus. "Come on. Give me a big breath."

I do as he says, releasing the tension from my body in the process. Ezra grabs a handkerchief from his pocket and wipes it across my cheeks, drying my face. We sit together in silence until my glass of water is empty and my heart finally settles down.

"I'm sorry you had to see me like this. I don't know what got into me." I ruffle my fingers through my hair, pushing the strands over my shoulders.

"Obviously Jonah," Ezra says, patting my knee with his warm hand. "I know he can be a bit much. He struggles with his emotions. He's quite sensitive and passionate and has always been that way."

"You forgot jealous and reactant," I quip, clenching my fingers into fists to stop my hands from shaking as I relive everything that happened after class.

"What has he done? Does this have to do with the beta in your class? The one Jonah told me he worries about bothering you?" Ezra remains expressionless.

I wonder how much he truly knows and what Jonah has said. I'm sure my five alphas talk about everything regarding me.

"Yes and no." I wish Leo would've already told him about my job offering, but it's too late for that now. Neither of us could've expected things coming up before dinner tonight when we finally all have a chance to sit together. "I was hired for a job painting some windows for Halloween that I had applied for before your proposal. Chaz happens—"

"Amore, you got a job to paint? How wonderful!" Ezra says, engulfing me in a hug.

I melt into him, my sadness fading away, fueled by his wave of excitement on my behalf. This was the reaction I was hoping for from Jonah. I didn't realize that it was the case until now.

"See, this is what I wanted. I told Jonah, and all he could focus on was the fact that Chaz worked at the coffee shop." I spill my heart to Ezra, telling him everything that happened after class. About Chaz getting my number somehow and how Jonah lied to me about how he knew Chaz worked at the coffeehouse.

"You must be so hurt. I'm sorry, amore," Ezra says, hugging me again.

"His intentions were good, but I'm just...I don't want to be lied to, you know?" I press my lips together, wishing the ache in my chest would fade already.

"I know it's not my place, but would you like me to speak with him?" Ezra rubs his hand across my shoulders, his closeness helping to keep my mind and body relaxed. "I have dealt with many of his tantrums over the years. He's always been so...he wears his heart on his sleeve."

I shake my head. "No, I'll be okay."

"The only way he'll learn your expectations is if you tell him. So please don't ignore this and hope that it goes away." Ezra smiles softly, his advice sinking in. "I want you to be happy. I know the situation isn't ideal, but we can control how we move from here...and now my age is showing." He chuckles, his face lighting even more.

I laugh and shake my head, patting his shoulder. "That's not a bad thing. Thanks for talking me down." I lean in and kiss Ezra, grazing my lips to his, testing him for a reaction.

And boy does he give me one, cupping my cheeks and deepening our kiss, exploring my mouth as if he needs to memorize every sensation and taste, every second of the passion exploding between us.

Just when I think he's about to rip my clothes off, he breaks away and rests his head on my shoulder, inhaling a couple of deep breaths of my scent.

"You're so irresistible. I can see why Jonah is quite overprotective. I'm not sure how I would react to seeing someone else give you attention freely when I can't. I hope you know I look forward to every moment I'll have to get to know you more. I hate to admit this, because I never want to see you hurting, but I'm thankful I caught you. I'm here for you."

A wave of warm emotions courses through me, and I kiss him again, caught up in our passion and his affection, things that I'm still unsure of how to handle. He hasn't been very open with me, but he also hasn't had much of a chance. I'm not the only nervous one, though he doesn't admit it.

"That means a lot to me." I release a breath and straighten my back. "Are you busy the rest of the day? Do you have more classes?"

Ezra pulls out his phone and taps the screen a couple of times. "Not anymore. No one will be sad that I'm postponing a quiz until next week."

I laugh. "I hate to admit that they're probably going to celebrate."

He takes my hand, pulling me to my feet. "And we will too. We'll do whatever you want, amore. I'm so proud of your achievements. I can't wait to shout our engagement to the world."

Scarlett

CELEBRATION

Mom: Call me when you get the chance.

I tuck my phone away, ignoring the text message from my mom. I don't really care what she has to say. If it were important, she would hound me about it. She probably just wants to know more about how I'm handling things and what my pack has offered me so far. Maybe even learn about a wedding date. But I don't know. I don't want to talk to her. A part of me is angry about her slip up, but another part of me is happy that it happened.

"Chaz isn't bothering you again, is he?" Jonah asks, staring at me from across the table.

"Of course, he's not. He knows she blocked his number. And if he was, you need to let Scarlett handle it until she asks for our help otherwise. It's best to let her navigate all the relationships she has in her life outside of us. He is a beta and not a threat. He's just a boy, Jonah," Ezra says, squeezing my hand under the table.

Jonah growls but doesn't argue. "He's a pain in my side. No one should harass her."

I pull my phone out and slide it across the table. "Tell that to my mom. I'm two text messages away from blocking her too."

"I'm sorry, Scarlett. I'm going to work on my jealousy. I already have an appointment with someone to give me better coping skills." Jonah slides the phone back to me. "I know my behavior is unacceptable, and I do apologize."

I grimace at his comment, surprised that he arranged for outside help. Most alphas I know would just mutter under their breath and play it off as an omega's fault. I've seen it a dozen times.

"Oh. Um, I don't know what to say." I turn my gaze to the table.

"You don't have to say anything. I just thought you should know. I don't trust that guy, and I worry about you. I know that as an omega, you've been trained to ignore a lot of things you shouldn't have to. I'm your alpha, and I want to protect you. I also want to be able to function without wanting to murder people as well."

Adrian barks a laugh. "Murder, Jonah? You grow faint during a blood draw. I highly doubt you're capable of murder."

"He could just torture the fucker by reading one of his ancient novels." Leo whacks Jonah on his shoulder. "Slowly, in his monotonous professor voice. I heard it once, and it was…I'm just happy I survived."

I can't help the smile crossing my face. "I happen to enjoy it when he reads out loud. I didn't realize as much until the last time, and I grew jealous that he wasn't reading to me alone." I stretch my leg and run my foot over his, playfully touching him under the table.

Jonah purrs deep in his throat. "Is that so?"

Leo slams his hands on the table. "Don't even get him started. This is a celebration and not a snooze fest." Turning to the ever-quiet Dominic, Leo waves his hand to him. "Play some music or something. I'll give Scarlett a celebratory lap dance."

I tip my head back and laugh. "I have to see this."

Ezra slides out from the table and sways his hips, offering his hand. "He's not the only one who can dance. Come on, amore. Dance with me."

Music hums through the hidden surround sound, the rhythm upbeat and catchy. Spinning me out, Ezra draws me back in, sliding his hand to the small of my back while cupping the other.

For the first time ever, I'm thankful to have learned basic dance steps at Omega Prep. I used to dance with Sapphire, my self-proclaimed perfect princess little sister, in the living room of our San Francisco home. She was a perfectionist, and I just wanted to work through the rumba for the Fall Ball or the waltz for a wedding. Neither dances fit this moment, so I do as I told my sister a dozen times—let the alpha lead. Silly, I know, but we were marked down at Omega Prep if we dared otherwise.

Another body slides up behind me, and Leo rests his hands on my hips, sandwiching me to Ezra. He leans in and sniffs my hair, nuzzling it out of the way with his nose. "Damn, dirty girl," he whispers. "Keep swaying those hips—"

I bump him with my ass, cutting him off.

Ezra spins me away, and Adrian cuts off Leo, laughing as he traps him in a two-step, forcing Leo to dance with him.

"You're going to need some practice to keep up with her," Adrian says, winking at me as he makes Leo spin.

Leo growls playfully, but instead of trying to break away, he takes the lead and dips Adrian. Dominic and Jonah laugh, getting to their feet. The five of them take turns twirling me around and dancing with me, and I find myself in Dominic's arms, close to him for the first time.

His dark gaze bores into mine as he holds me against him. "You are—"

The music lowers with the sound of a doorbell, and Dominic looks toward the others. They obviously aren't expecting a visitor.

"Mr. Raynard, please. Misters Hart have strict orders." The voice of one of the staff members shouts from down the hallway.

Adrian turns off the music completely. "Dominic, take her to her room."

Dominic doesn't hesitate, obeying Adrian's command. He pulls me toward the doorway to the kitchen, and we move past the staff and toward another stairwell used by their servants.

My heart races as he guides me in silence. I'm a bit nervous being alone with him, considering he isn't a man of many words. At least, not when the others are around. Or maybe they just are more vocal.

"Peter Raynard is head of Joe's department," Dominic says, slowing down as we reach the door to my suite in the dimly lit hallway. "He definitely doesn't have any business being here at this hour. There is nothing that important that couldn't be relayed by a phone call."

Now I'm nervous. A dozen thoughts cross my mind. What if someone saw me besides Chaz leaving Jonah's office? What if someone saw Ezra pick me up and carry me into his office? Fuck.

"Do you think it has to do with me?" I ask, waiting for Dominic to enter my room.

It's the first time he's been in here, and he doesn't move away from his spot by the door, but he does close it.

"I hope not, but if it is, it's not the end of the world. We will be okay." Dominic finally moves from his spot, closing the space.

I sit on the edge of my bed while he finds a spot a safe distance away, pulling the chair out from my desk. It feels as if the moment of carefree fun is over between us. I think he was caught up in his pack's excitement and affection toward me that he was more comfortable participating. But now that we're alone? He once again builds a wall around himself. Jonah made it clear from the first moment he realized I was his soon-to-be wife that he wouldn't explore a relationship with me. Dominic never mentioned it. I know he was as concerned as his pack mate, but now I want to know exactly what his boundaries are. I want to get to know him, but I don't want to push him.

Silence fills the room, and I think of a dozen things to say. It's not like I can ask him how his day was, because I already asked at dinner, and I don't want to sound dumb by bringing up the weather or some shit.

"You're nervous around me." It's not a question. Dominic swivels in the chair, looking around my room before focusing on me. "Is there anything I can do to help? I've never really been good at...socializing. Forgive me if I make you uncomfortable with my silence."

"You don't make me feel uncomfortable, Dominic. I'm nervous because of the visitor. Not because of you." I bounce my feet on the floor, keeping my gaze locked on his. "I keep thinking that maybe dropping out might be best. It's not like I have a ton of friends here. It was mostly just me and my sisters growing up, and my best friend moved away right before I came here."

The chair creaks as Dominic gets to his feet, finally closing the space. I scoot up on my bed, offering him more room to join me. He doesn't hesitate climbing on, stretching out his long legs and crossing his socked feet beside me.

"At first, I thought dropping out would be best, but then I realized how selfish that would be to demand such a thing. The only reason you'll drop out is if that's what you truly want and not because you're afraid." Dominic rests his hand on my knee, showing me affection. The simple gesture helps ease my worry, and I sink against him, happy we have this chance alone despite the circumstances.

"I don't want to. Not really. I'm so close to finishing. I kind of want to do it to prove that omegas can do it all. I can accomplish more than just graduating from Omega Prep, finding a pack, and breeding. I feel like my mom obsesses over our lives because she's now bored with hers, since she's no longer having children. My dads are constantly busy too." I rest my head on his shoulder, inhaling a soft breath of his scent, earthy like a forest mixed with the lingering fragrance of clay.

"Perhaps you could recommend a hobby to her. Do any of your dads paint? Is that where you found your interest in the arts?" Dominic rolls his shoulder and reaches behind him, pulling something out from underneath the pillow.

I realize I left my sketchbook on my bed, and now he's found my secret one. And holy shit. The last figure I drew was Leo in all his naked glory, his cock piercings sparkling.

I reach out to grab it too quickly, and I accidentally pull one of the loose pages free. As if he touches fire, Dominic drops my sketchbook on the bed, reacting to my sudden movement. I whip my attention to him, watching him look down, and heat burns across my neck and cheeks as a full-frontal self-portrait of me rests on his knee. I should really quit sketching myself. I've always done it because I'm my best and pretty much only model unless I accidentally catch sight of someone else, which is rare. There are a couple of drawings from some porn Emma sent me, but that's about it. It's mostly me and my fantasies.

"Scarlett, you're extremely talented. I don't think I've seen an artist able to capture an image so vividly. I thought it was a photograph." Dominic touches the edge of the paper but doesn't move to grab anything else.

I scoop up my sketchbook and close it. "I'm sorry. I have a thing for...nude figures. I don't know how to explain it. I'm so embarrassed."

I dip my chin, using my brownish-auburn hair to veil my face. Dominic shifts and combs the strands away, tucking them behind my ear.

"I'm sorry. I didn't mean to touch your sketchbook. I thought it might've been a textbook or something, and it was digging into my back." Dominic leans closer, the warmth of his breath tickling my cheek. "Your interests are nothing to be ashamed of. I've crafted many statues over the years. I can show you my work sometime. I find the human body just as fascinating and exquisite."

The corner of my lips curls up, and I tilt my head, focusing my gaze on his. "You do?"

He hums under his breath. "Absolutely. Especially yours. You're a living masterpiece, and I wish you would let me see more of your art. I don't get enough of it in my life because...as an alpha, art wasn't practical, which is why I teach Mathematics. If I could teach ceramics and sculptures full-time, I would."

I wondered why he had two very different teaching schedules. His one and only ceramics class is on a Friday morning, a day not many students would be interested in taking it, but it is always filled up.

"I'll show you my sketchbook if you show me some of your sculptures sometime," I say, smiling wider. "Maybe I should make you go first."

He chuckles and brings his arm around me, resting it across my shoulders. "If that's what it takes…I happen to have cast a mold of myself. If that doesn't ease your mind…"

My mouth forms an O. Damn. Now I have to see it.

I inhale a deep breath and bring my notebook to my lap, flipping it to the first page. My embarrassment vanishes the longer we sit together, and I appreciate his honesty. I realize it's okay to be vulnerable. He's going to be my husband. His actions have already proved that he wouldn't do anything I didn't agree to, including looking at my art. He could've stolen my notebook and flipped through the pages, but he didn't. He respected my belongings, and because of that, I trust him.

"I have to warn you. There is a lot of…male anatomy in this. I lived in a co-ed dorm. My best friend thought it was funny to send me porn, knowing I'd send her drawings of it back. I've always been intrigued, you know." My heart picks up pace as Dominic turns the page, staring at half a torso gleaming with shower steam.

Dominic shakes his head and chuckles. "This is going to sound terrible, but I recognize the beta. He was a volunteer model. My class tends to lean toward female enrollment, and they requested a male figure for one of the sculpture units."

I clap my hands once and laugh, my voice ringing through the air. "It's because you're hot. You should see how registration is. I tried enrolling twice, because I'm interested in all types of media, and my roommate said that your class is one of the most sought after because of who taught it."

Dominic's brows knit together. "I always thought it was because people considered it an Easy A."

I lift and drop my shoulders. "I won't lie. I was super frustrated over everything. I even snuck by your class to see for myself."

"I'll have to make it up to you. They only get me as an instructor for a semester. I'll give you private classes for the rest of our lives if you want. I've never really created anything with another person. Art has always been a bit lonely. It was an incredible and joyous surprise to discover that it's your focus." Dominic flips another page, taking a moment to appreciate every one of my drawings.

I study his face, watching his eyes drag across the pages, remaining longer on my self-portraits than anything else. I wonder what he's thinking, but I'm afraid to ask, letting him just drink in my private sketchbook that I have never intentionally shown anyone. His scent grows more intense, the hearty cologne of his lust triggering mine.

"I love seeing you through your own eyes, Scarlett. You'll have to let me create you through mine sometime. I'd really enjoy that." Dominic licks his full lips, shutting my notebook when the pages turn blank.

"I'd like to use you as a model as well." I reach up and caress my fingers over his shaven cheeks, stroking from his jaw and down his neck.

He drags his hand down my back, hooking it to my side and rolling me onto him. I crash my mouth to his. The sudden intensity of the moment consuming me completely. I don't want Dominic as a model. I want him as a man beneath me, exposed and as vulnerable as I felt a moment ago. I want to see the masterpiece created by his existence and discover what he looks like, feeling his hard cock pressing between my legs, his shaft pulsing with his excitement.

It's as if both of us were on the brim of exploding, and all it took was opening ourselves up to each other to unleash the passion felt between an omega and her alpha. My deep desire to bond with him grows, and I reach between us and unbuckle his pants, taking the initiative when he doesn't stop me.

"My attraction to you is unexplainable. I never knew something could hit me so hard and fast. I thought it would take much longer to cultivate a relationship with

you, but it's as if fate knew you'd be my perfect match."
Dominic kisses along my jawline, lifting me up higher
to bury his face between my breasts, nipping my supple,
sensitive skin. His hands lock to the back of my shirt,
yanking it over my head, and I follow his lead, dragging
his shirt up as well, my hands exploring the curves of his
body and how surprisingly muscular he is. He's always
worn a button-down shirt or suit, and I only knew his
arms were bulging in all the right places. He's as fit as Leo
and now just as bold, helping free his hard-on from his
pants, my desperation and desire to touch him giving me
the bravado to continue.

He moans as I lace my fingers around his girth, familiarizing myself with him. I can't help watching my
fingers glide up and down until his tip glistens with his
pre-cum. I capture the moment in my mind, studying
every curve and how smooth his body is as if he prefers
no hair at all on himself.

Engulfing my fingers with his, Dominic guides my
hand up and down, showing me exactly what he prefers.
I perch on his leg, rocking my hips and grinding against
him, needing the pressure of his body to help with the
growing ache between my legs. I've never been so turned
on in my life, the warmth blooming around my thighs.

Dominic trails his fingers over my breast, pinching my nipple through my sheer bra and working his way down to my torso. He slips his hands into my pants and growls, the vibration of his voice shooting tingles across my skin. He tears my bra with his teeth and sucks my nipple into his mouth at the same time he rubs his finger over my clit and sinks it inside me, feeling exactly what he does to me and how wet I am. I pick up my pace, using his pre-cum as a lubricant, rubbing it up and down in even strokes on his cock. The sensations explode through me, and I rock harder, getting him to stroke my insides just right as I fuck his hand in a way I have never done before. I use my free hand and grab his chin, bringing his head back up to my mouth to kiss me. He bites my lip and pulls it between his teeth, his deep purr of satisfaction the sexiest thing I've ever heard.

"You're so tight. So, so tight. I'm afraid I'll hurt you." Dominic moans against my mouth. "It'll take some time for you to take my knot." He moans with his words, his comment revealing what's on his mind, his thoughts open to me now.

"Don't be afraid. I know I can handle you. I want you so badly. Your finger feels so good, I can only imagine—" A zing of pleasure rushes through me, and I scream out, my voice ringing in the air with my orgasm. My body tenses and pulses, clutching Dominic's hand, and he silences me with his mouth.

I wiggle and moan, the ecstasy better than any toy I've ever used. Dominic grunts and moans as warmth splashes across my torso. He gasps a breath and slows my hand down, pulling me away to tangle our fingers together. I straddle him, his body so close to mine with only some fabric between us. I glide my tongue over his, kissing him until both of our hearts stop racing.

Dominic cups my cheeks, staring deep into my eyes, his gaze penetrating me as if he looks into my soul. "You're an amazing woman, Scarlett. Thank you for being so open with me. I was nervous that you wouldn't want me."

Someone knocks on my door, not giving me a chance to respond. Dominic quickly scoops me up and carries me to the bathroom, calling out that we need a minute.

He helps me clean off and picks me back up as if he never wants me to walk on my own again. I quickly discard my torn bra and shrug into a shirt.

Another knock sounds on the door. "It's fine if you're busy with Scarlett, but I wanted to tell you everything is all good and the douche is gone. Apparently, some shit went down with Pack Raynard, and Peter needs to go on hiatus. He wanted to tell Joe personally that he was stepping down from the department head position and giving him a head's up that he was putting in a referral for Joe to be his replacement." Leo's voice booms through the wood door. "Joe's not sure he wants it."

Dominic swings the door open, not bothering to put his shirt back on. "What do you mean Jonah doesn't want the position? It was his dream."

Leo's gaze darts to mine and back to Dominic. "Dreams change. It's all he said. But I think you should talk to him when you get a chance. He decided to retire to his study early, claiming he has a ton of essays to grade."

Dominic adjusts me in his arms. "Scarlett, do you mind if I go talk to him? He's lying about the essays. That man doesn't work after hours. That's always been his thing."

I slowly bob my head and look from Dominic to Leo. "Is there anything I can do to help?"

"Not tonight. Why don't you go enjoy your celebration with the others? I'll try to get Jonah to come back down." Dominic sets me on my feet and nudges me toward Leo. "I'll join you soon."

I stand with Leo, watching him walk away. I can't help but feel at fault for Jonah possibly turning down the chance to further his career.

I never want any of them feeling as if they gave up something, especially because they've done everything they could so far to ensure that I don't give up anything either.

"Don't stress over Jonah, dirty girl. This is your night. He'll get over it and join us. We just have to laugh louder and make it irresistible to sulk." Leo swings my hand back and forth.

If only I didn't hear Jonah holler at Dominic to leave him alone.

If only I don't feel as if after tonight one of my soon-to-be husbands will pull away from me.

The last thing I want is to break up their pack.

I want all of them. All of Pack Hart is supposed to be mine.

Scarlett

FAMILY SURPRISE

Hardass: You should really respond to Mom. She's talking about flying to San Diego to surprise you.

Princess: You're hurting her feelings.

Hardass: More like pissing her off.

Black Sheep: Whatever gets her off of my ass.

Psycho: Did you get your gifts? The packages say delivered.

Mother Hen: Give Scarlett a break, you girls. She's getting to know her pack.

Psycho: Or taking the D.

Mother Hen: Emma! That's my little sister.

Princess: Ew. And my big sis.

Hardass: Maybe she's in heat and didn't tell us.

Psycho: Don't act like you all weren't thinking it. Best friends share everything. Get used to me. I'm not going away.

Hardass: Unless you're arrested.

Mother Hen: Scarlett, ignore everyone. I'll cover for you with Mom. Love you.

I stare at the string of text messages from my chat with Emma and my sisters. It's been a while since all of us chatted at once, and I'm glad that Cyan decided to warn me about mom. She's always strived to be the badass rebel omega out of all of us, though sometimes, things don't come as easy. I miss being closer to my younger sisters, but I definitely don't miss our nagging mom. Or surprise visits. Fuck me.

Tucking my phone in my pocket, I turn back to the mirror and finish my makeup. I rub my suppressant lotion into my arms, focusing on my wrists and then I work my way around my neck down my torso to my thighs all the way down to my ankles, ensuring that any signs of me being an omega are diminished. I'm glad my omega birthmark hides on my lower back, kissing one of my dimples.

None of my alphas have mentioned it or complained, but I know that I'll eventually have to stop using it. I considered switching to a pill, but I heard those make your heat even more intense. The lotion will mess with me, especially since I skipped my last heat with a pill, but at least I know what to expect.

I head downstairs, listening to the voices humming from the dining room. I get excited hearing Jonah's laughter. I wasn't exactly sure what to expect from him after his hiding the last two days, but it seems that he's back to normal. No one has told me anything else, and I think they're waiting for him to tell me.

"Ms. Scarlett, you have some packages. They just arrived a couple of minutes ago. Would you like me to take them to your room?" Franny stands with her hands clasped together in front of a long table my guys use to set their personal belongings on, out of the way of any public space of the museum. I know they'll be opening the Clearwater Manor again soon to visitors, and I don't really look forward to it. At least no one will be going into our bedrooms or our personal areas.

"Ms. Franny, I'll take them to the dining room so Scarlett can open them there. I was informed by her pack that she'd be receiving something today." Adrian adjusts his tie, coming from the wraparound staircase. He's never first to breakfast, considering he doesn't have as early days as the others. Sometimes he doesn't even leave the manor and chooses to work remotely. I know he runs Clearwater University's finance department, but I know there's more to his position. He has talked about traveling soon, trying to arrange things to where we'd all be on break for Thanksgiving or Winter Break.

"Yes, sir. Let me know if you need anything else. I'll be putting up the ropes to keep the museum guests out of your private quarters. We have our first appointment scheduled for tomorrow." Franny curtsies and turns away, not waiting for Adrian to respond.

He grumbles under his breath and stacks four boxes. There are far too many packages for him to carry on his own without making a second trip, so I gather the largest box and set three bubble mailers on top.

"We can just take them up to my room. I think it's the rest of my stuff from home. My sisters mentioned my mom would be cleaning out my room completely."

I purse my lips, not reacting. I don't give a fuck what she does with my room. It was mostly just childhood belongings I don't care for anymore.

"One is an engagement gift from Pack Carlisle's leader. It has all of our names on it." Adrian adjusts the box in his hand. "I suspect the rest are gifts as well."

Dominic pops his head out from the archway to the dining room and strides forward, gathering everything from my arms. "Ezra made breakfast today. You want to eat it while it's still hot."

The sugary scent of pastries fills the air, and I gape at the huge collection of breakfast foods set out like a buffet in warming trays. A pile of scrambled eggs, sausages and bacon, potatoes, and a couple of other things I can't see under lids wait for me. A tower of donuts glitters with sugar and chocolate drips over buttery croissants. A huge carafe of coffee rests alongside a pitcher of orange juice. A mound of fresh-cut fruit finishes off the breakfast collection, and I nearly charge the table out of hunger.

"Amore, come sit down with me." Ezra smiles, standing from his spot across the room at the end of the table. "The chef sits at the head this morning and gets the honor of feeding our beautiful fiancée."

Adrian sets the four boxes at the end of the table, and Dominic stacks the rest on top, motioning for me to go to Ezra. Leo and Jonah sit across from each other. I love how everyone focuses on me. Jonah smiles softly and reaches for my hand, quietly pulling me in for a sensual kiss. The small affectionate gesture helps ease the tightness in my chest. I was afraid he'd ignore or avoid me, but he acts as if nothing happened the other night.

Leo moves around the table, kissing me next, and I laugh as Ezra spins me away, plopping down with me on his lap. He lifts a chocolate croissant to my lips, and I hum in enjoyment at the burst of sweet, buttery flavor.

"You made all of this?" I ask between bites, trying my best not to snatch the pastry away. Because it's fucking delicious.

"Yes, amore. I decided to make you a little bit of every-thing, but croissants are my specialty when it comes to breakfast. What do you think?" Ezra offers me another bite, and I watch as the others join us around the table. It's nice to eat together like this for breakfast and dinner, considering we don't all see each other during the day.

"Stop asking her questions and let her eat. She obvi-ously enjoys it. That little moan she keeps releasing is driving me wild." Leo stretches his arm out and smudges his thumb on my chin, wiping away flakes of croissant. He pops it in his mouth and winks at me, filling his empty plate. I realize everyone was waiting until I sat down. I wonder how long they would wait or if they would just starve if I took my sweet time. I wouldn't do that, though. I know it's customary for alphas to wait until their omega gets taken care of first. Omega Prep taught me that it was their duty.

"He's right, Ezra. Enjoy just feeding our beautiful omega." Adrian scoots closer, sitting in Ezra's usual spot. I stretch out my hand and let him kiss my knuckles. "It'll give us a chance to discuss a couple of things of importance. The first one is our engagement announcement. I'm planning to meet with Pack Carlisle's leader in regards to building a Clearwater University satellite campus just outside of San Francisco, and I feel it's important to show our upcoming union to strengthen our ties. I've been trying to get into Northern California for a while. I find this to be a splendid opportunity. We can also meet Scarlett's family too."

I crinkle my nose at the idea. I wonder how awkward it would be for my dads to realize that my new pack is around their age and that mom didn't care about reading over my profile, missing the typo. Does it matter? I hope not. I'm already comfortable. Mom made it clear that this was happening, and I accepted it.

I wouldn't change anything either.

"Do you think that's a good idea? Word might spread." Jonah tightens his jaw and sets his fork down. "We shouldn't use our relationship to secure it like that. I'm sure you can get the contract on your own, Adrian."

"When he puts it like that, Adrian, I have to agree. You know the publicity that will follow with the formal announcement. I thought we'd wait until spring." Dominic laces his fingers together, resting his elbows on the table.

"Her expected heat will arrive before then. The school has her enrolled under her alias Scarlett Carlisle since the Carlisles are Pack Steele's authoritative pack. I made sure that there were no ties to the Steele name. Now it's not necessary to include a bloodline if someone is forming a pack." Adrian straightens his back. "I want things to be official for her. It's important to me too. More important than appearances."

I stop eating and set down my fork, feeling tension rise in the air. "You can make it official, but I'll tell my mom that I don't want the media involved until we start planning the wedding."

"She was also asking about a date for that. She prefers it sooner rather than later because your pack won't release the dowry to her until our marriage certificate is turned in and you're officially a member of Pack Hart." Adrian twists his lips, his expression softening.

"Then maybe we need to offer her a stipend to hold her over." Jonah scoots back in his chair. "I don't want anything ruining our plans."

Adrian stops him from getting up, draping his arm over his shoulders. "You're right. I was being a bit selfish, and I don't want anyone feeling as if I'm doing things for my own sake or for Clearwater University over our own wants and desires. I would still like to meet with Scarlett's family. It would be a fun weekend getaway, don't you think?"

I bite the inside of my cheek, forcing my face to remain even. "I'd love to show you around San Francisco as long as we don't hang out with my family too long."

"That bad, huh?" Leo asks.

"Probably worse." I shrug my shoulders. "I'm just happy to be here. I hope you guys know that."

Ezra kisses the crook of my neck. "We just hope you know how grateful we are that you accepted us."

I rest against him, savoring the collection of their scents wafting around me, their happiness uplifting and pushing away all thoughts of my family.

Adrian claps his hands, not letting too much silence pass between us, ensuring that my mind doesn't wander. "You should open our gift from Pack Carlisle."

I can't imagine exactly what they would send us, considering we haven't made the formal engagement announcement. And now I'm curious. I've only met the mayor of San Francisco a handful of times, and he was more interested in mom and her fertility. A magical womb everyone hoped she passed on to us.

I guess I'll find out soon enough.

Adrian gets up and slides all the packages over. "It looks like I was wrong about them shipping your belongings. The rest of these are from your sisters."

"And Emma," Leo adds, peering at the packages.

I remember that Emma had mentioned she and my sisters sent me some things. "Which one is from Emma?"

"It's the big one." Adrian gives the box a shake, and something rattles inside.

"Put that one back. I know my best friend, and I don't think I want to open it in front of you guys." Blush blooms across my cheeks, and I peek up at them as they stare at me.

"Now you have to, dirty girl. I want to see what you're afraid of. Lingerie?" Leo chuckles and snatches the box from Adrian, shaking it. "No, definitely not clothing. Sounds like...a big ass dick."

Oh, my fucking God.

"Why on earth would her friend send her a sex toy?" Ezra asks, hugging me from behind.

"The same reason she sent me porn," I mutter under my breath. "Why don't you hand me Sapphire's first?" Hers might be the safest bet. Maybe Cyan's. They wouldn't want to send something that would create a bad impression for themselves in front of my pack. Raven is a bit unpredictable. Violet's could be safe as well, but she might just send a bunch of baby clothes or even aphrodisiacs. Depends on her mood.

I use one of the knives to cut through the tape and pull out a tissue-wrapped box with a sticker from my favorite bakery in San Francisco. Everyone watches me in silence as I pull it out and set it on the table. I tear the tissue and discover a handwritten card.

Congratulations on your new pack! Enjoy the peen party! —Sapphire

P.S. Emma demanded a specific theme.

Heat burns my cheeks as I open the bakery box, revealing five penis-shaped cookies and one vagina with a pearl candy as the clit. Fucking Sapphire, for going along with Emma.

"Damn, I never thought I'd want a cock in my mouth." Leo hovers over me, snatching a cookie from the box. "Here, my dirty girl. Take the first bite."

Ah, hell.

My mouth automatically opens for Leo, my shock turning me into a robot. I take a small bite, humming as sweetness crosses my tongue. Sapphire is so lucky these are delicious. Reaching up, I lock my fingers around Leo's wrist and bring the cookie back to my mouth.

"I'm going to need more than just the tip," I murmur, snapping my teeth hard to the sugar cookie.

"Damn." Dominic cocks his head at me, watching me devour the cookie.

Adrian chuckles. "Those look absolutely delectable. May I have one, Scarlett?" He's always been a bit formal with me.

"Make him eat a dick," Leo says, chuckling.

I laugh in exasperation, resting my head against Ezra's shoulder. "When you put it like that..."

"It wouldn't be the first time." Adrian lifts up a cookie, eating it in a couple of bites. His words swirl through my mind, and I wonder about them. He winks at me, daring me to speak my mind. I'm more curious than anything. It's not like it's uncommon. There are five of them and only one me, and I've seen some sword-crossing action in porn. It's hot.

And now it's on my mind.

"That's intriguing," I say, my face burning. "Have you guys..." I grin, my heart racing.

"Careful, Adrian. You might make our omega jealous with those confessions," Ezra warns, kissing my neck like he can't help himself.

Adrian inhales a breath. "Her scent says otherwise." He shakes his head and moves closer, kissing my hair. "I'll answer whatever you want to know. You never have to be shy with me, Scarlett. Plus, someone will thank me when your heat comes, considering there are five of us and one of you."

My heart skips a beat, his honesty and boldness getting to me in a good way. Many packs explore their sexuality together, and it's just something I haven't thought about until this moment. Dampness warms between my legs just thinking about it.

"I might thank you too," I say, tilting my head up and smiling. "I'm open to anything."

"As long as you come before us." Jonah smirks with his double entendre and picks up a cookie next, choosing the vagina. He plucks the pearl candy off and pops it in his mouth. "Always taste the best spot first."

My body buzzes at his words, and I can't help just watching everyone's interaction.

Adrian sets another package in front of me. "You better keep opening before you get distracted. I know I already am, and I have to leave soon. I don't want to miss out."

"Maybe you should just call in late," Dominic says, moving from his seat to stand behind me.

"I would if we weren't going to plan a trip." Adrian touches my cheek. "I hope you understand."

I nod my head without commenting and cut open one of the bubble mailer envelopes. I reach in and pull out a knotting simulator toy. I drop it on the table, fire licking across my skin. I didn't even check to see who it was from.

Little chickie, just in case you're nervous and want to fulfill your curiosity alone. An omega told me about them. —Vi

As if the phallic cookies weren't bad enough. I know Violet's heart was in a good place, but a fucking knotting vibrator? She's insane.

Ezra picks it up and inspects it, hitting a button and turning it on, the vibration so loud that it echoes. "They make an alpha one too. You fill it with a hormone cream, and it makes you knot."

He says it so seriously that it's hard to be embarrassed. I feel a bit better about my sister's gift, knowing that at least I don't have to explain anything. Maybe if they were my age, but they probably have a lot they could teach me. Actually, I know they do.

Leo pumps his fist. "I want to see what Psycho sent."

"Leo, she said she would open that one in private," Jonah reminds him.

I release a heavy sigh and grab Emma's box. "I might as well just open them. This will be one way to introduce you to her. A little payback. They're all going to regret mailing me this stuff."

I stab at the box from Emma, a little aggressively, and I stare at the colorful bubble wrap. She's always been a go big or go home type, and I stare at the small chest.

She didn't get me just one gift. She got me a fucking collection.

Scarlett, I hope you find your inner freak with your new hot daddies. Be a good girl for them! Or bad. You might get spanked. Happy engagement!

—Your favorite, Psycho

"She's wild, isn't she?" Leo messes with the lock on the box and pops it open. "I'm almost afraid to see what's inside."

Me too. I don't say the words out loud, though and instead, pull it closer to peek in first.

I tip my head back and release an exasperated laugh. Lacing my fingers around a dagger, I pull it from the box and shake my head.

There's a small note taped to it.

This isn't for what you think. Use your imagination. Isn't the textured hilt fun?

I drop the dagger, my mouth falling agape. This better not be an insinuation for what I think it is. At first, I thought she had sent it as a joke, because she would mutilate a male for being disgusting or something. But with her note? I don't even want to think about it. I wouldn't put it past her. And looking at the hilt, it's almost as if she had it custom-made for me. The grooves and shape of the hilt mimic a dildo.

"What am I missing?" Jonah asks, looking at the dagger.

Ezra rests his chin on my shoulder. "It's for her pussy. Looks like blood play. Sensation play. It's an interesting choice."

Interesting? Maybe.

"Freaky," Dominic says, his voice low.

I ignore the rest of the toys in the box and decide to skip everything else. I don't think my cheeks can handle the warmth of my blush any more.

"I think I'll just save the rest for later. Are you sure you guys want to go to San Francisco?" I suck in my bottom lip, trying to cool my cheeks down with my even breathing.

"After this?" Leo asks, grinning at me. "Fuck yeah."

Adrian rests his hand on my shoulder. "You don't need to be shy or embarrassed by your family. I'm sure they're more normal than you think. I've met a lot of strange and interesting families in my life."

I respond with a nod.

I just wish he didn't have to meet mine.

"Didn't you receive my message, Scarlett?" Ms. Sandy sets down one of the mini blenders. "My afternoon barista called in sick, so I had to ask Chaz. I know how your pack feels about him, so I figured you wouldn't come in."

I've managed to avoid Chaz by changing seats in my World Literature class, and because I stay a minute later than usual and Jonah always follows behind me as if he's leaving for the day, Chaz hasn't bothered me at all. I'm pretty certain he got the hint after I told him to leave me alone.

"It's fine. I want to get as much done as I can because I'm going away for the weekend." I pull my hair up into a high ponytail and secure it in place. "My pack is a bit overprotective."

"As they should be." Ms. Sandy knows I'm an omega and set to be engaged. What she doesn't know is that my alphas also have tenure at my university. "I wouldn't expect anything less, even though Chaz is harmless. A bit crude and entitled, but I'll make sure he doesn't bother you."

She also knows not to tell anybody about my order, which she has respected.

"Thank you," I say, heading around the counter into the stock room with all my supplies. I've spent the last time here sketching out my Halloween illustrations on huge pieces of paper that I can tape to the window.

Ms. Sandy also has me cover my work when I'm done, wanting to keep things a surprise. It's exciting how she treats this little project more as a revelation for a piece of art she's acquired. It's more fun that way too.

I grab my smock and window paints, heading to the front. Fake spiderwebs and skeletons pop up in new places around the coffee shop, and I love how much Ms. Sandy enjoys the holiday as I do. I put in my earbuds and turn on my music, tuning out the world around me. The cool, crisp ocean breeze plays with the loose strands of hair around my neck. I pull my sleeves down, working on mixing the paint I need for the first windowpane, inspired by Van Gogh with a gothic twist on my part.

A shadow grabs my attention, and I turn and spot a man in a suit watching me work. I flick my attention away from him, trying not to let his silent presence mess me up. It's not as if no one has ever watched me paint before.

I continue to work, splitting my attention between the silent man in the suit and getting my outlines in order. This window display will take a couple of layers for me to perfect, because I need to make sure it looks good on both sides.

The man moves closer, drawing my focus again. He taps his ear, motioning for me to pull out one of my earbuds. I pause my music and pull both earbuds out, letting them hang around my shoulders.

"I'm sorry to bother you, miss. I just can't help admiring your work. Are you a barista here?" the man asks, crossing his arms over his broad chest as he trains his gaze on the outline instead of me.

"No, I'm a commissioned artist." I offer a smile and turn back to the window, unsure of whether or not I should continue the conversation.

"That's wonderful news to hear. I saw you sketching inside the other day, which is why I came back, hoping to see the progress. I have my daughter's wedding coming up, and I would love to see more of your art. Do you have a portfolio?" The man steps closer, his fragrance trickling to my nose, the musky, woodsy scent of patchouli distracting my senses. He's an alpha. I can tell from feet away.

"Not with me, but if you give me your email, I can send it over. What are you looking for?" I set my paintbrush down, my heart rapping against my ribcage at the thought of another art gig. I thought this would probably be my only one ever.

"The reception is being held at the Clearwater Beach Club down the road. I'd love to have some of the windows painted to match her color schemes. Maybe flowers or something from nature. I don't know exactly, but I can also put you in touch with her." The man proffers his hand. "I'm Paul, by the way."

It takes everything in me to shake the man's hand, knowing that he'll leave his scent on my skin. He obviously doesn't know I'm an omega, considering that I'm using suppressant lotion. If he did, he wouldn't make such a gesture.

"It's nice to meet you, Paul. I'm Scarlett." I tug my hand away and turn back to my mural. "I'm a bit messy to grab my phone, so can you just write your email down and leave it with Ms. Sandy at the counter? I have to get back to work."

Paul smiles and takes a step away. "Yes, of course. I look forward to seeing the rest of this incredible mural. You're very talented, Scarlett."

Paul leaves me to my work, and I peek at him through the window, watching as he orders coffee and writes on the back of the receipt, handing it to Ms. Sandy. She turns her attention to me from across the counter and smiles, waving the paper.

"Won't your dad get pissed off that you're getting strangers' numbers, Dickasso?" Chaz's voice sounds from behind me. "Especially that old dude. He's a prick."

I spin, flicking paint across the front of his face. "Shit, I'm sorry." I grab a rag and toss it toward him. "You scared me."

He chuckles. "Sorry about that. But really, that guy, Dickasso? You know you don't have a chance with an alpha. Do you have one of those kinks? You want to pretend to be his little omega? You can do that with me, too."

Fuck me. This asshole. I know better than to engage, so I turn away from him.

"It's not like that. He was interested in commissioning some art." I ignore Chaz moving closer. "You know people don't always have the same intentions as you."

"If you say so, Dickasso." Chaz tosses his rag right into my paint pallet. "I see the way you look at me."

"That's all in your head." I snatch up the rag, my anger getting the best of me. He's about to swallow this damn cloth because he just messed up my color combinations.

"In your dreams too." Chaz wags his eyebrows, twirling his fingers at me. "You're only lying to yourself."

I glower. "Fuck—"

A horn honks, distracting me. Chaz laughs and turns away, striding to the door. The bells chime as he yanks it open and flicks his tongue between the V of his fingers, the gesture grossing me out.

"Scarlett? Is that the beta Jonah and Leo told me about?" Adrian hangs his head out of his window.

"Yeah, but it's not a big deal. Ms. Sandy warned me that she had to call him to come in for a shift. She won't let him bother me." I drop the paint rag back on my pallet. "What are you doing here anyway? I thought you were picking me up this evening. Is everything okay?"

Adrian tightens his jaw, looking past me into Beach Brew. "It's fine. Just a slight schedule adjustment. I know I told you we wouldn't be leaving until tomorrow, but there's been a change of plans. We need to go tonight. How much longer do you need? I can grab a cup of coffee and wait." He doesn't say it, but the look he gives the door behind me speaks volumes. He caught what Chaz did and might want to say something.

I release a deep breath. "I'm actually at a good stopping point. Just give me a couple of minutes."

Who knew I'd be thankful for a change in plans? Especially ones that involve going home.

I guess that's what asshole beta guys do.

All I want now is to get away.

10

Adrian

HOMECOMING

"**F**lowers, no. Wine, yes. Jewelry, yes. My mom loves anything luxurious. Consider her spoiled." Scarlett strolls in front of me, drawing her finger along the rack of scarves.

It's customary for all packs under the Pack Clearwater hierarchy to bring a gift any time one of its members is being hosted, even if it's a family of a pack we're marrying into. I hate to admit it to myself, but I do hope Scarlett's family approves of me. As a pack under Pack Carlisle's authority and a subset of them, I want to ensure everything goes smoothly. My allies within Carlisle have been clear about how special Pack Steele is. I know that they have already agreed and accepted the dowry for our proposal, yet if it turns out that any of her family has a problem with us, things will be difficult for Scarlett. She claims that she doesn't like to be home or around her mom, but she has never talked badly about her fathers or her sisters. I would hate for her to lose her bond with them, so I'll do my best to make a good impression. Even if it means showering her mother with material things and feeding her ego.

"What do you think about this?" I ask, motioning toward a designer handbag displayed on the wall of the upscale boutique.

Scarlett picks up the purse and poses with it. "Actually, this is perfect. My mom loves handbags."

I pick up a wallet and a diamond-studded compact mirror. "These will be an exquisite addition to the gift." As for her fathers, I'll bring an expensive bottle of tequila and whiskey, because Scarlett couldn't remember which they drink most of. And of course, wine. I'm counting on her mother drinking and hopefully turning in early.

Scarlett smiles at me, strolling around the boutique. She lingers at the jewelry case, looking at several sparkling pieces. She presses her finger to the glass above a ruby ring, her eyes lighting up.

"Why don't you pick out a couple of things for yourself?" I say, sliding my hands around her waist. She never asks for anything, and I want to know more about what she prefers. She didn't even glance at the diamonds, so I know her tastes are bolder and more vibrant than classic. She also gravitates toward vivid colors and whimsical prints. That is unless she's wearing jeans and a T-shirt.

Scarlett offers me a smile. "I wouldn't even know where to start. I've always done my shopping online and could only get what my mom approved of."

"Why don't you start with something to wear and go from there." I motion toward the racks of dresses displayed on the back wall. This boutique has everything a woman who enjoys fashion could desire. "And if you can't decide, we'll take whatever you choose. There are no limitations for you, Scarlett."

She beams a smile, turning toward the store, her gray eyes wide as she peers around.

Is it strange that I disapprove of her mom? Perhaps. I disagree with how obediently trained omegas are in our society. It's why I liked the idea of someone out of the normal age range of omegas looking for a pack. Though after meeting Scarlett, I realize how perfect she is. Because she might have been trained to be an omega, but she is also adaptable. She's a quick study and has really opened up since our first night.

It's strange. At first, I felt old due to my personal insecurities about the age difference. In reality, Scarlett makes me feel young. Giddy. I never thought I'd be excited about even glimpsing someone the way I do with her. My emotions run rampant like a mass of butterflies fluttering in my stomach. I get jitters over being alone together. I'm full-on smitten knowing she's a Hart. Has my heart, too. And watching her now gets to me in the best way possible. Who knew a man of my age and stature could have a crush? More, even. With each passing day, I fall harder for this spectacular woman.

Peeking over my shoulder, I wait for Scarlett to select a couple of dresses and then head toward the fitting room. I expect her to call me over, but she doesn't, and I'm glad for it. My favorite part of the morning is to see what she chooses to wear, and I admire every inch of her incredible body.

Plus, I want to get her a surprise too.

I wave my hand at an associate dressed in all black. "I'd like to see this ring right here."

The man unlocks the case and pulls it out for me. "This is a four-carat, pear-shaped ruby from Mozambique. Stunning clarity."

I take the white gold ring and study it with the eyeglass he offers me. "It'll look magnificent on my omega, don't you think? I'd like it to be a surprise, so please be discreet. She is in the fitting room."

"Yes, sir," the man says, retrieving the ring for me and gathering a crystal box to place it in.

I quickly go over the certificates and paperwork and give him Scarlett's ring size. "I can have it cleaned and ready this evening."

"I'll have someone from my staff give you a call to discuss insurance policies and whatnot." Because this is *the* ring. The second I saw Scarlett's face light up, I knew this was the one I would give her as an engagement present from our pack.

"Absolutely. I can also add whatever your omega chooses to your account." The man smiles at me. "We're very happy to be at your service, Mr. Hart."

This is one of those boutiques that you have to make an appointment to even enter, which makes things a lot easier and more private. We don't have to worry about tourists wandering in from the Wharf or being approached out of curiosity by someone who might recognize Scarlett. She is more reserved when it comes to socializing. I won't push her into uncomfortable situations if I can help it.

"Adrian, what do you think about this?" Scarlet's voice drags my attention away from the jewelry, and I swivel and catch sight of her standing in a full-length, low V-neck gown in a color fitting for her name. Her hair looks more mahogany in this light, but I'm sure if she were to step in the sun, the dress would bring out the auburn highlights of her tresses.

I whistle and smile, my heart picking up pace at the sight of her. "Hypnotic. Stunning. Incredibly beautiful."

"You don't think it's too much?" Her cheeks redden with her blush. "This is something I'd wear to a ball or a wedding."

"Or perhaps an unforgettable night on the town," I say, strutting forward to close the space.

I catch a whiff of her cherry-vanilla scent from a few feet away, and my muscles tighten, and my cock hardens, her closeness triggering my desire. She not only looks incredible, but she also smells so mouthwatering that I pull her to me and kiss her softly, needing to feel her body against mine.

She rests her hand on my chest. "Leo might complain about wearing a suit," she teases, smiling against my mouth.

"It's been a while since I've seen him in one. It shall be a night to remember." I slide my hand down her back and pull her even closer. "I've arranged a penthouse apartment. We'll only stay at your parents for an evening and not take them up for hospitality."

Scarlett's eyes light up. "Seriously? You're the best!" Engulfing me in a hug, she meets me for a kiss with enough passion that I can't help picking her up.

She hooks her legs around my waist, hiking up the dress. The heat of her pussy radiates against me, turning me on. Scarlett moans against my mouth, squirming in my arms, rubbing against me as if she needs more.

I break away with a gasp, my balls throbbing and my cock pulsing. "Let's get out of here."

"Mmmhmm," she murmurs, caught up on our desire. I've never been so out of control in my life. All I can think about is her and how she feels against me. How delectable she smells, her sweet scent filling my senses and triggering my innate desire to mate with her. I can already imagine her beneath me, ready and waiting. How tight she'll be when I knot with her.

Damn. I want her so badly.

Now is not the time or place.

But I won't let her suffer the same ache I feel.

I call out to the associate to bag everything in the dressing room and exit the boutique, heading toward my rental SUV with dark tinted windows and enough space for our pack. They aren't with us, preparing for our weekend, and I open the back and set Scarlett on the seat. I climb in and shut the door behind us, watching her pant and arch her back as she wiggles in anticipation of whatever happens next.

I drag her dress up higher and grab at her panties, yanking them down and flinging them. She gasps and grabs my shoulders, pulling me back to her for another kiss. I break away and work down her neck, sucking the sensitive spot on her throat, leaving a mark for both of us to remember. Scarlett scratches at my suit jacket, moaning and whimpering with her need. I reach between us and caress my fingers over her pussy lips, listening to her gasping reaction.

"Do you want me to taste you, Scarlett?" I murmur working lower to guide my tongue over her torso, gently teasing the seam of her legs. "Will you sit still and let me have my way?"

"Yes." Her breath barely makes a sound with the word.

"Tell me louder. I'm not sure if you really want me to." I ease just the tip of my finger between her legs, withholding without getting carried away. I want to hear her say it. I want confirmation that she wants to be with me. And she wants me to continue.

She tries to grab at me, running her fingers over my stiff cock, making me growl at the pleasure. But I want to deny myself. If she gets her way, we won't leave this SUV for hours.

Snatching her wrist, I raise her arm over her head and pin her. "Don't. This is about you and your pleasure. I need to abstain from enjoying you right now, but it'll be worth it. If you can't promise to behave and let me give you what you need, then I can't give it to you at all."

A whine escapes her lips, and she stops squirming, her breathing heavy as she lies on the seat beneath me. "Please, don't stop. I'll be your good omega. I'll hold still. Just don't stop."

My cock jumps at her words, and I release her hand only to reach down and unfasten my belt and free my hard-on. I might not resist her if she touches me, but I can take care of myself while I make her come. It's the type of control I need.

Her eyes drag down my body, drinking in the sight of me exposed, kneeling between her spread legs. Lust fills the air, and I ease my other hand under her legs, pushing up until she holds them for me.

"I'm going to taste you now. Stay still as I get my fill, or I'll have to stop. We'll never leave this vehicle otherwise. You're going to let me get us both off. Do you understand? I need this control right now. I need you." My voice rumbles with my desire, my muscles flexing as I watch her dig her fingers into her thighs, her body bent into position with her legs over her head.

"Then take me." Her bottom lip quivers, and she doesn't take her eyes off me, watching me lick my lips and ease down, turning her slightly in the seat so I can kneel on the floor.

I use her slick to lube up my hand to rub my cock, the sensation enough to make me growl a moan. I bow down and glide my tongue across her body, tasting the sweetness between her legs as she whimpers in pleasure, arching her neck, unable to resist watching me as I eat her out like the most delectable dessert. Her cream is as delicious as her scent, and I can live here forever if she'd allow it. I run my tongue over her clit, using my free hand to keep her open for me. She pants and moans, unable to continue watching as her back arches and she says my name, the sound so incredibly sexy it makes my balls tighten.

I suck her clit into my mouth, rolling my tongue over it in even strokes, despite the ferocity of my hand jerking my cock over and over again, my desperation turning me wild.

"You're coming for me first. You're my beautiful woman, Scarlett. My perfect omega." I growl against her pussy, feeling her thighs squeeze my head tighter. She reacts to the sensation and moans again.

I drag my tongue up and down the seam of her body, moving my head so she can feel more than just my mouth. I want her to remember what it's like for me to eat her out. I want her to think about this for days. I want her to feel it for days. I want the friction to set her off in a way where she can't walk straight without getting wet.

I dip my middle finger inside her, feeling for the rough patch of nerves that I know will make her squirt with enough attention. Her mouth parts open, her teeth biting and dragging across her full lip. She's getting close. I can smell it. I can taste it as her slick drenches my face, dripping down my chin. I stroke her G-spot softly, playing with her body as if she is my personal toy, and I can't get enough. I kiss her clit, rolling my tongue as I finger her and stroke myself, working my body harder, feeling on the edge of exploding.

Scarlett squeezes me with her thighs, screaming out in ecstasy. She releases her legs, resting them on my back, and she grabs my hair and twists, holding onto me as if she might float away otherwise. She comes, squirting over my face, and I purr and don't stop, pushing her to the edge as quickly as I can, wanting to lengthen her orgasm.

"Fuck, Adrian. Fuck!" She screams again, louder as she arches her back and kicks her leg against the seat like she can barely stand the pleasure.

She squirts across me again, her body so incredibly sexy and wet. It's enough that I force myself to pull away, my balls tightening as I grunt and come, splashing my seed over her pussy and pelvis.

I release a breath with the pleasure, imagining it being so much more intense when I can knot with her. I almost can't resist myself and climb on top of her, needing to feel the heat of her body against mine. But I don't try to enter. I kiss her, devouring her affection, putting my weight on her so she knows that I'm here. She won't float away, but I won't let her go until her heart settles and she can come down from the high of our passion without crashing. I don't care how long it takes. She is my omega, and she's my future.

She's the center of my world and my pack and nothing from this point forward will ever change that.

I feel it deep in my soul. I waited so long, because I was waiting for Scarlett. Our souls have been in search of each other only to be separated by time, and I won't allow another second to pass without having her in my life.

"You are mine, Scarlett. My perfect omega. My dream woman. You're everything I could ever hope for and more. You make me feel as if my life is just beginning. I promise to be everything you could ever need." I peer into her beautiful eyes, watching them sparkle with the bond we grow together.

"You're my strong alpha. My leader. My everything. I'll be everything you need as well." Scarlett whispers the words, clinging to me, kissing me again before she nuzzles her face into my throat, inhaling a deep breath of my scent.

Her words touch me deeply, and I savor them as I savor her closeness.

She's more than my omega and my perfect woman.

I can't wait to make her my wife.

I can't wait to grow a family with her.

If only I could stop the world for a moment. I feel as if the anticipation will kill me otherwise.

But Scarlett is worth the wait.

Standing outside of Scarlett's childhood home makes me feel as if I've gained back twenty years of my life. I didn't expect a man of my age to get nervous over meeting another pack. It's part of my job, and I've traveled many places and have met many distinguished and powerful packs. But meeting the family of the woman of my dreams? I feel as if it's my first day of college all over again. How I was nervous about whether I'd fit in or if it was the right decision to go or the right school. It feels as if I no longer know the direction my life is headed, and I also feel a bit out of control. Young and naive.

That is, until a man with auburn hair with streaks of gray opens the front door of the Queen Anne Victorian-style house on one of the prominent streets of downtown San Francisco.

He glances at me first, but Scarlett doesn't give him even a second to open his mouth before she launches forward into his arms. "Dad! I didn't know you'd be home. I thought you'd be working late tonight. Mom said—"

The man laughs and embraces Scarlett, spinning her around before setting her on her feet and cupping her cheeks to kiss her forehead. "Sage says a lot of things, darling. I wouldn't miss the opportunity to meet Pack Hart since they're taking my baby girl from me."

Fuck. Scarlett's dad glances at me, raising an eyebrow.

Scarlett giggles and pulls away, turning back to grab my hand. "No one's taking me from you. But you know I can't be your baby girl forever. I'm almost twenty-two. And I want you to meet my pack leader and one of my fiancés. This is Adrian, Dad. Adrian, this is my dad, Leroy."

Again, her father gives me another questioning look. He tightens his jaw and proffers his hand. "Please, call me Lee. It's a pleasure to meet you."

I shake his hand and step back to put my arm around Scarlett's waist. "To you as well. Scarlett has spoken so affectionately about you. I'm happy to finally meet her family. The rest of my pack will be here shortly. I thought it best to meet you first."

"Scarlett! You're here!" A blond girl runs to the foyer and engulfs Scarlett in a hug, forcing me to release her. "I've missed you, big sis. We have so much catching up to do." The girl pulls at Scarlett, only turning her attention to me for a moment to smile. "You must be Adrian. I'm Sapphire."

"Sapphire? You sent the cookies." I smirk with my comment, watching Scarlett's face scrunch up, dying to laugh.

Sapphire gawks in shock. "I—I hope you liked them."

I chuckle. "They were the talk of the night."

Her cheeks redden. "That's...good. It was all Violet's idea. We had a theme, and I wasn't sure what to get as a gift." Crinkling her nose, Sapphire turns to Scarlett, shaking her head. Scarlett will surely laugh about this later. "I hope you don't mind, but I've been dying for a moment with my sister."

"That sounds like an excellent idea, princess. I'd like to get acquainted with Mr. Hart, anyway. Why don't you and Scarlett go see if your mom needs any help?" Lee glances at his daughters and then at me. "If you don't mind."

I square my shoulders. "Not at all. It was nice meeting you, Sapphire. Scarlett talks highly of you. I'm glad to be able to bring her here."

Lee clears his throat, motioning his daughters away.

This is it.

I can see a dozen questions on his face, and he needs answers. I don't have to read his mind to know that he disapproves of me without even giving me a chance. I knew to expect this. A father will always be protective of his daughter.

And unfortunately, I'll have to stand my ground. Because Scarlett is mine now.

I'll have to prove to be a worthy alpha, and the first step is never backing down.

11

Scarlett

CHALLENGES

I yank away from Sapphire's hold and stop short in the hallway, giving myself a view as two deep, guttural growls challenge each other. My heart sinks into my stomach at the sight of my dad challenging Adrian in a pissing match. What does he think he's doing? He knows exactly what the terms are to keep mom happy and living in her lavish life of luxury. But worse, he's showing major disrespect to my alpha, and I can't stand around and tolerate it.

"Dad!" I yell, striding forward and back to them as they stand in the foyer. "What are you doing? What kind of welcome is this? Mom has been demanding we come here, but if you don't want us to be here, then we'll leave. I don't understand what has gotten into you."

"Your mother failed to mention that she betrothed you to a pack my age, Scarlett. You deserve someone better. Younger. He can only give you half a fucking life with him. I will revoke your contract. It is in my right, considering that your mother misinformed me." Dad shocks the hell out of me by shoving Adrian and pushing him against the door. "What kind of sick intentions do you have? You're far above the appropriate age for taking an omega."

"An appropriate age? You speak to me as if I'm elderly, and I'm not. I'm well established in Pack Carlisle and far more powerful than you, so I suggest you take a step back and cool off. I paid the dowry. I've done everything and more for your daughter to ensure that she is happy. I gave her the opportunity to back out if she were uncomfortable with our age difference. She didn't. She chose us."

I get between my dad and Adrian, my eyes filling with tears. This wasn't the reaction I was expecting. I thought he'd be happy. He knew how important it was for me to find a pack, especially because no one else offered. I press my hands to my dad's chest, getting him to stay back. He growls in my face for the first time ever, startling me.

I try to nudge him back, but he doesn't budge. "You need to stop. Mom arranged everything. At first, I was a little nervous, but it wasn't because of their age. You know how hard it's been for me. I have been rejected by basically every fucking pack, and now you're going to try to deny me the happiness I found? I won't stand for it. You don't get a choice in this matter."

"Do not disrespect me, Scarlett." Dad glowers, looking ready to snatch me up, but Adrian slides his hand around my waist and pulls me back.

"You've disrespected us first, and I will not let you speak to her like that. She is mine. She's my wife, and I don't care who you are. You will not talk to her in this manner. She spoke her peace, and it is clear we're not welcome here, so we'll go." Adrian reaches for the door, twisting it open without turning his back on my dad.

He drags me back, minding the steps as Dad watches from the doorway. I've never seen him so angry. So disappointed. But I don't give a fuck. He has no right to an opinion on my decisions any longer. He basically discarded me the second he sent me away.

The Harts are my pack now.

It's never been clearer

If only I didn't feel as if the bonds to my sisters must also be broken.

So much for my perfect life.

Once again, my family has proven that the only thing that matters is them.

Fuck them. I matter too.

I won't stand by as they try to push their anger on me, because it's not my fault. It's theirs.

And I'm happy.

My pack is happy.

And that's all that matters to me.

The crisp breeze wafts around me as I stand on the balcony and look over San Francisco Bay. Adrian, Ezra, and Jonah sit just inside, talking in hushed voices. Everyone knew something was wrong immediately when Adrian called them, and it has taken everything in me not to cry my eyes out.

I thought introducing my pack to my family would be awkward, but I didn't expect the kind of reaction it elicited from Dad. I'm sure he went to my other dads as well, and they're going to try to give us hell.

Princess: It's a mess here. I don't think I've heard this much yelling in a while.

I stare at the text message from Sapphire, wishing she had never seen any of it.

Princess: I'm sorry things went that way. Mom is getting everything in control. Stop worrying. You know how she is. All she'll have to do is whine, and they'll give in.

I rest my elbows on the balcony, clutching my phone for dear life.

Me: Thanks for saying that. I don't know why it's such a big deal.
Princess: It's not. Adrian was so handsome and protective. Things will settle. You know how Mama knows how to handle things.
Me: When did you grow up, Sapphire? You sound so wise.

Princess: Hah. I learned it from you. You were always so reasonable. It kind of wore off and helped me. Fake it until you make it, remember?
Me: No one will know otherwise.

I repeat the phrase I told her a couple of times when she came to me needing help with one thing or another. The stress of trying to be perfect to make up for Violet has weighed on all of us. Sapphire always wondered how I could remain composed, especially when I never got any interest from packs. I faked it—I didn't need a pack when I was passing as a beta.

Princess: Oh. Mama just stormed out.

Another text message pops on my screen, and I inwardly groan.

Me: Shit. She just texted me. She wants to come to meet with my alphas before we go.
Princess: Good luck, sis.

I sigh, stepping away from the balcony. I turn toward the open living room, spotting Leo and Dominic sitting on the couch. All five of my guys look up at me, and it's as if mom knows that I'm not going to respond in a timely manner, because all their phones go off at once.

I squeeze my eye shut. "My mom wants to come over. She and my dads have been fighting. I don't know what to expect. Maybe we should run while we still can."

Ezra gets to his feet and opens his arms, coaxing me to come forward. "Amore, it'll be fine. We need to do this. I know how important family is to you, despite the problems. I'll make dinner, and we will have a nice evening. Once everything calms down, we can try again."

"Shit. So that means I need to put on the damn suit?" Leo asks, rubbing his hand over the back of his neck.

"I'll grab the gifts. I'm sure it won't take her long to get here," Jonah says, patting Adrian on the back. "Why don't you pull up an additional proposal. You said it yourself. Money talks. We'll offer her something she can't refuse, and she'll help settle Scarlett's family."

Dominic comes to my side and tugs me away from Ezra, allowing him to head to the kitchen. He quietly guides me toward the master bedroom and what they've deemed my suite to make it easier for all of them to come in as they please without feeling possessive like they would be in their own rooms.

"Lettie, I feel how tense you are, and I want you to take a couple of deep breaths. We'll take care of everything.

This isn't the first dispute two packs have had during an engagement. I've seen it a dozen times with Pack Clearwater, and to be honest, I can't blame your dad for his reaction. He'll always see you as a little girl and not the beautiful woman you are. I don't think anyone could impress him." Dominic spins me toward the mirror and pulls my hair over my shoulders, hugging me from behind. "But it doesn't mean I won't stop trying. This is important to you, so it's important to me."

I turn around in his arms and cup his face, meeting his dark eyes. "But that's the thing. You're the ones who are important to me. That's what hurts me. My dad should see that. It's not about the damn paperwork or our obligations. It's about me finding my happiness, and it's as if he just can't see it."

"Then we will make him." Dominic kisses me softly and heads toward the closet, pulling out one of the dresses the associate from the boutique had delivered not long ago.

I let him help me dress, enjoying the sensation of his lips kissing my shoulders and neck, his gentle touch keeping my heart steady as he traces his finger over the small flower-shaped birthmark that darkened when I manifested into an omega. His fingers glide over my silhouette, and he smiles in the mirror at me, his eyes shining with affection and adoration. I could live on his attention forever.

If only the doorbell didn't ring.

My heartbeat skips, knowing that Mom is here.

Adrian opens the door, and Dominic guides me toward the living room. Mom strides into the penthouse as if she owns it, and Adrian bows slightly as he takes her hand and kisses her knuckles.

"It's an honor to have you surprise us this evening, Mrs. Steele. I want to apologize for earlier. It was an unexpected situation, and I do regret my behavior, but your daughter is important to me. I won't tolerate her being treated as if she is not my omega." Adrian takes a step back, towering over Mom.

She stares at him expressionlessly until he picks up a gift box from the table and hands it to her.

"I hope we can overcome these challenges. We have a gift to show our appreciation for your openness to visit despite your alphas' opinions." Adrian smiles and motions toward the rest of us. "Why don't you come in and make yourself comfortable? Ezra is preparing dinner, and I have a bottle of some vintage wine if you would like a glass."

Mom's face softens. She smiles, her eyes lighting up. She loves to be wined and dined, and I'm so glad that

Adrian really took the time to understand how my mom works.

I force myself to step forward and open my arms. "Mom, I'm so happy you're here. Thank you for giving us another chance. I don't understand what has gotten into Dad."

Mom hugs me and steps back, giving me a long once-over as she mentally picks apart my dress. "He's just being bullheaded. I told him as much, especially because he even signed the proposal paperwork. I just don't think he actually took the time to read over everything. Your alphas are quite handsome, Scarlett. I hadn't realized they would be so unexpectedly mature. My fault. I didn't read over everything. Just the financials."

Of fucking course. Anger sizzles beneath my skin, her admittance over just signing a paper to get the money getting under my skin. She couldn't care less about me or my future as long as I fulfill the obligation bestowed upon us. And now that she speaks of my alphas, I bristle. I certainly don't want her anywhere near them. She is a huge flirt, and I don't want her embarrassing me or making my alphas uncomfortable.

"You still did well," I force myself to say, knowing she loves praise, even when she's fucked up. "I'm very happy. Why don't you come and sit at the table to open your gifts? Adrian picked them out." I offer Adrian a smile as he pours seven glasses of wine, and Jonah and Leo help him carry them to the table.

Dominic pulls out a chair for mom, giving her the head of the table. "Mrs. Steele. Please take the guest of honor seat. It's such a pleasure to have you here. I'm Dominic. That's Jonah and Leo. As Adrian mentioned, Ezra is preparing dinner."

"I hope you like Italian. I'm cooking one of my mamma's favorite recipes."

Mom smiles as she carefully pulls out the tissue paper from the bag with the boutique's name clearly on the side. "I love it. How did you know it was my favorite store?"

"Because it's Scarlett's too," he says, winking and making Mom blush.

Her attention returns to the gifts, and she pulls out the box with the purse and gasps, covering her heart with her hand, her reaction over the top but normal for her. "How lovely! This is absolutely perfect." Mom turns to me and says, "I'm quite impressed. Your pack seems generous."

"We're quite happy about the small mistake with her paperwork. Who knew a typo would bring such a magnificent woman, who happens to have a brilliant mother, into our lives?" Adrian says, taking a seat beside me. He rests his hand on my knee, acting charming as hell.

Mom cocks her head, setting down the rest of the gifts. "I'm sorry? What do you mean by a typo?"

Adrian remains expressionless. "Her age was incorrect on the profile posted. It's what actually first drew us to her. But none of that matters. We're very happy. So much so, that we would like to offer you a special gift. Scarlett wants to prolong our engagement through the school year, so how could we ever say no? Because of that, I'd like to offer you a stipend. I understand how your pack won't give you the dowry until our marriage is official."

Mom presses her lips together, remaining silent for a minute. Sweat prickles on my hairline and I peek at Adrian and then at the others, taking a moment to study their anticipation.

"It'll be quite substantial, Mrs. Steele," Adrian adds. "I've had a very successful meeting with the mayor of San Francisco. The leader of Pack Carlisle has approved the expansion of our university. You will be pleasantly rewarded for agreeing."

My heartbeat picks up pace, my nerves getting the best of me. I've never seen Mom take so long making a decision. She's usually quick and rash about every aspect of our lives.

"That sounds lovely. A summer wedding would be perfect for my beautiful daughter," Mom finally says, offering the fakest smile I've ever seen. "Whatever makes my daughter happy."

Mom reaches out and places her hand on mine. Something strange darkens her eyes, and I feel the world crowding around me. I've seen this look before, but I can't place the meaning behind it.

She's acting, and I know it.

"Wonderful!" Adrian says, raising his wine glass. "Let's make a toast. To new beginnings, a beautiful bride, and a union of families."

"Cheers," Leo says, clinking his glass to mine.

"Cheers," everyone repeats, smiling with their relief.

Mom sets her wine glass down without drinking from it. We have a problem. I know it. I just wish I knew what to expect. Why does it feel as if she's going to mess up my life again?

Because she's mom, that's why.

All I know is that I can't wait to leave.

I need to set my life under the Steele name behind me.

It's the only way I'll make it through. It's the only way I'll have a future of my own making.

Scarlett

MISTAKE

Mom: Honey, can we talk? I know you're busy, but it's important. It's about Lee.

My chest clenches, Mom's text message igniting fear inside me. I ignored her last three phone calls, and now I worry something happened to Dad.

I quickly slide my textbook into my bag and rush toward the door, mouthing an apology to my Biology professor.

Rushing down the long hall, I race through the automatic glass door. Sunshine dims my vision. I head toward the shade of a tree and sit on one of the many benches. I rest my elbow on the table, watching students meander around campus. It's always super busy on a Tuesday. I know a lot of people squeeze all their classes in mid-week.

My cell phone buzzes again, and I summon my nerves. I don't read the text from Mom and just hit the call button. It rings far longer than I expect it to, considering I know she just sent me a text, and I think she might be doing it on purpose. It would be just like her to ignore my call because I did so to her.

Just when I think it's about to go to her voicemail, the line clicks on, and I hear a horn beep.

"Mom, is everything okay with Dad? I was in class." I keep my voice low, doing my best to remain even in tone.

"Of course, he's not okay. He feels as if you abandoned him. He's upset with how you left things. You know he loves you, and he wants the best for you." Mom's voice snaps at me, the annoyance hot with her unexpected comment. When she left the penthouse after dinner in San Francisco, I thought things were fine. She had promised to cool Dad off and also told my pack that she was happy that we were together.

I smack my hand on the table. "You made it sound like he was in an accident. I'm sorry, Mom. I don't have time for this. I have to go."

"Scarlett, don't you fucking dare hang up on me. This is important. Your father isn't budging in his opinion of Pack Hart. And now that he knows you made a mistake on your profile, he wants to reject their proposal," Mom spits out. Is she kidding me? She's blaming me for the mistake? I never even saw my profile. It's just like her to twist things instead of holding herself accountable.

"You better do something. You created my profile. You arranged the proposal. I've done nothing but be the obedient daughter you demanded me to be." I pound my fist on the table, my anger controlling me.

"You should've said something when you met them! I will not take the blame for this." Mom growls with her words, reminding me of the dozen times she had cornered me in my room, threatening me with a hairbrush because she was mad that I had told my dad on her when she was acting out and scaring me.

But now, it feels as if neither of my parents are on my side.

"Are you kidding me? You saw their profiles. They brought up the age difference even with the error. You can't do this shit. You've already agreed and approved. We have set a date. This is my life, and I will not let you ruin it. You took the stipend from the Harts." Panic seizes my muscles, and I grasp the table as if I will suddenly fall over.

"Come on, Scarlett. You can do better. We can do better. Now that we know of my error, we can fix it and find you another pack. You'll get scooped up so quickly, especially with your upcoming birthday. So many are anxious because of the time between proposals and breeding. This is a good thing. You cannot possibly be attracted to those old men," Mom says, contradicting herself with her admission. I wish I were recording her as proof. She had obviously told Dad it wasn't her fault, and now that she's angry at me, the truth comes out. She damn well knows this was her fault.

"You're fucking older than them, Mom. Don't give me that bullshit. You don't care. All you want is more money. So fuck off. This is set, and it's happening. I love them." My voice rings through the air, my anger turning into fury, burning my eyes with tears. "If you do anything to mess this up, you'll regret it."

Mom hisses through the line. "Scarlett, Goddamn it! You little—"

I hang up on her, not standing for her oncoming threats. I can't believe this bullshit. I can't believe that she has decided to seek other opportunities now that she realizes her mistake. She was absolutely fine before, even knowing they were older, and now she's trying to use my dad's opinion as an excuse. I can't believe this.

"Damn, Dickasso. Who pissed you off?" Chaz stands a foot away, crossing his arms over his chest. A smile tilts his lips as he stares down at me. "So, you're playing hard to get because you love someone already? I haven't seen you with anyone. Do I know him? His pack?"

I flare my nostrils and glower up, wishing I could disintegrate him with my eyes. At least he didn't catch that I had used a plural term. Because betas don't usually hook up with several people at once. Many are monogamous. There are a couple out there, but not enough for it to be normal. Not like with omegas and alphas.

"Stay out of my business," I mutter, sliding off the bench seat. I sling my satchel across my shoulder. "What are you even doing here? I saw you on the schedule at Beach Brew. Shouldn't you be there?"

"Miss Sandy switched me out for the evening shift again." Chaz steps closer. "It's nice knowing that you keep track of me."

I roll my eyes and turn away from him. "So I can avoid you."

A strong hand locks around my wrist and yanks me, causing me to stumble. Chaz catches me in his arms, not letting me go.

"You're a fucking bitch. I've been nothing but nice to you. I don't know what the fuck twisted your panties, but you need to lighten up. Appreciate my attention. It sounds like whoever the hell you were talking to doesn't like your boyfriend. You know shit never works out if a pack doesn't approve." Chaz surprises me by grasping my chin. "Maybe you should just give me a chance. I'll prove—"

A deep, guttural growl reverberates through my bones, and the world falls out from under me as someone snatches Chaz away, sending him sprawling. I catch Leo's scent before I see him tackle Chaz and swing his fist, punching him in the face.

"Don't you fucking touch her ever again. I'll break your hand." Leo growls and swings again, sending blood from Chaz's nose spattering across the concrete path.

"Don't you ever fucking touch a woman without her consent. Do you understand?"

Chaz freezes under Leo, shocked into submission.

"Leo, what's going on?" Jonah's voice echoes through the air. "Get up and let him go."

"He assaulted her. I saw it with my own eyes." Leo growls and shoves his hands into Chaz's chest, pushing him as he gets to his feet.

My mind whirls as I watch two of my alphas face each other, with Chaz on the ground between them. Jonah curls his fingers into fists, his face twisting with his fury. But he's not mad at Leo. He looks ready to join him in beating the shit out of Chaz. I scramble to my feet and take a step back, bracing myself for it. A part of me buzzes in anticipation. I've never seen something so hot as my alpha defending me in my life. It's as hot as Adrian standing up to my dad.

"Mr. Broderik, get to your feet." Jonah turns to me. "Ms. Carlisle, is that true? Are you okay?"

My mouth trembles, my body cooling as Chaz scowls at me, silently threatening me with his gaze. But I won't let him intimidate me.

I nod my head. "It's true. I was trying to go back to class, and he grabbed me. He's trying to coerce me into dating him. I've already told him no."

Tears burn the back of my throat. I had no idea how Chaz's approach really affected me until this moment. How dare he think he could just put his hands on me. How dare he think he has the right.

Jonah growls and snatches Chaz by his arm, pulling it behind his back and restraining him. "You'll be going to Dean Clearwater's office, Mr. Broderik. We don't tolerate harassment on campus, nor do we tolerate assault and ignoring another student's lack of consent."

"Mr. Hart, please. It was a mistake. This asshole is her dad. She's too scared to speak up against him. He's been trying to keep us apart." Chaz flares his nostrils. "You should kick him off campus. He doesn't belong here."

Leo loses his cool and charges Chaz in Jonah's arms. He grabs the front of his shirt and leans in. "I'm not her fucking father. I'm her fiancé. Now, leave her the hell alone, or you're a dead man."

Oh, shit.

Jonah shoves Leo back. I race forward and snatch his hand, pulling him away before he triggers Jonah into losing control and joining him. I can't let them beat up Chaz despite how much I want them to. They're faculty members. Chaz doesn't know Leo works in the Athletics and PE Department. He wouldn't, considering I doubt he's ever lifted a weight or participated in a sport in his life.

"Her fiancé? You better fucking prepare yourself, asshole. I overheard her talking with her pack. They hate you." Chaz flails in Jonah's arms, but Jonah doesn't let him go, pushing him in the direction of the administration building.

I squeeze Leo's hand and tug him with me, forcing him to walk. I'm afraid we've caused too much attention. I fear someone will recognize us together. But I also know he needs me right now.

"Leo, take me home. I just want to go home," I say, my voice quivering.

Leo scoops me in his arms and carries me in the direction of the staff parking lot. He doesn't try to hide me. He doesn't even care anymore.

Neither do I.

I'm tired of the world feeling against us, and now my family is turning against us too.

I can't let that happen.

I won't. I'd rather see the world burn.

"Just hug me. Hug me, so I don't leave you to murder that asshole." Leo buries his face into the crook of my neck, snuggling me and squeezing me as tightly as I do him. "I would have if Jonah hadn't fucking intervened."

"Then you'd be in prison. He's not worth it." I shift on the bed, straddling his lap, pinning him with my body.

"You're worth it." Leo growls, the vibration of his voice tingling over my skin.

"I need more than conjugal visits. Now please, just kiss me. Kiss me before my damn mouth whimpers. Kiss me until I forget." I grab Leo's hair, easing him away from my throat.

He bares his teeth with a rumble, but the noise isn't threatening. It's sexy as hell and demanding—like the sound of lust and desire with feral need. I tighten my fingers to the back of his neck, biting my nails into his skin. He flips me onto the bed and bows down, smashing his mouth to mine like our lips go to war for dominance.

I moan and spread my legs, letting him rest flush against my body. His tangy scent of lime explodes with flavor across my tongue, Leo deepening his kiss and leaving me breathless. He might win the battle for control now, but it won't last. Not when I make him weak in the knees. Not when I feel the heat of his body on mine. Not when he gives me his knot. My mind and body are set.

"My dirty girl, you know exactly what I need," Leo murmurs, stroking his fingers down my throat, leaving a trail of his scent behind.

"Which means you're going to let me take care of you. I'll make it so you never consider leaving this bed." I push my hands to Leo's chest, getting him to roll over again, giving me control back.

He grabs my shirt, pulling it up and over my head, exposing my bra to him.

"You've already made it so, dirty girl. I don't care who's on top. You'll be riding my face regardless." Leo grabs at my waistband, dragging me closer.

I press my hand to his mouth, smiling as I shake my head. Without a word, I flip around. I restrain his arms the best I can, squeezing them to his sides with my knees. His hard-on bulges from his workout pants, and I tug them down, exposing his pierced cock. My heart races. I've seen porn. Omega Prep spends several classes instructing us how to please our alphas. And now? I swallow my nerves and just go for it.

I lace my fingers around his base and suck his tip, tasting the tangy taste of his pre-cum. His scent sets me off with the sound of his moan, and I take a breath and deep throat him, humming as I take him in completely.

"Damn, dirty girl." Leo groans, moving his hips, pushing deeper into my mouth, taking a bit of control.

His barbells graze against my tongue, and I bob my head, slickening him with my spit. Leo breaks his arms free and grabs my ass, opening and closing my body as he massages me. I whine and wiggle, feeling his balls tighten against my fingers at the sensation of my voice.

He enjoys that. I can tell by his body's reaction and the intensity increasing in his scent. Moaning, Leo stretches and grips my hair, pulling it out of his view as he leans sideways to watch. I suck him harder, more desperately, and he tugs my pants down and slips his other hand between my legs.

"Goddamn, you're so fucking wet. You love sucking my cock, dirty girl," he mutters, fingering me teasingly.

"Mmmhmm." I moan, rubbing my thumb over the smoothness of his balls. I won't stop until he comes. I'm desperate to taste him. To know that I can get him off with my mouth.

"You're so sexy. You want to waste my seed, don't you? You want to swallow, or can I paint your hot fucking tits with it? Leave my scent on you for days. No one will ever fucking doubt you're mine." Leo increases the pressure between my legs, stretching me enough to make me gasp. "Tell me what you want, my dirty girl."

I lick my lips, my chest heaving. "Whatever you want.
"

Leo releases a deep, guttural noise and spanks me. "Tell me what you want."

My whole body buzzes, and I only think about it for a second before saying, "I want to taste you."

Leo guides my head back down, moaning as I take another deep breath and suck him in my mouth, feeling him in my throat. This time, I take complete control, sucking and humming, licking and letting his piercings rub my mouth enough to make my throat ache. I lose myself to his pleasure, my body singing with enjoyment. Satisfying my alpha is unlike anything I've ever experienced.

"Get ready, Scarlett. I'm going to come so hard." Leo thrust his hips up, fucking my face until he grunts with his release.

His cum fills my mouth, the thick, sticky texture citrusy like his scent but a bit saltier. I pull away and swallow, turning to meet his gaze as he watches me. He surprises me, locking his arms around me to spin me around only to flip me onto my back. He yanks my pants off completely and shreds the soft fabric of my panties, ripping them away as if he can't wait even a second to see me naked. He grabs for my bra next, unhooking it with one hand only to capture my nipple between his teeth. He nips me hard enough to make me gasp. I clutch his hair and drag his head to the side, sinking my teeth into the sweet scent glands on his neck.

"Careful now. You're testing my restraint. I like things a bit rough, and I know you need to be worked up." Leo cups my face, pinching my chin, holding me still to kiss me. "You need some attention before I leave my own fucking mark."

I roll my hips, silently begging for more. "You don't have to be gentle. I'm not fragile. Just fuck me. Fuck me until I can't think. Don't make me fight for control. I've been fighting all my life to get what I want, and right now, I want you."

An unfamiliar expression crosses his face, his brows knitting together, but it's not a frown. It's darker, wilder, and so fucking sexy that I nearly go placid beneath him. Who knew that one look could trigger my body into submission?

"You want me that bad, dirty girl?" Leo asks, his voice deepening. He buries his face to the crook of my neck, sucking my skin, teasing me before biting me back, our lust mingling, our bond growing more intense with our need. "If you want me, take me. I want to see how much you crave me. If you can claim me, then I will fuck you until you can't walk, so I can carry you around like my good little omega. I'll fuck you so hard that you will never want to leave this bed."

His words ignite the fire inside me, and I shove him hard, pushing him off. He could resist, his strength out-matching mine, but he does it for me. He wants to see how far I'll go, and I'll do exactly what it takes for him to claim me. To knot with me. It's all I can think about. My lust and desire are uncontrollable. I've felt horny a million times before, but never this much in my life without my heat, and it's as if it controls me.

I grab his shoulders and force him to the bed, gliding my body lower until I feel his hard cock tap against my ass. He licks his lips, watching me, and I raise my hips up only to adjust him beneath me. But I don't push him inside me. Instead, I slide my body up and down his legs, letting him feel how slippery my slick is, my body ready to be destroyed in the way I want. Because I want him to carry me around. I want him to care for me, feed me, and just love up on me as much as I need. It'll be that much more worth it if I give in to our deep-seated, wild nature as an omega with her alpha.

Leo flares his nostrils, watching as I rock my body, grinding against his without letting him slip inside me. "You like being a fucking tease."

Digging my nails into his chest, I scratch him hard enough to leave red streaks. "What are you planning to do about it? I don't need you inside me to make myself come."

I bite my lip and smile, the sensation of his hard-on and his piercings feeling so incredible that I might actually follow through with my teasing threat. I move harder and faster, using him like my own personal toy.

"Keep it up, Scarlett. Keep it up and see what happens." Leo reaches up and drags his thumb over my mouth, hooking it to my cheek. He pulls me down until our lips press together, and he grips my ass, spreading my body wider as he aligns me with his cock. "You're testing me."

"Because I want you. Fuck me. Fuck me like you plan to break me. Fuck me until I'm the only thing you'll ever think about again." I bite his lip and stretch it, making him growl. "Stop treating me like I can't handle you. Give me your knot. Now."

He smacks my ass, the stinging sensation radiating through my body. "You're in fucking trouble now." He thrusts inside me, holding my ass cheeks as he controls me while I straddle him. My eyes roll back as I scratch my fingers into his chest, the sensation an unexpectedly good ache, unlike anything I've experienced. The shock-wave of pain and pleasure rolling through me leaves me breathless. He turns wild with his passion, bouncing me on top of him, growling with each thrust. My mind spins with his intensity. I can't even think about anything except how he feels inside me.

My forehead scrunches, the world jostling as I cling on, my moans sounding like bursts of screams. "Fuck! Fuck!" It's all I can manage to say.

"Your pussy is so tight, Scarlett. You're so hot riding me," he mutters, sitting up and moving my legs around his waist, so we can face each other. "My dirty girl. You're mine. My beautiful, sexy, horny fucking omega. You ready for my knot?"

I gasp, my slick soaking him, turning the ache into unforgettable pleasure that buzzes throughout my cells. "Fucking give it to me. I want to know what it feels like to have you fill me with your seed."

"I can't wait to see how sexy you look with it dripping down your legs. Get ready." Leo snarls with desire, capturing my mouth hostage as he picks me up by my ass only to set me on my back. He kneels, digging his fingers into my ass cheeks while curling me up. I pant and moan, grabbing the blankets with each powerful thrust. His eyes never leave our bodies connecting. The way he holds me half-suspended, giving him the room to swing into me leaves me breathless. I scream in pleasure as his body knots with mine, the pressure more surprising than painful, bonding us together in the way I crave as an omega. The pleasure increases with a wave of pure ecstasy, his orgasm setting off mine, controlling me like his knot does. My body won't stop pulsing until he releases me, the act mind-blowing and unlike anything I could have imagined.

He moans loudly, lying on top of me as he rocks, his weight comforting. I kiss him fervently, desperately. I can't help it. It's the only way to silence my need to scream my pleasure. To whimper at its intensity. How wild and out of control I feel riding this wave of bliss. I thought I knew what to expect from knotting with an alpha, but the reality of the experience is something I could've never fully prepared myself for.

"You're doing so good, Scarlett," Leo murmurs, breaking from my mouth. His words come softer, gentler, instead of the teasing alpha he started as. "Just ride with me through it."

My vision shadows, heat filling me from between my legs, sending tingles over my skin. I can barely breathe from the pleasure, our orgasms intertwining, his hormones feeding mine in a never-ending wave that crests over and over again. Neither of us can pull apart, not that we'd want to, and the connection of this moment penetrates me on a soul-deep level. He truly is my alpha. It's more than my growing feelings for him. It's innate. Unending. Completely irrevocable.

Leo bites my neck hard enough to make me bleed, but it doesn't hurt. The raw act of marking me solidifies our bond as mates. The world melts away as time passes, Leo's body still locking me to him for what feels like an eternity of bliss.

Just when I feel as if I'll never leave this hypnotic state, I gasp as the pressure releases me, stealing away the warmth and bliss exploding from my fading orgasm until I'm left whimpering beneath Leo, glistening with sweat, the heady scent of our passion consuming the room.

He envelops me in his arms, stroking his hand up and down my spine. "You're so incredible. So strong and powerful. Let me draw us a bath, so we can soak for a bit. I only want you aching in a good way."

I release a breath and snuggle my face to him, my body more relaxed than it has ever been. Kissing me softly, Leo brushes his lips across my skin in a way that eases the freefall from the high my body rides. And this is only the beginning.

Leo cuddles me long after we bathe, never taking his arms away when I drift to sleep. I only stir awake for a moment with the whisper of voices. But Leo keeps the world away.

He'll always protect me.

He and our pack.

Forever.

13

Scarlett

Stalker

Ms. Sandy: Hey, Dickasso, you missed class. Want my notes? I'll leave them at Beach Brew for you.

My stomach twists at the text message, clearly not from Ms. Sandy. The last person I wanted to hear from was Chaz. He must've known that I blocked him and borrowed Ms. Sandy's phone while she was doing something else. I consider ignoring him, but I've been so anxious since the confrontation between him and Leo. Jonah told me that it had been handled, but he's obviously still attending class.

Ms. Sandy: Please talk to me. I'm sorry for what I did. I don't know what got into me.

I squeeze my eyes shut, wishing the messages away. He's persistent enough that he'll continue until I respond. I wish I didn't feel as if I had to. I can't exactly block Ms. Sandy's number either. I could tell her about Chaz stealing her phone, but I fear the repercussions. He might be apologizing now, but I don't trust him.

Ms. Sandy: I want to start over. Just as classmates and friends. I got the message loud and clear that you are unavailable.

I push up from my bed and stroll into the hallway. Voices hum from downstairs. I meander down, padding quietly with my bare feet. A collection of scents greets me first before I catch sight of all of my alphas gathered around Adrian's desk in his home office, the double doors wide-open. They excused all the household staff for a couple of days, giving us a chance to have privacy. They've also canceled all tour appointments, claiming that they were sick.

"I think we should wait it out. Sage obviously has an agenda, and she's using her own mistake as an excuse. She wants more money out of us, trying to blackmail us by canceling our contract and claiming that we misrepresented ourselves. Obviously, we can fight that," Adrian says, keeping his voice low.

"It could financially destroy us if she wins. The stress of it isn't worth it. Not to mention Scarlett would have to return home during the hearing. Not happening." Leo growls and smacks his hands on the desk. "We need to elope. It's the only way to ensure Scarlett remains with us."

"The only thing that could possibly solidify the situation would be if Scarlett was pregnant. Her mom knows her heat cycle. This is why she's hitting us hard now. She can lie to any prospects about Scarlett ever being with us." Ezra rests his head on his hands, leaning on the desk.

Jonah pushes to his feet. "She needs to stop using the suppressant cream. If she continues, she risks skipping her heat altogether. You know how that stuff is. Unpredictable. She can wear perfume instead."

I blink a few times, realizing he's right. I need to do whatever it takes. Mom is selfish enough to act on her threats, and I have to be considered used. She won't be able to hide me away, especially with who my alphas are.

"I think we're getting ahead of ourselves. I'd like to return to San Francisco and speak with all of Scarlett's dads. I think the shock of it should have worn off by now. It's the best way. They have the final say, and if we can prove how much Scarlett means to us and how happy she is, that will help ease the tension. We have to take the civil approach. Will you give me a day or two?" Dominic leans back in the chair. "If I'm not successful, then we will reconsider our options."

Leo stretches his arms over his head with a groan. "If it comes to a fight, I'm ready to drop everything and run with Scarlett. I don't give a fuck about the school or any fucking thing else."

Sighing, Adrian frowns at Leo and looks at Dominic. "No one is running away. I'll give you a day to see what you can do, Dom. You're right about your approach. Civility first. Thanks for being more clearheaded than me in this moment. I feel as if I'm failing."

Jonah drapes his arm over Adrian's shoulders. "No one is failing. We have handled so much shit in our lives that I know we can get through this."

I clear my throat, drawing everyone's attention to me. "He's right. No one is failing. I'll do what it takes to stay with you. I can call my sister and see what she can do." We could stay with Violet in Alaska. Sapphire can keep Mom busy. My sisters would be pissed off if they knew what Mom was trying. I just don't want Mom to know how badly she's messing with me. It's something that she'll feed on. She gets pleasure from my pain.

"It's probably best not to get more people involved," Leo quips, getting to his feet. He shuffles around the desk and opens his arms, waiting for me to fall into them.

My body hums the second I do, the memory of our passion rushing over me, sending heat between my legs. Silence fills the room. I don't even think any of my alphas are breathing. They watch Leo and me in curiosity, knowing that I took his knot first. It's not awkward, but I can feel the intensity and anticipation coursing through each of them. The scent of my lust ignites theirs.

I uncontrollably whimper and close my eyes, taking a moment to compose myself. "Shit. I'm sorry. My body is a bit out of whack."

"There's nothing out of whack about that, Scarlett. It's normal for a bonded alpha to set off their omega, especially when they expect their upcoming heat." Adrian remains expressionless with his comment, acting as if me fucking Leo isn't the huge deal it truly is. Because I know they all crave me now. More so than before. They can't help it.

I nod my head and pull away from Leo, puffing a breath out my nose to ease the intensity of the cologne drawing me back to him. "I overheard Ezra mention me stopping the use of my suppressant lotion. I think I want to do that."

I swallow my nerves, studying the various expressions crossing their faces—from lust to surprise and maybe an ounce of worry on Jonah's face.

"If that's what you want, then I support you fully." Adrian stands up and strolls to me, hugging me next. "I don't want you to think you have to because of the situation. Just know that."

"I know," I say, rubbing my hands over his cheeks, leaving my scent behind. "I want this. I want all of you. You're my pack, and I'm ready. I've been ready for a while."

The truth of my words hangs in the air. We all knew that my becoming their omega and wife also meant starting a family. I've always known the expectation and never wanted to fight against it, but it seems more important than ever. I don't want to resist our natures. I find it incredibly thrilling to think about.

"Fuck yeah, my dirty girl. You don't know how happy this makes me. You're already mine, but damn. This will declare it to the world." Leo spins me around, making me laugh.

The five of them surround me, engulfing me in a group hug that I can live in forever. I was afraid that my mom ruined things for us. I was afraid that the stress of everything would steal our joy. But it's made us stronger. It brought us closer.

"Scarlett, I wanted to wait until I had the chance to plan something more extravagant, but I can't wait any longer." Adrian reaches into his desk and pulls out a crystal box from his top drawer. "As the leader of our pack, I want to declare our lives and future to you as our omega. We vow a lifetime of love, passion, joy, and protection to you. You're a magnificent woman, and I will not live my life without you ever again. I love you. Will you accept our promise as your alphas?"

My heart flutters at the sight of the teardrop ruby I recognize from the boutique in San Francisco. I had no idea that Adrian bought it, and I tear up, burning trails of happiness down my cheeks.

I open and close my mouth, a whimper escaping as I struggle to find my words. "Yes. Absolutely, yes. I love you. I love all of you."

This moment is proof that I'm my alphas' omega. I'm the center of Pack Hart, and no one will change it.

Not my family. Not the world.

They are mine forever.

I'm theirs.

Unknown: Look to your right. I don't want Ms. Sandy to see me, but I want to talk to you.

My heart sinks into my stomach at the text message from an unknown number. I whip my attention to the side alley leading to the dumpster beside Beach Brew. Chaz leans against the brick wall, wearing a hat and sunglasses as if it's some kind of stealthy disguise.

I don't move from my spot and tap the screen of my phone instead.

Me: You look like a creep. Please, just leave me alone. I'm busy. I have to get this done by tomorrow.

Unknown: Just five minutes. Give me five minutes, and I'll leave you alone from now on.

I sigh and tuck my phone away.

"Amore, how incredible! Leo said you were talented, but this is extraordinary. Your reimagination of Starry Night is...wow." Ezra's booming voice startles me, and my soul nearly exits my body.

I flick my gaze to where Chaz last stood, but he vanishes like the stalker he is.

"And Fruit Basket? It's magnificently morbid. I love it." Ezra's jasmine and bergamot fragrance floods over me with his arrival.

"You do?" I know that rotting fruit, showing off skulls beneath the flesh, isn't exactly everyone's cup of tea, but I thought it was fitting for the Halloween theme. I couldn't wait to add ghosts and other creepy entities to starry night.

Ezra slides his hands around my waist, admiring the window mural from over my shoulder, his warm breath tickling the skin beneath my ear. "Absolutely. It's fantastic."

I turn in his arms and shade my eyes from the bright lights I set up to paint past sunset. "I couldn't get the idea out of my head. I only sketched it out in my notebook, but with such a big canvas, I've really been able to pour my soul into it. Just wait until you see what I came up with as an ode to my favorite artists." The last windowpane will have a collage of self-portraits of artists with skulls instead of their faces. It's been a lot of fun. I love Gothic and dark, and Halloween is my favorite holiday of the year.

Ezra beams, squeezing my shoulders as he peers behind me. "Perhaps the owner will let me buy the windows so I can frame them."

I laugh and shake my head. "This is just a fun piece. What I really hope is to get the contract for the permanent mural inside. I can't believe someone is willing to pay me for my art. Mom told me it was a pointless hobby."

"Something that feeds the soul is never pointless, amore. Your mother was and still is wrong about a lot of things." Ezra presses his lips to my forehead, stroking his fingers up my neck and to my cheeks. "I'd love to see more of your art sometime."

I haven't shown many people my artwork, especially because I've kept a lot of it secret my whole life. I've drawn my sisters things over the years and have sent Emma many unconventional erotic pieces to mess with her, but I don't even know what happened to any of them. "Yeah, sure. I haven't had a chance to do much apart from doodling recently. There wasn't any space in my dorm, and I don't have any art classes this semester.

I took all of those immediately, if you've ever wondered about my schedule."

"That needs to change. I have a studio at the manor. So does Dominic. You're absolutely welcome to use them. They're in the back houses." Ezra picks up a couple of rags from the ground, not caring that paint gets on his fingers. "Why don't I help you clean up, and we can head there? We can order some takeout, or I can cook you something. The others are out tonight until late." Because they were seeing Dominic off to the airport and ensuring he had whatever he needed to approach my dads with.

I push the thought away and meet Ezra's gaze. "I'd love that. Let me close up the paint and put it in the stockroom."

As much as I try to argue, Ezra doesn't let me clean up alone. He greets Ms. Sandy, offering to help her finish stacking the chairs. I smile, watching how he works quickly and meticulously. It feels so good not having to constantly worry here like I do on campus.

But then a shadowy figure passing by the front door reminds me that isn't true. Chaz lingers nearby, making me uneasy.

A hand rests on my shoulder, startling me. I jump, my eyes wide.

"Amore, what's wrong?" Ezra asks, lacing his fingers through mine.

I flick my attention to the counter, looking for Ms. Sandy, but she's gone to the back.

My cell phone buzzes from my pocket, and I swallow hard, not sure whether or not I should look at it.

"Amore, you're trembling. Please talk to me," Ezra murmurs, lowering his voice.

Sweat beads on my forehead, and I tug out my phone, glancing at the unknown number with a new text message alert on my screen. "It's Chaz. He's been trying to reach me. He was outside right when you showed up."

Ezra squeezes my fingers. "Why didn't you tell me?"

I slump my shoulders. "I got distracted. You were so happy that it slipped my mind."

I expect Ezra to yell at me. To get angry. He does neither.

Pulling me closer, Ezra hugs me in his arms, kissing my forehead. "Amore, I want you to stay here. If he's still outside—"

The front door chimes, cutting Ezra off. I tense at the sight of Chaz strolling into the empty cafe, no longer wearing his hat. He gives me a long once-over, raising his eyebrow.

"Hey, Dickasso. I didn't know you'd still be here. I came to pick up my check from Ms. Sandy. Is this yo ur...dad?" Chaz drags his gaze to Ezra.

It's clear that Ezra isn't, and we're obviously together. I can see the wheels turning in Chaz's empty head as he thinks through the situation. He knew that I was taken. But now he realizes there's more to it.

Ezra releases me and steps forward, straightening his shoulders as he gets into Chaz's face. "You're the one who assaulted Scarlett, aren't you?"

Chaz takes a step back and raises his hands in surrender. "I don't want any trouble. Like I said, I'm here to pick up my check."

"That's hard to believe, considering you were just texting her." Growling, Ezra remains stiff in his spot. If it were anyone else, they might throw a punch. He remains in control, though.

"Only to apologize," Chaz argues, nervously shifting on his feet.

"Do that here and now, and don't text her again. Don't look at her. Don't speak to her. Consider this your one and only warning. I will not tolerate this kind of behavior." Ezra steps back and takes my hand. "If you so much as even consider disobeying my order, I will make you regret it."

Chaz scowls, opening and closing his mouth. He looks like he's about to threaten Ezra, but for once, he's smarter than that. Nobody truly wants to challenge an alpha if they don't have to. Especially one like Ezra. He's not some young, hotheaded man going into rut and aggressive because of his order. He's intelligent, strategic, and has influence that Chaz can't even comprehend.

"Fuck. You aren't worth it." Chaz spins on his heels and struts out of Beach Brew without getting his supposed check.

Ezra drags me along, following behind him, leaving the coffee shop without saying goodbye to Ms. Sandy. My heart races as we head behind Chaz, stalking him like he had stalked me.

He's scared. I know he is.

He keeps peering at us over his shoulder, keeping his brisk pace until he reaches an old Ford Ranger.

Ezra smacks his hand against the hood as Chaz backs away, burning rubber as he puts the truck in drive and stomps the throttle.

"Please don't think you have to tolerate his harassment. I wasn't joking with my threat. I don't care who he is, or what my position is to him as a professor at the university. I will not stand for his behavior. I'll always protect you, amore. Always." Ezra turns to me, kissing me softly.

Lights beam over us, setting us aglow in the parking lot. Fear squeezes my chest at the sight of Chaz's truck barreling toward us.

He's out of his damn mind.

I don't even have a chance to react as Ezra shoves me out of the way and onto the hood of his car. I scream, fear blurring my eyes.

Chaz slams the brakes, squealing to a halt only feet away from Ezra. Smoke billows around us, and I cough, the scent gagging me.

"Don't you fucking threaten me, you bastard! You think you can scare me, but you can't. Let this be your warning. Next time, I will run your ass over." Chaz honks his horn, startling me. "And Scarlett, you're a fucking whore. I know your secret. You smell like a disgusting, slutty omega. Next time, answer my damn text messages. If you don't, you'll be the one regretting it."

Chaz shifts gears, reversing out of the parking lot. I can't move. I can't breathe. All I can do is sit frozen as Ezra scoops me from the hood and sets me in the front seat of his car.

What the fuck just happened?

Where does all of Chaz's animosity come from? I don't understand.

"Scarlett, listen to me. He's done for. I promise you that." Ezra squeezes my hand, barreling from the parking lot.

If only I could believe him.

If only I didn't feel as if my whole world was about to fall apart.

14

Scarlett

THE CLAIM

My pencil glides over the canvas as I pre-sketch the painting I imagine in my head. I vividly remember what Leo looked like as he entered me, the row of piercings on top of his shaft sparkling in the light. I squirm in my seat, taking a deep breath. That's all I seem to be doing lately. Breathing in and out. Doing whatever I can to calm my nerves and distract myself.

Now I have taken residency in Dominic's pottery studio, wanting a change of scenery while I lose myself to my art. It helps push my thoughts of Chaz away. The fucking psychopath. Jonah said he hasn't shown up for class, but it's not like I have either.

He's probably livid beyond reason, especially because Ms. Sandy fired him, spotting his behavior on her security camera. She gave it to Ezra in case he wanted to file a police report.

I'm not sure he will though. Not yet, at least.

"Lettie, Ezra said I'd find you here." Dominic's voice sounds from behind me, his nickname for me bringing a smile to my lips. "What are you sketching?"

Heat blooms across my face, and I spin around in the rolling chair and raise my palm to him, stopping him from getting closer. "You probably don't want to see. I...might be sketching something dirty. You know, it's kind of my specialty."

Dominic grins, knowing exactly what I'm talking about, considering that he has seen my sketchbook. "Now, I insist. Let me see what's going through your mind right now."

I giggle, covering my eyes with my hands. I should be more embarrassed than excited to let him glimpse the passion that refuses to leave my mind. He closes the space to me and looks at the canvas as he towers above me.

He intakes a whistling breath, the scent of his desire wafting around me, battling the pungent smell of clay. "Is that Leo?" he asks, his voice deepening. "Damn, Lettie. You know he's going to want to hang that on his wall."

I tip my head back and laugh, looking up at him. "He wouldn't." Except I know I'd be lying to myself. I've seen the self-portrait I left behind on his nightstand.

Leaning down, Dominic kisses me softly, smiling against my mouth. "If he doesn't, I will. It's going to be fantastic. So sexy."

"Yeah?" I ask, my voice turning breathy. "You know, I'm always looking for inspiration."

I don't know where I find my bravado, but I hook my fingers to Dominic's pants and pull him closer. I draw my finger along his zipper, feeling the hardening desire through his pants.

"And I'm always ready to be that for you. Whatever I can do to distract you. How are you holding up, anyway? I wish I could've been home sooner. I know it was only supposed to be a day, but your father requested I stay a bit longer." Dominic holds his hands out to me, tugging me to my feet. He lifts me into his arms and kisses me again, holding me close as if he can't resist.

Everyone has been so stressed and intense over Chaz that my family was really the last thing on my mind. I knew Dominic was staying longer in San Francisco, but I just didn't really put much thought into it. Adrian said everything was being handled and it was looking good.

I meet Dominic's dark eyes. "He did?"

Dominic smiles, his expression soothing the worry before it has a chance to explode through me. "Yeah, and it went better than we could've hoped. Your father agreed that the most important thing was you. He wants you to be happy, and I guess something your mother said kind of pushed him in our direction. He won't contest our engagement or marriage. It's only your family's alphas who get to give approval." Dominic sets me on his wide table, standing between my legs. "We've also set a date. We will officially marry in June. Our announcement will hit the press in January. Everything is coming together now. You don't have to worry any longer."

My mouth falls agape with his admission, and I squeal and grab his shirt, pulling him to me. He moans, pushing me back, gliding his tongue over mine as he drags me to the edge of the table, pressing between my legs, his hard-on throbbing and threatening to destroy our clothes if it doesn't get what it wants.

My lust grows out of control. It's even more prominent now that I haven't worn my suppressant lotion in days. The hormones within it have finally faded.

"Keep kissing me like that, and I'm going to beg you for more," I whisper, gliding my hands over his sides. "My desire has been...a bit out of control."

Dominic kisses me harder, set off by my words. "We can't have that now, can we? Let me help you. I've missed you, Scarlett. More than I thought possible."

His words dig deeply into me, and I grab his shirt and yank it up over his head, wanting nothing more than to feel the heat of his body against mine. It feels as if I'll explode if I don't get what I need otherwise. I arch back until I'm sitting on the edge of the table. Dominic matches my passion, tugging my shirt off before pulling down my pants, leaving them in a pile at our feet. Clay dust dirties my skin, but it doesn't bother me.

"Be my inspiration, Scarlett. Be my canvas." Dominic unfastens his pants and shrugs out of them, stroking his fingers along his prominent shaft, his cock hard and ready, flexing with his muscles.

"I'll be whatever you want, Dom. Do with me as you please. I'm yours." I bite my lip, easing my legs open wider, exposing myself to him as he stands in front of me.

He groans in his chest, the rumble vibrating to my core. He doesn't move closer, studying me for a long, hot moment. I squirm under his intensity, wishing I could hear what's on his mind.

"I want you to stay still. Don't move." Dominic holds his finger up and strolls around the table, heading toward his big metal cabinets.

I watch in anticipation, loving that creativity bursts from every aspect of his life. I don't know what I was expecting from Dominic, but wetness spills between my legs just thinking about it.

Drawing my hand down my pelvis, I rub my fingers between my legs, moaning softly. I can barely handle the wait, and the sound of my voice draws Dominic back to me as if he's caught in my magnetic field. He strokes himself, drinking me in. I masturbate, squirming because he takes his time to set up and moisten a slab of clay. He drips cool water over my breast, watching as the gray liquid streams over my nipple.

My body clenches, and I arch my back at the sensation.

"I'm almost ready for you, Scarlett. Let me see if you're ready for me." Washing his hand in a clean bowl of water, he glides his fingers over my thigh, the coolness from the clay sending tingles over my body. He caresses his fingers over my pussy and spreads me open to touch my clit before he slides his middle finger between my legs, soaking himself with my slick.

I moan and writhe at the sensation, closing my eyes and losing myself to the pleasure Dominic ignites in me. More cool liquid coats my breast, and Dominic massages clay over my nipples, painting me as if I'm his living statue.

"It feels so good." I roll my hips to increase the pressure of his finger. I want more. Need more. "I don't know how much more teasing I can take."

Dominic pulls me closer, setting me on my feet. He slowly turns me toward the table. Lifting my hair, he kisses my neck, nudging me to bend over. The thin slab of clay cools my breasts, pebbling my nipples. He flattens his hand firmly against my spine, pressing me down. I moan, his body aligning with mine. He teases me with his tip, sliding in and out of me as my body leaves an imprint on the clay.

"You're so hot and wet. You feel so good." Dominic teases me, working me up without thrusting inside. He massages his hands along my back, moving his way down to my ass where he squeezes, spreading my body wider as he slides in, moaning as he takes his time, far more gentle than Leo but just as amazing.

"Your teasing is killing me. I want more," I gasp, trying to take a step back to push harder against him.

He pins me in place, resting his hand beside me, digging it into the clay. "Art takes time, Lettie. It'll be worth the wait."

I swallow, trying my best to control myself. My vision hazes with my desire, and I reach out and grab Dominic's hand, lacing our fingers together. He continues to slide in and out slowly, the gesture driving me wild.

I can't take it. I feel as if I'm going to explode. As if I'm going to die if I don't get what I want.

Pushing my body back, I take all of Dominic's cock inside me and gasp at the pressure of his girth stretching me. He groans, giving in to my need, and I can't stop my scream of pleasure as he locks his fingers to my shoulder and pins me down, thrusting deep until his hips hit my ass, and it's as if I can feel him in my stomach. He moans, his resolve breaking. I whimper and scratch my fingers into the clay, the coolness sticking underneath my nails. The table thuds against the wall, Dominic's thrusts declaring our passion to anyone in hearing range.

It doesn't stop there.

He flips me over and sits me up, pulling my leg onto his shoulder as he pounds into me, his body flexing as he prepares to knot. My ass sinks into the damp clay, and I slap my hand down, bracing myself as he picks up his pace, his quick thrusts deep and passionate. His mouth finds mine, and he kisses me as the pressure builds and builds between my legs, his knot reacting to my body. I gasp as ecstasy floods through me with his seed, the pleasure so intense that I close my eyes and moan, my voice ringing through the air. I hadn't expected how much I'd want Dominic, but he's so incredibly sexy and talented. He makes me feel so very safe and wanted. I pant at the sensation of my orgasm consuming me, his rippling muscles flexing as he grunts, digging his hand into the clay, our bodies leaving behind outlines of our passion.

"I love you, Lettie," Dominic mutters, his voice grumbly as he moans, his orgasm as intense as mine. "I love you so much. We'll always have this moment. Our passion solidified in art."

Heat travels through my body, weakening every inch of me. I gasp my affection in return. It consumes me, pushing out the world around us.

The sound of the door slamming shut snaps me from the moment. "Hello? Scarlett? I'm sorry for—"

A strange, uninviting scent wafts through the air, prodding at my fear. I can't even move as someone enters Dominic's studio without waiting for a response. Fear shocks my heart, and Dominic growls.

"Get out!" Dominic hollers, his knot stopping us from moving.

I don't see the intruder, but I can smell him. His shadow stretches across the floor behind Dominic.

"Fuck." The uninvited man shatters my perfect world and my perfect moment with Dominic. "I'm sorry."

"Leave!" Dominic lifts me up and carries me toward a small office connected to his studio. He frowns and kisses me, doing his best to remain calm despite his racing heart and uncontrollable growl.

I wiggle and test his knot, the vulnerability and helplessness stealing away my ability to think clearly.

"You're safe. We're okay. I'm almost done." Dominic hugs me close, smoothing his hand across my spine. "I'm so sorry. I should've locked the door," he says, his voice hitching.

"We shouldn't have had to." I release a soft whine, my heart racing as his knot finally releases us. "Why did they just barge in?"

"I'll figure it out. Stay here, Lettie. I need to go after him. I'm so sorry," he repeats, kissing me softly.

I sit in shock, my body cooling as Dominic vanishes, leaving me alone after our moment of lovemaking.

What the hell just happened? Who was that?

A door slams, startling me, and I grab a smock and cover myself up, hearing footsteps run across the studio.

"Scarlett? Scarlett, Dominic said you were in here." Jonah's voice booms through the studio.

"In h-here," I stutter, standing frozen.

Jonah rushes into the office, not even hesitating to pick me up. I cling onto him, my body shaking as I come down from the high of being knotted. "I'm going to take you back to my room, okay?"

I nod my head, my voice refusing to come.

"Dominic caught the bastard. He's handling the situation now. You don't have to worry." Jonah pulls his jacket around my body, covering me. He jogs through the garden and heads toward the manor, not wasting a moment or risking my crashing in the studio, where I can't shake the feeling that my privacy was purposefully invaded.

"Who was he? Is he a threat? I don't even know how long he watched us. I feel sick." I hide my face against Jonah's chest, my mind whirling. Who fucking does that? Who watches someone have sex? Why was he even there?

"I'm so sorry you experienced that. It won't happen again." Jonah strokes his hand up and down my spine, smoothing out my trembles.

"How can you be so sure? Our house isn't private." I squeeze my eyes, trying to get my body in control.

"I have agreed to take over as director of my department. I no longer have the stipulation of keeping the manor open to the public year-round. It'll be only in the summer months, and during that time, we'll be traveling to our vacation home. It's going to be amazing." Jonah strides through the manor, quickly relocating me to his bathroom suite.

His comments distract my mind enough to save me from spiraling into a wave of darkness. "What? Really? I thought you didn't want it?" I bounce on my feet, watching as Jonah turns on his shower.

Jonah finally turns to me, shrugging. "I thought about it for a while, and I think it's the best decision for all of us."

I step closer to him, resting my hands on his shoulders. "As long as you're happy."

Jonah's face lights up with a smile. "Incredibly. I'll be happier if you let me clean you off and take care of you, though. Your scent is driving me crazy."

Heat flushes over my body, and I slowly slide off the smock and stand covered in clay before him. His eyes drink me in, his gaze smoldering over me, warming my body even more than the steam in the air.

A knock sounds on the door to his suite, drawing his attention away from me. I release a breath, shivering, craving his attention.

"Jonah? It's Dom. You have Scarlett, right?" Dominic shouts, knocking on the door again.

Jonah drags himself away from me, leaving me in the bathroom as he heads through his suite to answer. I can't resist the heat of the shower, my body growing colder than I like, and I step inside and take the initiative to wash myself despite Jonah's desire to do it for me.

"Lettie, I'm so sorry. I should've locked the door. I should've paid better attention. I wasn't expecting Paul to just barge into my studio." Dominic doesn't hesitate entering the bathroom and purses his lips together. "But that's not the strange part. He wasn't looking for me. He was there for you. He got your address from Ms. Sandy and said that she told you to expect him. That you've been in contact. Apparently, he was considering hiring you for a job?"

I rack my brain, trying to pinpoint the name. And then I realize who it is. The man whose daughter is getting married and the guy I sent my portfolio to. But feels like forever ago. I had forgotten about him completely.

I open and close my mouth, unsure of what to say. Something feels utterly wrong, and it's not just the fact that some stranger saw me with Dominic. It's more. "He couldn't have gotten my address from Ms. Sandy. She only has me down at the dorm."

Jonah growls, fisting his hands. "Are you sure?"

I thrash my head up and down. "Yes, I'm sure."

Turning to Dominic, Jonah puffs a breath. "Finish helping Scarlett get cleaned up. I need to make some phone calls. We need a pack meeting."

"What's up, Joe? What is it?" Dominic asks.

Jonah clenches his jaw. "Someone knows. Someone fucking knows."

"Calm down. You don't know that." Dominic tries to touch Jonah's shoulder.

He backs up out of the way. "I do fucking know. It's that asshole Chaz. I know it. I knew he wasn't going to just let shit go. He's coming after us now. He's crazy and setting us up."

Dominic rubs the back of his neck. "And we'll handle it. Just like we always have before. But you need to think rationally."

Jonah growls. "Ezra said he's unpredictable. He commented on Scarlett's scent as an omega, but he couldn't possibly know that without having more on us. He's a beta. There's more to it. Now, get her dressed. We need to be prepared. I'm not going to let a fucking beta ruin our lives and careers. That fucker needs to go down."

15

Dominic

Masterpiece

Paul: I can't apologize enough for my unexpected visit. I had no idea Scarlett was a part of your pack.

Anger rushes through me at the memory. Paul is lucky that his murder isn't worth losing me a lifetime with Scarlett or else he'd already be dead. There is no amount of apologizing that will ever fix what my beautiful omega went through. His actions ruined a safe space for us. It destroyed our moment of consummating our love.

I hate him for it.

Paul: When I met her at the coffeehouse, I assumed she was a beta.

That might be true, but his other message is full of shit. He claims he was there to meet Scarlett, but he'd have to be an idiot not to put things together, considering how long we've lived in the Clearwater Manor.

Me: Cut the bullshit. I've contacted Beach Brew and you never reached out to Sandy. What do you want, Paul?

Paul: It was another employee. A young man. He's friends with Scarlett.

Again, another fucking lie.

Me: Do you think I'm an idiot? That employee is no friend of Scarlett. He's been harassing and stalking her. What does he have over you?

Paul: I don't know what you're talking about.

Me: You really want to play this game? You're too damn high up in Pack Clearwater to mess with people like him unless he has something on you.

I growl and slam my phone down. It's pointless trying to argue with him over text, which means I need to confront him in person. I was far too distressed over Scarlett to think things through. I just wanted him gone.

My phone buzzes again with another text, and I can't resist reading it.

Paul: Come on. Let's move past this. It was an honest mistake. If you're able to, I want to offer Scarlett a job painting the windows at the resort for Bethany's upcoming wedding. It is a great opportunity, considering who will be in attendance. Consider it my apology for this debacle.

Again, with lying. The last thing I want Scarlett to do is to get involved with anything concerning Paul Miller, a cocky bastard of a man who left Clearwater University to pursue a political career and was elected City Treasurer of Clearwater. He's always been egotistical, rubbing in his win, but I was glad to see him go.

Me: I'll ask her.

Paul: Tell her to really consider it. My daughter has her heart set on commissioning her, and I refuse to disappoint her.

Me: Like I said, I'll ask her and let you know. Have a good day, Paul.

I turn on the *do not disturb* function on my phone, only allowing those on my approved list to contact me. Stepping away from my workstation, I stare at the thin slab of clay, imprinted with the perfect outline of Scarlett's body, now dry and ready to be put in the kiln.

The fragile masterpiece will look incredible glazed and hung on my wall. I've split the clay into two pieces, the one of her ass and hands scratching the clay my favorite, but the impression of her delectable tits pressed hard enough to display her nipples gets me hard just looking at it.

I quickly add the art pieces to the kiln plus a couple of bowls I designed for a student auction at the end of the quarter. The fundraiser will go toward an art scholarship, hopefully bringing more people into the department, and encourage the board to agree to add some more classes. I grow weary of teaching algebra and calculus. I hate that I was forced into something so practical.

I'd be happy if I never teach most students' least favorite subjects again.

I spot Scarlett heading in the direction of my studio, strolling through the garden. I lost track of time, my thoughts wasted on worrying about Paul instead of focusing on what's important today. Scarlett should be completing the finishing touches on the window display for Beach Brew. I'd be lying if I wasn't relieved for that project to be over. I know that Chaz was fired for his psychotic behavior, but I worry about Scarlett so much that I'll be escorting her the whole day. Leo took yesterday.

I quickly wash my hands and head toward the door, greeting Scarlett with a smile. She automatically steps into my arms and hugs me, inhaling a breath of my scent.

I give in to her need for affection and kiss her neck, working my way up until she eases away to meet my lips. I know everything has been so stressful for her. I'll do what it takes to keep her focused on the positive things in our life.

"My beautiful fiancée. How was class? Hopefully Joe didn't bore you to death." I caress my fingers over her jaw, wanting my scent to linger on her skin.

Scarlett giggles, patting my shoulder. "Never. I could listen to him read all day. I think he knows it because he decided to go off the syllabus and read a section from

The Golden Ass. I'm pretty sure it was to tease me and torture all the other students he dislikes. I mean, he read aloud what I can only describe as donkey-shifter porn. Ancient Roman erotica. It was fascinating."

I tilt my head back and laugh. Jonah always had a unique taste in literature. I'm sure he'll redesign the curriculum now that he plans to take over as the head of his department.

"Perhaps you can read me some later. Maybe sketch out a scene or two." I kiss Scarlett again, unable to resist her. "We have to get to the coffeehouse now, don't we?"

She groans in longing. "Last day. Ms. Sandy needs it finished for the store decorating contest for the Fall Carnival."

"Which she'll absolutely win." I tug Scarlett with me, guiding her to my motorcycle. It's a beautiful day for a ride along the coast. I could use the adrenaline that comes with the speed and rumble of the engine against my body.

"What is this?" Scarlett asks, staring at my bike in the lone garage stall. I don't trust my pack mates not to hit it, so I've claimed the old carriage house as mine.

"A CVO Road Glide." I bought the Harley recently, though I've been riding since I got my license in my youth. I've gone from crotch rockets to cruisers, and I'm excited to share the experience with Scarlett. The way she looks at the Dante's Red Fade design, biting her lip nervously, I can tell she's never been near a motorcycle.

"I mean—a motorcycle? You're not scared of all the crazy drivers out here?" Scarlett hugs her arms over her chest. "Of tipping? Road rash if you fall?"

My brows pinch together. "Twenty-one turning...what, fifty?" I tease, giving her a little shake. "If you're too nervous, I'll grab Leo's keys."

Scarlett huffs a breath, picking up on my dare. "I'm not nervous...I'm terrified...and curious. You promise not to do anything insane? Where's my jacket? Helmet?"

I raise my eyebrows and motion toward my gear hanging on the rack. "I'll pick you up some of your own stuff tonight. This will have to do for now. I can't promise there won't be assholes on the road, but I can promise I'm a defensive rider. We'll take the back way."

She shudders, shaking out her hands with her nerves. "No speeding."

I chuckle. "Come on, Lettie. Let's ride."

If Scarlett holds me any tighter, we might merge together as one entity. Her squeals sound over the rumble of my motorcycle every time I shift gears and pick up speed until we reach the stretch of road along the beach. I slow down, catching the scent of the ocean air drift into my full-faced helmet. I wish Scarlett didn't have to put the finishing touches on her window paintings so I could just pull over and carry her into the water. It might be a bit cold, but in this moment, I need some cooling off. I constantly feel on the verge of either yearning to claim her or wanting to burn the world down in her honor.

The fact that she stopped using her suppressant cream, her omega scent now inviting me to her body, just intensifies my deep-seated nature. I'm going into rut because she's going into preheat. It won't be long until we aren't able to resist each other.

It's not often that an omega walks pregnant down the aisle, but the thought sounds incredibly sexy to me. Seeing her swollen with life in a wedding dress. Knowing that she'll bring a baby into our family.

Damn.

What a beautiful life.

I focus my attention back on the street, wanting to kick myself for allowing my thoughts to consume me. Thankfully, the road is desolate this early and during the off-season. It'll pick up tomorrow with the kickoff of Halloween festivities.

Scarlett practically cackles, relaxing when I park my bike. She grips my shoulders and gives me a shake, the gesture feeling like she's trying to mount me from behind with her excitement. I laugh and slide off my bike, helping her to her feet. She looks ready to smack her helmet to mine for a kiss. I quickly unfasten it and pull it off her, setting it on her seat. She attacks my neck with her mouth, kissing and nipping me, her adrenaline running hot and seductive. I get a second to inhale a breath when I remove my helmet, and she steals it right from me, molding her lips to mine as she climbs up my body, making me hold her.

"Lettie, keep this up and we're going for another ride. Somewhere secluded," I mumble against her mouth, biting her lip between my teeth teasingly.

She groans and stretches back, waiting for me to release her. "Then let's do it. I have time. It'll be worth it."

I grin. "You know I'll never deny you. Let's get that helmet back—"

"Before I surprise you, I just wanted to make my presence known." Paul's annoyingly familiar voice sounds from behind us, and I tense, my muscles rippling. "I wasn't sure you had received my messages, Scarlett."

Rage rushes through me, and I break away from Scarlett to face Paul, ready to swing and punch him in the face. He knows better than to approach Scarlett, especially because he knows she's my omega. Yet here he fucking is.

Scarlett snatches my hand and tucks herself into my side, preventing me from starting a fight. "I did, and I already replied. I just don't think it's going to work out."

I blink a few times, wishing I had taken a moment to talk to Scarlett about Paul. I got so caught up in her presence that I forgot to mention he had approached me. No wonder he wanted me to tell her it was a good opportunity. The fucking bastard.

"I'd like you to reconsider. I've already doubled my offer for the commission. There will be many important people attending my daughter's wedding, including Pack Clearwater's head pack. You don't want to miss out on this opportunity." Paul repeats to her what he already told me, and he gets under my skin that he's refusing to take no for an answer.

"I'm sorry. I've made my decision. Maybe if there's something else next year. But for this November? I'm going to have to politely decline." Scarlett steps even closer to me, her body begging for me to step in front to hide her.

Paul growls and scrubs his fingers to the back of his neck. "I hate that I have to do this, but if you don't reconsider, I might have to pass on this little unannounced claim to the dean. My nephew told me that you were passing as a beta, Scarlett. He also said that you were engaged, but now that I realize who it's to... What do you say? Agree to this and make my daughter happy or I guess you'll find out. It's a shame you couldn't find some alphas your own age. My nephew would have been excellent for you. He has recently left my pack to start his own. Once he gets his inheritance, you'll all be well off. He just needs an omega my pack won't arrange for him."

My chest tightens with his comment. With his blackmail. I don't understand what's going on or who his nephew is, but this is utter and complete bullshit.

"What? Chaz is your nephew? What do you mean starting his own pack? He's a beta." Scarlett's voice shocks sense into me, and I put all the pieces together.

Now I know exactly what's in it for Paul. He's spoken about his wayward nephew getting expelled from the most prestigious Alpha Academy in the area. Because of it, his pack leader denied him the chance to move up ranks and claim an omega. He'd been disowned and renounced from Pack Miller's wealth.

"A beta? How funny." Paul smirks, training his eyes on Scarlett as if I'm not standing here. "You two have a lot in common. Chaz was a little bit of an embarrassment to the family, which is why he took on a new name and identity. Getting thrown out of the Alpha Academy doesn't bode well. Kind of like your inability to meet Pack Carlisle's stipulation. I looked into you, and I know you're one of the Steele omegas. I also know that you need to be married soon. I don't know if that will happen if word gets out. But I guess there's always Pack Broderik. Your parents would be quite happy, I think."

Scarlett screams and rushes forward, her fury triggering mine. I snatch her by the back of her jacket and yank her away only to jab Paul in the solar plexus, winding him. I might be known as a math geek or a shy artist, but Leo ensured we all know how to fight. And fight dirty.

I shove Paul again, knocking his feet out from under him until he lands on his back. I jam my knee into his gut, twist the front of his dress shirt between my fingers, and strike him in the nose. I bow to snarl in his face. "You don't blackmail Pack Hart without consequence. I think you underestimate our power and think too goddamn highly of yourself. Have you forgotten your true place? A reject. Only given a position of power to shut up your whining. You're nothing, and if you think you can hurt my omega or my pack, you're wrong. I can make your life fucking hell. Don't think we don't have records of your indiscretions. My teaching position means nothing to me. I can always find a new job. But you? This sort of behavior will get you thrown from office. So get the fuck out of here. Threaten me again and see what truly happens. I will never back down from a fucking challenge."

I growl and spit in his face, slamming my palms against him to get back to my feet. Paul lies in shock for only a second before getting his bearings together and dusting himself off. He wipes his bloody nose on his sleeve and glowers at me, but he doesn't attempt to threaten me again. All he does is jog away. If he had a tail, it would be tucked between his legs.

Scarlett whimpers, and I turn around, spotting tears glassing over her eyes. "I'm just going to drop out. Finishing my degree isn't worth it. It's not important. You and my alphas are important. Our pack is important."

My heart aches at her pain, and I scoop her up and carry her closer to the side of the building, wanting nothing more than to drown her in my affection. "Scarlett, if you do that, then they'll win. They'll see that they can push us around. Please, don't let someone like Paul or Chaz try to defeat you. Your passion is important.

They're pieces of shit that will never amount to something. They'll never have what we do."

"Oh, Dom." Scarlett cups my face. "A degree doesn't change my passion. I just...I don't want to be in this position. The worrying and stress I see you guys going through because of me isn't what I want. Let's just elope. It'll make everyone happy." Scarlett's mouth quivers.

I kiss her tenderly, stopping the shivers from controlling her muscles. "Give things another week. If you still feel the same way, then I support you in whatever decision you make. Just let things settle. They're trying to see what they can get away with."

Scarlett rests her forehead on my shoulder, breathing softly against my jacket. "Just a week. I can handle it."

I hug her close, petting my fingers through her hair. "Of course, you can handle it. You're my omega. You can handle anything."

I hope she believes me.

It's what I want most in the world.

I sit at a table, babying a latte as I watch Scarlett add in the finishing shadows on the collection of skulls mimicking the portraits of long-dead artists. Her talent never ceases to amaze me. I've seen her sketches with charcoal and pen, but now that I see what she can do with paint? I can't get enough. The world will soon see what I do. What she has kept hidden her whole life due to her omega order and the expectations our society thrust upon her.

"Goddamn. That is mind-blowing. I can't wrap my mind around how someone can paint like that." Leo's voice sounds through the empty coffeeshop, and I turn to see him enter through the back with Ms. Sandy leading the way.

Jonah, Ezra, and Adrian trail behind him, sneaking in so Scarlett doesn't know they're here. Ms. Sandy thought it would be a fantastic idea to throw a small gathering with us to celebrate the beauty Scarlett created just for her, which will surely bring in even more business and get recognition in the city.

"How much to purchase the windows after Halloween?" Ezra asks, staring at Scarlett's shadow as she pulls the masking tape away from the windowsill, unable to see us inside. We can see her silhouette because of the bright lights she uses.

Ms. Sandy laughs and shakes her head. "I was considering having Scarlett just paint some Christmas hats and lights to the scene for the holidays and keeping it up year-round."

"Smart woman. Something like this should always remain on display." Ezra rests his hand on my shoulder, smiling at me as I continue to watch Scarlett. "How has your day been, Dom? Any more trouble since this afternoon?"

I lift and drop my shoulders. "Not a single word from Paul."

"He won't bother us again. I found another student to take the commission, working it out with his daughter without his knowledge. She won't tell him that we arranged things. It should help ease the tension as well since Scarlett won't have anything else to offer." Ezra takes a seat beside me. "You did the right thing. We can't allow anyone to think they can scare us or blackmail us."

"It helps that we have quite a bit of information on Paul and his despicable nephew. They won't go to the dean or the police. I have ensured it." Adrian straightens his shoulders, adjusting his tie. "Laundering money doesn't look good for a treasurer. Neither does the surveillance of Chaz trying to run someone over. He has quite the record on campus as well, having his uncle buy off many people to stay silent. It's funny what you can find when you have access to finances for more than Clearwater University. Seems like Paul helps him because he's running low on his own inheritance."

His words bring me relief, and I drink the last bit of my latte and set it down in front of me. Adrian always knows exactly what to do when we're faced with unfortunate and undesirable situations. It's always been part of his character. He's never been big on sharing secrets or blackmail, but he's excellent at keeping records of anything that concerns him.

"Fuck yeah." Leo smacks Adrian on the back.

"You won't have to worry about either of them at my coffeehouse. They've been banned completely. From a lot of restaurants and shops around here. I don't tolerate that kind of nonsense. Scarlett is a sweet girl. She doesn't deserve the mistreatment." Ms. Sandy sets down several coffee cups and fills them. She adds a plate of pastries left over from the day, and I snatch one up and take a bite of the cheese danish.

"You're very kind, Ms. Sandy. We won't forget it. You'll always have our business." Adrian nods to the woman. She scurries away, grabbing a couple more things from the back.

I watch Scarlett's shadow hop off the ladder. She starts collecting her supplies, so I stride to the door to help her.

It chimes as it opens, and she greets me with a stunning smile, her eyes lighting.

"What do you think?" she asks, waving her arm at the windows. "I'm kind of obsessed."

I slide my arm around her waist and pull her to me, staring at her incredible work. She is far too talented to be painting windows unless she was painting every single one of them in the world.

"I'm honestly speechless. No compliment I could come up with could ever possibly capture the emotions that you elicit with this mural. It's truly a masterpiece, Scarlett." I kiss her temple and hug her. "Everyone's going to love it."

Her cherry-vanilla scent wafts over me, her joy intensified by my words. It's as if painting triggers the same adrenaline that riding my motorcycle or even kissing me brings her. It evokes passion and pleasure, mirroring the image of her very being. Of her soul.

"Why don't we go get Ms. Sandy. I can't wait for her to see." Scarlett tugs me toward the coffee shop door, practically skipping.

I hoist it open, sounding the bells. The others stand a couple of feet away, grinning and bearing gifts like flowers and a couple of balloons Ms. Sandy brought from the back. She holds up a cake and smiles.

Scarlett covers her mouth with her hand. "What is all this?"

"A celebration," Adrian says, popping a cork on the champagne. "For bringing this masterpiece to life. But also for bringing joy, love, and magnificence to our world."

"Here, here!" Jonah chants, raising his glass. "To Scarlett. "

"To Scarlett," everyone repeats.

I can't wait for the ecstasy and bliss we will bring to each other's futures.

I've never been happier.

Ezra

HAUNTED

"Are you sure we should be here? What if somebody sees us?" Scarlett sits in the third row next to Dominic while Jonah and Leo take the middle seats, and Adrian sits beside me upfront. I'm the only one who owns a vehicle big enough to accommodate all of us.

"Look out the window, Lettie. There are so many people here that no one will notice us. We're all in costume. Don't let your nerves scare the fun away." Dominic rests his hand on her knee.

She is the epitome of autumn with her green leggings, ankle boots, and the sparkly long-sleeved dress that matches the crown of fall-colored leaves on her head. She clutches her fairy wings on her lap, playing with the glittering fabric. Chilly night air trickles in through the window, mingling with the salty sea breeze. The marine layer hovers in the sky, keeping the moon away. Scarlett adjusts her crown, her hair spilling over her shoulders in waves of dark auburn ringlets.

"And if you feel the need for a kiss, amore, I'd be happy to sneak you away." I wink at her, grinning at the flush tinting her cheeks.

I love making her blush and wish I were next to her to feel the warmth of her skin. Like cherry pies fresh from the oven with a scoop of vanilla ice cream melting on top. My mouth waters just thinking about her fragrance.

"Or I could take care of you right here and now in the backseat, satiating you to hold you over, dirty girl," Leo says, stretching his arm to caress his fingers along her leg to her thigh.

She snatches his hand and links their fingers together, not even caring about the fake blood on his costume. "Don't even start. I am feeling…especially antsy."

I unbuckle my seatbelt and fling my door open. "Then perhaps some fresh air will do, amore. I have the perfect place to take you."

"Jonah and I will have to catch up with you later. We're representing Clearwater University and judging the pumpkin carving contest." Adrian opens the side door, stepping out before offering his hand to Scarlett. He sets a gaudy fake crown on his head and grabs his scepter from the floor, tapping it to the ground like a king.

I walk around the hood and pick her up, spinning her around to make her laugh. I'll do anything to see her smile. I know the last couple of days have been rough, and she can use some fun before the start of the week and Monday blues. That's why I don't teach on Mondays.

Leo pats my back, fixing my cape. "Take good care of our girl. I want to hear all about her fun time later. I signed up to haunt the corn maze. I know of a good dead end if you want to bring Scarlett for a quickie."

I scoff and shake my head, chuckling. "I think I could handle such a task."

He play-growls. "But I could make it doubly fun."

Scarlett groans at his words, her lust so strong it's nearly tangible. I swat him, getting him to step back. The five of us risk going into rut as Scarlett's heat approaches, and it makes us more aggressive. Irrational and volatile when it comes to others outside of us. I know Dominic is already facing the effects, especially when he told us that he punched a former colleague in the face.

Knowing that Paul is also Chaz's uncle doesn't help the situation. We're just lucky we keep tabs on the many packs within Pack Clearwater's Territory. It's the one thing that keeps things easier to hide unless we blatantly announce things ourselves. I wouldn't usually agree to blackmail, but I'm at a point in my life where I will stop at nothing to protect my future wife.

We just have to get through the next couple of weeks. Christmas break and a new semester will start soon enough.

"Ezra," Scarlett says, her voice soft. "If we keep standing here, I'm going to pull you back to the car. You said there's something you wanted us to do?" Running her hands over her arms, she pushes the cold away.

Jonah helps Scarlett with her wings before putting his aviator sunglasses on to go with his fake cop uniform that he added grammar police to. It's the nerdiest thing I've ever seen, but Scarlett laughed so much that I couldn't help appreciating the humor of it.

The others part ways, masking up in monstrous costumes, leaving me alone with Scarlett. I'm the only one who didn't volunteer to help out with one of the booths or contests because it's just not my thing. Plus, I didn't want Scarlett to be alone. I got lucky that the Fall Carnival fell on my night. I'm not one of the most popular professors on campus, so I don't worry about getting recognized. Not like Dominic. Maybe even Jonah. My specialty in art history isn't of many students' interests apart from a credit to fulfill.

I smile at Scarlett, and she tucks her arm into the crook of my elbow, strolling beside me. She wears more makeup than usual, her pouty mouth a beautiful shade of burgundy that complements her hair. Fake gemstones glitter along her eyebrows, and I poke the tip of her fake pointed ear, glittering with real diamonds on her lobes.

"How about we warm up with some hot chocolate first and then ride on the Ferris wheel? It has an amazing view on the pier."

A couple of young children screech and laugh, rushing past us and toward the walkway heading to the main street of the downtown area of Northern Clearwater. Bright lights string along the trees, glowing like stars descended to Earth. Haunting music fills the air, and I pull up my Phantom of the Opera mask, securing it on my face. That's the great thing about the Fall Carnival. Everyone dresses up. Scarlett has nothing to worry about when it comes to being recognized.

She strokes her fingers along my cape and up to touch the mask. Her eyes light up, her excitement obvious. Fake smoke fills the air as we pass the entrance to the corn maze, growing across from the strip of shops. Clearwater might be the only area that has farmlands that reach near the ocean. It's what keeps our people thriving as well, because we don't have to import a lot of food.

A collection of scents mingles around us, drawing my attention to the food booths set up on the closed-down street. I beeline right for the coffee stand Beach Brew has set up on this end to help keep the guests warm without having to go to the shop. An unfamiliar girl mans the stand, and I order hot chocolate for Scarlett and me, adding an extra tip for the barista.

"I didn't get to come to this carnival last year. My mom made me go home for the Fall Ball because that's where a lot of omegas meet alphas with Pack Carlisle. They come from all over." Scarlett sips her hot chocolate, the frothy whipped cream getting on her nose.

I stop her, leaning in to brush my lips to the sweet flavor, kissing the tip of her nose before holding my lips to her mouth, wanting nothing more than to give her some affection.

"I'm glad it didn't work out, to be honest. We haven't been to a ball in years. Adrian preferred to look at options in the omega database instead. We'd have kind of stuck out anyway." I nudge Scarlett to move again and point out a couple of the storefront windows, plastered with fake bats and party streamers. None of them compare to the art piece she painted for Ms. Sandy.

"Isn't that the point? To get attention?" Scarlett smiles at me, fluttering her long eyelashes. "You'd have stolen mine."

"Amore, what I wouldn't give to have met you even a year sooner." I clasp her hand, drinking her in as she smiles and laughs, pointing out different Halloween decorations. She tells me about how she used to beg her mom to buy stuff after the holiday for birthday decorations in November. For being such a kind soul, Scarlett enjoys the darker things in life, seeing beauty where others find fear. Only a special kind of person can still find light within the morbid, and I respect her for it.

"Look, there isn't a line." I point at the Ferris wheel on the huge boardwalk pier. Waves crash along the shore, the hum of the ocean roaring over the deep tones of an organ pounding out a creepy melody through the speakers.

Scarlett's eyes sparkle in the red lights, and she pulls me forward only to stop short when an ear-piercing scream rips through the air. A person in a costume with a fake chainsaw pops out in front of us, startling Scarlett. She screeches and laughs, ducking behind me to use me as a shield. Her closeness sets me off, and I spin and scoop her into my arms, letting her cling to me.

"I think we should go into the haunted house instead, amore." I chuckle and shift my mask, nuzzling my nose to the crook of her neck, kissing her hair.

"Only if you carry me if I get too scared," Scarlett says, pulling back. "My heart's still racing."

"Amore, I never planned to put you down." I spin her around, sending her wings fluttering.

She shivers with the caress of cool air, and I don't set her on her feet until she squirms and wiggles, playfully fighting against my hold the second we enter the pop-up haunted house. I wouldn't describe it as scary, but Scarlett startles every time something or someone pops out to jump-scare us. And I love hearing her laughter. Feeling her arms squeeze around me. She knows she doesn't need me to protect her, but she craves it anyway.

A dark archway leads deeper into the haunted house, and Scarlett shrinks behind me. She clings to my cape, using it as a comforting shield between her and the spooky noises echoing around us. Something drops from the ceiling, thumping in front of me. The lights suddenly flicker, showing a room of fake body parts. Scarlett screeches as a rubber hand bounces off her shoulder. She steps away from me, shielding her head as other rubber extremities rain down.

"Hurry, Ezra!" she calls, pushing her hands to my back.

I laugh and dig my feet into the ground, waiting for her to come back around. She jumps up, and I automatically catch her, feeling her body wrap around mine. She giggles and kisses my throat, her sweetness pouring over me. I love every second of her whole body hugging me that I can't resist drawing my hand down to squeeze her ass. She retaliates by guiding her tongue up my throat until she nips my ear, biting it between her teeth.

I spin her around in the dark room, propping her up against the wall. A huge fake monster blocks a corner, and I look around behind me, listening for people coming.

"Ezra," she murmurs, her breath feather light against my neck. "Let's get out of here and go back to the SUV.

You are setting me off. All I can think about is sex. It's driving me crazy."

My dick hardens, my balls throbbing at her whispering voice. Now that she puts it in my head, it's all I'm thinking about too. I feel along the wall, touching the curtain, pulling it aside to step behind it into a small space where the side of the trailer rests, the small hallway seeming to be an access point for the employees to get around if they need to.

"Why waste another second, amore? No one will catch us here," I murmur, lowering her enough to feel the hardness of my cock through my pants. "I mean if you're brave enough."

She shivers at my comment, easing her head back to meet my gaze, her eyes shadowed in darkness with only a couple inches of black light illuminating the area.

I expect her to deny me.

I expect her to resist.

But Scarlett reaches between our bodies and unbuckles my belt, relying on me to hold her up.

This wasn't how I imagined our first time together to be, and it's far more exciting. I thought Scarlett would be turned off by the idea of public sex or the possibility of getting caught, especially after what happened with the douche walking in on her and Dominic, but she kisses me with enough conviction that I yank her leggings down. Spinning her around, I press her to the wall, using my hand to test her body, feeling how hot and wet she is, her slick demanding I continue. With my other hand, I cover her mouth, silencing her moan as I work her over, feeling how her pussy clenches my hand, so fucking tight as it waits for me.

"Are you sure about this, Scarlett?" I ask, keeping my voice low. "We could get caught."

"I'll be quiet," she whispers, nipping my hand with her teeth. "I'm so horny. I don't know what's going on, but I feel as if I'll die if you don't give me what I want."

Her words set me off, and I lift her up enough to slide inside her, my cock pulsing as her tight pussy welcomes me as if this is where I belong. The pleasure ignited from our bodies coming together shadows my vision, and I bite her shoulder to stop from moaning.

I know exactly what has gotten into her. The suppressant cream has completely left her system, and she could be going into heat any day. The raw desire she experiences is what sets me off. It's what draws me to her as an alpha. And now, all I can think about is knotting with her. Wishing she were already in heat so I could fill her with my seed and knock her up. Know what it's like to breed and grow a family. I've been waiting so long for it. The thought becomes all-consuming.

I thrust harder, pressing my mouth to her shoulder as she sucks my finger, our breathing heavy but our moans in control. It's exhilarating, feeling the coolness of the air around us every time I pull back to thrust deeper and deeper until my knot expands and locks me to Scarlett, igniting a mind-blowing sensation that makes me gasp out and bite her again, my orgasm shooting electricity from my balls to my core and through the rest of me.

Scarlett remains quiet, breathing and panting, and a small whimper escapes from her mouth through my fingers. I reach around and stroke my finger over her clit, exploring her body as I bond with her on a level I've been craving. She arches her back and squirms, unable to stay still through the intensity of her own orgasm. I pin her to the wall, grabbing her hair to kiss her throat and using my other hand to play with her nipples.

"Amore, you're not going anywhere. You've taken my knot. Lose yourself to the pleasure. Let me drown in your everything."

A few screams sound through the haunted house as people pass by, unaware of the two of us hiding behind the curtain, caught up in our passion and our raw need as an alpha and omega. The moment feels endless, like eternal bliss, the minutes ticking by. How many exactly? I don't know. Enough for the haunting soundtrack to repeat.

I pump my body, wanting nothing more than to continue feeling Scarlett even when my knot releases, easing the intensity of her tight pussy around my cock. I slide out and spin her to face me, lifting her up and kissing her. I don't stop until her breathing slows and her fingers release me, her nails biting my skin, and she comes down from the high of our passion.

I snuggle against her for a moment longer, only setting her down to help her clean off the best I can with my cape. And now I will keep it forever, her scent so delectable that I can't wait for it to be all over my bed in my room. I want to make love to her again as soon as we get home. "I love you, amore. I can never deny you. I hope you know that. I wanted this moment to be—"

Scarlett kisses me, silencing my words. "This is perfect. I love you too, Ezra."

Another group of people's screams comes through the haunted house. I hold my finger to my lips, motioning for Scarlett to be quiet. I peer through a crack in the curtain, waiting for the next group to pass, and then I take her out, listening to her laughter fill the air.

A fake ghost drops from the ceiling, startling Scarlett, and I rush forward, my urge to leave all-consuming.

It's what knotting does to me as an alpha. I just want to get Scarlett back to our home where we won't be bothered or caught.

"Ezra, watch out," Scarlett says, sliding off my back.

I stumble, tripping over something on the floor, and catch myself on the wall. The flickering lights snap off completely, screwing with my vision. Scarlett screams, and I twist and reach for her. She snatches my cape, yanking me closer. An unfamiliar scent assaults my nose. I don't have a chance to react before my cape twists around my neck, tightening enough to shock fear into me. Scarlett yells my name again, her panicked voice setting me off.

I growl and swivel, swinging my arm out. I punch a figure, barely noticeable in the darkness of the haunted house. The figure yanks my cape again, choking me. I sweep my leg out, blindly attempting to knock the asshole's feet out from under him. I know he's male—an alpha too—but his scent leaves me in confusion. Who the fuck is this guy?

"Ezra! Where are you? I can't see shit!" Scarlett calls, her voice bouncing off the walls like there are microphones set up to throw off the sound.

I twist my body and elbow the fucker in his gut, breaking free of his hold. I gasp, intaking a sharp breath. The son of a bitch is going to get fucked up. I'm going to drag his ass out of here and beat the shit out of him. No one fucks with us.

"Ez—" Scarlett's panicked voice cuts off, striking me in the heart. I spin around, finding a pinprick of light coming from a sensor that sets off one of the fake ghouls that pop out of the wall.

"Scarlett! Scarlett!" I yell, searching the darkness for her silhouette.

She doesn't respond.

Fuck.

Something blankets over my head, and I realize my cape now twists around me. I catch the unfamiliar scent of the alpha again and this time throw my entire body forward, crashing into whoever gets in my path. I don't know what the fuck is going on, but I'm not going to let anyone hurt Scarlett.

I manage to pull my hand free of the fabric and punch something soft. A grunt hums in my ear, and I hear the scrape of someone pulling himself up to his feet.

"Scarlett?" I ask, raising my voice. "Scarlett, say something." My phone must've fallen out of my pocket at some point, because it's no longer there, so I can't use my flashlight. I smack my hands against the wall, searching around for anything that might light up.

The lights flicker on again, messing with my vision. I spot a shadow against the wall and then Scarlett whimpers.

I rush in her direction, spotting an old potato sack pulled over her head as she bends over, trying to get it off, but it's tangled with her ivy crown.

"Shit, Scarlett. Are you hurt? What happened?" My heart beats out of whack, my emotions getting the best of me.

"I—I'm okay. I tripped and hit the wall. It sent me into a different room. I couldn't find you. Then one of the monsters pushed me back, and I hit something. I don't know. A bunch of shit came down from the ceiling." Scarlett heaves a couple of deep breaths, clutching onto herself. "Are you okay? I didn't mean to scare you."

I try to process her words, looking in the direction that she came from. It's a hidden door. Maybe going to the back where the actors move around.

"No one touched you, right? No one tried to hit you or kick you out of here?" I don't want to freak her out more than she already is, but whatever alpha asshole I was in here with was doing more than being a monster. He was out to get me. To fuck with me because of Scarlett and her order. I know it. It's because she's going into heat soon.

"Only to guide me back to this room. I didn't say anything either. I couldn't see much." Scarlett ruffles her fingers through her hair, combing out the curly strands with her fingers, trying to fix the mess from the potato sack. "Why? Did something happen?"

I pull her closer and follow the glowing red light now visible through some curtains. "Nothing serious. I think one of the monsters got out of hand. I'm fine, though."

My biggest question is wondering if it was intentional. It's dark, and maybe the monster was really just messing with me. All they did was throw my cape around. Maybe it was me who choked myself. Maybe I hurt him without a real good reason.

I push the thought away. The incident has me feeling uneasy, and I want nothing more than to get out of this haunted house.

"I'm a bit over this haunted house." Scarlett moves closer, her body pressing against mine as she slides her arms around my neck. "Carry me the rest of the way? You promised if I got scared, you would."

I lift her up and let her wrap her legs around me, my body relaxing now that she's in my arms again. I manage to navigate the rest of the haunted house without any problem.

An attendant greets us at the exit, wearing a full mask and hooded costume. I catch his familiar scent and bristle, my anger getting the best of me. It's the asshole from inside.

"Sir? Did you drop your phone?" A voice sounds from behind me, and I spot another actor wearing bloody bandages and face paint.

I swivel to look at the masked and hooded alpha, but he strides back into the haunted house. What the actual fuck?

"Oh, that is your phone, Ezra. You must've dropped it when...thank you," Scarlett says, holding her hand out to the beta. "It was hard navigating in there. The lights kept going out completely."

The beta frowns. "Oh, thanks for letting me know. That wasn't supposed to happen. It's a safety hazard."

I clench my jaw, my instincts right. "You're welcome. Have a good night."

I set Scarlett on her feet and look at my phone, my whole body rippling with tension through my muscles. I study the photo, left on the screen, showing me pressing Scarlett into the wall. It's too dark to make out anything, but it's proof that we were being watched.

The fucking sicko.

"What's wrong, Ezra? You're tense," Scarlett says, stroking her hand over my bicep.

"Let's go find the others. Someone was messing with us in the haunted house. I want to get a list of who works here." I tuck my phone away without showing her the picture, not wanting her to get upset and freaked out where I can't properly comfort her.

"Shit. Someone was watching us, weren't they?" Scarlett squeezes her eyes shut. "Shit. Do you think it was…" She doesn't say it, but I know she's thinking about Chaz.

I engulf her in my arms. "His scent wasn't familiar. Don't worry, amore. There is no way anyone could've possibly seen anything. It was dark. I made sure you were covered."

She crinkles her nose. "You're right. Fuck them. I'm not going to let it get to me. It's probably just some dumb horny teen or something."

If only that were the truth.

A part of me knows it's not.

An even bigger part of me knows this wasn't random. I might not have recognized the alpha who attacked me, but it has to do with either Paul or his nephew. They're trying to get into my head because they can't do anything else otherwise.

But I won't let them.

No one will get between Scarlett and me.

No one.

Scarlett

Pack Priority

I clutch my pillow to my chest, standing in Adrian's doorway. He sits at his computer, scouring over the screen like whatever it is he works on can't wait until morning. I shift on my feet, anxious for no other reason than not being able to sleep.

"Is it okay if I sleep in here?" I press my lips together, wondering why I'm suddenly nervous. "I just—I don't know what's wrong with me."

Adrian stands from his desk and holds his arms open. "You never have to ask. I was hoping you'd come to me tonight. You never have to sleep alone again if that's what you want. Your personal space is for your comfort. As for mine? I don't want personal space. I want you."

My heart flutters with his words, and I bury my nose against the soft cotton of his pajama shirt. He scoops me up in silence, pressing his lips to mine. I devour his affection, his closeness easing the strange worry tightening my chest. I know my body is supposed to be a bit out of control now, but it's worse than ever. I've only allowed myself to have my first heat and skipped my second. It was too terrible going through it alone that I didn't want to experience it that way again.

Adrian sets me on his bed, and I automatically bury my face in his pillow, inhaling a breath of his scent that I can't get enough of. I don't know what it is about his bed, but exhaustion tries to take me out even though my mind spins wildly.

I yawn and stretch my arms over my head. "Come lay with me."

Adrian rubs his hand across my leg, adjusting the blanket on my body. "Just give me one minute. I need to finish up an email and then I will join you."

I puff out my bottom lip. I probably look pathetic, but I can't help it. He's so close to me. All I want is for him to hop in the bed and wrap me in his arms.

"If you're not going to join her this second, then I will. She looks like she might start whining like the sexy, needy woman I love. Isn't that right, dirty girl? Adrian should get detention or some shit for asking you to wait even a minute." Leo grins at me from the open door, standing in only a pair of boxer-briefs. Where Adrian is more modest, Leo would walk around the manor naked if his pack mates wouldn't mind. They do it for the staff, mostly.

I laugh and wiggle my fingers. "Maybe if you do, Adrian will join us faster. I wouldn't mind being sandwiched between the both of you. I'm a bit cold. Shivering." I force my body to tremble, faking being cold.

"Come on in, Leo. I'm assuming you weren't just looking to interrupt my night with Scarlett." Adrian kisses the top of my head and crosses his arms over his chest, remaining serious.

Leo strides through the room and hops on the bed, pulling me into his arms and making me giggle. "If I knew she was here, I'd have come sooner. And you're right. I sent you something you need to check out."

I narrow my eyes at him. "So you're going to give him a hard time for finishing up an email, yet you sent him something that you want him to look at? I think you're going to be the one in trouble, Leo."

He bites his bottom lip with a smile. "How do you plan to punish me?"

I snatch Adrian's pillow and whack him over the head with it, making Adrian bellow a laugh. Leo tries to steal it away, so I let him, using his gesture against him. I grab his sides, digging my fingers into his skin. I hadn't realized he was this ticklish, and now that he squirms to get away, I can't help the sudden need to drive him crazy.

Leo rolls off the side of the bed and hits the floor with a thump, his laughter ringing through the air. Holding up his arms, he silently calls surrender and stands before me, his body hard and erect, excited from my closeness.

"I hadn't realized that all it would take is a little tickling to make you submit," I quip, wiggling my fingers at him again. "Maybe I'll ask Adrian to pin you down so I can continue. Can you handle that sort of torture?"

Leo swings his attention to Adrian, standing at his desk, trying to focus on his computer while he watches us. I crawl to the edge of the bed and jump at Leo, managing to hook my arms around him while he stumbles in an attempt not to fall to the floor.

"Looks like a party," Jonah says, grabbing a pillow to whack Leo in the back with. "You're usually asleep by now, Scarlett."

He's right. Early to bed, early to rise because of fucking classes. His class, actually. It's the earliest one I have, and only because I needed it to finish up my degree.

"I just couldn't. It's...everything." I wave my hand at my body. "Omega shit." My face warms with the words. "I'm antsy. Hungry. Horny. Maybe I'm overtired, even."

"What can we do to help? Do you have enough pillows? Ezra said you took all of his. I have extras if you want," Jonah says, his voice deepening. "What about blankets?"

He's asking without really asking if I'm starting to create what I like to call my safe spot. The strange, all-consuming act of nesting has come and gone a couple of times tonight, but I just couldn't get my room perfect. It's why I came to Adrian.

"I like the blue one." I raise my eyebrow, watching his reaction, because I know that the blue pillow on his bed is his absolute favorite. It's the only one I've ever seen him use.

Adrian gasps a laugh, his shoulders shaking. "You better go get it for her, Joe. We all agreed that we will do whatever it takes to make her comfortable. Even if it means we lose all our bedding and have to sleep on the cold floor."

"Never. I might just ask for a cuddle pile. You can be my bed. All of you. I like to spread out." I spread my arms and hop back on the bed, pulling the blankets to wrap myself up like a burrito.

As if Dominic and Ezra know we're all in here, I hear their voices sound from the hallway. My heart picks up pace, my anticipation growing as all of my alphas unintentionally gravitate together in front of me.

My heart falters the second I peek out of my cocoon and meet Ezra's eyes. He shakes his head, forcing himself to smile. The others look at him, their smiles fading, sensing the same thing I do. That something's wrong.

"Amore, would you mind if I steal everyone for just a couple of minutes?" Ezra ruffles his fingers through his dark curly hair. "I promise I'll make it up to you."

I sit up, yanking the blanket off to free my arms. "What's wrong?"

Dominic steps forward and kisses my temple like he can't resist coming into the room without showing me affection. "It's nothing. Boring contract stuff."

I wouldn't usually call someone out, but I've grown comfortable and brave with my alphas. "Don't lie. I can smell your scent, and something bothers you."

Leo play-growls. "Come on, dirty girl. Cut him some slack. We just want you to relax. You're obviously stressed out and exhausted, so let us take care of you by keeping away anything that could possibly mess with your head."

Narrowing my eyes, I burn him a look. "You're going to stress—"

Adrian touches my shoulder, towering over me. "Give us five minutes. Let me hear what Ezra has to tell me, and then I will decide whether or not it can wait until morning. Please, Scarlett. Leo is right. You're exhausted and need to rest up. Save your energy."

I feel so small, sitting on the bed with the five of them towering around me, their scents practically enveloping me in a way that makes me comply with my nature as their omega.

I flick my hand and sit back on the bed, crossing my arms over my chest. I try not to look bratty, but I want them to know that it does bother me. Had I been able to sleep, they would've had a pack meeting without me.

But maybe it's because it is about me.

Fuck.

Ezra squeezes my foot through the blanket, and I watch as the five of them exit the room into the hallway. Adrian closes the door behind him. I listen to them stroll away, probably heading to one of their rooms or even the library.

Something buzzes in the bed, and I remember I had tucked my phone away in my pillow. It's a habit I can't seem to break, because I always want to be able to respond to my sisters if I have to.

Unknown: You alone?

Goosebumps prickle over my skin at the text. I fucking loathe unknown numbers. I don't even have to ask to know who the psycho on the other side of the line is.

Unknown: Don't be shy. I know you are.

I get up, wrapping the blanket around me.

Unknown: I could come in, and no one would even know.

Shit. Shit. Shit.

Unknown: Used bitches still make great fucks.

Heavy metal music booms through Adrian's surround sound, startling me. I scream and run from the room, my fear taking over. I run to Ezra's room and tug the door open, but none of them are there. So I keep going.

I call out for my alphas, expecting them to run down the hall to get to me. Music bumps through the surround sound, seemingly following me, though I know it's set up throughout the manor. Reaching the end of the upstairs wing, I rush downstairs and into Jonah's study. My heart can't handle what my mind keeps throwing at it, the haunting sensation of being watched leaving me practically debilitated.

Resting my palms on his desk, I stare at the pile of essays next to his laptop. I'm afraid to keep running and searching. I need to just find somewhere to sit down to let my heart chill the fuck out.

I spot the small storage closet with shelves of books. The floor beneath them is empty, so I grab a couple of pillows from his sitting area and arrange them across the small closet floor. I crawl in and pull my blanket around me, closing the door to just sit with only the glow from his desk lamp coming through the small crack. It only takes a moment for my heart to stop racing and for me to get out my phone.

Unknown: Freaked out enough? Don't worry, Dickasso. I'm just fucking with you. I bet you didn't know the manor has an unlocked Wi-Fi and Bluetooth connected to the university server. Easy to screw with shit.

Anger rushes through me, and I clench my teeth, glaring at my phone.

Me: Stop texting me and just leave me the fuck alone.
Unknown: She's not getting boned! Hallelujah.
Me: Fuck off.
Unknown: ...

A picture of a hard cock pops up on the text message, and I nearly drop my phone in exasperation. What the fuck is Chaz's problem? He already knows I've bonded with my pack. I'd never be interested in him. Never. Not even if he's an alpha—a terrible one at that. Alphas don't get kicked out of Alpha Academy for nothing. He had to have done something that proved him incapable of deserving the responsibility of a pack and claiming an omega.

Unknown: Something for you to draw later. Maybe when you get over your obsession over old, flaccid dick. Do they even work?

Me: What is wrong with you? You're a disgraced alpha with nothing. Give up. I wouldn't touch you even if you were the last alpha, and I was in an endless heat cycle. Fuck off!

Unknown: Keep telling yourself that. Just wait. You'll be screaming my name. Begging for my knot. You'll have to work for it after all this bullshit, though. I'll train you to be a good omega. You'll see. Start now and apologize. Give me a peek of your pussy. Maybe I'll let you have that shriveled old dick a moment longer before I claim you.

His text message ignites anger and disgust inside me. I can't keep replying, despite wanting nothing more than to tell him off. I close out the message, muting all text messages and calls from people that aren't on my approved list. I usually don't block everyone, because sometimes Emma will text me from a new number because she had to switch for some reason or another, but

I've had enough. I can't let Chaz take up even another ounce of my headspace.

Minutes pass as I remain frozen and hidden in the closet. My eyes grow heavy, my exhaustion kicking in completely. The scent of Adrian's blanket and Jonah's pillow settles my entire body, and I drift off to sleep for who knows how long.

"I think she's in here," Jonah whispers, his voice pulling me from my groggy state. "I can smell her."

I blink a few times, trying to wake up, but my eyes don't want to remain open. The floor creaks as someone crosses the room, and soft light shines around me. Jonah cracks open the door to the closet, peering down at me.

"Scarlett, what happened? We heard the surround sound go off, and Leo went to help you fix it, but you weren't in Adrian's room. We've been searching for you for over thirty minutes." Kneeling, Jonah fills the doorway of the closet. "You scared me."

Digging his arms beneath me, he lifts me from my makeshift hiding spot and into his arms. Adrian stands a few feet away, his worry pinching his face. Leo pushes past him, his expression a series of hard lines. I automatically stretch out my arms, sensing his desire to hug me.

"I'm sorry," I say, a small whine escaping my lips. "Chaz fucked with my head. I tried to find you, but couldn't, so I hid." I scrub my palms into my eyes, trying to push away the sleep. "I didn't mean to fall asleep."

Leo growls and takes me from Jonah, adjusting me in his arms like a blushing bride. "You guys need to handle him. If I do it, he won't be breathing tomorrow."

"Let me see your phone," Jonah says, looking around my nest until he finds my phone on the floor, tucked in the blanket.

He and Adrian look at the screen, their eyes darkening with their anger. My heart picks up pace, and nerves bunch my stomach. I'm not sure they're capable of handling Chaz any better than Leo in this moment. Their scents trigger something deep-seated in me, and I reach out and grab onto Adrian's shirt, dragging him closer.

"Can we just handle it tomorrow? I could really use some cuddles." I rub my hand along Adrian's cheek. "Please."

Adrian tightens his jaw and gives Jonah a silent look. He heaves out of breath and dips his chin, agreeing with my request. Voices mumble from the hallway, and I watch Ezra and Dominic enter Jonah's office.

It's as if the air leaves the room, the looks on their faces dark and even angrier than Adrian, Jonah, and Leo's. I can't help thinking that there's more.

Actually, I know there is.

This must involve the pack meeting they had without me.

"You guys need to tell me what's going on," I say, straightening my back, making Leo adjust me in his embrace. "Did Chaz do something to you guys? He's acting like a psycho, even more so now."

Dominic wags his head softly. "No, it's nothing to worry about, Lettie. I promise. Your mom asked for more money, claiming that our postponing of the wedding has caused unnecessary financial stress. It's been taken care of. We had to have a pack meeting, and all agreed on how to move forward, and we decided to add to the monthly stipend until the summer." He closes the space, his frown paining me. Of course, Mom would do something like this. She's always been milking everyone because of her fertility. "As for Chaz, I'll reach out to his uncle and demand that he gets him to stop harassing you or else we'll leak what we have on him. I'm done getting fucked over."

As am I. I just want to be left alone. I just want to be with my pack, celebrating our love, and preparing for our future.

It's in this moment that I realize what I have to do. I will put a stop to Chaz and his threats. I will put my mom in her place. It's my turn to take care of my alphas.

I'm done being a good omega for my family.

The decision feels as if I've been set free.

I just hope my alphas agree with me.

Because it's the only way.

Scarlett

POWER SWITCH

I turn over in Adrian's arms, stretching my back and sitting up as he sleeps against me, spooning me from behind. Leo breathes softly on my other side, but Ezra, Dominic, and Jonah have all left while I was asleep. I glance at the time on Adrian's alarm clock, seeing that they headed out for their classes. And once again, it looks like I'm missing one of mine.

A warm hand slides across my waist, and I peer at Adrian as he smiles at me. "You didn't get enough sleep last night. Lay back down, and I'll cuddle you some more. Don't worry about your morning class. It's been canceled by your professor. Supposedly, the custodian needs to fix a broken pipe or something." Adrian presses his lips together, suppressing his smile. "We can't have a leak, now can we?"

I crinkle my nose, laughter bubbling from my lips. "Did you have something to do with it?"

He lifts and drops his shoulders. "One of the perks of knowing everyone on staff. Don't worry. Nothing is actually broken. Now come here, Scarlett. You need to rest."

The second his fingers dig into my skin, sending a rush of tingles through me, I roll on top of him, planting my hands on his chest. "I'm no longer tired."

Leo groans, opening his eyes. "Damn, dirty girl. You going to show Adrian his place? Show him that he can't tell you what to do. That shit turns him on."

Adrian's body awakens beneath me, his hard-on now pressing between my legs. He liked the idea Leo put out there. It reminds me of one of our conversations where he had casually mentioned some of his turn-ons.

"I might need some help." I rub my hands along Adrian's chest and to his neck, scratching my fingers lightly against his throat, coaxing the scent of his desire into the air. "I'm not sure he'll obey me."

Adrian arches up and links his fingers to my shoulder, drawing them across my skin and to the back of my neck. He pulls me closer until our lips are an inch apart. "That's why you make me."

The guttural deepness of his voice shoots pleasure right between my legs. This wasn't exactly what I expected to wake up to, and I'm here for it. I never expected the idea to turn me on so much.

I grab his hand and pull it away from me, twining my fingers through his and squeezing. I close the space between our mouths and kiss him, inching my body forward until my weight guides him back to the bed. "Like this?"

"That's a start, dirty girl, but he's letting you." Leo hooks his arms around my waist and pulls me off Adrian. He flips me onto my back and pins my arms over my head with one hand while sliding his fingers between my legs with his other. "He wants you to take it. See how I am? How easy it would be for me to fuck you with my fingers? But I'm not."

I gasp at the sensation, my body dampening with my slick.

"Now, I'm going to get you to beg for it. That's what you need to do. Make him beg for that tight, wet little pussy." Leo bends down and kisses my throat, sliding his fingers between my legs, making me moan. He stops just as quickly and holds his hand in front of Adrian's mouth. "Give him a taste first. Don't you want to know what it's like to be with our omega?"

Adrian's muscles ripple, his reaction sexy as fuck as he snatches Leo's hand and sucks his index and middle finger into his mouth, moaning at the taste of my slick. "Mouthwatering," he murmurs, flaring his nostrils. "Give her to me. I want more."

I open my mouth to tell him yes, but Leo silences me with a kiss. He stares at me with lust in his eyes, weighing down his lids.

"Not yet," Leo says, his voice rumbly with his denial. "You're going to watch me with her first...if Scarlett agrees. I'm not sure our dirty girl is ready for this adventure. I don't think you're ready, either."

"Don't make me put you in your place too, Leo. I want this. I want you both. I'll always get what I want." I reach between us and grab at his throbbing dick. "Isn't that right, Adrian? We're ready."

"So fucking ready. All I think about is you. Ever since you teased me in San Francisco. How you let me devour you and satisfy myself." Adrian remains expressionless, his eyes locked on me, waiting for my reaction. "I wanted so badly to claim you. Give you my knot. It's been torture knowing you took my pack mates first."

The memory ignites lust through me, and I reach out and grab Adrian's neck, getting him to move closer. I kiss him passionately, attempting to steal his breath away.

"Is that so? You've been thinking about me for that long without acting on it? I think Leo is right. You're going to have to wait longer now. He's taking me first. You're going to have to face the consequences for hesitating. Now sit up," I say, my body trembling with anticipation.

"Look at him. He wants to be your good boy. Your good little alpha." Leo shakes Adrian, winking at me. "Tell him what he's going to miss out on. What his punishment is for not giving you his knot already."

I swallow with my nerves, the lust permeating through the air pushing me forward. Leo likes a little roleplay, and clearly, so does Adrian. And me. "I do love a good alpha. If you can obey me and watch as I ride Leo's face, I'll reward you."

Adrian flares his nostrils, licking his lips. "You have no idea what you do to me. Letting me switch. Giving you control is so freeing. A stress relief."

I press my finger to his mouth, smiling as I silence him. "I see exactly what I do to you. Now touch yourself. Give me a show."

Adrian responds with a grunt, adjusting himself until he sits up, showing his massive dick pressing against his pajama pants. Stroking his length through the fabric, he says, "Yes, Scarlett. Whatever you want."

My body burns with his words. I want so badly to do this for him. With him. To learn what he needs from me.

Leo grabs Adrian's face, pinching his chin. The way he handles him triggers goosebumps over my body. Adrian always carries an air of authority as leader of our pack, but here? Letting Leo manhandle him without even flinching? My pussy will never recover.

Leo bares his teeth, getting close enough to share the same breathing space. "You mean, yes, mistress. You will respect her authority. Do you understand?"

"Yes, sir." Adrian shifts his jaw.

He pats his cheek. "Good boy."

"Fuck," I breathe, inching closer.

"See how much she liked that?" Leo adds, dragging me closer. He leans close and presses his lips to my ear. "We can take it slow if you need. Don't feel pressured."

I turn to face him, feeling Adrian's gaze on us. Snagging Leo's lip with my mouth, I suck it hard and stretch it. "I need you to stop worrying about me and teach me how to handle this sexy alpha. Let me be who he needs. Who you need."

At Omega Prep, they don't teach this kind of thing. Not many alphas will give up control. It's both hot and exciting, especially with Leo guiding me.

I pinch Adrian's chin, loving the smoldering intensity of his blue eyes drinking me in. "Isn't that right, my very good boy? Now speak up if I'm too much for you to handle."

Adrian chuckles, rolling his shoulders and cracking his neck. "You could never be. My balls ache for the release you'll bring me. Sometimes, I just need to give up control. My pleasure is under your control."

"And this sexy thing craves it." Leo lets me up, shifting out of the way. "Don't you, dirty girl? You'll tell me when you need to give it back, right?"

I nod and climb onto him, stripping my shirt off as if it's about to go to war with my skin. I need the heat of their bodies beside mine. I need the pleasure to ease the ache growing with my need as an omega.

"Now shut up and lick my pussy," I say, my voice stronger with my demand. I grab Adrian by his hard-on, making him crawl closer. "You, show me your cock."

"Damn. Yes, dirty girl. Bury me beneath you." Leo hooks his hands to my knees and slides me up to his face, shifting my panties to the side.

I moan as his tongue flicks across my body, and he sucks my clit. My body takes control, and I rock, wanting more pressure. Adrian watches, stroking his hand over his cock. I watch him, memorizing the curves of his body and the V of his hips. A patch of silver hair peppers the blonde curls of his chest hair, and I reach out, linking my fingers to the short strands to pull him closer.

"Kiss me." I part my lips, letting him glide his tongue into my mouth before I sink my teeth into his lip and pull back.

He growls but doesn't complain. He strokes himself harder, letting his tip caress my side, dripping his pre-come onto me.

My muscles tighten and spasm with my orgasm, and I scream out, squeezing Leo's head between my legs. I bounce slightly, riding the wave, feeling the sensation of his fingers digging into my ass cheek.

He grunts and nudges me back, licking his lips. "Do you think Adrian's been a good enough alpha? Why don't you give him a little reward for giving you a show?"

"Do you think you've earned your reward?" I ask, sliding off Leo and onto the bed between them. I don't know what comes over me, but it's as if Leo's encouragement and Adrian's anticipation give me the bravado I need to dive into this adventure.

Adrian shakes his head. "No, I haven't. I haven't made you come." Linking his fingers to my side, he pulls me flush against him, his cock resting on my hip as he kisses me softly, guiding his fingers down my body and between my legs. He glides his thumb over my clit, playing my body like an instrument for pleasure. Leo kneels behind me and kisses my shoulder, working his way lower until he pulls my panties off completely for Adrian, exposing my body.

He spanks my ass. "God, you're so sexy. Do you know how badly I want to share you? Or would you prefer the power? I think Adrian has a toy or two around here."

I gasp as Adrian picks up the pressure, playing with my clit as he uses another finger to dip inside me.

"Let that be my reward. Show me what a magnificent, powerful woman you are, Scarlett." Adrian grabs my hair and captures my mouth, kissing me until I scream out, his finger sending me over the edge. "Fuck me. Fuck me how you want me to fuck you. Take control. Dominate me."

My mind whirls with his desires, and I slowly nod my head, wanting nothing more than to experience what it would be like if our roles were reversed.

"Are you sure?" I ask, panting as I shift on my knees. "What if—" Shoving my worry away, I turn toward him. Adrian wouldn't ask me to do something he didn't enjoy. "Show me. Guide me. Teach me what you want."

Adrian moves to his nightstand and opens the top drawer, pulling out a couple of different toys. I swallow as I look at them, excited and curious about what to expect. My body was always intended to be used. I have never even thought about using toys with someone else. I glance at Leo and Adrian, drinking them in for a moment, watching as their own anticipation hardens their bodies in a way that turns me on. I can smell their desire. I can smell their need.

They're giving me something I never expected, and I won't take it for granted. This is the kind of trust you build with those you love, and I trust them more than anyone in the world now.

"Take control and give me some reprieve. I want this from you, Scarlett. Sometimes I just need someone else to take care of me. Being the leader of our pack...I want you to fuck me." Adrian grazes his fingers over my wrist, working his way down to squeeze my thigh. "Show me how powerful I know you are. I crave it."

Leo grabs what looks like a harness and kisses my shoulder, unfastening it only to wrap it around my waist. "I'll help you, dirty girl. You don't have to be nervous. Adrian is strong, and you're going to make him feel so fucking good...while I do the same for you. Now show him how you want to be fucked, and then we will fuck you together."

I nod as Leo slides the dildo to the strap-on between my legs, slickening it with my body. I'm so hot and turned on, dripping wet, that they choose to use me to bring Adrian pleasure.

"Look at that good alpha," Leo says, taking my wrist and guiding my hand to touch Adrian. "He's so excited for this."

I trail my fingers over his back and down to his ass, massaging my fingers into his smooth skin. "So hot. Look at how hard I make him." I reach around and stroke my fingers over his length.

Leo playfully smacks his ass. "Tell him you're going to fuck him until he comes." He murmurs the words in my ear.

I use my slick to wet my finger and tease his ass, gently testing his body. He moans, the noise so incredibly sexy. It's unlike anything I've done with the others. They feel good because of my body. Now, I have to figure out how to make Adrian feel good with what I do.

"You want me to fuck you until you come, don't you?" I ask, letting Leo coax me. I smile at him, reaching behind me to glide my free hand over his cock. I summon my gall and bravado from him, using both his and Adrian's excitement to slip into a role I never ever considered. A position Adrian craves.

Adrian growls at me, arching his back, exposing his body even more. "So bad. I want to come for you."

"You heard him, dirty girl." Leo positions himself behind me, guiding my hands to the strap-on. "Give him your dick."

I tap the strap-on to Adrian's ass cheek, listening to him breathe, his anticipation wafting through the air with his berry scent, warmed with the cinnamon spice of his lust. Leo squirts on extra lube, only helping me guide the strap-on an inch into Adrian's ass before he focuses his attention on my breasts, rolling his fingers over my pebbling nipples.

I moan at the same time as Adrian, starting slow at first, recalling everything I know about sex with a male omega I learned from one of the many sex-ed classes at Omega Prep and using it to satiate my alpha. My alpha. I love the sound of that.

Bowing down, I reach around and stroke Adrian, jerking him off as I rock my body, controlling his pleasure. I've never felt so powerful. Adrian switching into a submissive just for me gets to me in a good way, more so than I could've ever imagined.

"Look at him take it," Leo murmurs, aligning his body to mine, sandwiching me to Adrian. "Tell him how good."

Tingles burst between my legs, the pressure building as Leo slides inside me, teasing me with his tip. I gasp and thrust deeper, listening to Adrian release a guttural noise from deep in his throat. His cock pulses in my hand, his muscles rippling.

"You love this, don't you? You're taking it so good, my sexy alpha," I say, moaning with the words. "Come for me. Come for me, so I can have you like I want."

Leo slides deeper, bumping his pelvis to my ass, guiding my thrusts with his body. I bite the back of Adrian's shoulder, pressing my body to his, working my hand over his cock as Leo fucks me.

"Come for me," I repeat, my voice turning breathy. "Do it before Leo knots."

"Make him, dirty girl." Leo locks his fingers to my hips, guiding my body to thrust into Adrian. "Tell him if he doesn't, then he'll have to fuck your ass. He won't get to knot with you."

I release a whimpering breath as Leo slows down and slides out of me, denying himself the chance to knot while using the idea to turn me on even more. I work the strap-on into Adrian, picking up my pace, listening to his bursting moans grow louder and louder. His cock pulses in my hand, and I pull back and stretch my neck, watching him come all over the bed.

I hug him from behind, resting my breasts on his back and kissing his throat. "So good. So, so good," I murmur, my heart still racing.

Leo hooks his arms around my waist, lifting me up and allowing Adrian to roll on his back. The smoldering look he gives me sets my soul ablaze, and I cup his face and kiss him. I reach out to Leo, craning my neck to kiss him next. I feel so incredibly sexy and loved. All I can think about is giving my alphas what they want—me.

"You're so perfect, Scarlett. My beautiful omega. The woman of my dreams," Adrian whispers through another kiss, blindly unhooking the strap-on and sliding it off.

"Of our dreams," Leo says, sliding into me, wetting his cock.

Adrian's body awakens again, flexing against my thigh. "We're the luckiest alphas alive."

I squirm on top of him, pushing up on my knees enough to grind against him until he positions himself to me. I sink down on top of him, moaning at the sensation, my body welcoming him. Leo latches his fingers to my ass, bouncing me up and down, controlling my movements. I close my eyes, giving into the moment. Adrian pulls me close, our hearts out of control and beating frantically. Pressure builds between my legs, and I scream out as his knot locks me in place, triggering an orgasm so intense that my eyes roll back.

Leo massages my ass, kneeling between Adrian's legs, and I groan at his tip teasing my ass, my body slickening even more to intensify the pleasure. This moment is all pleasure and no pain, my alphas giving me what I need, kissing and loving me as they move in even, rhythmic thrusts. My body was made for this. My slick ensures so much pleasure, allowing them to claim me at once, getting their fill.

"How do we feel, Scarlett?" Adrian asks, combing his fingers through my hair, kissing my jaw, hugging me through the wave of ecstasy cascading over me.

"Ah-amazing," I gasp, my voice coming out as a moan. I can barely see straight, every molecule on my body exploding with bliss.

Adrian hums with pleasure, whispering his affection as Leo moans with each of his thrusts until he grunts as he comes. I pant and squirm, my body singing and screaming in pleasure until Adrian's knot loosens from holding me in a state of bliss longer than ever.

No one moves, cuddling me and kissing me, ensuring I don't crash from the high of their love. My heart flutters, my body humming in a way I never want it to stop. I feel so incredible. Sexy and wanted. Cherished.

I've spent almost my entire adult life feeling unwanted. I felt like a disappointment.

But now?

I know I'll never feel that way again.

"You're my world, Scarlett. I hope you know that," Adrian murmurs, massaging his fingers to my spine. "I'll do anything for you."

I smile and rest my head on his pec. "I know. I'll do anything for you too. All of you. I promise."

And I'll know I'll never break it.

That's the one thing I'm absolutely sure of. Nothing will ever change.

19

Scarlett

THREATS

Me: Where's Mom? My call keeps going to voicemail.

Hardass: Probably ignoring you. She's been whining about how unfair Dad is being, not letting her intervene with you anymore.

Me: She's so selfish.

Hardass: She is a narcissist. Apparently, it's all our fault that she made a mistake on your profile.

Me: Sorry you have to deal with that.

Hardass: Not for much longer. Just focus on your pack. She'll move on.

Me: To you four. I wish her shit would just end with me.

Hardass: We'll all get through it. Maybe tell Dad she's ignoring you. You know she hates that.

Me: Thanks, Cyan. If she's too much, come visit. I miss you.

Hardass: Miss you too!

I ruffle my fingers through my hair, pushing it out of my face. I haven't heard from my mom in days, which isn't like her. I know that she's been harassing my pack, asking for money, and I want to confront her. I know she's not responding or speaking to me because she wants me to go to San Francisco and face her, but I don't want to give her that sort of pleasure. I just want her to stop being a bitch.

I take Cyan's advice and decide to reach out to Dad. I haven't talked to him since my last visit to San Francisco, and I'm not even sure what to say. Ezra mentioned that he was over the whole age thing, but he still hasn't reached out to me either, which speaks volumes. He's disappointed. Not necessarily in me, but I'm caught up in the aftermath of Mom's mistake and her current psychotic behavior.

Me: Hi, Dad. It's been a while. I hope everything's okay. I love you.

I lean back in my desk chair, staring at my phone as if it'll suddenly explode. I know better than to just start complaining about Mom. He's always been hands-off, letting her deal with all of us, so I just remind him that I'm still here, living and breathing, being a disappointment because I fell in love with men he doesn't see as a good fit for me.

Dad: What do you want, Scarlett? Your mom said you've been avoiding her. Until you can grow up and be mature, I'm staying out of everything. You can't expect me to accept your pack if you can't even act like an adult.

My mouth falls agape at his response. Is he fucking kidding me? Of course my mom would play the victim. She's always a goddamn victim, blaming us for every single one of her mistakes or for not being her obedient daughters, ensuring that she continues her life of luxury now that she's no longer popping out babies. She can't rely on her own damn pussy, so she wants to control ours.

Me: I don't know what Mom has said, but I've been trying to reach her for a while. She keeps contacting my alphas and asking for money. If you guys are so hard up, maybe she should demand the pack gives her more. It's the least they can do, considering we're the ones doing all the work. They should be the ones to deal with her. Not me.

Dad: Your mom said that your alphas were trying to sweeten her up because she disapproved of them.

Me: We want nothing to do with her. She's greedy and constantly threatens to ruin my life.

Dad: Perhaps it would be best if you just came home. You'll get over your infatuation with these alphas. They're not the only ones in the world. It will make life for all of us easier. You think you love them, but it hasn't been long. You can fall in love again.

Fury rushes through me, and I dig my nails into my palms, stopping myself from chucking my phone at the wall. I can't believe this. I don't even know why I bothered. He would never take my side. Mom would never stop harassing him if he did. She'd withhold sex or something, going to one of my other dads. She's always been manipulative. Using her body to her advantage.

But she's not going to use it against me.

I won't allow it.

Me: Never mind. Forget I tried to reach out to you. If you see Mom, tell her that she's a cunt.

My phone rings, my dad choosing to call me for the first time in who knows how long. I decline it, knowing that he's going to try to yell at me and defend my mom.

I block him. There's no point in trying to ask him for help when he clearly doesn't want to give it to me. He might have always been more mild-mannered and mostly an acceptable father, but his lack of involvement speaks volumes. It really shows where my place is with him.

Tears burn my eyes, and I blink them away. This isn't how I wanted to start off my day. I need to be left alone. I want my pack to be left alone. They're doing everything they can to ensure I'm happy, and I wish I could ensure that they are as well. I don't want them to have to deal with the bullshit of my life.

My phone rings again, and I sigh, seeing my mom's contact flash on the screen. It takes everything in me to gather my will to accept the call because I'm just so over her, but this needs to be done.

"Before you say a goddamn word, you're going to let me speak. I've had enough of your bullshit. I have done everything that you have asked of me my entire life. I will not sit back and let you threaten and coerce my pack into giving you more than you deserve. They paid the dowry for me. They've taken the time to ensure you were happy, and they deserve me. I have already accepted their marriage proposal, and it's time for you to back off. If you don't, then I will go to Pack Carlisle's leader. I think you have a lot more to lose than I do, and I'm not going to let you scare me into compliance anymore." My body shakes with my words, my anger seizing my muscles.

"Oh, Scarlett. Why do you have to be so mean to me? I have been looking out for you. I have given up so much to give you a good life, and you repay me with hostility and a bad attitude. You didn't even let me speak to know that I was only calling to apologize. I'm sorry, honey." Mom's voice whines through the phone, her words cracking. "It's so tough being a mom of seven omegas. You don't know how much work goes into arranging everything to give you such a good life. I'm sorry if things came across as they have, but I'm just looking out for you, my sweet baby. I don't want you in a situation you'll regret later. I know that those alphas of yours are probably pressuring you to do this, so I want to make sure you know that you have options. Take some birth control for your upcoming heat. You don't want to get knocked up before you're married. You don't know their intentions just yet. They keep pushing off something that should've already happened. They know what's at risk, and they don't even care."

Mom gasps a breath, sniffling into the phone.

I see past her fake concern. Something dark lies within her words, setting off my fear instincts. Why would she say such things? Why would she mention my heat and pregnancy? It happens all the time if an omega gets engaged to her alphas too close to their season. It's not a dealbreaker and never has been, because the betrothal and paying the dowry have always been enough. That's why we must be engaged before our twenty-second birthday and allowed to marry after.

"They do care, Mom. You don't even know anything. They have been nothing but kind, respectful, and loving, and they make me happy. I make them happy too." My mouth dries with my words. I shouldn't have to defend myself or my alphas.

"They say they do, but actions speak louder than words, honey. All I want to do is protect you. These men are far older, and the only reason why they want an omega is to breed with. They could just knock you up, take claim of their heir, and toss you aside. They could ignore you for the rest of your life. You will be out of everything, especially if something happens. They don't care about you. They only care about their own bloodline. There's no other reason why alphas would wait so long in their lives to take on an omega. It was very clear in the arrangement that they were ready to finally have children." Mom groans under her breath, sniffling again as if she's been crying over the whole situation. "Your daddy agrees with me. He thinks that this engagement is wrong. But he wants you to fail and see the mistakes you've made. I care about you. So please, take some birth control and protect yourself. See what happens after your heat when they realize you were not knocked up. They'll call off the wedding. They'll see about finding someone else."

A tap sounds on my door, and I swivel in my chair, watching as Dominic peeks his head in at me. Tears spill across my cheeks, my emotions getting the best of me. I can't contain them any longer. It's as if his presence alone is enough to trigger my body into knowing that he will hug me and take care of me as everything spills over, my mom pushing me over the edge.

"You're wrong," I argue, my voice cracking. "You're so fucking wrong. They love me. They aren't using me to breed. You are. You're making money off me and my body. So don't give me this bullshit. You don't care about me. You care about no one but your damn fucking self."

Dominic strides across the room, growling deep in his throat.

"Goddamn it, Scarlett! Just do as I say. You're going to regret it otherwise." Mom's attitude flips, the fake concern in her voice turning into annoyance. "I promise you that."

Dominic snatches the phone from my hand, another deep, guttural noise escaping his throat. "Don't talk to my omega like that. She is no longer of your concern. If you continue to threaten us or blackmail us, I will go to the public. They will see just what kind of woman the mother of the Steele sisters really is."

"Don't threaten me!" Mom's voice sounds out through the speaker, her scream getting under my skin.

Dominic disconnects the call and sets my phone down, scooping me up into his arms to cradle me close. I break down, everything crashing over me, threatening to drown me. How could everything be so right when the world outside us is so wrong? How could my family be so fucked up?

"I'm done with them. I'm so fucking done with her." I tremble with my words, my anger and fear threatening to swallow me whole. "I don't know what the fuck she's planning, but I don't like it. She kept mentioning for me to take birth control."

Dominic relocates me to my bed, holding me on his lap as he rubs his fingers across my cheeks, smearing my tears away. "I won't let her do anything crazy. I have been keeping track of every single thing she has done and said."

"I don't think you understand. She's insane. She's done some fucked up shit to my sisters too. I don't trust her. She's going to try to ruin our lives." I rest my head on his shoulder, breathing in deep breaths, trying to get my emotions in control.

"If she tries, she'll face heavy consequences. She's just trying to use everything as a scare tactic to get more money." Dominic nuzzles his nose to mine, kissing the trembling from my mouth.

"She keeps insinuating that you are purposely pushing off the wedding, and I'm afraid she'll use that to her advantage. I think I should drop out. A degree isn't important to me. I only came out here to hide. You're important. Our pack is important." I rub my lips together, tasting the saltiness of my tears.

Dominic sighs. "We both know that's not true. If that were the case, you would have wanted to do so sooner. You've worked so hard already, and you're so close to finishing. Don't give it up because of her. That's what she wants."

I scrub my hands over my cheeks. "It's not because of her. I'm just—"

My phone rings again, cutting off my comment. My heart stinks into my stomach at another unknown number. Why did I even take it off do not disturb? Why can't I catch a break? It's like I need to keep the whole entire world blocked out. I just need to change my phone number. Maybe even use a burner phone like Emma.

Dominic taps the screen, choosing to answer it instead of ignoring it and sending it to voicemail. "Hello?" he asks, his brows pinching together.

I listen to the soft sound of a feminine voice, but I can't decipher if I know who it belongs to. It's not Emma or any of my sisters. It's not Mom either.

"Yes, she's available. May I ask what this is regarding?" Dominic glances at me, rubbing his big hand to my knee. He listens to the woman speak, pressing his lips into a thin line. "The art piece was extraordinary, wasn't it? I'm so happy you enjoyed it. Scarlett is a very talented artist."

I tilt my head, my curiosity growing as Dominic gushes about me, his deep voice turning soft. It helps steady my racing heart. I lower my guard and grab his hand, getting his attention.

"Yes, of course. I'll put her on the line right now." Dominic hits the mute button. "It's a woman by the name of Talia from Pack Xavier. She saw your artwork at the Fall Carnival and wanted to reach out to you."

I take the phone from him, clearing my throat and composing myself before I unmute it. "Hello, this is Scarlett."

"Hi Scarlett, thanks for taking my call. My name is Talia Xavier. I'm the new director of the Art Department at Clearwater University and saw your Halloween piece at Beach Brew. The woman at the coffee shop gave me your information and said you were a student, so I looked you up and was pleasantly surprised that you're graduating soon."

I purse my lips. "Yes, I am. I'll be graduating in the spring."

"Wonderful, that is exactly what I wanted to hear. I'm looking for an assistant who is familiar with Clearwater University, and I have been allotted a great budget to reform and expand the art department. Pack Xavier has recently created ties to Pack Clearwater, and I think you would be perfect. You wouldn't have to relocate, the position will have benefits, be paid full-time, and it could set you up for a lot of future opportunities," the woman, Talia, continues.

An assistant? Expanding the art program? Her words spin through my mind. "Oh, I wasn't planning—"

"Before you decline, I want you to take some time to think about it. It's not often that a beta is given this kind of opportunity. Your art is amazing. You're incredibly talented, and I would hate to see it wasted. I can help mentor you. Please, just think about it." Talia cuts me off. "It'll look good on your résumé and will open many doors for you. Getting your degree is nice, but having this experience? Just think about it."

Dominic shifts beside me, grabbing my attention. He nods his head.

"Okay, I'll think about it." I can't believe this. I was so excited about getting commissioned for the window paintings at Beach Brew, but this? This is something beyond my wildest dreams.

"Excellent. I'll be sending all the information to your school email. I will need an answer by the end of the semester." Talia hangs up, her words still spinning through my mind.

Dominic pulls me to him, touching my face and kissing me. "Oh, Scarlett. This is incredible. It is unheard of for someone to be offered an assistant position right out of graduation."

Graduation. But that's the thing. I need to drop out. I already had my mind set.

I frown, the excitement over the unexpected phone call drifting away as my dark thoughts grab hold of me once more. "But..."

"Don't just discard this opportunity. We can talk about everything." Dominic hugs me tighter. "This is so incredible."

This moment proves just how wrong Mom really is. My guys don't want me just for my fertility. If that were the case, I'd have already been pulled out of this university. I wouldn't have been given the ability to make my own decisions. I wouldn't be encouraged now to break the norm.

And now I feel stronger than ever.

I don't feel afraid to face her.

I'm going to rub this in her face. I'm going to prove just how amazing Pack Hart is.

She can threaten us all she wants, but she will never bring us down.

20

Scarlett

surprises

"Keep your eyes closed, my beauty. No peeking." Jonah squeezes my hips with his fingers, nudging me forward. A blindfold rests over my eyes, and I look downward, staring at my glittering heels in the soft lighting. I can't see anything though, unless I tilt my head back, but he stands so close that I bump his chest when I try.

"This is too much. I thought we were going to just have something private at the manor." I stretch my arms out, my legs quivering with each step.

"You've been cooped up for days. It's your birthday, and there's no way we weren't going to celebrate in a manner you deserve. Stop worrying. You're going to love it." Jonah's warm breath tickles the nape of my neck, and I spin in his arms. I tip my head back and peeked at him through the sliver of view I get where the ribbon drapes over my nose.

He scrunches his face, narrowing his eyes, and I stretch up and plant my mouth to his, kissing him softly. He groans deep in his throat, sliding his hand down my spine and to my lower back, pulling me closer.

I stand flush against him, feeling his body awaken. Lust consumes me, my body tingling and begging for more. A whimper escapes my mouth, and I trail my fingers down the front of his dress shirt and to his pants, cupping him. "Not as much as I love you. You know what I want for my birthday?"

Jonah glides his hand lower and squeezes my ass. "The semester is almost over. You make it so hard to wait, but we have to, Scarlett. With everything going on, I don't want to risk something else being held over our heads."

I pout out my bottom lip at his rejection, trying not to let it get to me. The more time that passes, the antsier I get. I've already bonded with his pack mates, and now all I can think about is what it would be like to be with him. He teases me and showers me with affection, but he never goes overboard and always stops himself before either of us gets carried away.

And now it's driving me wild.

Snagging my lip between his teeth, he nips me softly and stretches it as he eases away. "You're really testing my restraint now. We better hurry. Our pack is waiting."

I sigh and pull off the ribbon, meeting his gaze. "Just one more kiss?"

"I'll make it two." Jonah kisses me again, lacing his fingers into my hair as he glides his tongue across mine, deepening our passion as he explores my mouth. Heat builds between my legs, setting me off, and I jump up on him, wrapping him in a full-body hug.

He moans and strolls forward, blindly walking as I refuse to stop kissing him, skewing his glasses. He gives into my affection, his body and heart against mine and his lust permeating the air.

"Just fuck her already. Denying her only makes it worse." Leo's salty, lime scent engulfs me a moment before his arms do. He presses his face to my neck, breathing in my hair. "Better yet, hand her over. I'll bang her on your behalf. You deserve to smell our sex for the rest of the night for this."

"We'll take her together and show him what he's missing. He'll learn from his mistake." Adrian laces his fingers to the back of my neck, guiding me to kiss him next.

I shiver, the memory of their moment with me sending pleasure straight to my clit as if they had already touched me.

"Don't worry, Lettie. Once you go into heat, he won't be able to resist. He'll be all yours. He won't even remember why he denied you." Dominic comes to my other side. "He'll kick himself for years to come."

"Give him a break. He's doing us a favor, giving us more of Scarlett's attention to devour. Isn't that right, amore?" Ezra completes the circle around me, kissing me from Jonah's arms.

"Maybe he'll just give me a show." I smile at Adrian. "You know how much I like that."

Adrian roars a laugh and whacks Jonah on the back, grinning at us. "Indeed, I do...mistress," he whispers, his voice tickling my ear. "Careful what you start. We've arranged this birthday celebration, and I want you to enjoy at least dinner and cake."

"Only if you feed it to me," I say, finally looking around.

"Fuck yeah, we will. I'll even let you use me as a plate." Leo play-growls and kisses my cheek. "Let me be your present."

"One of many," Adrian adds, taking me from Jonah to set me on my feet. "Because this is your day, and you'll get whatever your heart desires."

"Except that asshole," Leo mutters, flicking Jonah on the pec. Dodging out of the way of retaliation, Leo fills the empty space by my side and drapes his arm over my shoulders. Leaning in, he whispers, "But don't worry. I'll give you another gift later. One of seduction. He will cave."

I grin with a laugh, my heart bursting with the happiness wafting around us. "You think?"

"I know." Leo pulls me from the others.

The brilliant sunset sparkles across the ocean, the puffy pink and purple clouds painting the sky with breathtaking color. Twinkling lights wrap around the tall palm trees of this cliff top restaurant, and I bounce on my feet, smiling at the glowing sign of the Mermaid Lounge.

"We have a balcony view," Ezra says, adjusting his tie. The swanky restaurant hums with music from a live pianist.

"Happy birthday, Lettie." Dominic kisses my temple, squeezing his head between Leo and me as he walks behind us.

The stained-glass door swings open as the maître d' greets us, offering my pack a bow in respect. Adrian and Leo both take one of my hands, walking with me between them, not hiding the fact that we're together. It helps that we're outside of Pack Clearwater Territory and away from campus. They wanted this night to truly be ours without having to worry about drawing attention.

Jonah is even comfortable enough to kiss my cheek and show me affection. His moral standing cracks, and it takes me a bit not to push him. But I want to. I know he wants me to, but he won't initiate things.

"Surprise, Scar! Happy birthday!" Familiar voices ring through the air, and I whip my attention to the huge balcony extending over the cliff side. The sunset lights everything in cotton candy colors, and I spot Emma, Sapphire, and Violet standing at a long table with balloons and confetti scattered across the top.

I turn to my pack with wide eyes. "What is this? I can't believe you arranged this!"

"A special visit for our beautiful omega. Happy birthday, my beauty," Jonah says, nudging me forward.

I squeal and stride across the balcony, opening my arms for my best friend and favorite sisters. It's been a while since I've seen them, and I feel so loved that my mates arranged this for me, especially with the family drama.

"We've missed you, sis," Violet says, pulling me into a hug. She kisses each of my cheeks and nuzzles her nose to mine. "When Ezra called, there was no way I could decline the invitation. I wish I could've managed to wrangle everyone, but you know how it goes. Jade is MIA as always. Cyan, Raven, and Amber are keeping Mom busy. They wish they could be here. How are you holding up? I heard about the fallout with Mom. Sapphire told me what happened."

Sapphire pops out her bottom lip. "It's even worse now. I couldn't wait to get away."

"You have no idea, but it is what it is." I squeeze my eyes shut and shake my head, wanting nothing more than to push the thoughts away. "You know how Mom is. She's mostly pissed off that she can't get her way by throwing a tantrum with me anymore. I'm better now that I get to spend my birthday with you girls. How did you even manage?"

"The cunt doesn't control me," Emma says, rubbing her fingers through my hair. "I helped Ezra arrange a plan. We kidnapped Sapphire, disguising this as a pack-finding mission. It's been fun."

Sapphire laces her fingers through mine and tugs me closer. "Let's not talk about Mama anymore tonight. I get enough of her at home. We don't have a lot of time to spend, so I don't want to waste another minute."

Emma shakes me. I wasn't sure I'd ever see my best friend again, and here she is, helping bring my sisters to me too. "She's right. Let's pretend that bitch doesn't exist and celebrate your vagina liberation day."

"You're too much, Em," Violet says, shaking her head.

"Be thankful I'm not related." She sticks out her tongue, reminding me of a dozen times before. Emma was there when Violet and Jade ignored me at Omega Prep because I was their dorky, artsy little sister. I know Violet regrets it most, but I've forgiven her.

I laugh and hug my sisters again. The only thing that could be better than this as if all seven of us Steele sisters were together, but I'll take what I can get. If Mom had it her way, we would probably never get to see each other again.

"You're ridiculous, but I love you, princess," I say to Sapphire.

"I love all of you." Violet guides us toward the table. "Let's have a drink, eat, and celebrate."

I glance at my alphas. "This is the perfect birthday."

Leo pulls me onto his lap. "For a perfect woman."

"I wish you all didn't have to go." I stand near the limo my pack arranged to take everyone back to the airport. "I miss spending time with you."

"Maybe you can elope in Vegas. It's close enough for me to travel without issue. Stick it to the cunt," Emma says, grinning. Her brown eyes sparkle in the string lights hanging from the trees.

I laugh and shrug my shoulders. "Just her reaction alone would be worth it."

"Don't worry about her or anyone else. Focus on you and your alphas. She'll lose interest. I promise." Violet caresses her knuckles to my cheek.

"She's right. Cyan, Amber, Raven, and I will keep her busy." Sapphire squeezes my hand. "You're basically free now. I'm happy for you, by the way. We all are."

I hug my sisters and Emma one last time, my heart happy apart from the shadow of sadness I push away as they climb into the limo and the driver shuts the door.

I don't get more than a moment to pout before Dominic spins me toward him and dips me, dancing to the soft music coming from the Mermaid Lounge.

A bright flash of light pops from over Dominic's shoulder, and I catch a figure with a camera sitting in the front seat of an old sedan.

"What the fuck?" Leo asks, his voice deepening.

Another camera flashes, stealing my vision with the blinding light, and two men laugh and snap more pictures. Dominic pulls me close, covering me with his jacket protectively. Ezra and Jonah straighten their backs, creating a wall.

"Dickasso! Smile for me, baby! I want to make this a birthday for you to remember!" The car door slams, and Chaz steps out, waving an expensive camera with a long lens. "It'll go with the ones from Halloween. You know, these old asses don't fuck you enough. Maybe they can't get their dicks hard for you."

I bristle, my chest tightening. This is another level of psycho. I thought he'd back off. My pack said they had stuff against him and his uncle that would keep him away.

"Come on, Chaz. You promised you'd get her to show her tits." This comes from one of the other men who came from the other direction. He's not stalking me alone.

"You son of a bitch!" Leo breaks away and charges the two guys, spreading his arms wide as he knocks both of them off their feet. They underestimate him, thinking that just because they're older that they won't fight back.

But I know that isn't true.

They have far more to fight for.

Swinging his arm, Leo punches the blond asshole in the nose.

Chaz whistles through his fingers. "I wouldn't do that if I were you, professor. Don't you recognize him? Chris is the quarterback on the football team. Rumor has it that the Athletics Department director has been giving the team steroids. It would be a shame for that sort of information to come out. But we can make arrange-ments."

Leo growls again, spitting in the guy's face. He snatch-es him by the front of his shirt and glowers. The man smiles, blood pouring down his nose. He's just as de-ranged as Chaz.

"What is it that you want?" Adrian steps forward, balling his hands into fists. He puffs his chest out, his demeanor changing from one of sophistication to threatening.

"I want to see her tits," the quarterback, Chris, says with a laugh. "What about you, Nick?"

"I want more than that. Let me give her a ride. Show her what it is like to be with a real alpha," the other man says, pushing to his feet.

Dominic sucker punches him before he can even step a foot closer. Chaz's camera flashes again as he snaps picture after picture, getting under my skin.

"This will make a great scandal. Clearwater's professors assaulting students. Buying an omega out from under a more worthy pack." Chaz steps closer, taking a dozen pictures.

Something explodes inside me, the edges of my vision reddening. I scream and rush him, planning to beat the shit out of him. Jonah hooks his arm around my waist and yanks me back, not letting me get within Chaz's reach.

"Let us handle it, Scarlett," Jonah says, spinning me behind him protectively.

"He can't handle shit, Scarlett. Come on, now. Be the obedient omega you were born as. Come to me. I'll let you give me a blow job, and maybe I won't turn these pictures over to the dean." Chaz stares at me, reaching into his pants and pulling out his hard-on like he gets off on tormenting me. He strokes himself and wags his eyebrows. "It's that easy. Don't be shy, Dickasso. I'm sure you'll love my dick far more than their flaccid cocks."

"You disgusting sicko! I'll kill you!" I yell, dodging around Jonah.

I can't see anything through my blurry tears except for Chaz's figure, and I slam into him, knocking him off his feet. I swing my hand out and punch him in the groin, just as Emma taught me. She always despised her order and ensured that I couldn't be pushed around.

Howling, Chaz locks his fingers to my hair and yanks my head. I twist and buck my body, managing to get Chaz in his groin again before Jonah rips me off. The scent of my alphas' anger permeates the air. Their aggression blazes like Chaz even laying a hand on me sets off a nuclear weapon inside them. Someone yells from the restaurant, shouting that they are calling the police, and Adrian grabs the camera, smashing it on the floor. My alphas don't hesitate to pin Chaz and the two other guys down, yanking their phones from their pockets, ensuring they don't have any incriminating evidence against us.

"Misters Hart, get out of here. I'll ensure the police know that these men had assaulted our patrons. There's no need to get involved. I'll handle it from here." The maître d' motions toward two servers in uniforms.

Chaz kicks Jonah, knocking his legs out from under him. None of us see the car until the horn honks, dragging our attention away. Ezra grabs Jonah, and Adrian tosses me on his shoulder, spinning out of the way just before the car collides into us. Smoke fills the air, the distraction enough to give Chaz and the other two guys a chance to fight against the two servers to get to the vehicle.

"One of them was the asshole from the haunted house. He's the one that attacked me," Ezra says, flaring his nostrils.

"This makes more sense. Chaz needs a pack and an omega to get is inheritance. He's buying people off. She's an easy target and his uncle has enough influence. They probably made a deal of some sort. It's why he's obsessed with Scarlett. Especially now that he knows she's been claimed by us." Dominic dusts off his hands on his slacks and fixes his tie.

I inhale and exhale a couple of breaths, my body trembling. I close my eyes as a deep ache burns in my middle, rolling through me. I feel so sick to my stomach. They are utter monsters. The way they talk to me. The way they treated my alphas. We can't let them get away with us. We just can't.

"He's out of his goddamn mind. I don't think we can continue to just wait things out. We need to go to the dean and get ahead of ourselves. I have Chaz's threat on video." Ezra waves his phone.

Adrian shudders and hugs me tight. "I think you're right, Ez. Not even just for our sake. But for the rest of Clearwater University and any potential omega. He proved this isn't only some obsessive game over Scarlett. It's more. What do you the rest of you think?"

"Agree," Leo, Ezra, and Jonah all say in unison.

"Agree," I whisper, my voice barely managing to escape my lips.

"Then it's settled. We will formally announce our engagement to the dean and set an appropriate plan of action into motion." Adrian rubs his hand over my back. "Now let's take our birthday girl home. This was not how we were going to celebrate. Let's give her what she needs."

Unfortunately, they can't give me the one thing I need right now.

To end Chaz's entire existence.

To ensure he never does anything to hurt anyone ever again.

21

Adrian

revelations

Dean Clearwater sits at his dark mahogany desk, sipping golden whiskey in a crystal tumbler. Cigar smoke taints the air, hiding his usual filthy musk. I suspect he doesn't shower as often as he should, but I know the gesture is purposeful. He wants every student and staff member on campus to catch a whiff of his alpha stench.

I pull a wad of fabric from my pocket and dab my nose, the fragrance of Scarlett's panties enough to settle my annoyance.

"Where is the rest of your pack, Adrian? I thought they'd be joining you." Dean Clearwater sets his tumbler down and motions to a decanter of whiskey. "May I offer you a drink? I think we're beyond the stuffiness of professionalism after two decades, don't you think?"

Which is why I thought it was acceptable calling upon him at this late hour. I should be used to his casual behavior, but in a moment like this, where I need to discuss serious matters and not some power shift occurring in the main branch of Pack Clearwater and those I serve under, he acts as if we're here to socialize.

"They'll be here soon," I say, strolling forward, tucking Scarlett's panties away again. "I wanted a moment alone to prepare you for our visit."

Dean Clearwater sits straighter in his chair, cocking his head. "Is this not good news about the expansion of the university in San Francisco or about the English department head position? I assumed this would be a positive meeting. A celebration."

Because no one chooses to talk to Dean Clearwater about issues to his face. The man has overserved his time at the university and should have retired a decade ago.

The bastard is pushing close to eighty. But some men can't give up control or power.

"My apologies, Dean Clearwater. You must've misheard my call when I said it was urgent." I sigh and sit in the chair across the desk from him. "San Francisco is still under contract as well as Jonah's decision on whether or not he wants the position."

Dean Clearwater rests his elbows on the desk. "I'll offer him a thirty percent increase. I need someone I can trust."

Jesus Christ. The man can't think of anything outside himself.

"Which is why I've come to you. We've been working together my entire career. You're a most trusted ally, and I wanted to address some possible issues that may come to light." I crack my knuckles, meeting Dean Clearwater's brown eyes. He was the man who recruited me after I graduated from Alpha Academy. "We've found ourselves in...a bit of a predicament and need your allegiance."

A knock sounds on the door, dragging Dean Clearwater's attention from me. Without waiting, the door cracks open, and Jonah, Ezra, and Dominic stroll in, remaining expressionless. Leo and Scarlett aren't behind them, their absence striking a nerve inside me.

Dominic closes the space and rests his hands on the back of my chair, leaning down. "Scarlett wouldn't leave the closet. She's not feeling well, and we didn't want her stressing out."

I remain expressionless despite his words sending a cool wave down my back. She needs all of us with her, and it kills me that I have to deal with such bullshit because of some entitled, psychotic douche. I'm too damn old for this. If I didn't have so much to lose, I'd have beat the Pack Miller reject into submission. The fact that he doesn't have as much to lose makes him dangerous. We must get ahead of things.

Dean Clearwater crosses his arms over his chest, glowering in silence as Jonah, Dominic, and Ezra pull chairs from the wall to sit in front of him. I feel younger under his scrutiny and like a frat boy who fucked up and must beg for forgiveness and a second chance.

I'm better than this.

My pack is better than this.

"Misters Hart, it's getting late. Had I known this wasn't going to be the meeting I expected, I'd have postponed until an appropriate hour." Dean Clearwater swigs his whiskey, draining the glass. "Please make it quick."

"This should take great precedence to you, considering we're respected members of the staff and Pack Clearwater." I open my hand to Ezra, silently asking for him to hand over his phone and the evidence. "We have been keeping such personal matters quiet, but it seems things have gotten out. As you know, we have been in search of an omega and were planning to marry this year. We found Scarlett and proposed to her a couple of weeks ago. Her pack works under Pack Carlisle."

Dean Clearwater sits up straighter, his eyebrow shooting up on his head. "Oh, I suppose a congratulation is in order. This is quite fantastic news."

"Yes, it's absolutely thrilling for us. Our fiancée is everything we could've imagined...except we thought she was older. We assumed her pack had graciously allowed her to pursue a career instead of obligating her to find a pack right out of Omega Prep. Like how things went with us." I shake away my nerves. "However, it seems there was a bit of a mistake on her profile."

"A mistake? What do you mean? Is she widowed? Rejected?" Dean Clearwater leans forward, engrossed in our personal matters.

I side-glance Dominic. "Not exactly—"

"I'm just going to spit it out." Jonah groans and links his fingers together, resting his elbows on the desk.

"Scarlett was sent to Clearwater University to hide the fact that she wasn't engaged yet. This was due to the mistake with her age on her profile. You know how societal standards are. Her pack was ashamed."

"I don't think I'm following," Dean Clearwater says, swigging another mouthful of whiskey.

Jonah stiffens. "What aren't you getting? Scarlett's a student here, and we have already completed negotiations and have arranged a summer wedding."

Dean Clearwater furrows his brows, tightening his jaw without saying a word. Silence blankets the office, and I wish I could hear what goes through his mind. Just from his change in demeanor, I know I've lost a bit of his respect. This is something I should've addressed immediately, but I didn't want to. I find my personal relationship and pack issues to be no one's business.

"You're engaged to a student?" Dean Clearwater scrubs his hands over his face, processing our admission. "There's an omega enrolled here?"

"You know there are no order requirements. None of this is the issue. The problem is that we're being blackmailed by a former student who has recently been expelled for disgusting behavior. He has gotten several other students involved, and they're trying to create a scandal to tarnish our reputations, including Clearwater's." I hit the video icon on Ezra's phone, setting it in front of the dean.

His expression morphs from confusion to shock to anger as the video replays, capturing Chaz threatening us and Leo with the idea of encouraging steroid use on the football team.

I clench my fingers, my anger rising again, watching the video unfold. It doesn't show any of us, nor does it show the violence, which I'm thankful for. But damn it. Reliving this is just as bad as the first time, if not worse. Because all I can think about is what else I could've done to prevent any of it from happening.

Dean Clearwater slides the phone back to me and stands from his chair, pouring himself another glass of whiskey. He paces, mumbling to himself. His musky scent grows more intense, and I push my chair back and rise to my feet, uncomfortable that he stands taller than me while I'm sitting.

"This is quite the predicament. If it were any other professors on this campus, I'd have no choice but to demand a leave of absence while I discuss this with the board. Because it's you, Misters Hart, and you have done nothing but great things for the school, I would like to keep this discreet. The first thing you must do is pull your omega from this university. We can backdate the paperwork to prove that you took appropriate action immediately." Dean Clearwater glances at me before returning to the rest of my pack mates. "Then we must handle the Athletics Department. We cannot let such things reach the media. We'll threaten immediate expulsion unless they sign NDAs and contracts that they're at fault and go through drug testing weekly."

Jonah gets to his feet and crosses his arms. "Scarlett is nearly finished with her education. We would like to hold out until spring. She's been offered a position right here with the new Director of the Art department. She can't accept it unless she graduates."

Dean Clearwater scowls. "Now what is that of any use? She's young and fertile and is ready to start breeding, is she not? That is why you have decided to claim an omega, right? You know that it's important. You're not getting any younger either."

"A pregnancy will not interrupt the rest of her education. You do know it takes nine months to have a child, or have you never taken the appropriate sex-ed classes?" Leo asks, growling with his words.

"Do not disrespect me!" Dean Clearwater shouts, erupting in anger. "You have put this mess on me and this university, and I'll not allow such a scandal. My decision is final. You either pull her out of CU, or I will expel her."

Ezra smacks the desk. "You—"

Dominic grabs his shoulder and pulls him back, spinning him around and getting in his face. The last thing we need is for Ezra to act on his anger, especially because we're more volatile now that Scarlett has been threatened and our lives as we know it are being jeopardized.

"Control your pack, Adrian," Dean Clearwater says, his voice rumbling with his wrath. "I will not stand for this disrespect."

"I'm their leader, not their authority. We're equals in our household. And as for what you're demanding? No. I will not waste all the work Scarlett put in just to appease you. You need to handle the students here more appropriately. There needs to be stronger consequences for poor behavior such as stalking, assaulting, and being disgusting human beings." I stand my ground, crossing my arms over my chest. "I came to you as a courtesy. I wanted to get ahead of the situation so we could handle it appropriately together. I did not come here to have you demand such things from my pack. And if you insist, I will not hesitate to break our alliances. You know that the mayor grows weak. I'll not hesitate to run for office or resist informing all of my personal network and allies of the many discussions that you have ignored over the years. Don't test me, Franklin. Do you understand? We will be discreet with Scarlett, and she will not be in any of my pack mates' classes next semester. I demand the same courtesy you would give one of your own family members. Just like you did with Jonah's predecessor in his department."

Because I've done some digging. Jonah's department head was caught cheating on his wife with a library assistant, and they were caught fucking in the room used to hold some of our most ancient books. He had been transferred, so he could hide the scandal, but he was not fired. His wife has also been paid off to hide his foul behavior. His only real consequence was giving up his position as department head.

"How dare you try to coerce me, Adrian," Dean Clearwater snaps, flaring his nostrils.

"I'm not trying. That is how the situation will be handled, because you can't see outside your precious position. You know I'm the best at my job, and I bring in millions of dollars for Pack Clearwater. I would prefer to stay here, but if it comes down to it, I could always find a new position elsewhere. My omega is highly regarded up north with Pack Carlisle." I bite the inside of my cheek with my words, hoping Dean Clearwater doesn't call my bluff. Because there's no way in hell that I'd ever ask Scarlett to return to San Francisco or be near her family if she didn't want to be.

Dean Clearwater holds my gaze, staring at me as if he could possibly intimidate me. But in a battle of wills, I would win. I have my pack by my side, standing tall and giving me the strength to get what we want.

"Don't make me regret this, Adrian. If I so much as hear anyone whispering about Pack Hart or your omega, I will not hesitate to destroy all of your careers." Dean Clearwater averts his eyes, submitting to my demand. He damn well knows that he couldn't mess up my career. He's not innocent either. Every damn alpha in power has something to hide, and Dean Clearwater has an entire house of skeletons, his closet not nearly big enough to hide his bullshit.

I nod my head and offer my hand. "You have my word. Everything will be handled accordingly. I'll send you the information about the students if you want to handle them yourself."

Dean Clearwater ignores my hand and turns toward his bookshelf. "Get out of my office. This will not be forgotten, so you better ensure you get the contracts in order and you accept whatever position and do any favor Pack Clearwater asks of you for this university."

I motion to Ezra, Dominic, and Jonah to head out before me. They exit Dean Clearwater's office, giving me a moment alone.

I surprise Dean Clearwater by grabbing his shirt and pulling him close. "We don't take threats lightly. Be careful what you say, Franklin. We both know you're not innocent, or should I bring up—"

"That won't be necessary, Adrian. As long as we have a mutual agreement, then we will handle whatever scandal thrown at us. I will not lose this position." Dean Clearwater straightens his suit jacket. "I didn't think you had it in you, but you have always been full of surprises, haven't you?"

"Because I see things differently. Be aware, Franklin. Things are changing. You need to decide whether you will step out of the way or..." I smirk at him, letting him fill in my silent command.

I don't wait for him to respond. He will not get the last word. Not anymore.

Because the most important thing to me right now is Scarlett.

I will not let her down.

22

Leo

MAKING A POINT

Fuck, Scarlett looks so fragile, curled in on herself as she sleeps in Jonah's office closet. Out of all the places, I wasn't expecting her to choose this. It's a tight squeeze for me, so I crawl in and lay on my stomach. I slide my arm under her and spoon her.

"Dirty girl, can I carry you to your room? I think you'll like what I've done." I kiss her earlobe, feeling her stir. "It's okay if you don't want to go. I get it."

Whimpering, Scarlett grabs my hands and pulls me closer, rubbing her nose to my wrist, scenting me. "Will you bring all this stuff too?"

"Of course. I'm at your service. Whatever you want or need. There are no limitations when it comes to taking care of you." I wiggle my way back until I have enough space to sit up. Scarlett doesn't even move as I slide my arms behind her legs and around her back, picking her up with her small pile of blankets and pillows. My balls tighten, spotting one of my shirts tucked in her collection. She's not in heat yet, but it's going to happen anytime. She needs to get as much rest as she needs. I can already tell it's going to be intense. I feel it deep in my bones. In my emotions. I'm already rutting, and it takes all my willpower not to just camp out with her. There's too much to do. Usually, we'd have to put in a notice, but no one wants to cause any more suspicions. Douche Clearwater might not have much on us, but I'd prefer not to deal with him.

My phone buzzes from my pocket, and I hold Scarlett in one arm and pull it out with the other. She snatches it from my fingers.

Litdude: Your presence has been requested in the Athletics Department. You're to assist Dean Clearwater with the active investigation. I'll meet you at your office.

I grumble deep in my throat.

Litdude: Bring Scarlett. The dean wants us to make a point. I'll take her to class with me after.

Scarlett purses her lips, silently reading the messages. She taps her finger to the screen, messaging Jonah with my phone.

Me: There's only one way I'm leaving this house. I need food.
Litdude: Don't worry, my forbidden beauty. You won't have to speak to anyone. I'll have lunch ready as well.

Scarlett clutches the phone as I carry her the rest of the way to her suite and to her bed. I abandon her to grab something for her to wear from her wardrobe. Her shadow falls over me, and she hugs me from behind.

"What is all this?" she asks, peeking at the mountain of blankets, pillows, shirts, towels, and whatever the hell else I could easily steal from everyone.

"My effort to lure you out of Jonah's office," I say, grinning at her. "Hopefully, it's acceptable."

She laughs and hugs me tighter, clinging to me so I can't turn around. "It's perfect...but now I don't want to leave. I want to bury myself and sleep for the rest of the year."

"But then, however will you seduce Jonah? Teach him a lesson for even suggesting you go to class when you're not a hundred percent yourself. I can't sit and feed you, snuggle you, or give you full-body massages if you're listening to him explain why the blue bedding in whatever old-ass book you're reading is a metaphor for the author's loneliness. He should just accept that it's the only color the writer could think of and it means nothing."

Scarlett giggles, her melodious voice wrapping around me in a comforting melody. "I'll tell him that."

"You're going to be sexy as hell while doing it, too. Make him regret his poor decisions of both denying you his cock and torturing you with discussions." I dangle out the plaid skirt I snuck into her wardrobe for...other purposes. "What do you think?"

Scarlett raises her eyebrows. "Sounds like we're going to both get in trouble."

I laugh. "It'll be worth it."

"Thank you, Professor Hart, for joining me today. As I've already informed your coach, there has been an anonymous reporting that brings me great concern. I'll be issuing drug tests to the entire team." Dean Clearwater stands in the locker room, his arms folded across his chest.

Scarlett hides behind me, and I tug her along, motioning to my office where Jonah stands and waits.

Murmurs erupt from the football team, and I remain expressionless. I recognize the two alphas who crashed Scarlett's birthday party immediately. Rage swells through me, and I grind my teeth, fisting my hands.

"Would any of you like to come clean about your usage? If you do, the consequences will not be as severe. I only do this because I care about this team and our school," Dean Clearwater says, pacing in front of the bench where the mixture of betas and alphas sit at attention. There aren't many alphas on campus, but the ones who enroll tend to need a more narrowed education outside of Alpha Academy. Or they've run out of options because they're fuckups like Chaz. I know it's why he pretended to be a beta when these douches don't.

"I'd like to come clean about something." The smug asshole from Scarlett's birthday, the kid I remember named Chris, smirks at me. "I won't pass the fucking drug test because Professor Hart was the one to encourage the 'roid usage."

The poor idiot has no idea what he's just gotten himself into. It's exactly what Adrian had told the dean would happen.

"Yeah, Dean Clearwater. I didn't want anything to do with it, but he made us," the other douche says, the one I have no fucking clue what his name is. I don't even think he's been on the field this year.

Dean Clearwater glances at me before turning back to the football team. "I find that hard to believe, considering I have trusted evidence that says otherwise. If you insist on accusing the Athletics Director, then you'll be immediately expelled. Would you like to redact your accusations?"

Chris slams his hands to the bench. "You son of a bitch! You shouldn't even be here. You should be fucking fired for—"

Scarlett's small gasp from my office sets me off, and I lunge at the lying asshole and yank him off his feet. I stand several inches taller than him and probably work out twice as much, because he can't even break free of my chokehold as I spin him around and slam him face-first into the locker.

I snarl in his ear, shoving my hand to his upper back, winding him. "Be careful what you say from this point on. You underestimate my power and authority. My private life is no one's business, and if you so much as try to ruin my reputation, I will ensure your future is ruined."

Chris stiffens in my arms, drawing placid as he submits to me. There are too many goddamn hotheaded assholes who just don't know that they must earn their places. You can do so illegally or with threats and violence, but that leaves alliances shaken. I've learned long ago that people who actually deserve respect get it. They don't scare people into giving it. He's about to learn that real quick.

"Now, go back to your seat and shut the hell up. Say anything again, and you will never be able to show your face on this campus again. You will shame your pack." I swing him around and shove him back down.

The locker room falls silent with my motion, and Dean Clearwater clears his throat. He adjusts his suit jacket and dips his chin in a nod of affirmation.

"Would anyone else like to speak up?" Dean Clearwater gives each member of the team a hard look.

No one responds. No one looks at the dean or me.

"Very well. I'd like to make something clear. Blackmailing or coercing the faculty will not be tolerated. You have the privilege to attend this university, but it is not a right. You will respect all faculty's privacy and personal lives. We will do the same for you as long as you earn such courtesies. Do I make myself clear?" Dean Clearwater holds his ground, towering over the football players.

"Yes, sir." Several mumbles sound in the locker room, parroting each other.

"From this moment on, I'll also be enforcing sterner punishments when it comes to student harassment. We're adults, and that sort of behavior does no one any good. If you want to join reputable and respectful packs, you will take my advice to heart." Dean Clearwater motions to a steel rolling tray with enough plastic cups for the entire team.

The last thing I wanted was to fucking mess with piss, but I bite my tongue and do as expected. Adrian warned me that our alliance with the dean was shaken, and it's important that I keep my cool.

I catch movement from my office, and I offer Jonah and Scarlett a stiff smile as they exit to stroll back by the football team. This is a silent warning to anyone who is considering exposing Scarlett as an omega, and I watch each football player closely for their reactions. Only Chris and his buddy glower, but they remain silent. It helps me know that no one else on the team is in on this bullshit.

"All right, team. Everyone piss in the fucking cup. I swear to fucking God, if you spill a damn drop, you'll be scrubbing this entire locker room with your bare hands." I pass out the cups, stopping at Chris one more time. "And don't forget to pass the warning on. You don't fuck with faculty. You don't fuck with things that are none of your business or don't belong to you." I smack my hand to his cheek, purposely leaving my scent behind. "Also, keep each other accountable. Got it?"

The team grumbles, most of them looking confused as fuck, which makes me feel a bit better about the situation. Dean Clearwater stays until the cups are gathered and put back on the tray, and he thanks everyone for their cooperation.

"I expect that no more problems will come my way, Leo. I have far better things to do than clean up your mess," Dean Clearwater grumbles, thinning his lips as the locker room clears out.

"We all do, Franklin." I follow him out, shielding my eyes from the sun. "Just know this courtesy won't be forgotten. You have our back, and we have yours."

"I wouldn't expect anything less. Have a good day." Dean Clearwater shuffles away, leaving the piss cups behind. He wasn't actually going to test anybody. He doesn't want to waste money or resources on something he doesn't actually care about.

I shove the tray to the side of the building, where dumpsters hide behind brick walls. I get rid of everything and jog out, wanting nothing more than to just take the rest of the day off.

A horn honks, drawing my attention to the student parking lot, and I tense at the sight of Chaz waving at his two asshole friends. I heave a breath, my rage consuming me. He's not even supposed to be on campus. I'm going to fuck him up for showing his face after what he tried to do.

I hit the asphalt, but Chaz stomps his throttle and peels out, leaving white smoke in the air. I catch his eyes in his rearview mirror, and I know this isn't over.

I'm going to have to call in some favors.

Some people won't give up.

I'm just going to have to make him.

23

Scarlett

NAUGHTY STUDENT

Me: I think I need someone to pick me up.

I wiggle in my seat, antsy and unfocused. I knew it was a bad idea to leave the manor, but Leo needed me to rile up the fuckers that attacked us at the Mermaid Lounge. Dean Clearwater wanted to see me for himself as well. Maybe to confirm what my alphas told him or because he's nosy. Whatever reason, I wish I had asked Jonah to take me home instead of to class.

Because dull cramps seize my stomach, stealing my focus. My body hums, my skin sensitive in a way that drives me crazy. Every shift of my legs causes my body to throb unexpectedly.

Good Boy: Where's Joe?

I smirk at Adrian's nickname in my phone. Leo must've changed it.

Love Machine: He better be standing right in front of her.

Fucking Leo. I scoot back in my seat, the fabric of my plaid skirt brushing my naked body. I was too caught up in my own worries that I hadn't really paid much attention until I was already halfway onto campus. I look like Leo's dirty fantasy in what could pass as a sexy school uniform. Now that I think about him...fuck me. I'm horny.

But worse, I'm going into heat.

Me: He's in the middle of a lesson, but I want to bail. I'm exhausted. Achy.

Good Boy: I can be there in forty-five.

Me: I'm so fucking horny.

Love Machine: Shit. I'll be there in thirty.

A book smacks on the floor, startling me. I whip my attention to the front of the room. Bending down, Jonah quickly picks up his paperback. My heart races, my body tingling. His movement wafts his scent in my direction.

He shakes his head and moves something on the podium. Not something. His phone.

Lit Dick: Scarlett, can you hang in for a bit longer? I'll excuse everyone early.

Me: I'm not sure. I ache. I think I'm soaking the chair. I'm so horny.

Love Machine: Goddamn. You better take care of her, Joe.

Jonah clears his throat, leaning his elbows on the podium. "Sorry about that. Family matters. Where was I at?"

I clutch my book, and though I follow along, my phone rests between the pages. "One-oh-seven. Paragraph five, Professor Hart," I murmur, my voice soft.

Me: He's too busy reading. It's torture. I don't think I can stay much longer.
Good Boy: Go to Joe's office if you need to.
Clayman: I'll excuse my next class. Sounds like you need us all, Lettie. Ezra, can you swing by early?
PapaMia: Anything for my amore.
Me: Bend me over?

"Thank you, Ms. Carlisle," Jonah says, his voice snapping my attention away from the phone.

I smirk and nod my head instead of responding with my voice.

Me: Since Jonah won't.
Love Machine: Do what I told you, dirty girl. You'll get out of there faster than he blows his load from his self-proclaimed abstinence until the end of the term.

Jonah flips through the pages of Blanca's Barcelona, another novel not on the syllabus but one he claims to use as an example of a modern allegory tale for this week's unit. His muscles bulge against his suit, his body flexing.

I don't know how he manages to remain expressionless as his phone buzzes, but I can't help my sudden need to get his attention.

"Steam filled the shower, the fragrance of their passion mingling with the scent of the lavender candles." His tongue glides over his bottom lip as he peers up from the book to glance at me. "Blanca laced her fingers through Jorge's wet, midnight hair. Burying his face into her body, as if the sweet nectar of life flowed from her..."

I squirm in my seat, his deep voice husky and filled with the same passion the characters feel in the moment. I can't concentrate another second on his reading. The pressure of squeezing my legs together does nothing for the ache growing in my middle.

So I do the only thing I can think of. I take Leo's advice. I uncross my legs, slowly and quietly, grabbing Jonah's full attention as I flash him my pussy.

Jonah clears his throat and pulls at his collar. He clutches the book hard enough to crack the spine. But he remains composed. Still collected and expressionless.

"Heaven. It's the only word that swirled through Blanca's mind," Jonah continues, his eyes only staying on the page of the book for a second.

I slide down lower in my desk, clutching the hem of my skirt. My heart pounds, the cool breeze of the air conditioner chilling my hot skin. I shiver, feeling feverish and achy but not because I'm sick. It's my deep-seated nature as an omega, now silently begging my alpha to give me what I crave.

Drawing my foot in a circle, I spread my legs open again. I bite my cheek, stopping a moan from trying to escape.

I have Jonah's undivided focus now. It's as if the rest of the class no longer exists, though I know they're probably wondering what the hell is wrong with Jonah.

Scratching the back of his neck, he says, "I'm sorry, class. I need to excuse you early today. I have a pack emergency." Jonah sets his book down and messes with his phone.

Lit Dick: You're in so much trouble, Scarlett.

"If I can please speak to Mr. Kane, Ms. O'Brian, and Ms. Carlisle in my office before you leave," Jonah adds. "I'll see the rest of you next class."

Jonah waits by the door until everyone files out, murmuring in small groups. Someone wonders out loud what the hell was up with Jonah, but I can't hear the other student's response. Mr. Kane and Ms. O'Brian stroll beside Jonah, their closeness to him getting to me. I stay behind a couple of feet, each step making it clear that I'm going to be consumed by my intense need to breed. It's even worse than my first time. It's not my fear of uncertainty or if I'll make it through my heat. It's worse because my alpha talks to two betas a few feet away when he should be fucking me senseless.

Fuck. Even my thoughts sound whiny.

What is wrong with me?

"Ms. Carlisle?" Jonah asks, interrupting my moment of self-loathing. "Here's the feedback you requested." Reaching on his desk, he hands me a stack of papers. "Do any of you have anything else you need help with?"

"Actually," I say, stepping forward. My palms sweat as I fold the papers. "If you have a minute—"

Jonah turns to the two betas. "Go on and enjoy the rest of your day. Excellent work."

I bite my lip as Jonah practically throws the two of them out of his office, standing in the frame until they vanish through another door leading back into the main building. I can barely process what's going on, my thoughts refusing to ignore my throbbing clit. The door shuts with a loud click, and I release the most pathetic whimper in existence.

"Fuck, Jonah. Fuck, fuck, fuck," I say, combing my fingers through my hair. "I'm so sorry. I—"

Smashing his mouth to mine, Jonah steals away my apology, sliding his hand under my skirt as if he'll die if he doesn't get to touch my body.

"Do you know how badly I want you? Why do you have to be so damn irresistible?" Jonah groans, sliding his fingers over my slickness. He's talking more to himself, moaning as I shift my body wider for him. "You're forbidden to me, but how can I deny you?"

"You can't," I say, reaching between us to stroke my fingers over the hard bulge pressing against his pants. "Fuck me. I need you to fuck me. It's all I want. Claim me like you'll never get me again."

Grabbing my wrist, Jonah yanks me away from him, spinning me around to bend me over his desk. Cool air caresses my body, and I lay flat on the glass top. Tingles rush through me in anticipation. It would be so easy for him. My skirt is short enough that I'm sure he can see my naked body.

And then his hand smacks my ass cheek, the sting of his palm radiating through me, making me cry out in pleasure and pain.

"That's for what you did in class, Scarlett. You know when we're in that room, I'm your professor. You nearly caused me to give the class a show. The way you exposed that hot, perfect pussy...mmm. It's all I can think about.

You're going to lie there and let me taste you. You're going to be a good student from now on, because you were just too damn naughty for me." Jonah stands behind me, massaging his fingers into my hot skin.

It's as if my very being understands what he craves, and I automatically submit instead of rebelling. I can't help it. I just want him to fuck me. I want the one man who has been resisting me. Who has denied himself the bond of an alpha to his omega.

"I'm sorry, Professor. I deserve your punishment. What are you going to do to me? Are you going to spank me again?" I scratch my fingers against the glass, squirming as Jonah presses his palm to my lower back, holding me still.

"You want that, don't you?" He smacks my ass more softly.

"Mmmhmm." I wiggle under his hold. My body throbs for his attention. I feel as if I'll explode if I don't get what I need.

"Too bad. Only good girls get what they want. Now hold still. Be quiet. If you make any noise, I'll stop. You'll have to wait until we get home." His breathy voice tickles my ear as he rests on top of me, pressing me into the desk. He's half playing and half serious. Because he's right. If I do get too loud, somebody could hear. We could get caught. Enough dumbass people already know about our engagement.

"I'll be good. I promise." I shift my ass, pressing it against him. "Please, take care of me. I ache so bad. I want you, Jonah."

All it takes is me saying his name out loud for him to flip me over and pull me up, combing his fingers through my hair as he kisses me passionately, breaking his game of professor and student.

I wrap my arms around him, sliding my tongue in his mouth. He tastes of mint and something sweeter, like he might've had a piece of chocolate before class.

"My beautiful omega. My forbidden love. I can't ever truly deny you, even though I know I should. I don't know what I was even thinking, trying to wait. I don't care anymore. You're more important. I'll take care of you. Forever." Jonah rubs his fingers over my cheeks and down my neck, lowering himself to the floor in front of me. He massages his warm hands into my knees and works his way up my thighs, hiking my skirt as he pulls me to the edge of the desk.

I lean back on my palms, letting him spread my legs wider to rest on his shoulders. The dull cramps in my stomach fade with his slow, sensual touch as he spreads me open with two fingers and kisses my clit, his demeanor turning from hot and passionate to caring and attentive like he knows it's what I need from him in this moment.

I gasp and bite the inside of my lip, closing my eyes as the pressure of his mouth builds, his tongue tracing my body as if he can kiss the ache away. As if he can kiss away my need.

"Jonah," I whisper, curling forward to run my fingers through his hair. "You're so good to me."

"I can't stand waiting any longer." Jonah groans between my legs, shooting pleasure to my core.

"Then don't. I need you now. Not in a couple of weeks. Your hesitation…" I swallow my words, my breath panting. It's unfair to pressure him. I knew he wanted to wait until I was out of his class, but I feel as if I'll shatter without him. My desire steals away my sense of reason. It denies me the ability to be patient.

"Scarlett, you're cracking my resolve. I've been a bad alpha. I should've never put my career first. You're my everything." Jonah kisses up my pelvis, abandoning the spot I need his attention most. "My beauty, this moment should've been better. More romantic. It—"

I cup his cheeks, dragging him to me. "I don't care about any of that. Just fuck me."

A growl vibrates against my lips, Jonah's alpha nature taking control. My nipples tighten, my lust fogging my mind. His mossy, jasmine scent envelops me, mingling with my own cherry-vanilla. Our passion will linger in his office for days. I hope it lingers even longer in our minds and bodies. In our very souls.

Jonah grabs my shirt and yanks it over my head. I latch my fingers to his pants, unbuckling them as he shrugs out of his suit jacket, ripping the buttons of his dress shirt in a rush to beat me. I giggle and lace my hand around his cock, my body singing with excitement. He's so sexy. Even more so than I imagined. I trace my finger down his shaft to his balls, exploring him as he kicks out of his shoes and pants, undressing completely while leaving me in my plaid skirt.

"The way you look at me, Scarlett... I've never felt like this. I wasn't sure if you could ever find me as attractive as I'd hoped, but damn. You look ready to devour me, my beauty. My heart." Jonah bows down, kissing me softly, sensually. "My love for you grows with every passing second."

"Never doubt what you mean to me, Jonah. You're my sexy alpha. You get to me in ways no one can. Now let me get to you. Make love to me. Claim me." I slide my hands over his hips, guiding them across his hard ass, his body better looking than any beta I've ever seen. And his scent? My mouth waters. Just his closeness helps ease the ache trying to steal my breath.

"I love you," he repeats, shifting closer as he aligns his body to mine. "You're mine. Mine to have and to hold. Mine to protect and cherish. Mine to teach and to guide. Mine to build a family with. Mine to adore and appreciate forever."

I whimper, my mouth trembling, his slow movements driving me absolutely insane. I try to pull him into me, but he resists, teasing me with his tip. I bite my lip to stop myself from moaning, from crying out that I need him to hurry. Instead, I remain fidgeting and wriggling on his desk, watching his cock stretch me wider.

"Jonah, please. Please. I need you. I need your knot." My pleas come as a whisper, and I scratch my nails into his skin, sliding to the edge of the desk until he pushes me back to stop me from jumping on top of him to fuck him how I want.

"Don't worry, my beauty. Let me just savor you for a moment longer. Your beautiful body is a work of art, and the sound of your pleasure is poetry to my ears. I will enjoy you. I will play you like a melody until you come." Jonah rubs his thumb over my clit, bending my knees to spread my body even wider. I let go of his sides and rest back on my palms, my body begging for more.

"Harder," I plead, reaching down to cover his hand with mine, using my strength to increase his pressure. "I ache. Make it stop."

Jonah strums my clit in even strokes, increasing the pressure while he watches my expression. Sliding in an inch deeper, he awakens my body even more, and my slick drips onto his desk. How he can resist me, only teasing me, is beyond my comprehension. If I had my way, he'd be on the floor as I rode him until I was weak in the knees.

"Come for me. Come for me, and I'll give you what you desire. You have to come first. On your own." Jonah groans under his breath, rocking his hips a little faster without sinking into me completely.

I don't take my eyes off our body connecting, the act imprinting in my mind to hold onto forever. He thinks my body is a work of art, but together, we are a masterpiece. One of the most breathtaking sights I've ever seen.

Heat blooms between my legs, my orgasm rising, the sensation stiffening my muscles. I arch my back, squirming at the intensity. It's almost here. I feel as if I'm about to detonate.

Tightening his fingers on my knees, Jonah thrusts inside me, covering my mouth with his hand, silencing my scream. I bite his palm, unable to control the wave of pure bliss crashing through me in electric waves. My back hits the glass desktop, the cool sensation making me gasp. Jonah stretches my legs up, holding them against his chest as he braces me, swinging his body with enough friction to lengthen my orgasm. I gasp in quick pants, unable to catch my breath. He growls deep in his throat, tightening his jaw, his lovemaking turning into furious passion that I can feel deep in my cells. In my soul.

Pressure builds between my legs, and Jonah spreads me open again, sinking in as far as he can, his knot locking us in place. I cry out but cover my mouth with my hand, trying my best to be quiet, but it seems impossible. Jonah slides me back, climbing on top of me, sending papers scattering. He lies on me, adjusting my legs to hook around him, and he kisses me deeply, the intensity of his knot making me come again as he fills me with his seed. His body claims me, easing the ache between my legs. This is only the start of my heat, and I know it's just going to grow more intense. I'm going to need more. The only thing that helps is the sensation of him on top of me, giving my body what it wants with his orgasm.

His passion pushes my thoughts away, and I lose myself to the pleasure. To the ache and the pain of my stretching muscles. I lose myself to everything Jonah is and everything he wants to be for me.

He doesn't stop kissing me, stealing my breath, until his knot releases and the pressure fades, but the memory of the pleasure lingers. He holds me in his arms, picking me up so that I sit on his lap, our bodies still together as if he doesn't want to let me go.

I don't want him to let me go.

"More," I whisper, bouncing slightly, awakening his body again. "Please, I need more."

Jonah cups my face and looks into my eyes. "Let me take you home. Our pack will take care of you."

I swallow and bob my head, my mouth still trembling. "It's all I want."

Jonah carries me to his small bathroom, preparing to clean me up. "I know, my beauty. We are going to help you through this. You are ours. Ours."

I puff out a breath, shivering. "And you're all mine."

24

Jonah

Irresistible

Adrian: Don't come home yet. There's been a threat to all faculty members. We believe it's Chaz messing with us, but we must ensure everything is safe.

Me: What am I supposed to do? Scarlett is in the first hour of her heat.

Adrian: Head to the Marina Hotel. I'll be there as soon as I can. I'm meeting with Dean Clearwater and the police. We hope to have it handled swiftly.

Scarlett moans from the passenger's seat, sitting up to look out the windshield. "What's wrong? Why have we stopped?"

I inhale a long breath, a part of me wanting to keep all this a secret. Scarlett doesn't need this kind of stress right now. What she needs is a hot meal, a warm bath, and to let us all take care of her.

I nearly ignored Adrian's message on the way back to the manor, but a line of police cars flew past me, and I got stuck at a traffic light leaving campus.

Scarlett purses her lips, messing with her bag. "Jonah? What's wrong?" she asks again, her voice rising.

I force my mouth to smile. "Adrian booked us a suite at the Marina Hotel. He thinks—"

"I want to go home. I'm uncomfortable. My muscles ache. I need my room. My stuff." Scarlett pouts out her bottom lip, her emotions from being in heat cresting over me in a hot wave.

Clenching my jaw, I command my hands to remain glued to the wheel, though I want to smack it in frustration. Not at Scarlett, but at everything. "I know, my beauty. I'm so sorry." Keeping an omega from her nest during her heat leaves her feeling vulnerable. I hate this. "We'll go home soon, but right now, we can't."

"Can't?" Scarlett sucks a breath between her teeth. "What happened?"

"I don't have all the details. It's just not safe to go back to the manor right now. I know it's pointless to tell you not to worry, so let me do my best to take care of you. The others will come shortly." I squeeze her hand, driving toward the marina. I hope that the breathtaking view of the Pacific Ocean is enough to distract Scarlett from what are undoubtedly dark thoughts. None of us need this right now. The threat to the alphas on the football team should've been enough. Chaz shouldn't have this sort of control. He is a nobody. A denounced alpha with a temper. His uncle promised as much. There's a reason he's going to Clearwater University instead of following his family's path. He has been denied power and opportunity because of his shortcomings.

That's why he's bitter.

I just hope his threats are now enough to take action. Because if they aren't, we'll have to handle him our own way.

I stroke my fingers on Scarlett's leg, listening to her groan. She shifts in the seat, messing with the air conditioning vents, and then she opens the window and sticks her head out. The salty sea air floods my Volvo, and I stretch my arm, squeezing her thigh, trying to comfort her.

She moans so incredibly loud that I swerve. My balls tighten, the noise indescribably sexy that I stomp the throttle and run through a stop sign, not even caring about getting a ticket or breaking the law.

It's as if her body screams at me to hurry up. All I can think about is how incredible her pussy tasted when we were in my office. How mind-blowing she felt, her body clutching my cock as I knotted with her. I growl deep in my throat and turn into the parking lot of the Marina Hotel. I blindly glide my fingers higher up Scarlett's skirt, feeling her slick drenching her skin.

"Ouch," she says, arching forward. "Damn it. Jonah, I need you."

Her soft voice kicks me into action, and I park away from the building, under a tree. I barely have a chance to unbuckle my seatbelt and push the seat all the way back before Scarlett's on top of me.

Leaning in, Scarlett tilts her head, kissing me so desperately I'm sure I'll have bruised lips for days. Electricity courses through me, igniting such a fierce passion that I slide my fingers against her scalp, deepening our kiss in a battle for control.

A soft whimpering purr meets my moan, her need all-consuming. Her hands roam over my thighs, rubbing the length of my cock as she unzips my trousers. I recline my seat completely, giving her better space to do as she pleases. She bows down and kisses me again, rolling her hips. She grinds against me, knocking all hesitation about fucking her in this parking lot from my mind. She craves me. Needs me. Acts as if she can't live without me even though I'm the one who can't live without her ever again.

"I want you inside me," she murmurs against my mouth, sucking my bottom lip between her teeth.

I growl and hike up the skirt, spying her damp thighs. She's so sexy, groomed short but still natural like I prefer. It'll guarantee I linger on her, marking her as mine.

"I shouldn't claim you again just yet, my beauty. My forbidden omega. We can make it to the room. Let me taste you to hold you over." If she takes my knot now, I'll never leave the car with her. I'll fuck her again and again.

Do I care that my pack mates will meet us soon? Not a single damn bit anymore.

"No. It's not enough." Scarlett reaches between us, pulling my cock free. "I need you now. I ache too badly."

"And I'll kiss you better," I growl, sliding my hands lower on her body.

I lock my fingers around her knees and drag her up my body, her slick hot as she soaks my half-buttoned dress shirt, her desire irresistible. She gasps and tenses, but she doesn't stop me. She braces on the seat, moaning as I draw my tongue over her clit, dying for another taste of her as much as I throb to knot with her tight pussy. I haven't felt so alive in what feels like forever, my reserve shattering with the sound of her pleasure, how her thighs tighten around my head, smothering me as she squirms until she screams out with her orgasm.

I kick my shoes to the dashboard, using my strength to shift us to the backseat. I nudge Scarlett to her back, my muscles rippling as she strokes my cock, her cool fingers shocking me with the sensation in the best way.

"You're in so much trouble. I'll never get enough of you. I want more than to claim you in the backseat of a car or my office. We can—" I snap my mouth shut as Scarlett guides my tip inside her, stopping me from my half-hearted attempt at persuading her otherwise.

She wants this. She wants me as I am in this moment. I could never deny her now.

"Spank me if you have to. I'm not waiting." Her breathy voice wraps around me, seducing me with the fragrance of her desire.

I sink deeper into her, her pussy drowning me with the slippery heat of her body. I moan, tempering my thrusts, even if all she wants is to fuck her hard and fast. "Then I'll take my time again. You're so tight. Hot. Mine."

A groan purrs through her lips, her unashamed desire conquering any shyness she had toward me when we first met. I devour how she yearns to explore everything I have to offer. The way she captures my gaze and slides her hand to the back of my neck. Pulling me closer gives me the bravado I need to throw my hesitation away. Nothing matters in this moment except for her and me together, familiarizing ourselves with our raw nature, knowing everything else will fall in place. The attraction is undeniable. Unavoidable. How I resisted her this whole semester is beyond me. I'll never resist her again.

"Does that feel good, my beautiful omega? My soon-to-be wife. My mate." I kiss her again, stealing her breath as I thrust inside her, moaning at the incredible sensation of her body welcoming mine.

"Mmmhmm." She scratches her nails into my back, pulling my shirt up to feel the warmth of my skin against her. Is it romantic fucking her in the backseat of the car, half-dressed, with the risk of getting caught? Fuck no. Is it exciting and hot? God, I can already feel my body on the verge of coming.

"You're so beautiful. So stunning. Tell me how much you want my knot." I thrust evenly, staring into her heavy-lidded eyes, her mouth pouting with each breath.

"I want it so—" Scarlett sucks in a deep breath, her eyes widening with a raspy scream of pleasure.

Her body squeezes my cock, my knot engorging and locking her to me. I grunt and close my eyes, my seed filling her how her body craves.

"Oh, God. Fuck. Fuck." Scarlett's whine digs into me as hard as her nails. "I'm going to explode. Fuck. It feels so good." She trembles beneath me, her body pulsing and orgasming with mine. I've waited my whole life to bond with my omega in this way.

"You're mine," I repeat, capturing her lips with mine. "This is only the beginning of our amazing life. Just give in to whatever you're feeling. I'm yours."

Scarlett breaks from my mouth, locking her legs tighter around my waist, squirming and arching her back like she resists truly giving in to the pleasure. Her mouth finds my neck and she nips my skin, releasing my pheromones even more.

The windows steam with our passion, the tint blocking the view of any people passing by. I could stay in this moment forever, listening to Scarlett moan and how sexy my whispered name sounds on her lips.

I stroke her cheek, kissing her and nuzzling my nose to hers until I finish, my knot releasing us despite my desire to stay together.

Scarlett pants with her heavy breathing, remaining on the seat as I slide out of her, taking a peek at how sexy she looks soaking wet with my seed and scent, everything that makes her mine beyond the societal expectations we ignore.

"We need to hurry. I feel like I'm going crazy. The need is so intense. Will you take me inside?" Scarlett asks softly, her cheeks tinted with her blush. "Fuck, people will know—"

I silence her doubt with my finger, leaning in to kiss her. "The only thing they'll know is how madly in love I am with you. Adrian arranged everything. The code is on my phone."

"So you can fuck me on the elevator?" Her salacious confidence returns, lighting her eyes like a bright sliver of the sun breaking through storm clouds, and she strokes me again, biting her lip, completely and unashamedly ready to go at it again.

If a car horn didn't blare from the street, I might've given in. I stretch up, peering through the steamy window at the parking lot. An old Ford Ranger pulls in behind me and blares the horn again. My chest tightens at the sight of Chaz.

"Scarlett, you fucking whore! Get out of the car. Now." Chaz's voice bellows through the air.

Scarlett gasps, her gray eyes widening. "What the fuck? How did he find us?"

I adjust my pants and reach for my phone. My best guess is that he's been tracking us. He's not an idiot, after all. He's a psycho with a death wish. "Stay down. I don't trust that he won't do something."

"Scarlett! Last chance! I'm tired of waiting for your fucking pack to get their shit together." Chaz pulls out a baseball bat.

The son of a bitch.

He swings and smashes the back window, shattering the glass. Scarlett screams, scrambling onto the floor between the seats. I growl and release the seat, reaching into the trunk. I pull a heavy metal flashlight from my emergency kit and fling the door open. He's not going to fucking intimate me.

"Jonah, stop!" Scarlett cries, reaching out to me.

"Stay here. Lock the doors." I slam the door shut without waiting for her to respond.

Chaz swings the bat again, denting my trunk. "Oh, look at you, professor. You really think you're a match for me? Give me my omega. Hand her to me, and you can go back to your pathetic life."

"Fuck off! She's mine!" I rush Chaz, ducking as he swings the bat over my head.

I smash my flashlight into his knee, dropping him to the ground. He hollers in pain, his bravado and cockiness getting to his head. He has a lot of fucking nerve.

I growl, glowering at the pathetic piece of shit. He rolls over, pushing to his feet. I swing the flashlight again, missing him on purpose. I want so badly to beat him senseless. I want to ensure he never fucking dares look at Scarlett again, but I can't have his blood on my hands. I don't have the resources to get out of a murder charge. It's the only thing that stops me.

"Jonah, he's not worth it. Please get me out of here," Scarlett cries, peeking through the open window as she sits behind the wheel. "I hurt so bad."

My insides twist at her pain. "I'm so sorry. We'll go. I just need to call—"

Scarlett's eyes widen. "Jonah!"

I spin, catching sight of Chaz. He wasn't running away in defeat. He was running to get a knife. Jerking my arms, I swing the flashlight, getting him to hop back out of my way. He jabs the blade, his eyes narrow. Baring his teeth, he growls and tries charging me. I dodge out of the way, and he rushes toward the driver's side door of my Volvo. Scarlett screeches and starts the engine, putting it in reverse.

Chaz smacks his hands to the window. "You slut!"

Clenching my jaw, I attempt to swing the flashlight again, but Chaz catches my reflection in my tinted window. I hit the roof of my Volvo, opening myself up. He rams into my gut, knocking me off my feet. The flashlight rolls out of my reach.

Shit. Shit. Shit.

Chaz latches his fingers around my neck, aiming the blade at my throat. "Fucking back down. I'll make sure you don't fucking breed ever. I mean it! She doesn't belong to you anymore. You've lost your fucking—"

Scarlett screams and swings the flashlight against Chaz's head. Blood peppers my face, and I stare at my beautiful savior for only a second. Shoving my hands into Chaz's chest, I push him off. His eyes roll to the back of his head, Scarlett's strength knocking him unconscious.

"Jonah, fuck. Fuck! Let me see you." Scarlett pats her hands over my chest and neck, working her way up to my cheeks. "Did he hurt you?"

I huff out a ragged breath, my heart crashing around my chest. "I'm okay. Come on. We need to get out of here. We'll call a car. I'm not going to risk him following us. There's probably a tracker or some shit."

I push to my feet, grabbing Scarlett's hand. Chaz remains slumped on the ground, his knife near his hand. I kick it as hard as I can, sending it into the bushes lining the parking lot. I'm not letting him take the fucking evidence. I just hope the pack authority can get here soon enough to see him.

Scarlett jogs to keep up with me, and I guide her around the vast property of the Marina Hotel and to the pathway that will take us to the harbor. All I can think about is getting away. Getting space between that monster and my beautiful woman.

We don't stop until we reach a long drive that travels around the harbor, the shops busy and full of life. I find a table outside a small food stand, and I slump into it. I pull Scarlett onto my lap, knowing that she's probably going crazy. I know I am. It takes everything in me not to return to the hotel to find and finish Chaz. Scarlett should've never been put in this position. She should've never been the one to have to save my ass.

But I'm so damn proud of her.

Me: Where are you? We have a huge problem.

Adrian: We're heading toward the marina now.

Me: You need to call a car instead. Chaz showed up. I think the fucker put tracking devices on our vehicles.

Adrian: Are you okay? What about Scarlett?

Me: We're a bit shaken, and Scarlett is most definitely in heat now. We need to find somewhere to hide out. Chaz said some concerning things.

Adrian: Ezra's arranging things now. We'll pick you up shortly. Just hold on as best as you can. Tell Scarlett we are coming.

Scarlett reads the text messages and releases the quietest of whimpers, resting her head against me. I know she feels sick, and her hormones are out of control. She's doing her best to remain calm, but I know she's close to her breaking point. I'll do whatever it takes to ensure she doesn't shatter.

I hug her close. "It'll only take them ten minutes tops."

She rubs her legs together, digging her fingers into my thigh. "I can't believe this is happening. What have I done to deserve this? Why is he trying to ruin our lives?"

My heart aches for her. I wish I had answers, but all I can do is hug her tighter and kiss her hair. Because I'm wondering the same thing.

I can't shake this nagging feeling. Chaz said some things that I don't understand. And we need to figure it out. Soon.

But Scarlett comes first. I will not allow this to ruin what should be days of passion and love. Of bliss.

I don't want her to even think about the world outside of us. I just have to get her somewhere safe. To prove that I'm a worthy alpha.

I will ensure Scarlett doesn't have to face Chaz again.

I just hope I can follow through.

Scarlett deserves the world and pure happiness. And looking at my beautiful omega, feeling her closeness and sensing her body calling to mine, I know I deserve the same.

We deserve a perfect life together.

Scarlett

BONDING MOMENT

"You need to eat something, amore." Ezra kneels on the floor outside of the small empty closet of our temporary apartment. "Leo said you haven't eaten since you left this morning."

I clutch the feather pillow to my chest, trying not to think about the fact that he's offering me something to eat in this moment.

I moan and reach down, petting my fingers through Jonah's hair. "I'm not hungry. I just...come join us. I'm so fucking horny."

"Amore, I don't think I can fit." Ezra stretches forward and caresses his knuckles to my cheek.

"That's not what she said," Jonah mutters against my apex.

I gasp a laugh, moaning as he returns to sucking and rolling his tongue across my clit, the act pacifying both of us in the heat of the moment. Jonah hasn't left my side for even a moment, carrying me to the bathroom when I need to go, cleaning me off when I'm there, and returning me back to the place I chose, not letting the pain of my heat return.

"Amore, I promise if you let me feed you, it'll be worth it. Jonah would never admit it, but he could use something to eat, too. Don't unintentionally deny us the satisfaction of being with you. It's so easy to get lost in the moment until it's gone." Ezra closes the space, kissing me softly. "Plus, Leo is about to snatch you out of here and pin you to the bed."

I squeeze Jonah between my thighs at the thought. "He can—"

Leo growls from outside the closet, locks his hands to Ezra's sides and drags him away. Everything happens so fast that I can't even release a whimper at losing the pleasure of Jonah's mouth before my back hits the bed. Climbing on top of me, Leo slides his hand behind my head and into my hair, bowing close.

"Listen, dirty girl. You've been coddled enough. You're going to be good and allow us all the honor of taking care of you. Do you understand?" Growling against my lips, Leo inhales a breath, keeping an inch of space between us.

I huff and squirm, feeling the length of his arousal against my leg. "Give me your fucking knot. That's the only way I'll be good for you."

The bed shifts as Adrian appears in my line of sight. The intensity of lust pouring from all my alphas circling around me sets me off in an unexpected way. It's as if I'm their sexy little prey to be devoured. I purr and grab Adrian's hip, clawing my nails into him.

"Teach me how to be good for him," I murmur, my desire fogging my mind. "For all of you. Claim me as you please. Show me what you need." Where this sudden audacity and demand comes from? Well, the ache inside me. The deep-seated need to breed with my alphas. To show the world that they're mine and no one else will ever mistake otherwise.

"Come here, Scarlett. You can lay on top of me. I'll hold you how you need for Leo," Adrian says, hooking his arm around me.

"Nice and still. I'm going to fuck you and fill you with my seed, dirty girl. We won't stop until you're knocked the fuck up, and no one will try to mess with us again. You're our omega. Our beautiful, horny omega." Leo locks his hand to my ankle, hoisting me up. He smacks my ass, sending hot tingles through my body. "Isn't that right?"

Dominic steals my attention, kneeling so close that I can reach out and grab his cock. I do, stroking my fingers over him, getting him to moan for me. He pinches my nipple, making me arch. "Unless I knock her up. Because I'm next."

Talk about teamwork.

We never discussed my heat in detail, but we all knew we'd want to start a family immediately. It's been an innate desire I've dreamed about. Not because it is my duty, either. I felt so lost after my first heat, knowing that nothing would come out of it, and it hurt me on a soul level. I've desired children for my short adult life. I wanted to do better than my parents. I wanted more than the incentives or obligations. I wanted—and still want—the freedom of raising a pack against societal norms. I want this moment, this act, to be one that changes everything.

Some of my sisters don't want to bring life to the future because of our obligations. I want to as a way of breaking the cycle. I know I can do it. My alphas and I can make waves, starting here and now with our love and loyalty. With our unending devotion to each other, built on sensibility and not power.

"Nice and wet. God, you're soaking." Leo ignites pleasure between my legs, banishing my thoughts of everything apart from him.

"Let me see," Ezra says, kneeling beside him.

I tip my head back and moan, the sensation of Ezra pushing inside me like ecstasy. The two of them take turns, slipping inside me, teasing me and working me up. Adrian tightens his hold on me, spreading my legs open. He pushes his tip against my ass, my slick dripping, inviting him to enter me from behind. That's all I want now. I want them to fill me up. To stuff me in a way that leaves me breathless and feeling so perfect. Feeling as if I'm everything to them.

I part my lips with another moan, reaching out and pulling Dominic's cock to my mouth. I lick my tongue over his balls and across the bottom of his shaft, setting him off. He holds my head up, resting my chin on my chest, and he slides his cock deeper into my mouth, his length touching the back of my throat.

"She wants all of us, don't you, dirty girl," Leo says, thrusting into me. "If you tell us, we'll give you what you want."

I hum my agreement, the vibration sending Dominic's hand tugging my hair. I ease back enough to say, "Just fuck me. Fuck me until you're all I can think about. All I can smell. All I can feel. Just fuck me. Fill me with your seed. Let me be your good omega. Let me be everything of your dreams."

"You already are, my beauty," Jonah says, sitting beside me. He touches my cheek and draws his finger to my nipples, giving each of them attention.

I squirm, opening my mouth again, tasting Dominic in a way I crave. Adrian lifts me up slightly, and I feel the pressure of his cock enter my ass. He moans in my ear, his pleasure battling against mine, and then Leo slides inside me as Ezra holds my hips. Kneeling in a way that he can join Leo as he fucks me, feeling the sensation of their bodies together, stretching me in a way that makes me whimper, but it feels incredible.

Jonah touches my clit, stroking his fingers over my hot body, wetting his hand. He strokes his cock until I blindly reach for him, gliding my fingers over his length.

Dominic moans, rocking his hips, taking control of my head. I scream through the wave of pleasure, the five of them using my body to satiate their desires while also feeding mine.

Ezra pulls out and bows forward, gliding his tongue over my clit at the same time Leo grunts and knots with me. He bounces me back and forth, controlling the motion of my body as Adrian slides in and out of my ass, the both of us at the mercy of his movements, how I bounce on his knot, locking me to him as he fills me with cum, our orgasms in sync. I relax my body and just lose myself in everything they are.

Dominic comes in my mouth, his taste tangy with a hint of sweetness, and he whispers his love for me. He mumbles his desire and how he can't wait for his turn.

I gasp, screaming in ecstasy, and Jonah slides his cock into my mouth next, silencing me while stroking his fingers through my hair. The pressure in my pussy releases only to have Ezra take Leo's place, working in sexy tandem, knowing exactly how to keep the ache of my heat away.

Adrian tenses beneath me, and I moan at the sensation of his nails scratching my skin as he comes in my ass. Ezra rolls with me, holding me with our chests touching as he knots in place, not letting Jonah slide into my mouth just yet. He kisses me softly, and Dominic smacks my ass, straddling both mine and Ezra's legs as he slides inside me, getting his fill and giving Adrian a chance to clean off.

"Open your mouth, my beauty. Ease my need as I wait again," Jonah murmurs, tipping my head up as he kneels next to me and Ezra, using my mouth as a vessel of his pleasure.

"She's so fucking sexy. Look at how deep she takes you." Leo watches, stroking himself, his body ready and waiting his turn to have at me again.

I never expected such a moment, none of them fighting for their spot, sharing me equally and managing to continue to love up on me in ways to make me feel as if I'm not just here to mate and breed. I'm so much more.

And they're so much more to me.

The intensity of my orgasm steals my breath, making it impossible to do anything except for scream in bursts, listening as Adrian returns to swap places the moment Ezra releases me, my body so wet and dripping, my heart full of everything they elicit from this moment.

Hours pass, the five of them ensuring that my pleasure doesn't stop. They'll ravish me for the days my body demands. They ensure I get what I want and what I crave, their bodies my path to pleasure, and I savor their attention. I savor how well they take care of me, ensuring that I never starve of their affection. Their love.

"You're doing so good, Scarlett. You need to eat. Here, let me help you." I sit up, Jonah beneath me, his knot locking me to him as Ezra guides his finger along my mouth, getting me to open up. I taste the sweetness of fruit, the smoothie filling my mouth, and I swallow, loving that even through the pleasure, they ensure I'm safe and tended to on every level.

Leo massages my legs and calves, keeping my muscles from cramping. Dominic cleans off my body, using a warm washcloth and water, helping me from crashing.

"She's so incredible. So strong. Our beautiful soon-to-be wife. Our omega. I can't wait to see your belly swell with our family." Adrian touches my cheek, leaning in to kiss me. "Tell me if there's anything you need. I'll be your good boy."

I roll my neck, my heart beating, my body so relaxed and my soul humming in anticipation. "I want to see you on your knees."

Adrian play-growls. "Is that so?"

"I want to hear you moan. I want to see you be claimed on my behalf. I want to share you the way you share me." I lick my lips, my desire igniting again, pushing away the exhaustion threatening to leave me a puddle.

"Damn, dirty girl." Leo kisses my throat, stroking his cock. "Do you want me to make him a good little omega for you?"

"Mmmhmm. Fuck him how you like to fuck me." I moan and stroke my fingers over my clit, looking at Dominic and Ezra, their attention still drawn to me, their bodies hard and ready. "Fuck him and make him watch me get claimed. It's what you want, right, my good alpha? "

Jonah growls and sinks his teeth into my shoulder. "Keep talking like that, Scarlett. I like seeing you boss him around."

"I'll gladly participate. You want my knot again, don't you, amore?" Ezra shifts me on Jonah, watching him release me. "He can have your ass now. Your pussy is mine."

"For now. She's mine next. I'm going to give her what she wants, and then I'm taking what I need." Adrian kneels on all fours in front of me, wiggling his ass.

"Make him come, Leo. I don't think I'll come until he does," I murmur, moaning and resting against Jonah as he slides into my ass, his body still hard and ready.

Dominic stands beside me, reaching for my hand. I caress my fingers over his length, licking his tip keeping my eyes locked on Leo as he strokes his cock and winks at me, claiming Adrian in a way that sets me off. It's so fucking hot watching him slide his cock into his ass. I wish it was me. I wish I were the one with my strap-on, making Adrian moan. I wish I were the one bending in front of Leo, feeling the pressure his cock does when he stretches my body.

"You're so fucking hot. You're such a good alpha," I whisper, my breath huffing. I know they like when I talk like this. Leo always encourages it, especially when it comes to our leader, a man who is in control of our pack who also needs time to decompress. He needs time to let someone else handle things, and I feel so incredibly blessed that he trusts me to help him, even with Leo, who gives in to whatever I want.

Adrian crawls closer, Leo bumping his hips to his ass, riding him until he's within reach for me to touch. I grab Adrian and get him close enough that I can stroke his cock.

"Come for me," I say, bouncing on Jonah, making Ezra bend to the side as we tangle ourselves into a cuddle pile. I stretch over Ezra's body, rubbing my hand over Adrian's tip as he bows slightly as Leo fucks him.

With a grunt, Adrian comes, his seed spilling across my face. I moan and lick my lips, my whole body tingling with another wave, the endless pleasure gripping my soul.

"You're so incredible to me. All of you," I moan, my body slackening, my heat beginning to ease up where I no longer whimper and ache between them as they take turns. I can't even fathom how much time has passed. Hours. Over a day.

"You're our omega, Scarlett. We'll do anything for you. We're a pack and family," Adrian says, stretching over Ezra, our bodies locked together. He strokes my cheeks, leaving his scent permeating the air. I can smell the lust of my alphas mingling together. And it smells like hope and love. Like passion and promise.

It smells like home.

It doesn't matter where we are or what's happening outside of our bonding moment together. The only thing that matters is each other.

I'll cherish this moment forever.

Just as my alphas cherish me.

26

Scarlett

summons

"You've been summoned to stand before Pack Carlisle," Adrian says, staring at the letter with the Pack Carlisle crest that was taped to the apartment door.

My alphas have taken a leave of absence for the last two weeks, waiting for news on Chaz's whereabouts. The five of them have been working remotely, leading lectures with a couple of student-teachers, arranged by Dean Clearwater.

I tilt my head, frowning. "What for? They're not my pack anymore."

Adrian tears the paper off and crumples it in his fist. "I'll remind them as much. We've gone above and beyond for Pack Steele. I'll call the mayor immediately. He wouldn't want to jeopardize ties with us. Not with the expansion."

Because he got the contract for the university. I don't know much about it, but it will bring a lot of jobs and opportunity to San Francisco.

"Go ahead and go to Dominic. He's going to take you to the studio for a bit before we have dinner with Talia and a couple of potential clients who are dying for a moment with you." Adrian opens the door to the apartment, motioning me inside. I've been so excited to meet the new director of the Art Department. If only a shadow didn't cling to me with my nerves. "I don't want you to worry about Pack Carlisle and whatever business they have. Let's focus on you. You make me so proud, by the way. My talented fiancée."

He kisses the top of my head, and I smile and kiss his throat, squeezing him as he guides me inside. I know everything outside of this apartment has been tense and worrisome, but I try my best not to let it bother me. There's only so much we can do. The authorities, including Chaz's pack, know what a psycho he's been. He's a fugitive, and we're just waiting for him to fuck up.

I have a restraining order in place, and if he breaks it, Pack Clearwater law says that I have every right to do whatever is necessary to protect myself. I'm a claimed omega, and they will not jeopardize my life.

Everyone knows that it's possible I could be pregnant. His bullshit won't go unpunished. There's far too much evidence against him.

The university basically is turning a blind eye now, because it's almost the end of the semester, and then I only have one more to go. We're now following a don't ask, don't tell policy. Dean Clearwater ensured my alphas' positions. It's my degree and future job at stake. As long as I pass all my classes, keep under the radar as I have been by continuing to use suppressant lotion, and not get caught fucking anyone on campus, everything will be fine.

I'm just lucky that Dean Clearwater wasn't willing to risk the money Adrian brings through his position as a financial advisor and the one in charge of expansion. Had it been anyone else, we'd have had to find other leverage. And my guys just aren't those types of people. They aren't criminals or crooked. Not like some of the heads of Clearwater.

"Lettie, I didn't think Adrian was ever bringing you home. How was your lunch date and shopping? Did you find anything nice?" Dominic sits at his desk, grading the math test distributed by one of the aides in his classes.

I hold up my shopping bag and shake it. "Just a few things. Mostly some undergarments, considering how many have been destroyed."

He chuckles and rolls back in his chair, getting to his feet. "There is an easier solution."

I laugh and hold my arms up, waiting for him to step into them so I can hook them around his neck and pull him closer for a kiss. "I have to make you guys work just a little bit, don't I?"

He groans and kisses me. "You wouldn't wear anything at all if I had my way. Especially with that masterpiece constantly teasing me." He motions toward our strangely beautiful ceramic slab, my body silhouette glazed over in shades of red as an ode to my name.

My phone chirps, drawing my attention from the ceramic piece deemed Scarlett's Claiming, and I reach into my pocket and pull out my cell.

Hardass: I know you don't want to talk to Mom, but she's on a rampage, demanding we find your number.

Me: Please don't give it.

Princess: She's trying to steal our phones.

Mother Hen: Make sure none of you have her contact listed under her name.

Hardass: Aww, you remembered my advice.

Me: I'll text her from our burner phone. Thanks for giving me a warning.

Hardass: Anything for my sister.

Cyan sends a couple of black heart emojis, and I show Dominic the string of text messages about my mom. I was hoping she'd give up on her bitchiness. It's been nice not having to worry about her texting me since we all got rid of our phones and got new ones in case Chaz was tracking us that way.

"I'm sure she just wants to ask us for more money or something," I say, playing with my hair. "It probably drives her crazy that she doesn't have direct contact with me now that she's been cut off."

Dominic rubs his lips together, not responding right away. He stares at my phone and the conversation with my sisters for another moment. "I hope it's only that. You know we've been a bit disturbed by Chaz's threats."

Damn. I tried pushing those thoughts from my mind. I don't want to think about how he tried to assault Jonah with a baseball bat. How he'd have probably run us over or killed him if he had the chance. The amazingness of having my alphas support me through my second heat had suppressed all of the bad shit. I was hoping it could stay forgotten forever.

"I'm sorry, Lettie. I didn't mean to upset you," Dominic adds, rubbing his fingers on my cheek.

I blink my burning eyes, not realizing that a tear spilled on my face. I can't help the cresting emotions. It's as if just the mention of my mom shattered the wall I built around myself to protect my mind from her trying to mess with me. She has caused a lot of emotional damage, and I'm only starting to really process and heal from it now.

I blow out a breath and shake my head, getting myself in control. "You didn't upset me. Promise. And you're absolutely right. Chaz is still on the run, and he could try something insane. He has it in his head that I'm supposed to be his or whatever. Fucking stupid."

A knock on the wall startles me, and I whip my attention to look at Adrian standing just outside of Dominic's room.

My heart sinks into my stomach at the sight of him. He runs his fingers through his blonde and silver hair, messing up the strands. It's as if he's aged in the past few minutes, his forehead wrinkling and crow's feet pinching the corners of his blue eyes.

"We need a pack meeting. Immediately." Adrian doesn't explain anything, turning on his feet and striding back toward our small living room.

I grimace, meeting Dominic's gaze, and he shrugs his shoulders and presses his palm to my back, getting me to follow behind Adrian.

I shuffle into the living room, meeting Jonah, Ezra, and Leo's gazes as they all sit together on the couch. I make my way with Dominic to the recliner, and Adrian sits on the coffee table, completing our circle.

He doesn't speak right away, scrubbing his face, his usually well-trimmed beard longer than normal. I wish there was something I could do to help ease the stress. I know he's been keeping things to himself to not worry me.

Obviously, something happened.

I slide off Dominic's lap and onto Adrian's, hugging him closely so he can feel my body and my support. It's enough to get him to release a ragged breath. He snuggles his face against my throat, inhaling and exhaling as he composes himself. Silence fills the room, and I listen to Adrian's rapid heartbeat. I don't think I've ever seen him so frazzled. He's usually stoic when it comes to the world. He only exposes his tender side when we're alone.

"You know you can tell us anything. We're a pack, and if something is wrong, we'll face it together." I graze my knuckles across Adrian's cheek, getting him to meet my eyes.

His blue irises glow against the redness in the whites of his eyes, and I can't help wondering if he had been crying. He never shows such a thing in front of us. A part of me breaks, wishing I could somehow kiss him and make things easier. I don't have that sort of magic, though. Not the way he can do such things for me.

"I know, Scarlett. I'm just...I feel as if I've failed us as a leader. Things have grown more complicated. This was supposed to be the easiest time in our lives. We have worked so hard to earn respect, ensure financial stability, and solidify ties to the most powerful within Pack Clearwater. And it seems that all it takes is one god-awful person to say something negative to send everything crashing down." Adrian closes his eyes, summoning the strength of his pack mates.

My stomach twists as sickness rolls through me. I already have a suspicion about what he's talking about, but I don't know to what extent. This has to do with the summons from Pack Carlisle. He said he was going to make a phone call, and he probably got answers.

"Does this have to do with my mom? My sisters said that she was harassing them. She was even trying to take their phones." My mouth dries, my words sticking on my tongue, my voice hoarse. I hate that all the current problems our pack faces are because of me. I'm the root of all their issues, but they would never blame me. I don't really blame myself either, but it doesn't stop me from feeling bad.

Adrian tips his head up, thinning his lips, and scrunching his brows. He eyes the others in his peripheral vision, but he doesn't take his attention away from me. "Partially, yes. It seems that she is not satisfied with our current arrangements despite everything that we have done. She has gone so far as to go to the leader of Pack Carlisle and accuse us of withholding information. She claims that we didn't immediately disclose the error when we found out your age. She has deemed us unfit to be your pack and has requested that we send you home to be appropriately betrothed to a younger pack."

Leo slams his hands down on the coffee table, shaking it. "Are you fucking kidding me? Scarlett could be pregnant. We have already claimed her. We have paid the dowry, and it was accepted. She can't just twist things around and take her back. She is not a possession. They don't own her. We didn't buy her from them. We paid the dowry to prove that we were serious and nothing more. It's illegal to buy or sell omegas. It even makes it clear in the contract that this isn't anything other than a gift."

Adrian clenches his jaw. "That's exactly what she's betting on. She's claiming that Scarlett is still part of the Steele family since it's illegal to buy an omega. She is using our extra support to twist it around, claiming that we were buying her off, leaving out the fact that it was part of her demands."

Fury explodes through me, and I hiss a breath, my anger powerful enough to turn my vision red. My mom is out of her goddamn mind. She can't do this.

"I'm not going back. I'll call her. She's just trying to mess with me. She's probably upset that we went to my dads." I stand up and hold my hand out to Adrian. "Can

I please use the burner phone? I don't want her having access to me without my permission."

"Scarlett, amore. Let us deal with this. You don't need that kind of stress, especially if you're pregnant." Ezra scoots to the end of the couch, reaching to grab me.

I dodge out of his way. "That's exactly why I need to do this. I need to call her out on her bullshit. We can send it to Pack Carlisle. They shouldn't care about who I end up with as long as I pop out babies. That's their whole thing. Me and my glorious, supposedly fertile uterus. They don't care how it's done as long as it's done. It's why we've been pampered our whole lives."

Jonah growls deep in his throat. "Those fuckers. They don't have that sort of right. That mentality is why things are the way they are."

"Which is why we need to fight. We need to change things." Adrian stands up, reaches into his pocket, and pulls out his phone, handing it to me. "Be careful with your reactions, Scarlett. It's what she wants. She will try to use anything she can against us."

My heart pounds, threatening to explode through my ribcage. Mom always has a way of poking at my emotions, leaving me feeling out of control, but I can do the same to her. I'm my mother's daughter, after all. She has emotionally manipulated me all my life, so much that I recognize it. I can fight it. Mostly, I can use it against her.

I stroll away from the table, needing to move around. My nerves tense my muscles, and I stretch and bounce on my feet. Only Adrian comes to me, the others giving me space. I lick my lips and shake out my hands. This shouldn't be so hard. I know what I must do. I shouldn't be so intimidated by the woman who clearly cares about only herself.

"Like we said, we can handle it, Lettie," Dominic says, his voice deeper than usual.

"I know, but I don't want you to. I can do this." I summon my bravery and tap in Mom's number, turning on the speakerphone for everyone to hear. Ezra pulls out his phone and starts recording to capture the entire conversation.

The line rings and rings until Mom finally connects as if she was waiting for the last possible second.

"Mrs. Steele speaking," she says, her voice sweet.

No hello. No who's this. Just her announcing she's on the other end.

I clear my throat, my palms sweating, making the phone slippery. "Mom—"

"Oh, Scarlett. It's nice of you to have finally reached out to me. I thought I was going to have to travel all the way there. It would've been such an inconvenience, considering that those bad alphas are keeping us apart. I've been informed that you're no longer staying at the Clearwater Manor. Where are they keeping you?" Mom's voice turns from sweet to sharp, her anger remaining in check.

Adrian touches my shoulder. "Take a breath and don't react. Tell her that you are not interested in leaving. Tell her you could be pregnant and that you're happy. Nice and calm," he whispers, his soft breath tickling my ear.

"Scarlett? Is everything okay? Are you in trouble?" Mom continues speaking, not missing a beat. "Do I need to call the Clearwater authorities?"

My whole body trembles with my anger. "No, that isn't necessary. There were some safety concerns about the manor, and we thought it was best to stay somewhere else until it was properly handled. My alphas are taking excellent care of me. I don't know if you know, but I went into heat."

Dead silence greets me, and I check the phone to make sure Mom didn't hang up on me.

"The proper people at the university know our situation and have been more supportive than we expected. I've been offered a job upon graduation, and our wedding date is set. We're all very happy. Just another week, and we will be able to find out if I'm pregnant." My mouth trembles as I try to remain calm. All I want to do is confront her about Pack Carlisle's summons.

Again, Mom doesn't say anything. I hear her intake a low breath, though.

"I hope you're as excited as I am. I'm so grateful you ensured that I stay with the Harts and the exceptional Pack Clearwater. My alphas have a chance to take leadership soon. Aren't you proud of me?" I know I shouldn't push her, but I can't stop the pettiness from coursing through me. I want to rub it in that my life will be better than hers. My alphas are more powerful, and I will not be considered worthy based on my fertility.

"Oh, Scarlett. Has Pack Hart not told you?" Mom groans with her words, faking concern. "It has been agreed upon by Pack Carlisle that they're unfit to be the alphas of you. I have arranged a far superior and more fitting pack. It's still within the Clearwater Territory, so you won't have to be concerned about moving. But I do need you to pack your things. You'll be coming home until everything is official."

My boiling blood cools, and I clutch the phone in my fingers. If I were any stronger, I'd probably break it into pieces.

I squeeze my eyes shut. "Pack my things? I don't understand. I could be pregnant—"

Mom scoffs. "Even if you are, things will be fine. The pack I have chosen for you doesn't care that you're clearly used. They would be happy to care for someone else's child. That's how incredible they are. I'm sure the Harts wouldn't do such a thing. They were probably especially happy that you were the perfect omega. Untouched and desperate."

"Are you fucking kidding me? I'm not leaving. I have my perfect pack. And so you know, I wasn't untouched. You're out of your damn mind if you think that I was going to remain a virgin. Don't twist things to make them seem wrong. I'm an adult. I'm not your precious little omega who you can trade around for more money. Back off or you will regret it." My shoulders shake with my deep breathing, my anxiety through the roof. How dare she think she could do this.

"Don't you threaten me, Scarlett. I'm your mother. I know what's best for you. You're obviously not worthy of calling yourself an adult. You're a spoiled brat who can't see the bigger picture. You won't have as many children with the Harts. You'll be a disappointment to everyone and then alone. Do what is expected. You will be taken care of. Pack Miller has ensured it. They offered so much more than expected. You need to accept this gift and move on with your life." Mom smacks something, the sound reverberating through my bones. "Now pack your things. You will be coming home even if I have to drag you here kicking and screaming."

Her words stun me, and I can't stop thinking about the pack she said she arranged a new proposal with. Pack Miller. That can't be possible. It's a common pack name, but a part of me dies inside of just the name alone.

"Did you say Pack Miller?" I ask, my voice cracking.

"Pack your things, Scarlett. You're coming home," she repeats.

Her call drops, and I stare at the screen in shock and fear. I can't move. I can't breathe. I feel as if I will die at any second.

Warm arms wrap around me, scooping me up. Adrian spins with me, strutting toward the couch. He squishes in between Leo and Jonah, and a moment later, I'm engulfed in the weight of my alphas' bodies as they try to hug away everything negative rolling through me.

"Oh, Scarlett, listen to me," Adrian says, pinching my chin and getting me to meet his gaze. "No one is taking you anywhere. I promise. I'm going to call in some favors tonight. We're eloping immediately."

I blink a few times, trying to comprehend his words.

It's as if my mom stabbed me in the soul, and I stand frozen, bleeding out. It feels as if no one can save me now. Not my alphas. Not Pack Clearwater. Not myself.

All I know is that I'd rather die than leave them. Is it dramatic? Not to me. They are my life, and I am theirs.

"Scarlett, did you hear me?" Adrian asks, getting into my face so he's the only thing I can see. "You're ours. The world will know it."

If only I thought the world would care.

If only I had the same hope as he did.

Right now, I'm hopeless.

All feels lost.

27

Dominic

confrontation

"Paul, come on. How long have we known each other? Do you truly think I'm an idiot? You're the Pack Miller leader. I don't understand why you're doing this. You have a family. You have everything you could want. Why even humor the idea of taking Scarlett?" I stand outside the city office, clenching my fingers into fists. "Let's discuss this. Please call me back."

I growl and stare at the security guard, monitoring the entrance. All I wanted was to have a civilized conversation with Paul. It's unbelievable that he could've initiated all this bullshit with Pack Steele. Unfortunately, the bastard's assistant said he wasn't here. I tried to argue that his car was parked in the garage, and then security gave me trouble and asked me to leave.

If Paul thinks he can avoid me, he has another thing coming to him. I know where he lives. I know where his vacation homes are. I know the residency of his three sons and his daughter. I'm not going to just act as if none of this is happening. He will fix this even if it means me risking my reputation and good standing. I will not allow Scarlett to go through this sort of stress and torment, all because of greed and personal vendettas.

My phone beeps and I look at it, hoping it's Paul.

Unknown: Leave my uncle alone, old man. This has nothing to do with him.

My muscles tense as I read the text message from the unknown number. I know it's Chaz. This is the first time the fucker reached out since he attacked Jonah and Scarlett.

I ignore the text message, screenshotting and sending it to my pack mates. They need to know and plan accordingly.

I turn back to the office building, watching as the security guard strolls away, the shift change finally happening. The new guy won't know that I've already tried to reach out to Paul. I'm not falling for his personal assistant's lie. I know he's in this building. He can't hide like the coward he is. He obviously knows something has gone down.

I push open the door, my phone vibrating in my hand.

Unknown: You're making a mistake.
Me: Fuck off.

I pull out my Clearwater University identification card and flash it at the new security guard. "The meeting on the third floor with Paul Miller. He's expecting me. I just got off the phone with him." I hold up my phone log, showing that I had called him.

The security guard nods his head, takes my phone, wallet, and keys, and waves me through the metal detector. I thank him and tell him to have a good day, acting as if I belong. No one is going to stop me now.

I stride to the elevator, hitting the call button. I wait for it to come down and smile at the man in a suit exiting. I haven't been in the city office in years, but nothing has changed. It's like those in power refuse to do anything to improve things, freezing the place's décor during the height of their careers.

They can easily forget the world outside progresses and moves forward, even if they try to remain stagnant within this time capsule of a building.

The elevator halts on the third floor. It belongs entirely to Paul, and I catch the receptionist texting on her cell phone while watching something on her computer. She glances up and quickly shuts it off, bringing a document to the screen.

"I think you have the wrong floor, sir. Mr. Miller isn't seeing anybody today." The receptionist glances at her landline. I can see her consider calling security, and I close the space and hold my hand up.

"So, Paul is here," I say, keeping my voice low. "His assistant told me he wasn't in. I have something important I need to bring to his attention. If you even consider calling security, you will be blackballed within this county. Mr. Miller straddles a thin line between being a lawful treasurer and being a white-collar criminal. You wouldn't want to get wrapped up in that now, would you?"

I don't take my eyes off hers, testing her resolve. She automatically rolls back from her desk and gets up, fluttering toward what looks to be a bathroom.

That's a smart idea. She can't get in trouble if she didn't know I was here.

I straighten my suit jacket and stride around her counter to the double doors with Paul Miller etched into the frosted glass. I shove it open.

"Tina, I told you not to disturb us—" Paul growls, widening his nostrils at me.

I cock my head and spot a woman on her knees under his glass desk, giving him a blow job. Of fucking course.

I strut forward and slam my hands on the desk. "You fucking bastard! What do you think you're doing messing with my pack?" Pulling my phone out, I snap a bunch of pictures of Paul in his scandalous state and immediately send them to Adrian. "I don't know what kind of games you're playing, but you better fucking withdraw your interest from Scarlett."

The woman squeaks from under the table, wiping her mouth on the back of her arm. She scrambles to get to her feet. I meet her eyes and snap a picture, making sure that I have the evidence I need to blackmail this son of a bitch if I need to. I don't know who the woman is, but she is someone else's omega.

"Dom, please. Settle down. I don't know what you're going on about. I have no interest in Scarlett. I've already done my part with my dearly beloved. You know I have no interest in another." Paul rolls his shoulders and zips up his pants, muttering the words as he watches the women leave the office.

I throw my hands out. "Then who the fuck is that?"

Paul leans back in his chair and stretches his arms over his head to rest on the back of his neck. "Just someone to play with. Now, I expect your discretion. You shouldn't be barging in here anyway."

Fury floods through me, and I reach over the desk and grab him by the tie, yanking him forward and slamming him down. I latch my fingers to the back of his neck and squeeze, feeling his pulse beating against my fingers.

"You need to fucking tell me what is going on. Pack Carlisle contacted us, demanding that we return Scarlett. They claim that we were not truthful with our proposal. They should be all fine and fucking dandy, but Scarlett's mother says that she has arranged another marriage. To Pack Miller of the Clearwater Territory." Leaning down, I get in his face and meet his eyes. "Which you are the leader of."

Paul mutters under his breath, the noise vibrating on my palm. "Dom, you're mistaken. I have not made any arrangements for another omega. You should ask my nephew. I'm not the only available alpha with Pack Miller. Chaz filed for emancipation from my leadership because he felt I was purposefully preventing his claim to power. His inheritance relies on him marrying an omega. He's using the Miller name despite legally requesting to be leader of Pack Broderik."

The psychotic, sneaking fuck. He must've used the prospect of his inheritance to persuade Scarlett's mom. "You could've warned us."

Paul sighs. "I didn't know he'd take things this far. But believe me, I had nothing to do with any of this. We both know he's unstable. Clearwater University was his last hope after his expulsion from Alpha Academy. We thought he would straighten up not being around so many hot-headed people. I don't know what Scarlett did or if they have a history that she's not telling you about. Maybe you should start there. There must be a bigger reason he wants her so badly apart from money."

I stiffen and slam my fist against his desk. "You will not blame his behavior on Scarlett! You said he has a history. He's been hiding who he was and passing as a beta. He didn't even know Scarlett was an omega when they met.

I will not stand for you trying to twist this onto my mate. It's sick."

"It's reasonable to think that. You know how available omegas are, especially ones passing as betas. I bet they were drawn to each other, but she had to change her mind because of your proposal." Paul sits upright and straightens his suit jacket. "I'm sorry, Dom. I wish there was more I could do. I can't control my nephew. He's an adult."

"He's a criminal and needs to be handled appropriately. You have connections to the right people. Get him to stop and put him in his place. Tell Pack Carlisle you don't back him and that he's a fraud." I fist my hand, clutching my phone. "If you don't, your career is over. Even if it's the last thing I fucking do. You're done."

I don't give Paul a chance to respond and stomp from his office, slamming his door. The receptionist remains hidden in the bathroom, and I take the stairwell instead of the elevator back to the lobby. I manage to make it outside without anyone stopping me, and I stride around the building and head a couple of blocks over to where I parked my motorcycle. I wasn't going to have it seen at the city office.

My phone vibrates in my hand, and I climb on my bike and start the engine, the rumble shaking me to the core.

Or maybe it's my nerves. I'm pissed off. I'm worried. I feel like I have lost all control of my life.

Unknown: What did I tell you, old man? You weren't supposed to go to my uncle. You know packs stand stronger together when they have a common enemy. You don't think I know my uncle's secrets? It would be a shame if he thought it was you who spilled them.

Me: Come face me, asshole. Show me what kind of alpha you really are. You keep hiding like the weak, pathetic bastard you are. You can never be good enough for Scarlett. You aren't a real alpha. That's why you passed so well as a beta.

Should I be testing him? The smart, practical part of me knows better. But he struck a nerve.

I send a screenshot to Paul, hoping that if he sees Chaz's threat, that he'll try harder to control the asshole and do what is right.

I don't hang around for a response, knowing that Chaz probably followed me and lingers nearby. I barrel forward on my bike, weaving in and out of lanes and making turns to take me in circles until I hit the Pacific Coast Highway and speed, letting the adrenaline of riding my motorcycle push away the tension clinging to my muscles.

Chaz might be bold. He might have the audacity to pull a fucked-up stunt like this, but he doesn't have the intelligence or the capability to succeed.

He will get what's coming to him.

He will get what he deserves.

And if he doesn't, then I will take care of him myself. Because if Scarlett gets taken from me—I can't even think about it.

I'm not afraid to watch the world burn.

I'll light the match myself.

"Our lawyer says we must submit all our paperwork and stand before Pack Carlisle next week to plead our case. They've requested we send Scarlett early." Adrian crosses his arms over his chest. "Scarlett denied them herself and informed them that they'd have to arrest her, but Pack Clearwater stands firmly on our side for now. They will not use their resources to aid the Steeles."

Thank the fucking fates. At least our good standing is useful for something. I'm sure Adrian had to pull a helluva lot of strings like I have. Right now, no one will come within a mile of Scarlett and risk scandal.

"What about Chaz? Have the authorities located him?" I ask, swiveling in my chair.

"No. He was last seen leaving the territory with three other alphas. Two of them were the football players. The third one was unknown and most likely not a member of our territory. They have a summons for their appearance in front of Pack Clearwater." Adrian purses his lips, crinkling his forehead. "I wish I had better news on that front. As long as he's not attacking us, they won't do anything. Worthless."

"Things need to change," I say, smoothing my fingers over my cropped hair.

Adrian steps forward and squeezes my shoulder. "I know. We have to focus on getting through this hurdle first. At least we'll have time to find out for sure if Scarlett is pregnant. It'll be more reliable if she waits a couple more days."

"It's just a confirmation. I know she's pregnant. I can feel it deep in my soul. It kills me that she has to deal with this when it should be the happiest time of her life. Of all our lives." I hang my head, staring at the floor.

Adrian kneels beside me and then embraces me, comforting me in a way he hasn't done or needed to do in a while.

"Keep that up, and you're going to make me jealous." Scarlett's soft voice hums through the air.

I chuckle and hold out one of my arms. "There's plenty of room right here between us, Lettie. Did you have fun shopping with Jonah? Did you find anything you liked?"

Scarlett holds up a garment bag. "I can't wait for you all to see it. Jonah was a bit annoyed that I didn't let him take a peek, but I thought it was only fair that you all had to wait until tomorrow."

A smile brightens her face, her cheeks flushing with the thought. We were planning a summer wedding, but things have changed.

And everything is set for tomorrow.

Excitement buzzes through me, melting away the negative feelings arising from talking to Adrian about Chaz and Pack Carlisle.

I can't possibly be worried when Scarlett slides onto my lap, presses her lips to mine, and fills me with all her love in a single kiss. Adrian wraps his arms around both of us, sandwiching us together, and I laugh and inhale a soft breath of her cherry-vanilla scent.

"One of the many reasons why I love you. You always know how to make us feel special. I could never be jealous of any of our pack mates because of it. My beautiful bride," Adrian says, kissing her temple. "I'm sure your dress is stunning."

"Enchanting," I say, kissing her other temple.

She giggles and shifts on my lap, setting off my body in a way that makes her hum.

"And this is one of the billions of reasons why I love you. I could survive on your affection forever. Actually, I plan on it, my grooms. Tomorrow will be one of the happiest days of my life. All because of you." Scarlett rests her head on mine, closing her eyes as if she's daydreaming about it.

I kiss her again. "And you. We're happy because of you."

28

Scarlett

HAPPIEST ALPHAS ALIVE

Mother Hen: I wish I could be there today! I'm so happy for you, chickie.

Hardass: Send pics!

Princess: I hope you like the cake! I promise no peens this time.

Baby girl: I made sure it was perfect.

Loner: XOXO!

Little bird: Love you, sis!

Me: Thank you all! I'll have another wedding in the summer.

Mother Hen: Before you go...did you take a test?

My best friend's face pops up on my phone, cutting off my chance to respond to Violet. I hit the call button, smiling as Emma squeals through the line, her video shaking.

"Fuck, Scarlett. You look so hot! I bet you won't even get down the aisle before you take the D." Emma grins with her words, filling the screen with a closeup of her mouth. "I'm so mad I couldn't be there."

I stare at my screen, tears glazing in my eyes, but I refuse to let them fall. "We'll have a public one soon."

Because today is my wedding day, and as much as I want my sisters and best friend here, we couldn't risk my mom finding out. So this intimate occasion will only have two witnesses. Dean Clearwater for my alphas, and Ms. Sandy for me. I was so relieved when she agreed to be here. The more I get to know the woman, the closer I feel to her. She already has so many projects she wants to hire me for. Because of her kindness and how much she believes in me, I have accepted commissions for the next four months until I take the assistant position with Talia, the new Art Department director.

"I know. It's just—fuck. I wish I could do something more." Emma swipes her arm over her cheeks.

"You've done so much already. I can't thank you enough for helping me stay in touch with my sisters. It means the world to me." I release a long breath.

"You'd do the same for me," Emma says. "Now send me lots of pics and go get that D. I'm so happy for you, Scar."

"I'm happy too," I say, blowing her a kiss.

Emma disconnects the line, and I stare at the string of new text messages from my sisters. As much as I want to catch up and chat like we used to, I can't. My heart hurts because Mom put us all in this position.

Princess: You know she'd tell us if she did.
Hardass: Not if she took my advice.
Mother Hen: You're paranoid, Cyan.
Loner: You mean smart.

"Ms. Sandy? Will you take a picture of me?" I ask, closing out the text messages from my sisters.

Ms. Sandy stands up from the small couch where she adds a ribbon to my bouquet. "Absolutely. Let me help you with one more thing." Lifting my veil from its spot on the vanity, she pins the flower and jewel arrangement to my hair and straightens out the soft tulle material. "Perfect."

I smile at myself in the mirror, feeling as if I'm a new version of myself. I'm not the same omega who came to San Diego to hide the fact that no one had proposed or wanted her. I'm a well-loved and taken care of omega with five strong alphas who will do whatever it takes to protect me.

"Now hold these," Ms. Sandy adds, lifting the bouquet from the table.

I take the colorful arrangement of deep yellow sunflowers, red hydrangeas, and burgundy and black roses. It's a perfect autumn bouquet, and I absolutely love it.

I bring it to my face and inhale a slow breath, peeking up as Ms. Sandy snaps a picture. I send it to my sisters and then to Emma, smiling to myself. Only a couple more minutes. A couple more minutes and I will officially be Scarlett Hart.

Me: No test, but Sapphire's right. I'll let you guys know when I do. Now I have to go. It's time to claim my grooms.

I set my phone down on the vanity and let Ms. Sandy help strap on my heels. My toes and fingernails glitter with the ruby polish, matching the color of my lipstick.

My heart beats rapidly, picking up pace as I look at the time, knowing that my alphas will be standing in the small chapel. I'm sure they're anxiously waiting for me.

"You look absolutely beautiful. I know that this might not mean much, but I hope you know how much you are loved. I haven't seen a pack so smitten and devoted until I met yours. You're going to make a fantastic wife and an amazing mother." Ms. Sandy squeezes my hand.

I pull her to me and hug her. "That means everything to me. You have been so kind. I don't know how I'll ever repay you."

She smiles softly. "Friends don't owe friends anything. I'm just happy that you came into my coffee shop."

A knock sounds on the door, and I suck in a shuddering breath, my stomach flipping with my nerves. I'm more excited and antsy than anything, but no matter what I do, I don't think I'll ever be able to shake the dark feeling. Not until—

Adrian cracks the door open, whistling under his breath as he drinks me in. And just like that, the blip of negativity vanishes as I stare at my alpha and pack leader standing before me, more handsome than ever in a tuxedo with a small sunflower pinned to his lapel.

"Are you ready, my beautiful bride? I'll be the one walking you down the aisle." Adrian leans in and kisses me softly like he can't resist even a foot of space between us. "I'm so honored to be your alpha. This is the best day of my life, Scarlett."

"I've never been more ready. I can't wait to officially call you my husband. To have and to hold, for the rest of my life and for all of time." I rub my hands on his cheek and down his neck, letting him kiss me once more.

Ms. Sandy smiles and pats Adrian on the shoulder, sliding past us with her own bouquet, acting as my bridesmaid and witness. I open my arms to Adrian, hugging him close for a moment as soft piano music trickles through the air.

Adrian pulls my veil down over my face, smiling at me as he offers his arm. I stare at my princess-style dress, the skirt sweeping with my movements. The sweetheart neckline accentuates my cleavage and tiny crystals glitter from the bodice. It was the first one I tried on and fell in love with it immediately. It's as if we aren't rushing to wed but as if this is our destiny. My perfect alphas. My perfect dress. The perfect day with soft white clouds, azure skies, and sunshine sparkling through the rainbow mural of the stained-glass windows.

Ms. Sandy strolls ahead of us, entering the nave of the chapel. She announces my arrival, drawing Jonah, Dominic, Ezra, and Leo's attention my way. Leo whistles between his fingers, catcalling me. Heat blooms in my cheeks. Adrian chuckles, his deep voice melodious with his happiness.

"I can't believe this is really happening," I whisper under my breath, my heartbeat erratic with anticipation.

Adrian strolls with me down the aisle, watching me in his peripheral vision. "You're already ours, so believe it. I'm the happiest man alive."

"That's questionable," Ezra says, stepping forward from his spot between Jonah and Leo. He holds his hands out to me, grasping my fingers. "I'm nearly certain that title belongs to me."

"It's not a competition, is it, Lettie?" Dominic asks, lifting my veil and flipping it over my head. He tilts his head and studies my face, drawing his gaze to my lips a moment before he kisses me.

"Because you know I'm the happiest man alive. I fucking scored. She's stunning." Leo kisses me next and traces his finger over my collarbone.

"Irresistible and magnificent. What love looks like in tangible form. My beautiful, incredible omega. I can't wait to call you my wife." Jonah smiles at me, gently taking my bouquet and handing it to Ms. Sandy. She sits next to Dean Clearwater, who remains utterly silent and expressionless.

I've never seen the officiant before, but the old man seems warm enough, his smile easing my worry about having a stranger among us. But Dean Clearwater assured that the justice of peace was an ally and a prestigious member of Pack Clearwater.

"It's a joyous day for such an incredible occasion," the justice of peace says, standing before us. "I'm honored to unite Pack Hart with their perfect omega in matrimony. Happily ever afters are usually the end of a romance, but as you stand before me today, I'd like to declare that it is only the beginning. Through time and work, you have found comfort and safety within one another. And today, we celebrate such a union. Under the recognition of the Pack Clearwater law and upon your vows, I will happily declare you as husbands and wife. Misters Hart, please surround your bride, showing her what strength comes from her being the center of your pack. You may each recite your vows."

Adrian turns me to him first as the others encircle me between their bodies, not allowing the world outside of them to see me. He clasps my hands between his. "Scarlett, it is a great honor to stand before you as the leader of our pack. You are the woman of my dreams, and I'm so fortunate to be able to share you in a union with Jonah, Leo, Ezra, and Dominic. I know we've had some rough times, but we've also had incredible moments. From this point forward, I can't promise that our life will be perfect, but I can promise that our pack will fulfill your every dream and fantasy. And we will not stop. We will continue to grow and learn and navigate this world in a way that satisfies us on every level. I promise to always protect you. To cherish you. To love you even at the worst of times and always love you during the best moments. You are my everything. You are our world, and you will always be. I love you."

Leo clears his throat and takes my hands next with a wink. "I don't know how I'm going to follow that, but I will always try my best to be a good alpha to you. I will carry your sexy ass around for as long as you let me. I will make you sweat in ways that you enjoy. And mostly, I will always try to make you laugh, fighting against any sadness that could dare threaten you. I love you more than I ever knew possible, and with every passing day, that continues to grow. I can't wait for the beginning of the rest of our lives. I love you, my dirty girl."

Heat flushes my face, and I giggle, patting him on the shoulder. His vow was so perfectly him that I savor the moment. One by one, each of my alphas spills their hearts to me, filling me up with love and affection and everything I need to move forward, stronger and better than ever. Because I'm not just their omega. I'm their wife and companion. I'm their friend and their pack mate. And soon, I know I will be the mother of their children. I will be everything to them as they are everything to me and more.

I stretch out my arms, coaxing them to all step closer and smother me between their bodies. "I know that being with me has been a challenge, and I can't promise that things will get easier. But what I can promise is that I will always be loyal and give you whatever you need on any level. I will be your confidant and your shoulder to cry on. I will be the vessel for your strength and your pleasure. I vow to satiate more than just your desire. I will learn from you and grow with you. But I will also teach you. I will keep you on your toes and support you through all our life stages. Through the messy. Through the sick or injured times. And through our most joyous moments. I love you all, and I will remind you of it every second of every day. For the rest of our lives, and longer than that."

"Now, with these vows, under the authority of Pack Clearwater, I must ask you to formally agree to this union. So please, Misters Hart, do you take Scarlett Steele as your lawfully wedded wife?"

"I do," the five of them say, grinning at me with enough happiness that it fills me up, sending energy through me.

"Ms. Scarlett Steele, do you take Adrian, Jonah, Dominic, Ezra, and Leo of Pack Hart to be your lawfully wedded husbands?" The justice of peace nods his head at me, a soft smile playing on his lips.

"I do," I say, my face lighting up with a smile that hurts my cheeks.

"With the power vested in me under the authority of Pack Clearwater and in front of the witnesses close to your heart, I now pronounce you husbands and wife, a union of the daughter of Pack Steele and the alphas of Pack Hart. You may now kiss the bride." The justice of peace holds his hands up and steps back.

My guys smother me with kisses, peppering every inch of my face and shoulders and arms. I giggle and squirm between them, capturing each of their mouths one at a time until I have kissed all five of them and now stand so excited and relieved. Flying on the adrenaline of finally getting what I want.

The justice of peace claps his hands along with Ms. Sandy and Dean Clearwater. "It is with great pleasure to formally announce Misters and Mrs. Ha—"

Glass shatters, cutting off the justice of peace, and I don't have a chance to react as a metal canister thuds on the aisle between the pews. Adrian hollers and scoops me up, the canister exploding in a cloud of smoke that obscures our views.

"Head out the back!" Jonah yells, his voice hoarse as he coughs.

Panic swells through me. What the fuck is happening? This has to be Chaz's doing. He's a goddamn psycho. He's the type to ruin someone's wedding day.

"Hand over Scarlett Steele. Do so without fighting, and we won't have a problem." A grumbly, unfamiliar voice booms through the air, and a silhouette stands at the entrance to the chapel, sunlight and smoke obscuring his appearance.

Dean Clearwater growls. "What is the meaning of this? You're on—"

Blood splatters across my white dress like rosebuds blooming on the fabric. Dean Clearwater crumples to the floor, the wound on his head showing brain matter. I gag and cough, the shock of watching a man get shot and die before my eyes leaving me frozen in Adrian's arms.

"Like I said, hand over Scarlett Steele. I have been ordered to bring her back to Pack Carlisle on behalf of Pack Steele," the man says, aiming his gun at Adrian next.

My mouth trembles in recognition. I know him. I know the bastard that just crashed what was supposed to be one of the best days of my life. And I can't believe it. Rip Fernando is the leader of the pack that saved my younger sister Raven when she was kidnapped years ago. He has helped my family whenever they were in need. He was supposed to be a hero. He has done such good for us, being able to manipulate the law in our favor. I know he is a criminal, but I never expected this. I never expected him to turn against me. He was always kind.

But now? He's a monster. He's a fucking monster.

"How could you!" I scream, wiggling in Adrian's arms. He's not going to let me down willingly, and fear grips my chest, squeezing my heart. I'm terrified that this monster of a man will come after my beloved next.

"Scarlett, sweetheart. Your mama said you've been a disobedient girl. You have a nice, powerful pack all picked out for you, and you go behind your mama's back and do this? What a disappointment. I thought you were supposed to be the good one." Rip strides forward, grinning with a wicked smile. He waves his gun as if it's not a lethal weapon. "Come on, now. It's time to go home. You've played enough with these men. I never knew you were the one with the daddy kink. Maybe you can sit on my lap on the way back to San Francisco. Be a good girl for your Mama, and I can reward you." His raspy voice strikes me right in the heart, and disgust trickles down my back in a cold wave.

"I don't understand. I thought you cared about my family. You helped Raven." My voice quivers with my words.

"That's why I'm taking you home to your mama. I care about your family and what they can provide me with. Now, be a good girl. Come here. Don't make me kill these bastards. That's a lot of bodies to have to clean up, and I don't want to waste any extra time." Rip holds his hand out to me, a leer on his face.

"Please," I argue, crossing my arms over my chest.

Leo growls. "Scarlett—"

Rip bares his teeth, raises his gun, and pulls the trigger. I startle at the loud pop, my whole body shocked with fear. If I didn't know any better, I'd think my soul had just evacuated to save me.

"Leo!" I scream, spinning around.

Hands lock around my waist and drag me back, the smoky tobacco scent of Rip pushing away the comforting fragrances of my alphas. Adrian shouts, rushing toward Leo on the ground, shielding himself. Dominic shoves Jonah back, stopping him from chasing after us.

Ms. Sandy cowers between the pews, her wide eyes staring at me as Rip slings me over his shoulder. Two other men open the doors for him, standing outside on guard with guns.

I don't see Ezra anywhere. The smoke still lingers in the air, and my breathing quickens, turning into gasps as I silently sob.

How could this be happening? How could my mom be so cruel?

"Look at my beautiful bride." The cocky voice stabs me like a knife in the back. "Good job, man. My mother-in-law was right. You were well worth the price." Chaz stands by the black SUV, ogling me.

I scream and thrash, bucking my body. "No! No, please! Not him. Don't do this for him!"

Rip snarls and points to Chaz. "Other vehicle. Now. I told you to stay put."

Chaz glowers and twitches his fingers, joining a couple of guys at another vehicle. My whole body tenses. I should've known it was more than Mom throwing a fit to have her way. If Chaz can buy off Rip, then there's still hope.

"Please, Rip. You don't have to do this. We can negotiate something. My pack has the money. Whatever you want. Don't work for that asshole. He's a psycho. A failed alpha from Alpha Academy. He's not deserving of me. We have power in Clearwater. If you just hear me out, I can offer you something better." I smack my hands to Rip's back. I feel so helpless.

"Sorry, sweetheart. I promised your mama I'd help the little douche. If she finds him suitable, then so do I. Just keep your mouth shut and behave. It's going to be a quick flight. You'll see that your mama is right. You need a better pack. You need alphas that you're not going to have to fucking care for when they're too old to do anything for themselves." Rip opens the back of an SUV and plops me on the seat, pushing me over to sit next to me. He smacks his hand against the driver's seat, signaling for him to go.

"You say that like it matters. I know what I'm getting into, and I don't care. There's more to life than what you imply. There's more to love, too." I don't know why I bother because Rip just shakes his head and turns away from me, playing with his phone.

I twist in my seat, looking out the back window. I spot my alphas leaving the chapel, looking around frantically.

"Put your seatbelt on. Now." Rip reaches around me, grabbing it.

I ignore him and hang forward, refusing to sit properly. I won't make it easy. It's what Emma always told me. If I'm going down, I better give my enemies hell.

"Scarlett—"

"Leave me alone!" I scream, stomping my heels into Rip's boots, getting him to put space between us. "Leave me the fuck alone!"

He growls and turns away.

I kick something with my shoe, and I can't stop myself from shifting my dress out of the way. What the hell? It's a phone. Ezra's phone.

Now I realize why I didn't see him.

The part of me that wanted to break heals with the hope flooding through me.

This isn't over.

No one has won.

29

Ezra

promise

"**I** did it. I fucking did it," I say to myself, peering from the bushes.

The horn honks twice as the two SUVs barrel away. Fury edges my vision in shadows. I can't believe those monsters took her. Scarlett's screams etch into my brain. I don't think I'll ever get rid of them from my mind. It took all my willpower not to put up a fight. I know I could've taken down one guy, but the others would've sent me down with him. I'm no match for a bullet. My love for Scarlett can't defeat a gunman no matter how much I will it to be true.

I'm just a man and an alpha. I'm not invincible.

My heart hammers, my nerves shot. The second the smoke bomb went off, I knew shit was going down. I took advantage of the smoke and ran, breaking open the window behind the altar. The driver was too busy keeping an eye on the door of the chapel that he missed me tossing my phone through the open back window.

"Come on, Scarlett. Find it. Find my phone." I wait until the two SUVs vanish, burning rubber at the signal from the parking lot. I don't know if my plan will work, but I had to try something. If anything, we can track my phone.

"You guys! Scarlett's calling from Ezra's phone." Dominic's voice rings through the air. "Where is he? Do you think—"

"Over here," I call, shaking the dirt from my trousers.

"Shit, Ez. Are you okay? How did Scarlett get your—"

A scream rips from Dominic's phone, Scarlett's voice stabbing me through the heart. She sounds more pissed than scared. It's the only thing keeping me from losing my shit.

"Fuck! Fuck! They're torturing her!" Adrian hollers, rushing to grab the phone from Dominic.

"You fucking assholes! I'll destroy you! I'll cut your balls off! You can't do this. I don't belong to Pack Steele anymore. I'm married." Scarlett's screams turn into a slew of swearwords, competing with something I've only ever heard from Leo. "Turn this piece of shit vehicle around. Do it or I'll kick your asses! You're weak little bastards who hide behind weapons. You let an omega push you around and tell you what to do. If I couldn't smell the damn stink of your order, I'd think you were betas. Fuck, maybe even omegas. You—"

A man hollers, his voice turning a pitch I didn't think possible. "Goddamn it, Rip! She kicked my dick."

"Scarlett, don't fight! Please, you have to stop. They'll hurt you." Adrian snatches the phone from Dominic, yelling into the mic.

"Adrian, no!" Panic shocks me, and I dart my hand out, yanking it from Adrian. I spot the mute on, thankful that Dominic thought to do so. If these men discover that I managed to sneak my phone to Scarlett, they'll take it away.

"I'll fucking do it again! None of you will ever get to breed. You assholes!" Scarlett's voice hums through the speaker, her anger nearly palpable.

Adrian growls, preparing to fight me for the phone. "She needs our help. We have to tell her what to do. They'll hurt her! They'll only put up with so much."

Jonah flings his arms around Adrian, pulling him back, breaking his focus on me. "Calm down, Adrian. They won't hurt Scarlett. It sounded like those guys worked for Pack Steele. She knew them."

"Then we need to hunt them down. They can't be far." Adrian loses control of his sensibility. He's thinking with his alpha instincts and not his mind. If I didn't worry about losing contact with Scarlett or jeopardizing our chances of getting to her, I'd join him on the manhunt.

"Take a breath. You're supposed to be our leader, not the one to throw together impossible plans with grim outcomes. That's Leo's job, especially after he faked getting hit to ensure they didn't shoot at him again." Dominic helps Leo to his feet, patting him on the back. "Which I'm thankful for. If we go after them now, they won't hesitate to kill us. We can't do that to Scarlett. Those bastards took advantage of the element of surprise. We can do the same. We'll make the appropriate phone calls and plan from there. They killed Dean Clearwater, and I'm sure Pack Clearwater will not tolerate it. They will help us."

"He's right, Adrian. I know it's tough not to act, but Scarlett needs us alive." I scrub my fingers through my dark, curly hair, trying my best to remain calm as I face my leader. I should fall in line, but Adrian's never been the type to use hierarchy against us. "I feel your need too. All I want to do is jump in the car and chase after her, but there's no way we can fight a bunch of armed criminals right now." Dealing with rowdy students is one thing, but an armed psychopath? It's out of my damn repertoire. We need a plan. We need to ensure our safety as well as Scarlett's. She could get hurt in the crossfire.

"Don't underestimate us! We can handle them. We have to!" Adrian hollers, punching his fist into the stained-glass door of the chapel, shattering it to pieces. Blood coats his hand from the cuts, and I pull out my handkerchief and stanch the bleeding, forcing him to stay still by tightening my hand around his.

"We will, but not like this. They messed up. We signed the marriage certificates before the ceremony. We're legally married to her. They can't keep her. Everything is in order, and our certificate has been backdated to prove that we have been serious, and Scarlett's mother's accusations are unfounded." Dominic dusts his suit jacket off. "Now, get yourself together. We need to focus.

We need to get Sandy and Harold out of here. They're witnesses to this all."

Dominic's comment draws my attention to where Ms. Sandy hugs the officiant of our wedding. Blood sprinkled across both of them from Dean Clearwater. I stride closer and lace my fingers around Ms. Sandy's arm, feeling her trembling.

"I'm so sorry you had to go through this. I won't ask if you're okay, but I need you to listen. You need to go to the manor and wait for the authorities there. You're a witness to what happened, and we're going to need you to address it. You'll be safe. Those bastards took who they wanted, and they won't come back."

Ms. Sandy bobs her head, her eyes wide and glassy. She tries to say something, but she chokes up and releases a cry instead.

"Get her to the car," I add, motioning to Jonah. "I'll call in some favors to use Pack Clearwater's private jet. We'll need an escort team and protection detail. Pack Carlisle won't be able to ignore this with the death of the dean."

Scarlett screams, her voice screeching from the phone again. I tense, my muscles rippling through me.

"This is your last chance! You'll regret it, Rip. Take my fucking offer and forget about my mom. She and Chaz will take you down with them. You're supposed to be a good guy. You're supposed to save us, not ruin—"

A growl reverberates through my bones. "Enough, Scarlett! Shut your goddamn mouth, or I'll tape it. Be a damn good omega and move the fuck on. These are Sage's orders. She arranged a good marriage with Pack Broderik. Count your blessings. If you were mine, I'd—" Pack Broderik. Fucking Chaz clearly recognizes his mistake about using Pack Miller without their authority, now choosing his alias.

Scarlett screeches and hisses a moment before a groan sounds through the air. "I said don't fucking touch me! I'll take your balls next time."

Silence falls over the line, though it doesn't disconnect. Scarlett grumbles under her breath, whispering out what I think might be street names. I've never been so proud in my life. She's no longer the shy woman I met. She's my fierce wife, and I swear on my life I'll get her back.

"Fuck yeah, my dirty girl!" Leo punches his open palm. "She'll give them so much hell they'll want to leave her on the side of the road."

I can only pray for it to be that easy.

"Scarlett's a fighter." Adrian manages to compose himself, cradling his bloody hand. "The actions of Sage will benefit us. She's proven unhinged, and the authorities will consider our actions from here on absolutely justified."

The death of Dean Clearwater proves how volatile the pack who kidnapped Scarlett is. The Steeles can face omega endangerment charges if it's put in front of the right people, especially since Sage proceeded to make arrangements before the court-ordered appearance.

Dominic clenches his jaw, rocking on his heels. He shrugs from his jacket, dropping it to the ground. "I'll reach out to Paul and see what he can tell us about Chaz's plans. The fucking psycho won't get away with this. Not this time. He can't hide behind the power of his pack."

"He won't be able to because I'll kill him. I'm going to fucking kill him." Leo fists his hands, finally snapping out of his shock over what happened. The man can go from easy-going to intense in seconds.

I swing my arms around him, squeezing him to me. "Save the anger for that moment. We have to move. Go with Jonah. I'll take the justice of peace where he needs to go and have a flight up north on standby."

"I'll alert the authorities and wait with Dom," Adrian says, cracking his neck. "We'll reconvene in thirty."

Fuck. Thirty minutes sounds like forever.

I just hope Scarlett knows we're coming for her. We swore our lives, our love, and our loyalty. We will keep our promise.

Scarlett

FIGHTER

I pretend to sleep, clutching the phone within the skirt of my dress. The flight to San Francisco was longer than I remember, and every second feels like a minute as I keep my eyes shut.

I refused to exit the plane on my own, not making it easy on Rip. He carried me all the way across the tarmac to where a van awaited.

I haven't seen Chaz since San Diego and a part of me knows I'll face him soon. He was in on this. He and my mom.

I've never hated two people more in my life.

"Wake up, sweetheart. Mama Steele is waiting for you." Fingers latch onto my shoulder, shaking me.

Rip's crazy to think I'll stop being difficult now.

I snap my eyes open and glare at Rip, wishing that I had the power to shoot lasers or bullets or acid from my eyes. I want nothing more than to burn the cocky look off his smug face. How could I ever mistake him for a hero? My naïve ass. Just because he did something good for my family doesn't mean shit about his character.

I swing out and smack his arm, knocking it away from me. "Don't touch me. I don't want your gross stench lingering on my skin."

Grabbing my chin, he strokes his thumbs over my cheeks, shocking me. "I hope you smell me for days, sweetheart. You have grown up to be a pretty little thing. Too bad you've already been used. Count your blessings that your new alphas don't give a shit."

It takes everything in me not to sucker punch him in the face. "Go to hell!" Fuck my hesitation. My rage grabs hold of me, and I give in to the fight burning inside me. Jabbing my fist, I punch him right between the legs.

He howls and tries to snatch me, but I duck out of his reach and shove into him, knocking him into the sidewall. I kick his knee and rush out of the side door of the van. The driver raises his hands and backs up, keeping out of my way. No one wants to mess with a pissed off bridezilla. I never thought I'd be the type, but they ruined my wedding day, and now I want to ruin their lives completely.

I nearly eat shit on the sidewalk outside of a two-story townhouse. I spin around, tucking the phone between my cleavage into my bra to keep it safe. Lifting the skirt of my dress, I kick off my heels and make a run for it. I have no idea where the hell I'm going, only that I'm going. I need to get out of here. If I can just find somewhere to hide, I know my alphas will find me.

A heavy body slams into me, knocking me off my feet. I skid across the ground. Pain slices over my arm and shoulder, the road rash burning my skin. Tears sting my eyes, but I don't let the agony stop me from fighting. I slap and punch and scratch Chaz, using my anger to push me forward. How dare he do this. How dare he feel so entitled to me that he'd go as far as to ruin my life because I rejected him. How dare he use me like my mom to gain wealth.

Lacing his fingers around my throat, he squeezes, cutting off my airway. "Fuck, Scarlett. Stop fighting. You've lost. If you don't quit it, I have every right as your alpha to put you in your damn place. You don't want to embarrass your mother now, do you?"

"Scarlett, honey. Why do you have to be such a disappointment? I've been doing everything to give you an incredible life, and you sit here and fight it. Stop acting like a child. You don't want him to hurt you, now, do you?" Mom's sickly sweet voice chimes through the air, freezing my heart like ice.

My chest heaves, my body relaxing. I was less afraid of Rip, which says something. Chaz will hurt me. I know he will. The strength of his hand around my neck proves as much. I'm sure I'll have bruises that'll linger for days.

Fuck. Fuck. Fuck.

I didn't expect to have to comb through my memories, pulling out all of the tidbits I was taught from Omega Prep on handling an angry alpha.

"I'm sorry," I whimper, my voice barely managing to escape.

Chaz's features soften, and he releases my neck only to squeeze my face between his thumb and index finger. "See. That wasn't hard. We don't have to fight, Scarlett. We're going to have a good life together. You get to be close to your family. You won't have to worry about anything apart from popping out those powerful children we'll have together. You'll be taken care of. You'll whine and beg for forgiveness soon enough. Just wait until we have you on your knees."

I cringe, biting my bottom lip to stop it from trembling. "Can I please get to my feet? I haven't seen my mom in a while."

Chaz smiles, though wicked darkness still lingers in his gaze. He slides his arms under me and lifts me to my feet, purposely adjusting the bodice of my dress without my permission. I want so badly to slap him, but he would be the type to slap me back. Instead, I need to reason with the only person that can help me right now. The one who has also betrayed me the most.

"Mom?" I say, my soft voice cracking. I spin on my feet and catch sight of my mom in a skimpy, tight-fitted black dress and big sunglasses. Diamonds glitter from her neck, earrings, and wrists, along with the sparkling buckles on her stilettos.

She lifts her sunglasses up, pushing her hair back. "Oh, Scarlett. My darling. I knew once you could catch your breath that you'd settle down."

I'm only settling down enough to get them to let their guards down so I can strike them like a fucking snake, going for the kill shot.

"I'm so happy I managed to stop that horrid wedding. I mean, look at that dress. That is gaudy and not fitting of one of the Steele women." Mom touches the skirt of my dress and stretches it out. "Have you gained weight? You look a bit chubby."

I bite my cheek, stopping from retorting with something similar. "What does it matter to you? My weight doesn't affect your life. And I love my dress."

"You never did have the best taste. But that can be fixed. I'm sure Pack Broderik will help train you into a respectable omega. Scarlett Broderik. It's so much nicer than Miller. I'm the one who suggested Chaz make the change. I know they have some trouble with the law in San Diego, but I managed to work some things out here. Pack Carlisle will be happy to have them in the territory, especially if you're anything like me. They can't wait to see if you can beat my record for omega girls." Mom motions me toward the open gate leading to the stoop of the townhouse.

Rip and his pack watch us in silence. I try not to react as Chaz hands him a thick envelope, and the two of them shake hands. Rip hops into the van, not waiting a moment longer.

I've never felt so disappointed and disgusted in my life. I should've known better. My mom and dads have done some shady shit. Of course, they would have someone like Rip at their beck and call.

"Won't she make an incredible mother, Chaz?" Mom asks, letting him help her into the back of the limo instead of waiting for the driver.

"And I can't wait to turn her into one. When's your next heat, Scarlett? There's no way in hell those old men could give you the child you crave." Chaz grabs my hand and yanks me to him, sliding his arm around my back.

His words ignite blinding fury inside me, and I jerk my knee up and strike him in the balls. Swinging my hand, I slap him across the face and shove him.

I won't let him take me.

I won't let him turn me into the obedient omega of his dirty fantasies.

So I run.

I run, and I don't stop.

I will never be his. I belong to Pack Hart, and the world will see. It's what pushes me forward. It's what will save me.

It can't end here.

It just can't.

"Scarlett!" Chaz yells, barreling behind me. The quick thuds of his footsteps kick my heart into overdrive. "You can't run from me! I'm one of your alphas. I bought you! You're mine!"

"Scarlett, honey. Please stop. You're being childish," Mom calls, her voice laced with annoyance.

I scream in anger, using it to push me to move faster. There is nothing childish about taking control of my life. Or setting boundaries. Knowing what I want and doing whatever it takes. I will not bow to Chaz. I won't let him break me.

"Scarlett!" Chaz hollers. "You're going to regret this!"

"Fuck you!" I yell, my breath panting, my body aching. I'm almost at the end of the block. I just need to get out of sight.

A shadow stretches across the ground from the corner house as Chaz's shadow shortens behind me, him closing the distance faster than I can put it between us. If it weren't for this dress, I'd manage.

So I cut across the street between cars and yank the side zipper enough to free myself. The gown falls to the ground, leaving me in a slip. Chaz growls and yells my name again. He thinks he can scare me into submission, but he can't. All it does is ignite my will to fight.

I come to another corner, now too focused on getting away that I don't see the car until it honks and skids to a stop, sending smoke through the air. A man thrusts open the door, his face twisted in anger.

"Help!" I scream, rushing toward him. "Please, help! I've been kidnapped. I just escaped!"

I clutch onto the man's T-shirt, getting into his face. He frowns, his eyes looking behind me. I pray to the universe that he helps me. I know not many people would, but I don't know what else to do. I can't keep running.

"Get in," he says, motioning to the passenger seat. "Tell me where you're from. I'll take you to the—"

Blood splatters across my face, and I scream, shoving against the man as he falls to the ground. What the actual fuck? I spin, catching sight of Rip still in his van as if he's been following me this whole time. He winks at me with a smile, and I don't even have a chance to react as Chaz hooks his arm around my throat and squeezes.

I gasp for breath, my body trembling in shock.

This is it. Maybe I'm not worth his trouble.

Maybe this is his revenge for rejecting him.

The world goes dark.

"You didn't have to do that, Chaz. You could've killed her." Mom's voice rings through the air, the same anger directed at me now focused on Chaz. "You know she could be pregnant. There were better ways to handle her."

Chaz growls. "Shut the fuck up and sit down. You're lucky I even let you come with me. You said you would get her to see things clearly, and you've done nothing but annoy me."

Mom huffs. "You didn't give me—"

"I said shut the fuck up and sit down!" Something crashes, and I peek through my eyelashes to see a figure stride past me before a door slams.

Another voice captures my attention, and someone mumbles under their breath.

"Miss Broderik, can you hear me? I would like to hurry and finish this examination so I can get out of here. Your alphas are a bit irritated, and I didn't sign up to be put in danger." A silhouette stands over me, and a woman shines a light in my eyes. "I've already bandaged up your scrapes, but I need you to take this pregnancy test. I don't have access to a lab, or else I would've drawn your blood."

I don't move. I'm not going to make it easy for her.

"Please, Ms. Broderik. I don't want to have to put in a catheter because you want to resist. Let's get this over with so we know, and then we can move on. Your alphas are outside, waiting in anticipation." The woman touches my hand, pulling me up, knowing that I'm aware.

"You have to help me. They are not my alphas," I say, hissing.

"Scarlett, she knows the situation. Stop trying to use people's compassion to get what you want. Just do what she asks so I can get the rest of our money. Your sisters would be so upset if they knew that you were purposely trying to hurt their futures." Mom speaks up from a folding chair in the corner of the dirty bedroom with clothes piled on the floor, trash and dishes on every possible surface, and a blanket tacked over the window instead of curtains. "I'd also like to get out of here. The sooner you stop trying to resist and accept these men as your alphas, the sooner you can go to a far nicer place. You don't want to spend the rest of your life in this shithole, do you?"

I blink a few times, trying to process everything she says.

"They are only fugitives because of you. You've caused so much trouble. I don't understand why you couldn't just do as I asked." Mom gets up and places her hands on her hips. "They also wouldn't have had to hurt you if you had just complied. I hope you remember that. It's as if you never graduated from Omega Prep. What a disappointment. Your fathers would be ashamed."

I clench my fingers, digging my nails into the palms of my hands. It's pointless arguing with her. She will never see beyond her own selfishness.

"Come on, Ms. Broderik. There's no time to waste. Take this cup to the bathroom. I'll do everything else." The woman hands me a clear cup. "Try not to spill."

It just makes me want to pee all over the fucking place to spite her. If only my modesty didn't put me in check.

"And leave the door open, honey. I don't trust you." Mom motions to the small bathroom.

I peek into the disgusting bathroom, crinkling my nose. I couldn't even escape if I wanted to. There are bars over the tiny window. I spin and glower at her, holding the door half open in case she tries to charge me.

"Fuck off, Mom. I will close this damn door if I want to." I slam it shut and try to twist the lock, but it doesn't click into place. I push a rolling cart with toilet paper in front of the door, blocking it, but somebody could probably just bust it open.

My bra buzzes, the vibration startling me. I was too distracted by everything that I didn't notice that the phone stayed in place. At least my boobs come in handy for something else besides looking good in a low-cut shirt or turning my alphas on before they turn into milk makers.

Adrian: Call me.

I know Adrian asks because he can't be certain that I still have the phone otherwise.

I hit his contact, listening to it only ring once before someone breathes on the other line. I clear my throat, doing my best to whisper without my voice shaking.

"It's me," I say, afraid that Adrian can't hear me. "I'm scared."

A little growl sounds through the line, Adrian's worry reverberating through my bones. "We have you located. I need you to hang tight. There was a shooting nearby, and one of our police escorts was attacked by a gang."

Tears burn my eyes, and I squeeze them, releasing a breath.

The door rattles on its hinges. "Scarlett! Hurry up! You can't take that long to fill up a cup."

I grip the phone harder. "Please hurry. Chaz choked me out. I don't trust him. He's working with Pack Fernando. They want me to turn against you. They want me to say that I want them."

"I need you to hang on, Scarlett. Do not do anything that will get you hurt. I know you're scared, but you're tough. You are a part of Pack Hart. These criminals won't get away with it." Adrian releases a little breath. "Now, keep me on the line. I'm here for you. We all are."

"Scarlett!" Mom screams, banging her fist on the door.

I startle and sit down on the toilet. "Give me one fucking minute!" I scream back, tucking the phone away again without hanging up with Adrian.

I do what I'm asked and force myself to move the cart out of the way to join my mom back in the disgusting bedroom. The woman in scrubs takes the cup from me, her gloved hand shaking. I know she's complying because she's been coerced into this. I still hate her, though. I hate my mom even more.

"Go sit down on the bed. You're not going anywhere." Mom points at the sheetless mattress with a throw blanket hanging off the edge.

I cross my arms and remain standing in my place, staring at the pregnancy test the woman dips into the cup. She sets it down flat on a tray, setting a timer. My heart pounds, my whole body going haywire at the thought. I'm terrified to find out the results. If I had taken the test yesterday, I'd be over the moon excited if it were positive. But now? I'm terrified. What if I am? What if Chaz and his new pack get away with this?

The bedroom door flings open, smacking against the wall. Chaz sneers, whipping his gaze at me, and I catch sight of two familiar guys standing a couple of feet away. They were the assholes that ruined my birthday. They were the same ones that were on the football team and threatened to ruin Leo's reputation.

"Well?" Chaz asks, baring his teeth.

The nurse releases a small whimper under her breath. "It's p-positive. Congratulations, Pack Broderik."

"My beautiful daughter. Pack Carlisle will be thrilled with the news. Following in my footsteps. This is amazing." Mom wraps her arms around me, her demeanor changing.

I get whiplash with the ups and downs of her attitude. But worse, I feel as if I will die at any second. I'm pregnant. I shouldn't be shocked. I knew that the possibility was high. It's what I wanted with Adrian, Ezra, Leo, Dominic, and Jonah. It's what we all wanted. A family.

But now? One look at Chaz proves that my entire life and future are in jeopardy.

He strides closer to me and grabs me by the neck, swinging me toward the wall. Bowing forward, he growls in my face. "You're excused, Nurse Cindy."

The nurse grabs her things and rushes out, pushing past the two alphas in the hallway.

I shrink back, testing the strength of Chaz's hand. "Please, you're hurting me."

"Maybe you should've thought about that before ruining my entire life. I had everything I could ever want, and I would have inherited a position of power with my uncle, but you just had to be such a bitch." Chaz growls, his voice vibrating across my mouth. "You have a lot of making up to do. First, I want to start with the bastard. You will fix this, or I will do what it takes to ensure that the Hart bloodline ends before it can begin."

Mom gasps. "Chaz, it was not in our agreement. You said that you wouldn't care. That baby—"

Swinging his arm, Chaz backhands my mom, sending her sprawling across the floor. She releases a cry and scrambles away, cowering in the corner.

"It isn't mine. It'll never be mine." Chaz snaps his teeth in my face, his eyes dark, lifeless almost. "But if you do as you're told, I will allow the Harts to pay off all of my debts. They won't have it, but at least it will exist."

My insides freeze at his psychotic words. He has no right to put me in this position. He has no right to try to control not only my life but my body.

His fingers tighten around my neck, and I gasp, trying to suck in air that doesn't come. I'm afraid he will knock me out again. I can't trust what he will do if I can't defend myself. And my mom is now a coward, hiding in the corner as if she's the victim in all of this. She probably blames me.

"Will you do as you're told?" Chaz asks, releasing his thumb enough to let me breathe.

I release a gargled cry, nodding my head. My mind whirls with a dozen thoughts. The edges of my vision shadow. I'm terrified of what's to come. I know my guys said they would get to me, but when? Can I hang on that long?

I don't want to find out.

"Good." Chaz motions to the bed. "Now go sit down. I have some business to take care of with your mother."

He takes a step back, giving me the space I need. Without thinking, I jerk my leg up as hard as I can, kneeing him in the balls. I throw myself forward with all my weight, landing on top of him.

Chaz grabs the fabric of my slip, tearing it. "Chris! Nick! Get your asses—"

I punch him in the face.
I don't stop.
I won't. If it's him or me, I choose me.
I will make him pay.

Scarlett

PACK HART FOREVER

"Don't touch her!" Mom yells, swinging a chair hard enough to knock Chris into the other alpha, Nick. She screams and grabs a lamp next, using it like a bat.

Chaz digs his nails into my legs, scratching my skin. Blood trickles over the wounds as he tries to fight me off.

Throwing himself upward, he latches his fingers into my hair and flips me over his head. I land with a gasp on my back. Pain explodes through my scalp, his fingers tangled and refusing to let me go. He drags me a couple of feet, the carpet burning my skin.

"Damn it, Scarlett! I could've made you happy had you just given me a chance." Chaz rips me off the ground and slams my back into the wall.

The world blurs, starbursts peppering my vision. Mom screams out in a way I've never heard. Chaz doesn't give me the chance to catch a glimpse of her. He tosses me on his shoulder, the sudden gesture knocking my phone free. It thuds against the floor, feeling as if it takes my heart with it.

"Fucking shit! We have to move. Now!" Chaz spins, pointing at Chris and Nick. "The bitch has a phone. Rip was supposed to search her. The fucker!" Roaring, Chaz punches the wall, leaving a crater.

Mom screeches, throwing a book near Chaz's head. "Stop! You haven't paid—"

Swiveling around, Chaz growls and knocks my mom away, sending her into the bed. Chris and Nick run forward, and Chaz stomps his boot into the phone, smashing it. I cry out, my panic seizing my muscles. If we leave this house, it'll be over. My alphas won't be able to track me. Who knows what will happen next.

"No!" I scream, throwing my weight. *Don't make it easy. Don't submit. Don't take shit from anyone.* My mind snaps at me, repeating the anthem over and over.

Flailing, I thrash, kicking and hitting. I bite Chaz's shoulder and then his hand as he tries to get his fingers around my neck.

Sirens blare from somewhere in the distance. The muffled ringing tenses Chaz's muscles.

"Fuck! Fuck! Nick, go out front. We need a distraction. They'll let you go with a warning. I'll get Scarlett out of here." Chaz grinds the words out, his voice guttural.

"Yeah-fucking-right, man. We're a pack. Make Chris. I don't trust you won't keep that sexy thing for yourself." Nick blocks Chaz, curling his fingers.

"You know he will. This was his plan all along," I say, managing to grab Chaz's shirt, pulling it up to block his view.

I throw my weight again, this time managing to knock him off balance. Hands link through my hair and drag me to my feet. I scream in pain, bucking my body, trying to break free of Chris's hold. Nick throws punches, herding Chaz toward the wall. Tears burn my eyes.

My muscles ache as exhaustion swallows me whole, demanding I rest, even for a moment.

But I can't. If I stop fighting, they'll take me.

I'll never see my pack again.

Chaz snarls and charges Nick, knocking him off his feet. He locks his hands around his throat, squeezing.

"Cool it, man. You're going to kill him," Chris says, holding me away from him.

I grip his wrists, digging my nails into his skin.

"That's the plan." Chaz whips his head up, sadistically smiling.

Chris steps forward, loosening his hold. "What? N—"

I thrust my leg back, kicking Chris in his cock hard enough that he drops me. Scrambling forward, I push to my feet, heaving a breath. My survival instincts consume me, and I peek over my shoulder, catching a glimpse of Chris trying to pull Chaz off Nick.

"Scarlett!" Mom cries from the doorway to the bedroom.

I cringe at her squeaking voice. It's enough to turn Chaz's attention to me. Without hesitating, I dash toward the open kitchen. The slider off the breakfast nook leads to a patio. My bare feet slap the linoleum floor, and I search for something to protect myself with. Dirty dishes fill the sink, but I don't get the chance to look.

"Stop, Scarlett! Don't make me hurt you!" Chaz shouts from the living room.

I charge toward the sliding door, flicking the lock open. My heart thrashes in fear, wanting me to look for Chaz coming after me. My brain won't allow it. I slide the patio chair to the block wall, using it to hoist myself up. Chaz smacks the glass, thrusting the door open. I jump from the patio wall and tumble across the dry grass, scraping my hands on the sidewalk to hop to my feet.

From here, the sirens shriek louder, but I don't know which direction to head. I can't stay here. I can't fight Chaz.

I've never felt so helpless.

"Help!" I scream as loud as I can. If I can't hide, at least I can do is make some noise. Draw some attention to me. "Help!"

I glance behind me. Chaz lands on the grass with a grunt. He scrunches his features with his rage. Bolting forward, he chases after me, not giving up. I scream again, pushing my feet to move. If he catches me, he'll hurt me. Worse, he'll kill me. Men like him are dangerous because he has nothing to lose except for the power he thinks he holds over me.

Keep running. Don't stop. Stop, and you'll die. I follow the pathway curving through the complex, cutting left when I hit a fork and run toward where voices hum through the air. The familiar noise of a bouncing basketball catches my attention, and I spin and run toward the high-fenced courts where a couple of teens play.

"Help! I was kidnapped! He'll kill me!" I yell, waving my arms. "Please!"

Arms lock around me, lifting me off my feet. "She's lying. Mind your fucking business or I'll send Pack Fernando to shut you up."

"No!" I jerk my head back, head-butting Chaz in the nose.

He yowls and drops me, slamming me hard to the sidewalk. He can't get away with this. He's out of control. A psychopath. Threatening children is beyond monstrous. How dare he think he has that kind of power.

Chaz lunges to grab me, but I sweep my leg out, knocking him into the bushes. I crab walk backward, screaming as loudly as I can. I hit my back on the building wall, the rundown complex needing serious renovation as paint flakes rain down on me. I dig my fingers into the dirt, scratching the concrete fountain jutting out from the laminate siding. A chunk breaks off in my hand, and I clutch it for dear life.

"Scarlett, you fucking bitch!" Chaz dusts his hands on his pants, jogging toward me.

I can't find the strength to get up and run. My hope dwindles away with every foot he closes between us. My life might end before it ever had the chance to truly begin. Bad omegas don't get perfect packs and dream lives. They get screwed over, degraded, and left in pieces to be put back together by monstrous alphas.

"Leave her alone!" a kid yells from the basketball court.

I blink my eyes, clearing the tears from my vision. A teen boy chucks his basketball at Chaz, hitting him in the back. Then another boy follows his lead.

Chaz scowls and snatches the ball, hollering like a lunatic out for blood. The small distraction is my saving grace. These teens aren't tainted by the orders of our society yet. They haven't been brainwashed or tricked into conforming.

And it's all I need.

I use the side of the building to get to my feet. My instincts scream to run, but my body refuses. I'm too tired. Too hurt. The only way I'm getting away from Chaz is if I stop him myself. I clench my jaw, silencing my mouth from whimpering as I creep up behind him.

I raise the hefty piece of concrete up and slam it to the back of his head as hard as I can.

Chaz bows forward, stumbling from the blow. I could run. I could get away. From here, I see the parking lot. The sirens ring so loudly that they might even be here, surrounding the place I'm no longer at.

"You bastard! You fucking bastard!" I scream, kicking Chaz in the ass, knocking him onto his hands and knees.

Blinding rage consumes me, and I smash the piece of concrete to his skull again and again. I can't see. I can't catch my breath. All I can do is slam the concrete over and over again, coating my fingers in Chaz's blood.

"You monster! I don't belong to you! I'll never belong to you!" Up and down. Up and down. All I can think about is ensuring Chaz doesn't get up. He'll never hurt me again. He'll never hurt my pack again.

"Drop your weapon and put your hands up!" a sharp voice snaps, breaking through the sound of my heart pounding in my ears. "Do it now!"

"Back down," Adrian growls, his strong, rumbly voice circling me. "She's not a threat. That's her. That's our wife."

Pounding boots boom against the asphalt, and a shadow blocks out the sun overhead. The familiar scent of citrusy bergamot mingling with the lightness of jasmine trickles to my nose, freezing my muscles in relief.

"Amore, stop. Put it down. He's gone. He's not going to hurt you ever again." Ezra's pleas wrap around me with the weight of his arms, and I crumple to the ground, my body recognizing that I'm safe. I'm no longer in danger. My alphas have me now.

"We need a medic," Dominic calls, dropping down beside me. He scoops me off Chaz's body, his breathing as hard as mine. "Move!"

I close my eyes, breathing in his scent, heightened by his fear and relief. The world jostles as he strides forward. Ezra stays close, kissing the top of my head. Adrian's familiar spicy berry scent engulfs me next, dancing through the air with Jonah's green floral and Leo's salty lime. The collection of fragrances soothes me on a soul-deep level, easing my racing heart and mind.

Dominic doesn't set me down and instead hops into the back of the ambulance for one of the paramedics to look at me. He holds me on his lap, combing my messy hair out of the way, kissing me a dozen times, the magic of his affection breathing life back into me where I thought I had lost it.

"You'll have to take her to her GP for a more thorough check-up. Most of her injuries are minor scrapes and bruises." The medic adds a couple of bandages to the ones the nurse had already put on me and takes a step back. "Would you like us to take her?"

Adrian shakes his head. "No, we have a doctor on our payroll. We'll handle everything from here."

Adrian takes me from Dominic, cradling me in his arms. I sink against him and listen to the sounds of his heartbeat, the rhythmic thrums are the most beautiful thing. It's what I need to hear in this moment. Jonah and Leo close the space and shower me with kisses as Ezra and Dominic put their arms around the four of us, cuddling me in the middle, squeezing me as if they alone can keep me from falling apart. And they do.

I can barely process what happened today, and my mind refuses to even think about what I've done.

"I killed him," I say, my voice cracking. "I didn't want to, but he wouldn't stop. He wouldn't let me leave. He threatened me and my pregnancy."

My words hang in the air, none of my alphas moving or speaking. I'm not even sure if they're breathing as everything sinks in.

"The nurse confirmed it," I add, pressing my lips together to stop my mouth from trembling. "He lied to my mom. He threatened to use it against me. He wanted me to make up lies about you guys or else he was going to—" A small cry escapes my mouth, and I bury my face against Adrian.

He strokes his hand down my back, adjusting me in his arms. "Take a breath, Scarlett. You've been through a lot today. You don't have to say anything right now. Just let me hold you. Let us take care of you."

I bob my head and wipe my eyes on his shirt. "That's all I want. Get me out of here. I just want this to be over."

Ezra touches my cheek, getting me to look at him. "It is, amore. We promise. You've done amazing. You're so strong, but you don't have to be anymore. We've got you. We'll never let you go."

Adrian rests his chin on my shoulder, cuddling me from behind as we eat in the penthouse apartment in San Francisco. "Another bite, Mrs. Hart. You're eating for two, possibly three—"

"Make it an even six, and maybe Scarlett's womb will have welcomed all our swimmers." Leo chuckles, stabbing a grape with his fork. "Her magical pussy is a gateway to bliss, so I wouldn't put it past us."

I play-smack him on the shoulder. "Please don't manifest that. One at a time is good for me."

Ezra groans and squeezes my hand. "But if you could get it all over with—"

I whack him on the leg. "You'll just knock me up another five times during my next heat. We don't need that kind of attention. I don't want to turn into my mom."

My heart aches at the thought. How could she have put me through this? I know she never intended for me to get hurt or for Chaz to try to murder me, but her actions have consequences that I have to live with now. I have blood on my hands. I'll never forget the feeling of ending someone's life and how awful it was.

"That will never happen. You are so compassionate and empathetic. You know there's more to life than materialistic luxuries. You don't put people on pedestals because of who they are. You will never be that woman. Ever." Jonah stretches his arm across the table and touches my chin, getting me to lean closer so he can stroke his fingers over my cheek. "I mean it."

If only I could shed the fear. People change as they grow older, and I've already changed so much over the last year. Even over the last two months.

I don't have the will to argue the possibility, so I just nod my head and let Adrian feed me a bite of the pasta.

Ezra cooked a little bit of everything, trying to ensure my meal was nutritionally balanced, and I can't help smiling at the thought.

The doorbell rings, drawing our attention. The last one who showed up was a reporter for the Pack Carlisle newspaper. Before that, it was the leader himself, wishing me a speedy recovery and thanking my alphas for taking action.

"Tell whoever it is to go away. They'll have to schedule an appointment to talk to us." Dominic leans back in the chair, looking at Leo, silently volunteering him.

Leo stands up with a nod, flexing his arms, showing off his bulging muscles. He's always the one that doesn't give a shit about being rude or maintaining proper appearances.

I hunker down on Adrian's lap, my nerves getting the best of me. It's going to take me a while not to fear the world outside of my alphas. I hate that just someone knocking on the door unexpectedly gets to me. It shouldn't be like this. I shouldn't want to run and hide in the closet. Hopefully after I take some self-defense classes with Leo, I'll feel more confident.

"Scarlett!" My sister's familiar voice echoes through the room, and I turn my head up and catch Cyan striding forward with Amber and Raven behind her. She fidgets with a deck of cards, her eyes narrowed into slits with her concern.

I get up from my chair and open my arms, my whole body freezing when a fourth figure comes in after them, and I meet mom's gaze. She is bruised from Chaz's attack and her face scrunched with wrinkles, making her look older than when I last saw her. I'm not even sure if she put on makeup or not or if it's just residue of her cried-off mascara darkening beneath her eyes.

Three pairs of arms wrap around me at the same time the cherry-vanilla scent of my sisters engulfs me. It feels like forever since I've seen them, and I'm so happy that they came here.

If only Mom's shadow didn't loom over us.

"Make some room for Mama," Mom says, standing a foot away. "The best hugs are the ones from me. I just wish you hadn't attracted such a psychopath, Scarlett. I knew you going to that university would lead to—"

Something dark inside me snaps, and I whip my attention toward my mom.

"Are you kidding me?" I ask, pushing between my sisters, the warmth they brought me frozen now that I face the woman I hate most in the world.

Mom sighs. "Oh, Scarlett. You can't blame me for not seeing the truth. That alpha had me convinced that you would be properly taken care of. I had no idea he had been harassing you. You know how things are. It's not like anything bad happened. You're strong just like me, and I knew you could handle—"

Swinging my hand out, I slap my mom so hard across the face that her head turns sideways and she stumbles back. She falls to the ground with a cry, her face twisting in surprise.

"Get out! Get the fuck out! I'm done with you. You will not come into my house and try to make me feel as if this whole situation was my fault. I have done nothing but everything you've asked of me. And when I was finally happy, you tried to ruin it. You nearly cost me my future. Now get out." I point at the open door where Leo stands.

Mom touches her chest, her mouth open. "Scarlett, you're being unreasonable. You can't just—"

"Get out or I will throw you out myself!" I clench my fingers with my anger, narrowing my focus on my mom. "I hate you. I hate you so much. The only thing you care about is yourself. I have had it. I don't need you anymore. I have my own pack who loves me and will treat me like a queen without anything in return. Now get out. I never want to see you again."

Mom scowls. "But—"

"And don't expect any money or help with anything. Be grateful that I don't turn you into Pack Carlisle for your actions." Because I want to so badly. I get great satisfaction thinking about the trouble Mom would get into, but my dads need her. My sisters still need her. But she will realize how grave her mistakes are when she has no one left in the end. Because no one will need her forever.

Mom throws her hands in the air. "They won't believe you. You better—"

Leo snatches my mom by her underarms and yanks her off the floor, dragging her out of our penthouse apartment. She hollers like a wounded animal, struggling against him. I think she's angrier about the fact that no one will let her finish a word. But I've heard enough. I've heard her excuses all my life, and I won't accept them again.

This truly is it. I'm cutting her out of my life completely.

"Girls, you better get out here. Scarlett made it clear that she is no longer a part of our pack. Come along. You don't want to end up following in her footsteps. Such a disgrace." Mom points at Amber, Cyan, and Raven, who stand in silent shock.

They don't move for a second, and I think they might finally stand up to her. But then Cyan nudges Amber and Raven and the three of them frown at me. They follow Mom.

But I don't blame them. She still controls their lives and their futures. I just hope that they don't face the same fate that I did. I hope they don't have to fight or face unthinkable challenges and enemies. I hope they can find their happily ever afters like I have without the drama and pain.

At least in the end, it was worth it. I wouldn't change anything if it solidified my life with Pack Hart.

They are my forever and always. We have made vows, and together, I know we will make a difference in the world. We will create change.

And it's already started.

I touch my hand to my stomach, blinking away my tears before they can spill, watching my sisters leave with our mom. Their mom. She's no longer mine.

But sometimes, you have to cut off what hurts the most. I owe her nothing. Blood doesn't make a family. Love and respect, appreciation and time—the things that help build the foundation of a pack, and I will cherish every brick I put together for my alphas and myself.

Starting now. With this pregnancy and all of our future children.

They are why I won't stop fighting for change. Why I plan to teach them how to finally stand up against these ideals of what is right.

Because no one can know what that is for another, and that's why Sage Steele struggles so much. I'm not my mother's daughter, after all. I'm like my sisters, born of steel, but forged from the challenges we have faced.

And no one can take that away.

Absolutely no one.

Scarlett

New Beginnings

“The creativity flowing through this room is absolutely magical, amore. Your vision enchants me. I could watch you work forever.” Ezra stands in the doorway of the empty classroom. He offers a dreamy smile, turning his gaze back to the outline of the new mural for my soon-to-be boss and art director, Talia.

"She's incredible. Surprises me every minute." Talia wipes her hands off on her paint-splattered jeans. "I'm so happy to have her coming onto our staff. I can't wait for her to be eligible for a teaching position."

"Unless she decides to color the world instead. She's quite sought after." Ezra steps forward, holding his hand out to me.

I take it, letting him spin me in his arms. He rests his hands on my growing belly, now peeking out from my raggedy shirt. "There's always the summer for that." Because I desire to share my love of art with whoever I can. Teach those who've been denied creativity and help them express their own visions in a world of conformity.

"That's what I wanted to hear." Talia waves her paintbrush, flicking teal paint in my direction.

I laugh and reach for the spray bottle of water, squirting her in retaliation. "I'm just so thankful for this. For everything."

"You're thankful? I'm thankful. The new changes Pack Hart is introducing—well, you know. You have somewhere to be, don't you? I'll clean up here if you want." Talia waves the paintbrush again.

I bob my head and smile. "Thanks, Tal. I'll do the clean up tomorrow."

Ezra holds his hand out, scooping me into his arms. "Come on, amore. We have to hurry, or we'll miss the announcement."

I kiss his cheek. "Then run."

"It is with great pleasure that the board of trustees announces Dominic Hart as the new dean of Clearwater University and all satellite campuses." A man in a suit stands at the podium in Clearwater Hall, waving his hand out to Dominic.

"What?" I whisper, peeking over at him. "You guys didn't tell me this. I thought this was to award Adrian for the expansion."

"We didn't want to say anything until the contract was final." Jonah presses his lips to my ear. "Dominic has wanted to move from the math department for years and into administration with Adrian. He'll finally get to focus on the changes we need to make."

I clap my hands, bouncing in my seat far more excited than the rest of the stuffy room of some of Clearwater's most prodigious.

Leo joins me, whistling. "Yeah, Dom!"

We might sound foolish, but I don't give a fuck. I'm so happy for Dominic. For everyone. He'll be incredible.

Dominic shakes the board member's hand and acknowledges the crowd. My stomach flips and flops in anticipation, my heart filling with incomparable happiness. Jonah rests his hands on my belly, feeling what I do, and he motions to Ezra and Leo to join him. I bite my lip to stifle my coo and catch sight of Adrian standing off to the side of the stage. He tips his head to the door, and the second Dominic finishes, Jonah lifts me up with him. I guess there isn't more for us to see or do because I've never seen my guys rush so fast from a building.

Leo's laughter echoes through the air, the cool spring night flourishing with the scent of blooming roses from the huge, luscious gardens around the building.

"What's the rush?" I ask, clinging onto Jonah as he spins me around, more lighthearted than I've ever seen him.

"This is where the true celebration begins, Lettie. We have a surprise for you." Dominic snatches me from Jonah, cradling me in his arms to curl me up to kiss my belly. "We couldn't wait until tomorrow."

Ezra brings the SUV to the curb, and we all climb in. I sit in the front seat as Adrian covers my eyes from behind. I tremble with excitement, my heart beating wildly.

I have no idea what they're up to. Now I wonder if they arranged for me to help Talia early so they could be the sneakiest cute alphas. Their excitement reminds me of children on their birthdays, the joy of the special day unforgettable. They act like giddy teens even, laughing and joking around, kissing me and teasing me.

"I don't think I can take this much longer. Where are you taking me?" I ask, prying at Adrian's fingers.

"We're almost there." Adrian chuckles, leaning over the seat. "It'll be worth it. But you have to promise to keep your eyes closed until we are ready. Okay? Just another minute."

I don't want to wait. I'm excited but they know I will do anything for them. "I promise."

The SUV slows as Ezra parks it, and I shift in my seat, refusing to sit still as everyone exits except for me. Cool air caresses me as Adrian opens the door, his scent incredible with his excitement. I step from the SUV with Adrian staying behind me, his hands covering my eyes again.

The strange whine of metal catches my attention, and I cock my head, listening to what sounds like a gate opening.

I grab Adrian's wrists and pull at his hands. "Let me see," I demand, bouncing. "Pretty please. I'm going pout otherwise."

Adrian's husky laugh rumbles against my back. "We can't have that now, can we? Before I show you, I just wanted to remind you that things have changed substantially for us, and we thought it was best to finally get something unaffiliated with the university."

His words pique my interest, and I spin, facing him. "You guys bought a house?"

Leo chuckles. "Only the staffing units could be called houses, dirty girl. We bought a mother-fucking mansion. Somewhere big enough to raise all of our babies. I'm sure we're gonna have at least thirty."

"We wanted somewhere we could protect them and you." Jonah stands next to me and kisses my shoulder.

"But mostly, we wanted somewhere that we could thrive as a pack. Somewhere that we could all have a place for our hobbies and our interests along with the ones we share." Dominic pushes my hair over my shoulder.

"Whatever. You know you just wanted suites big enough to fit the double Alaskan king beds. You should see these fucking things, Scarlett. We could live comfortably in a blanket fort." Leo takes my hand and spins me around, finally showing me the massiveness of our new home.

I thought the Clearwater Manor was huge, but this is twice the size.

I open and close my mouth, taking in the beautiful architecture of the granite façade fit for a palace. The covered drive sparkles with a crystal chandelier and glittering concrete paths. Instead of guiding me through the front door, my alphas lead the way through a wisteria-covered path and into a courtyard that sits in the middle of the mansion, protecting us from the outside world yet bringing the outdoors into our personal sanctuary.

A huge veranda with a spiral staircase greets us, and the six of us head up to double glass doors. I cover my mouth with my hand, spotting the spacious living area filled with all sorts of furniture—cribs, rocking chairs, playpens, and so much more.

"We thought this would make a perfect nursery. There are rooms connected, and we can all be close together." Adrian rubs his hand up and down my arms, nudging me to walk forward.

"What do you think, amore?" Ezra asks, waving his hand. "We didn't want to set it up or decorate without you. We want to do this together."

Leo motions toward an open door with an empty closet. "And look, there's your nesting room. Look at that cuddle bed in there. It's like a human-sized dog bed. You can fill it up with whatever you want."

I smile and throw my arms around him, kissing him with enough passion to make him moan. I grab Dominic by his tie and pull him closer to me next, nipping his lip, letting my desire take control. Jonah lifts me off my feet and carries me inside, and Adrian and Ezra start stripping me down, leaving a trail of clothes in their wake.

I blindly kiss and touch each of my alphas as they surround me, passing me between them instead of fighting over who gets my attention. They all know that I love them equally and in their own ways, and I'll give in to whatever they desire. I am theirs. Their pleasure. Their love. Their everything, just as they are mine.

"Whoever gets me to the bed the quickest gets to knot with me first." I laugh, tipping my head back as Leo spins me around and away from everybody.

"Whoever helps me can have her ass," Leo says, propping me higher in his arms to spank my naked skin.

Ezra gets close and kisses my ass cheek, spreading me wider on Leo's shoulder. I wiggle under his attention, moaning as I scratch my nails across Leo's back.

The world spins as he sets me on the bed far more gently than he would before. He laces his fingers to the back of my neck and pulls me up, kissing my throat until he sinks his teeth in, marking me the way he wants.

The others undress around me, their delectable bodies sending tingles between my legs and spreading throughout me. And then I see the swing. My eyebrows peak in fascination as Leo grins, pulling me to the edge of the bed to strap a harness around my naked body.

"We have to test this out. Soon your belly will be bulging so much that we'll have to be creative." Adrian hooks the straps to the anchors above the wide doorway of the suite that leads to a grand bathroom. I spot a slanted rectangular pillow along with a few other toys sitting on the dresser. That's all that's unpacked, and I know that they've been planning this.

This is our own private celebration.

We finally have everything we want. Power, love, and the beginning of what will be an amazing future.

Leo carries me to the swing and lifts me higher, pulling the straps to help me hang. "What do you think, dirty girl? You're ours now. I'm going to make you come so hard that you'll fucking squirt all over the floor."

I gasp, my excitement growing as he positions the swing, and Dominic and Jonah stand at my slides, helping to spread my legs wider, leaving me exposed to them how they want. Adrian leans me back, and I arch, opening my mouth upside down. I grab his hips and pull him to me, sucking him into my mouth and taking him all the way until my nose touches his balls.

"Damn," Dominic says, his voice rumbling. "That's so fucking hot, Lettie."

"Just wait until she swings." Leo maneuvers between my legs, rubbing his fingers across my clit. I moan at the sensation, my mouth vibrating over Adrian's cock.

Warmth blooms between my legs and Leo teases me with his tip, rocking his hips back and forth, bouncing me in the swing until Jonah and Dominic push me by my knees, sinking me onto Leo.

I scream out in pleasure, the ecstasy from having them control my every movement so hot and sexy. I've never felt so beautiful and wanted in my life. I'm theirs to keep.

Leo thrusts, swinging me just a bit to help me bob my head up and down Adrian's cock. He moans as his muscles ripple, and Leo tightens his grip on my hips as his knot locks us in place, throwing me over the edge as my orgasm mirrors his, the pleasure making my eyes roll back.

"Sit her up, so Ezra can slide into her ass. Hold her still, you two," Leo commands, taking charge of my pleasure and of his pack mates' desires.

Adrian pushes me back up, and Leo steps up on Jonah and Dominic's knees, giving Ezra room to join him as he balances like a goddamn performer.

Ezra fingers me, testing how slippery my slick is, and he moans as he slides inside me, him and Leo so close, but neither of them complains. This isn't about comfort. This is about getting and giving. This is about bonding as a pack in ways that will make us stronger. Even more powerful.

The six of us lose ourselves to the pleasure, and I moan and scream out their names, moaning as they take turns sucking me and making love, letting me taste them and kiss them and touch them all I want in the process. I'm like their sun as they gravitate around me, working together like the magic of the universe.

My body sings and quivers with each orgasm, loving how hot and wild and wet everyone is in this moment. What makes this moment even more special and intoxicating than my heat is that we're not controlled by our hormones. This is just the raw, feral need that we share together, loving each other on every level and being together as a bonding pack.

"My hypnotic omega. You are so perfect. So intelligent and creative. So strong and willful. I'll never get enough of you," Adrian murmurs, his knot loosening as he finishes, his body gleaming with perspiration. I don't even know how much time has passed and only that I could survive on their pleasure forever.

If the world didn't need us, I know I'd try.

But things have changed, and we have to embrace everything we fought for. We've already shaken the foundation of the university and of Pack Clearwater. Maybe even Pack Carlisle too. I have proven that omegas thrive better without being brainwashed into a breeding mentality. And now, we will change the world.

For our children. For my family. For everyone's future.

And the lessons will never stop.

We will always push for a brighter future.

We are the Harts of our territory. With us comes love, compassion, and knowledge.

We will make the world better, stronger. Equal. And it starts now.

Scarlett

Bright Future

"Look, Sienna. Mama's here to watch you paint. Show her what you're working on." Dominic grins at me from the floor of my art studio, where he rolled out canvas across the room.

"Hey, you got to give me some credit too. Look what I made." Leo grins at me, showing a rainbow ass print in the corner. "We made matching ones over there."

I watch as our daughter scoots across the canvas, covered from head to toe in paint, splattering it everywhere. She catches sight of me and stretches her plump arms up, cooing as she crawls on her hands and knees before pushing up to stand.

My eyes widen, and I take a step back, excitement crashing through me as she waddles a few steps toward me and wraps her arms around my leg.

I screech, bend down, and pick her up, not even caring that paint gets all over my button-up shirt and black pants. I had just finished a staff meeting with the art department.

"Did she just...?" Ezra steps into the studio behind me, shrugging out of his suit jacket. "Ragazza, my beautiful girl! You just walked!"

I grin and spin around, looking for Jonah and Adrian following behind us. We always meet in my studio before dinner every night, just being together.

"We got it on canvas!" Dominic says, pumping his fist in the air. "I can't believe it!"

I sit down on the floor, snuggling with Sienna as she wiggles from my arms and continues to make handprints as she crawls toward Adrian. He chuckles and scoops her up, blowing raspberries on her tummy, getting blue and green paint on his face.

"Isn't this incredible? Life is so perfect. It's a mess in the most creative way, and I wouldn't change it for anything." Jonah gets on the floor beside us, and I reach out and poke his nose, leaving a spot of red paint.

"I wouldn't either. This is everything I could've hoped for. My life is full of love and family. You all make me the happiest omega in the world." I open my arms for them, letting them squish Sienna and me between them, every shift and moving of our bodies decorating the canvas with the streaks of paint Dominic put out.

It's magical.

It's mine.

Our art captures the beauty we have found together. As a pack.

And we will never stop creating. Never stop pushing for change.

If my life as an omega taught me any lessons, it's that we don't have to conform. We don't have to submit and be somebody we're not just to appease others. Because love blooms from honesty and being true to who we are. For never turning our back on what we want most in the world.

Whatever that may be.

Life isn't always easy, and it can be maddening. Scary. Wrong. But it can also be full of laughter and hope. Reaching dreams and loving endlessly.

Life is about living and learning. Growing with those worthy of your love. And passing on the lessons you've learned to help others do the same.

But mostly, life is whatever you want it to be, and I plan to make it unforgettable. Everything good, bad, and sometimes beautifully chaotic and messy. Those moments add up to create a masterpiece out of our lives. With my alphas and our pack, life will be priceless. It'll be completely ours.

Always.

The End

Other RH Books

OMEGAVERSE SERIES

Saint Vista Pack Regimes
Bonds of Steele Omegaverse

PARANORMAL

The Seven Sinners of Hell's Kingdon
The Pack Mates of Lunar Crest

The Wolfpacks of Shadow Moon Island
The Fated Mate of the Dragon Clans
The Divine Vampire Heirs
The Royale Vampire Heirs
The Academy of Vampire Heirs
La Vega Vampire Showstoppers
Rise from the Flames

CONTEMPORARY

Fame

About Ginna Moran

GINNA MORAN IS the *USA Today* Bestselling author of over seventy novels, including the popular The Pack Mates of Lunar Crest and The Seven Sinners of Hell's Kingdom reverse harem novels.

She always carried a fascination for all things paranormal and wrote her first unpublished manuscript at age eighteen. Her love of the supernatural grew stronger through her adult life, and she now spends her days with different creatures of the night. Whether it's vampires, werewolves, dragons, fae, angels, demons, or mermaids, Ginna loves creating and living in worlds from her dreams.

Aside from Ginna's professional life, she enjoys binge-watching TV, crafting and design, playing pretend with her daughter, and cuddling with her dog. Some of her favorite things include chocolate, mermaids, anything that glitters, learning new things, cheesy jokes, and organizing her bookshelf.

Ginna is currently hard at work on her next novel and the one after, and the one after that.